A HARD FALL

Gunfire slashed through the cottonwoods. McCan aimed, but the forms shifted and he did not know friend from assailant.

Someone cursed; a rifle fired. McCan pushed upward, over the rock, but his foot slid on the damp ground and he crashed down hard. His head struck something, night closed in, and he was out.

He came to moments, maybe an hour later. His head was bloody and throbbed. He struggled for perspective. He pushed up on his forearms and looked across the campsite, and suddenly his view was blocked by what appeared to be twin tree trunks. Focusing, he saw they were legs. His eyes lifted—a rifle butt descended toward his face . . .

TIMBER CREEK

CAMERON JUDD

St. Martin's Paperbacks

TIMBER CREEK / RENEGADE LAWMEN

Timber Creek copyright © 1989 by Cameron Judd.
Excerpt from *The Glory River* copyright © 1998 by Cameron Judd.
Renegade Lawmen copyright © 1992 by Cameron Judd.
Previously published under the title *Fiddler and McCan.*

For information address St. Martin's Press, 175 Fifth Avenue, New York, NY 10010.

ISBN: 0-312-94556-6
EAN: 978-0-312-94556-5

Printed in the United States of America

Timber Creek Bantam edition / May 1989
St. Martin's Paperbacks edition / November 1998

Renegade Lawmen Bantam Domain edition / December 1992
St. Martin's Paperbacks edition / March 1999

St. Martin's Paperbacks are published by St. Martin's Press, 175 Fifth Avenue, New York, NY 10010.

10 9 8 7 6 5 4 3 2 1

To Rhonda

PART I

DEADWOOD

CHAPTER 1

As Luke McCan strode through the gate of the Tol-liver & McClelland freight yard, a black man scrub-bing mud from a wagon turned to watch him. McCan nodded a greeting, but the big fellow gave not even a grunt in return.

At the doorway of the unpainted building of rough lumber, McCan took off his hat. Shifting it in his hands, he tried to swallow his tension; he couldn't. He straightened his shoulders and walked inside.

It was dark there, and musty. McCan stood blind a couple of moments as his eyes adjusted. He found himself facing three somber men on a bench against the opposite wall. They slumped more than sat, ex-pressionless as tomcats. McCan nodded, and got no more reaction than he had from the man outside. Like wooden Indians in a cigar store, he thought.

"Could you tell me where I'd find Ira Tolliver?" he asked.

Wooden Indian number three raised a hand-rolled smoke to his lips and took a slow drag as he tilted his head toward a door at the far corner of the room. It was ajar, and beyond it McCan saw the corner of a big pigeonholed desk, as cluttered as a postmaster's, and an equally paper-laden oaken filing cabinet. He nodded his thanks and headed for the door.

Inside the office sat a fat man with an unlit cigar stub jutting over an impressive collection of chins. He looked up; the chins danced gelatinously beneath broad jowls.

"What is it?" he gruffly asked.

"Are you Ira Tolliver?"

"I am."

"I'd like to speak to you a moment."

The man shrugged, and McCan entered. The office was cramped, and looked as if it had never been cleaned. It was a refuge for stray odors. Tolliver shuffled papers as McCan looked for a seat. The businessman's rubbery mouth wrapped itself around the well-chewed cigar, a duplicate of any one of a score of others that lay about on the floor.

McCan evicted an ancient gray tabby from a chair and took its place, then waited until Tolliver turned his somnolent gaze to him.

"You got business?"

"My name is Luke McCan. I'm looking for work."

"Uh-huh. Somebody say I'm hiring?"

"No, sir. I just figured to ask."

Tolliver dug out a match and lit his cigar. Through the smoke, his face was that of a bulldog, fat and lazy. "What work you after?"

"I'd like to be a teamster." He anticipated the follow-up question. "I've got experience—I hauled freight in Missouri almost a year."

"Oxen?"

"Mules."

"We use oxen." Tolliver looked to his papers again,

conversation concluded. The cigar made a four-inch roll to the other side of his mouth.

"I can drive oxen, Mr. Tolliver. I've done it a time or two, and I can pick up what I don't already know."

"How long you been in Pierre, son?"

"About a week."

"Where are you from?"

"St. Louis."

"You're young."

"Twenty-five. I'm told I look younger."

"You got folks?"

"No parents. They died just over a year ago, a wagon accident. I've got one sister living in Independence."

"What brought you to Dakota?"

"I just wanted to come, and saw no reason not to."

"You know where my freight line runs, son?"

"Deadwood, I hear."

"That's right. Black Hills. Gold country. A lot of young bucks looking for a way to get there." He leaned back in his chair; it creaked and moaned as if in pain. McCan caught his implication and shook his head.

"I'm not looking for a ticket to Deadwood," he said. "If I wanted to go there, I'd get on my horse and ride." He didn't mention he had lost his horse in a poker bet a week ago.

Tolliver flipped an ash. "This line cuts through Sioux country. There's highwaymen too. We got a one-mile-wide right-of-way through to Deadwood, but that don't mean a lot to the lower types. And Deadwood, once you get there, is about as dangerous as the trail."

"I'll try to take care of myself."

"Bill Hickok tried too. He's moldering in his grave on Mount Moriah."

5

McCan saw Tolliver was trying hard to sell him on *not* deserting the freight line in Deadwood. It was not something he had thought of doing, but all this talk was making him wonder if he *should*.

"I'm just looking for a job," McCan said. "Can you use me?"

Tolliver pondered. "A teamster quit me last week, and we got a shipment going out Monday. You come back in a couple of days, and we'll start breaking you in."

They talked pay, shook hands, and McCan left. He headed to a café and, in celebration, ordered a steak, biscuits, and coffee. As he ate, he looked out the café window at the busy street.

Pierre stood at the bend of the Missouri in the southern Dakota Territory. Since the discovery of gold in the Black Hills, the freight business out of Pierre had flourished, for the Black Hills had only two links to the world beyond: freight lines and stagecoaches. By those conduits people and goods were funneled into the Black Hills, and carried out again were stories of goldmining towns such as Deadwood. Talk had it that Deadwood was a place of intense living and easily found death. The murder of Wild Bill Hickok there a few years back had only bolstered the gritty mystique of the town.

McCan sipped coffee and tilted his chair back against the wall. He was a slender man and rather tall, his features smooth and appealing if not outright handsome. He dressed well for one who had been without a job for a year; his inheritance from his parents had been modest, but enough to finance a few months of wandering. He should invest what was left in something practical, he knew, but such was not his way. He had dreamed of roaming like this from the

6

first time he'd toddled across his nursery. Had he not gambled away his horse, he might have been content to remain jobless a bit longer; applying for work with Tolliver had been a momentary inspiration, a way to get in a little more travel with no investment of his own money.

Now McCan was thinking of Deadwood, and wondering why he had not thought of it before. Tolliver, in his eagerness to steer his thoughts from it, had instead turned them to it.

McCan left the café and walked without aim along the street. In front of a store whose window sign read MINING TOOLS—HIGH QUALITY AND LOW PRICE, he paused to roll a cigarette. The door opened and a man emerged, arms filled with supplies. Blinded by his load, he walked directly into McCan, and tools and other goods fell all around.

The man cursed, but it was directed at the situation rather than McCan, so McCan took no offense.

"If I had seen you coming, I would have moved," McCan said.

"Not your fault."

"Let me help you," McCan said. He and the man picked up the items and loaded them into a small covered wagon parked by the curb of the boardwalk.

McCan thrust out his hand and said his name. The other man took the hand and said, "I'm Caleb Black. I'm obliged for your help."

McCan gestured toward the wagon. "You're bound for Deadwood?"

"Like everybody else."

"I'm heading that way myself. I'm a teamster for the Tolliver company yonder. Just hired on."

"Maybe I'll see you in the Black Hills then."

"Maybe so."

Caleb Black climbed to his seat and rode away. Luke McCan watched him depart, then looked westward toward the horizon that hid the Black Hills.

McCan wrote a letter that night by candlelight.

Mrs. Martha Hyatt
Independence, Missouri

My Dear Martha,

As I write you now, I'm a teamster. When you hear from me next, I likely will be a gold miner in the town of Deadwood. That is where the freight line that has given me a job runs, and likely I will stay on once we get there, for it is the talk of everyone I see. There is money to be made there at honest labor, and I will be glad to make my part.

Our father would have been proud of me, would he not? "Make a living with the sweat of your brow" always was his theme—with me at least—though as a female you probably were spared some of that, it being more your duty to marry well, in his eyes, than to work hard. You've done both.

It is late and I will not write you long, but you will hear again from me when I am settled at the Black Hills mines. To answer the question of your last letter: no, I have not gambled away all my inheritance, though I have kept to my poker-playing ways. I see no harm in it, though I know in your eyes it is the fatal vice that will ruin my life, if not damn my soul, for you were well-taught by Mother about the wicked ways of men.

But do not worry about me, and be sure you will
hear from me soon.

> Your affectionate brother,
> Luke

CHAPTER 2

McCan labored through Saturday night, filling canvas sacks, heaving crates, stacking goods, covering the loaded wagons with tarpaulins. It was grueling work, with more to come on Sunday, for the loading was behind schedule.

McCan worked with Bob Webster, the black man he had seen washing wagons in the freight yard. Webster was talkative now, warmed to McCan through the brotherhood of labor. McCan asked questions, and Webster answered them in detail.

Tolliver, he said, would not come along on the journey. He was a businessman—at home behind a desk, but a stranger to a freight wagon seat. Ira Tolliver had founded the company three years before with a man named Zeke McClelland, and the latter had actually led the freight runs. McClelland had died after the first year, and Tolliver had kept the company running alone, amid rumors that he had swindled McClelland's widow. Now the freight runs were led by an employee named Benjamin Weaver.

Webster pointed Weaver out to McCan; he was thin-featured, with a mustache that drooped around fleshless lips. The left side of his face was ballooned incessantly with hot-twist tobacco. But he never spat; Webster claimed he swallowed the juice as if it were sugar water.

"Weaver is a good man to have leading," Webster said. "Better than Zeke McClelland was on his best day. Listen to him and you'll learn a lot about this business."

On Sunday the crew headed to the plains north of town to round up and herd in the oxen grazing there. It was easy; the oxen were accustomed to the process and all but fell into line. They plodded willingly back to the freight yard, where they were penned in a make-shift corral. Webster and McCan watered them and gave them hay, and the big beasts consumed both in placid contentment, watching the crew finish preparations for the Monday run.

Webster began McCan's education in the freight business. He gave a rapid-fire description of the train: ten teams of twenty oxen, each team pulling three wagons hitched together, each wagon carefully weighted. Lead wagons would carry seven thousand pounds, middle or swing wagons about five thousand each, and trail wagons about three thousand.

Before dawn Monday the train began its roll toward the Missouri. Ben Weaver led, followed by McCan. McCan sat astride his lead wagon, traces in his hands and the whoops and curses of the teamsters behind him ringing in his ears. The earth made a sodden, crushing noise beneath the big wheels of the wagons. As the sky turned from black to lavender to pale gold, a sense of adventure filled McCan.

The wagons reached the Missouri, and Weaver halted his team near the ferry that would convey the entire train across. Morning rays splintered over the river's chopped surface, brightening as the sun rose. Weaver's figure etched itself against the silver background as he talked to the long-bearded ferryman. McCan threw the brake and leaned back, knowing the crossing would be slow.

Indeed, it was almost noon before the chuck wagon at the end of the train was parked across the water, with a huge kettle of stew bubbling beside it. None of the teamsters had eaten that morning, because of the early departure from Pierre, so they accepted the food with the eagerness of dying souls grasping a sacrament.

Webster sat beside McCan, who was propped against a wheel of his swing wagon. Webster pulled away his hat and wiped the sweat off with his sleeve. "Mighty hot," he said.

"It is. How long will we stay here?"

"Most all day. The oxen can't take a lot of heat. We'll travel from the later part of the afternoon until we can't see no more. Then we'll camp, get up before dawn, and roll until it gets hot tomorrow. Good thing about this business is, you don't work much the hot part of the day. The bad part is, you don't get breakfast until about noon."

"How many miles will we cover a day?"

"It depends on the ground and the weather. On a good day, maybe almost twenty miles. On a bad one, maybe five or six."

McCan swatted a fly on his knee. "Slow way to get to Deadwood."

Webster looked at him sidewise. "You in a particular hurry?"

"I don't suppose. But I hear it's quite a place."

Webster smiled vaguely. "Oh, it is. You thinking of becoming a miner, maybe?"

"Would I tell you if I was?"

"There's nothing wrong with mining," Webster said. "A man sure can't get rich driving a team of oxen."

McCan had a sudden insight. "You're not coming back, are you, Webster?"

Webster's dark eyes flickered around. "Don't say that so loud. Old Weaver listens for such, and there's the devil to pay if he hears. I've thought of leaving, sure, but it can be hard for a colored man to get work if the mining goes bust. I can't let go of what I've got without a lot of thinking."

They passed the hot hours around the wagons. Men napped, smoked, talked among themselves. Except Ben Weaver; he stayed alone, staring at nothing, whittling a stick of pine.

"He's always like that," Webster said. "Either he's had some hard times in his life, or one of these oxen kicked him in the head. He's a smart man and a good leader, but he's always alone."

When the afternoon waned, the teamsters yoked up and rolled out. The oxen were full and rested and made good time. Weaver's wagon left deep ruts behind, so McCan pulled off his trail. Others behind him did the same, and soon the train stretched a quarter of a mile long and a sixth of a mile wide.

Dark came, but the sky was clear and moonlit. Weaver called back to McCan, and he in turn passed the message back: "Clear night! Roll on!"

Roll they did, a good two hours past dark. Such a thing was rare, McCan would learn. Usually darkness marked the end of the working day.

The wagons finally halted, and the oxen were freed to graze. Leftover stew was served, bedrolls came out, and Harvey Lane, the night guard, emerged from his sleeper wagon, which trailed along after Webster's wagons. He went to work as the others lay down, and sleep swept in with the song of crickets and the whisper of grass.

Lane's jarring call awakened McCan just before dawn. He crawled out, longing for coffee, knowing there would be none until they were far down the trail.

It was while the teamsters yoked their oxen under the paling sky that the first hint of trouble came.

CHAPTER 3

—❦—

It was a freakish event, but it set off hard feelings that had stewed, mostly unnoticed, for months.

Webster was yoking two oxen when Roy Sturley, a teamster from Arkansas, passed him. One of Webster's oxen moved suddenly and threw him off balance. Webster staggered back against Sturley, who dropped a yoke he had been carrying. It hit his foot.

Sturley spat, "Watch yourself, nigger!" and threw a hard right against Webster's jaw.

Webster squarely faced the man who had uttered and done what he would tolerate from no one. Sturley stared back, brushed dirt from his sleeve, and breathed loudly through his teeth.

"Nobody calls me that, Sturley," Webster said.

The teamsters gathered. Some grinned, others looked worried. McCan edged in and touched Webster's shoulder; Webster pulled away as if it burned him.

From the other side of the circle emerged Jimmy Wyatt, one of the youngest teamsters. He was a short, slight fellow with flame-orange hair and a ruddy face dotted with pancake freckles. He looked at McCan and said, "Stay out of it. It ain't right for a nigger to push a man."

"It was the ox moving that done it," somebody said.

"No. He pushed me a-purpose," Sturley interjected. "You seen it, didn't you, Jimmy?"

"Sure did."

McCan turned to Bob Webster. "Bob, just walk away from it."

Webster glared at him. "Shut up, Luke. I fight my own fights."

"Listen at that!" Wyatt chortled. "You gonna let a nigger talk that way to you?"

McCan was going to respond, but suddenly Sturley lunged forward, swinging wildly. Several blows connected against Webster's neck, chest, and jaw. A gout of blood squirted as a final swing hammered his nose. He fell back, and Wyatt whooped in tent-revival ecstasy.

Webster recovered quickly. He threw himself on his opponent, slammed a hard fist against his eye, and pounded a left into his gut. Sturley grunted, cursed, and groped for Webster's neck. He gripped it and squeezed until his fingernails were white, but Webster seemed unaware of the hands at his throat.

The black man pounded two more bruising punches into Sturley's stomach, then brought up his fists and spread them between Sturley's forearms, knocking the hands from his neck. He heaved forward, head lowered, and butted a granite forehead against Sturley's skull. The crack was like mountain goats colliding.

Sturley fell, but rose with a knife in his hand.

"Yeah!" Wyatt exulted. "Cut him!"

The men nearest Sturley parted suddenly, like a stand of wheat divided by a twister. Weaver came through the gap, walked up to Sturley, and punched his jaw with one hand while deftly taking the knife with the other. Sturley fell back two steps, then looked into the train leader's cold eyes. His face flared livid, then drained to funeral-parlor white.

"But the darky pushed me," he said feebly.

"Bob's my best teamster," Weaver said. "I won't have you cutting him up. And as for you, Bob, I won't tolerate troublemaking or folks with chips on their shoulders. The rest of you, clear out. We're losing time."

Sturley straightened and turned to Webster. The two stared like wary cats as Weaver walked away, confident from experience that his warning was enough to end the fight.

The atmosphere crackled with back-and-forth tension until at last Sturley turned away, muttering. Webster watched him go, then dug out his handkerchief and wiped away the blood. The other teamsters scattered, knowing Weaver meant what he said.

Webster returned to his oxen. McCan thought of going to him, but didn't. He hitched his own team and awaited the order to roll.

The journey continued until the sun raged hot. They stopped the wagons, and the cook provided beans seasoned with big hunks of bacon. The men lined up with pewter bowls in hand; McCan fell in behind Webster.

The cook, Sterling Slater, dished out huge portions and fat biscuits. When Webster received his, he stared first at his bowl, then at Slater.

"Where's the rest?" he demanded.

"What are you talking about?" Slater's confusion was justified, for he had given Webster the same amount as the others.

"You heard me."

Slater twitched thick brows and emphatically spit a

dollop of tobacco juice earthward, but he dished out an extra heap for Webster, who then stepped down the line. He was a volcano seething toward explosion.

Jimmy Wyatt thrust his bowl under Slater's nose. "Fill it up. As much as the nigger got."

McCan's eyes darted to Webster. The big teamster sat with his back toward him, shoveling beans into his mouth. He hadn't heard, or at least didn't let on.

For two days there was no further trouble. Webster calmed down, but remained brooding and distant. McCan spoke to him only a little, for most of the time it was obvious Webster wanted to be left alone.

Rain came, and the going was slow. The daily mileage dropped to six, and often the wagons had to be pushed through mud. Streams swelled to twice normal size, and Weaver worried aloud about the Cheyenne River farther on.

On the fourth day out from Pierre, the train encountered an emigrant wagon beside a stream. McCan recognized it as Caleb Black's.

"Stuck trying to cross?" he asked Weaver.

"Could be. Or maybe redskins, or bandits. If you know this fellow, come with me."

As they drew near, McCan pointed out two dead mules lying nearby in blackened blood, covered with flies.

"He was jumped for sure," Weaver said. "Keep a sharp eye."

McCan could see now that the wagon had bullet holes in the sides and rips in the canvas. From inside it a voice rang out: "Hold it there—come around where I can see your faces."

It was Caleb Black's voice, coming over the long barrel of a Henry that jutted out of the wagon. McCan and Weaver raised their hands.

"Easy, friend," Weaver said. "We're teamsters, here to help you if you need it."

The flaps moved and Black peered over the tailgate. He lowered the Henry. "Come on, then."

He stepped from the wagon as they approached. He recognized McCan, even remembered his name.

"Redskins?" Weaver asked.

"No, white men. Dressed like redskins to try to fool me, but I seen their faces. I'll know them when I see them again."

Weaver said, "You won't see them. Most of the highwaymen keep hid out. A few turn up in Deadwood from time to time—Tom Branton and Evan Bridger, mostly. Nobody bothers them. The law has no proof on them, and most folks are scared of them."

Black snorted contemptuously. "I'll teach 'em scared!"

"You can ride into Deadwood with us," Weaver said. "We'll hitch your wagon behind McCan's team. You can pay your way as an assistant night guard, or by helping the cook, or whatever."

"I'm obliged."

They tied on Black's wagon and moved on; Black rode in the seat beside McCan. The sun grew hot, and the oxen slowed after a few miles. At last Weaver signaled the halt.

CHAPTER 4

When they stopped, Caleb Black crawled inside his wagon and went to sleep. By then, McCan had received a nutshell history of Black and kin.

Black's brother, Walter, was already mining in the Black Hills, and had invited Caleb to join him. The brothers had one younger sister, who lived in Minnesota with her husband, a farmer. Caleb hoped to persuade them to join him in Deadwood after he became settled with Walter.

He answered McCan's questions: No, he had not mined before. Yes, he had read all about it. No, Walter was not rich—not yet. But yes, he would be, and Caleb too. He was sure of it.

The rains stopped, but the mucky land—called gumbo by the veteran teamsters—continued to hamper their progress. The Cheyenne, however, had receded by the time they reached it, and fording was easy. From there on the journey went speedily.

The first sight of the Black Hills reconfirmed to McCan his plan to stay. From a distance they truly were black, because of the pine and spruce on their summits. They crumpled the land like a scuffed-up carpet for a hundred miles on the western border of the territory, down to the Badlands farther south. At places, the hills humped like knuckles or pointed like fingers at the sky.

They approached Deadwood through the Centennial Prairie, where the oxen would graze after the wagons were unloaded. There would be only one day of rest and one night of carousing in Deadwood before the trip back to Pierre—a trip McCan would not make.

McCan had picked up some of Deadwood's history along the way. The town had been founded in 1875, after the discovery of gold there, and at first had been called Deadwood Gulch. The latter title was appropriate; the town was bordered by hills, and thus had grown in a long strand. Along its rutted course sprouted businesses—some legitimate, others not. There were those who called Deadwood the Gomorrah of the west.

Deadwood prospered. The Black Hills swarmed with prospectors; the town was populated with those who made a living, in a variety of ways, off the earnings brought in by the miners.

Deadwood had a decidedly lawless streak, and every kind of human castoff infested its alleyways and dark corners. Prostitutes, gamblers, thieves, murderers— they were plentiful in this hell-pit of a town, and many were those who predicted that one day the Almighty would swallow Deadwood into the bowels of the land and be done with it. The straight and narrow did not pass within a hundred miles of the Black Hills. Deadwood was a rough and cruel town, a place men did not go if they valued their mortal lives and immortal souls. Naturally enough, it was crowded.

The freight wagons rolled into Deadwood late in the afternoon. Unloading them proved difficult and slow. McCan had time only to glance over the town before the return to camp. The narrow street was little more than a wide gully with squatty buildings along it, all of them drab and crude, some consisting more of canvas than lumber.

McCan noted Carl Mann's Saloon, supposedly one of the wildest in town, where Jack McCall had blown out Bill Hickok's brains. They had buried Wild Bill behind the saloon at first, but later moved him to Mount Moriah, overlooking the town. He had plenty of company there; violent death happened frequently in Deadwood. "When the gold pans out," Webster observed, "they can start mining lead out of the corpses on the hill."

Weaver didn't hand out pay until the teamsters were back on the Centennial Prairie; it was his way of making sure they returned. A few slipped back to town immediately, but McCan was exhausted from the day's work. He crawled into his bedroll and fell asleep.

Caleb Black had remained in town. McCan thought about him just before he went to sleep. Probably he was looking for his brother right now. A stake waiting for him—a lucky man.

In the morning, McCan and Webster took two horses from the train remuda and rode into town. Weaver stayed behind with the wagons, ostensibly to guard them, but McCan figured that for an excuse. Weaver seemingly had no need for recreation or release, even company. He was a mystery McCan never would solve, for he knew when he waved his good-bye to him he would see him no more.

McCan and Webster sought out Hardin Crowley, a fellow teamster Webster said was honest, and gave him payment for the horses. "Take it back to Weaver when you leave," McCan said. "We'll not be thought horse thieves by any man."

Crowley pocketed the money. "Good luck to both of you," he said. "Next run, I'll be staying on myself. Wish I could now."

They left their horses at a livery and took to the street. Webster said there were days Deadwood was lifeless as its name, others when it teemed even at noon. This was one of the latter.

Men walked the boardwalks and muddy street, horses milled about, wagons creaked by, merchants sat in the doorways of their shops or tended customers inside. It was an incredible jumble, alternately thrilling and exhausting to observe. As the sun rose, the drab town took on a surreal light that made it almost beautiful, in a primitive way.

McCan stopped; approaching from the other end of the street were Sturley and Wyatt. He felt Webster bristle.

The pair approached and stopped, keeping out of reach of Webster's long arms. Wyatt grinned cockily. "You're keeping some bad company, McCan."

McCan said nothing. Wyatt and Sturley smelled like whiskey, even at this early hour. Wyatt weaved where he stood.

"Can't you talk?" Wyatt said. "It ain't polite to stand and stare at a man like a bug-eyed jackass."

"Just move aside and don't cause trouble," McCan said.

Wyatt presented a look of offended innocence. "Trouble? Did I talk about trouble, Roy? We're just trying to be nice. We're nice to everybody. Even to niggers like you, boy. I'm talking to you, Webster."

Webster moved almost imperceptibly, but managed to squelch whatever he was about to do or say. Wyatt saw he had touched a nerve. He grinned broadly.

"What's the matter, black boy? I make you mad?"

Webster nodded. "You did." His hand flashed out with amazing celerity, and his whole body lunged like a rattler's to within striking distance. Bone crunched horribly as Wyatt's nose went flat under Webster's fist. He grasped his injured face; tears poured out to mix with blood. Sturley gaped, open-mouthed and silent, at his injured partner, who now sat on his rump in the street with blood gushing down his shirt.

Wyatt struggled to his feet again, gripping his nose. He pointed at Webster and said, "You're dead, nigger."

His hand fell to the ivory-handled Colt he always wore. He drew and leveled it, clicked the hammer, and aimed the pistol between Webster's eyes.

McCan pushed the barrel aside as Wyatt squeezed the trigger. There was an empty click. Wyatt raised the pistol and stared crazily at it.

Webster laughed. "They don't work unloaded," he said. He kicked upward and caught Wyatt full force in the groin. Wyatt's body rose a foot off the street and fell backward. His eyes bleared; he tried to scream, but couldn't. As for Sturley, he backed off, then ran.

Webster knelt beside Wyatt and gently took the pistol from his hand. "I unloaded this while you slept the night after you decided mine and Sturley's business was yours. I never take a chance with a fool. And I figured you to be fool enough not to bother to check your own pistol before you came to town. You won't make it here, Wyatt. There's men what can eat you alive."

Webster tossed the pistol into an alley. A drunk scurried to it, stooped, then he and the pistol were gone.

Webster stood and he and McCan walked away. Sturley was gone. Wyatt still writhed in the dirt.

"It isn't over, Bob," McCan said.

"I know it." Webster paused. "Maybe I ought to get me a pistol."

"Both of us," McCan said.

They heard laughter, and McCan turned. A tall man with graying hair and a leathery face stood in the doorway of a tent saloon, a painted girl under his arm and a beer in his hand. He laughed at McCan and Webster, and when McCan looked at him, raised his beer in salute. The man turned back into the dark saloon interior.

"Who was that?" McCan asked. But Webster didn't know.

CHAPTER 5

—

The gunseller was a small man with a monocle; he smiled throughout the entire transaction. "Good choices indeed," he said as he passed two Colts over the countertop. "It's been a good day for Mr. Colt. I sold a pistol identical to these earlier today—only minutes before you arrived."

Webster and McCan exchanged a glance. "Let me guess—a shrimpy little fellow with a busted nose, maybe a funny way of walking?" McCan said.

"Why, yes. A friend?"

"An acquaintance."

Webster was silent a long time as they walked the street. The appeal of Deadwood was greatly diminished by the trouble with Wyatt and Sturley. Now McCan felt they were merely marking time until the next encounter.

Neither he nor Webster were gunfighters, and they knew it. Wyatt, by high standards, probably was not, either. But his quarrelsome nature and the fact that he routinely carried a pistol indicated he was at least oriented toward violence. McCan wondered if he had ever killed a man.

Night fell and brought out Deadwood's balance of human refuse. They reminded McCan of roaches scurrying from beneath his grandmother's old iron stove as she stoked it at the old Missouri homestead.

He and Webster went into a saloon and crowded the bar. The place was packed; poker games under way all around—an enticement for McCan any other time. Plump saloon girls who looked bad and smelled worse moved about with pitchers of beer and bottles of whiskey. In the corner, a piano player and fiddler pounded and sawed their instruments, each racing the other for the final crescendo.

"Take a look," muttered McCan.

Wyatt and Sturley came through the front door; both were very drunk. Sturley's eyes were sunset red, his hair matted on top and sticking out ridiculously on the sides. Wyatt's face was pasty, his nose puffy. The swelling from his suffered blow of the morning made his eyes squint in the middle of a fist-sized bruise spanning his nose.

"You did a real job on him, Bob," McCan said. "I'd say more than his face is swollen."

"I wish he'd just go off and let it be," Webster said.

"He won't. Well, he just saw us."

Wyatt stared at them. His eyes, made ugly by his bruised face, narrowed and became uglier. His fists clenched, unclenched, the right one near a new Colt in his belt. Sturley tried to look threatening too, but a shadow of fear in his expression spoiled the charade.

"Let's go over to them," Webster said.

"No," McCan said. "If anyone starts trouble, let it be them."

The stare-down went on another minute, neither side moving. Then the saloon door opened, and a drunk came in and stumbled against Sturley. That broke the back-and-forth eyeballing, and Sturley and Wyatt left.

Webster and McCan found a table and sat down. Webster ordered a beer, but as he lifted it to his lips, he stopped and shook his head. "Better steer clear of it tonight," he said.

"Both of us," McCan noted.

Webster said, "There's no reason for you to get any deeper into this. It's my fight."

"Not just yours anymore. They've drawn a bead on me too, just for being your friend."

Webster smiled. "Maybe we ought to work a claim together when this is done."

"I'd thought of that myself. We'll talk it over when we get all this behind us."

The conversation waned. They watched the head of Webster's beer dissolve and go flat. Finally Webster took a breath and said, "Let's get it done."

Together they left the saloon. McCan toyed with the butt of his Colt, fingers sweating. The pistol felt heavy on his leg.

Outside, the street was crowded, all of Deadwood's usual nocturnal action under way. McCan looked around, but did not see Wyatt or Sturley. But they were there—he'd bet on it.

As they passed the door of a brothel, Wyatt and Sturley stepped from an alley and faced them. "We're going to settle it right now, nigger," Wyatt said.

"Move aside," ordered McCan.

Wyatt laughed. "You'll die too."

McCan turned to Sturley. "What about you? Are you brave enough to draw on two armed men?"

Sturley, as usual, looked scared; his courage lived and died based on the momentary fluctuations of temper.

"Let's let 'em be, Jimmy," Sturley said. "I don't feel like killing nobody."

Wyatt saw his chance at battle slipping away. He flung a bitter frown at his partner, paused a moment, then grabbed at his pistol.

He was clumsy, inexperienced as a gunman. That gave McCan and Webster time to leap to either side. Wyatt's first shot plowed the dirt, succeeding only in drawing attention. Men appeared at windows and doorways. A woman screamed. The street around them cleared.

McCan drew and aimed at Wyatt, but the freckled redhead dodged back into the alley. Webster's pistol homed in on Sturley, who ran off wildly into the darkness.

Everything yielded to silence and racing pulses. Webster and McCan were alone. Then someone yelled "Look out!"—and a rapid series of things happened.

A shot roared, and Webster spasmed as if bolt-struck. His pistol fell to his feet, and blood dripped and pooled around it as he swayed. McCan saw Wyatt—he had come around the building and shot Webster in the side.

McCan yelled and swung his pistol around as Wyatt sent two more slugs into Webster's body. McCan fired but missed; Wyatt turned to him as Webster collapsed.

Suddenly, something loomed between McCan and his foe. McCan saw a dirty white shirt stretched over broad shoulders, a head of collar-length gray-black hair, a pair of canvas-clad legs spread in a fighting stance. The man raised a Remington and fired; Wyatt's body kicked back and he was dead, with his pistol smoking in his hand. The tall intruder holstered the Remington and turned and smiled at McCan. It was the man McCan had seen laughing in the saloon doorway earlier in the day.

McCan went to Webster. His brown eyes stared sightlessly skyward.

Another man came to his side. It was Caleb Black. He touched Webster's bloodied chest, felt for a heartbeat, and shook his head.

"He's gone," Black said.

CHAPTER 6

McCan sat in the darkest corner of the darkest saloon he could find and brooded over a beer. A tired-looking undertaker had carted away Webster's corpse an hour before, muttering and cursing the dead man for interrupting his supper. He had eaten later than usual because of a knifing death early in the afternoon. Webster's murder forced him to cut short his time at the table; he took it as a personal imposition.

Though McCan and Webster had not known each other long enough to be truly close friends, McCan had sincerely liked the man. Webster once told McCan he had been born a slave in Alabama, and though freed as a boy, had never really felt like his own man. Mining in the Black Hills had been more to Webster than a chance to make money. It had been his doorway to the most freedom he ever would have known. Wyatt had stolen that from him.

Caleb Black entered the saloon and found McCan. "I'm sorry about your friend," he said. "At least the Wyatt boy got what was due him. But let me tell you something: I recognized the man who shot Wyatt."

"Who?"

Black sat down. "I don't know his name, just his face. He was one of the bandits who robbed me along the Deadwood Trail. I'll find his name, just you wait."

"His name is Evan Bridger." The speaker was Hardin Crowley. He joined them at the table. "Luke, I never went back to the wagons. I got to thinking about you and Webster staying on, and I just couldn't leave. I sent your money for the horses back by Sterling Slater. I heard about Webster. What a shame."

"Tell me about this Evan Bridger," Black said.

"Nothing to tell but his name. I heard it called by somebody who had seen what happened. I've heard Ben Weaver mention him as one of the bandits along the Pierre-Deadwood route."

"I owe him my life, I suppose," McCan said. "If he hadn't cut in, it's even money whether it would be me or Wyatt dead right now."

"I owe him too," Black said in a different tone. "The man tried to murder me on the trail."

McCan saw a change of topic was called for. "Did you find your brother?"

"I did. He has a place out toward Lead. Just a shack, but on a good claim. I'm welcome there, and that's what counts."

"I wish I was in your shoes," McCan said. "Some hard work is what I need to take my mind off what happened. That, or a good poker game."

"At the moment, I'm mostly interested in Evan Bridger," Black said.

"What are you hinting at?" McCan asked, for some reason beginning to feel irritated.

"It's personal. Not your worry. Suffice it to say you don't harm a Black unless you're ready for the same in return. Eye for an eye—that's in the Bible."

"So is Balaam's jabbering ass," McCan said. He stood and walked out of the saloon.

Hardin Crowley grinned philosophically at Black. "I don't think he means it personal. He's worked up about Webster."

Black unlimbered his long legs beneath the table and wrapped his body across his chair. "I don't really care. I know what I need to do, and I'll do it. Evan Bridger should've never took the first shot at me."

Black didn't show up when they buried Webster. Hardin Crowley and McCan stood by as a hired preacher assured them that the colored brethren do have souls, yes indeed, that Webster was as much a man as any of us, and McCan, never having thought otherwise, merely shrugged and gave the man two dollars. The preacher tucked it into his heavy Bible and walked away, smiling like an aged cherubim.

Crowley left too, and McCan meandered alone about the grave, trying to figure out just what was nagging at him. He wandered over to a spruce grove and sat down, slumping into the shade. He went to sleep, and when he awakened an hour later, he thought he had it figured out.

It was that Sturley had gotten away clean after starting the whole thing. Wyatt might have dominated the dispute at the end, but Sturley had been the catalyst. And so far, he had taken not so much as a fist in the jaw for starting a run-in that had cost a good man his life.

Well, God help him, McCan would make Sturley pay. McCan hefted his Colt and studied it. He looked around for a target, and settled on a pine knot many yards distant. He carefully aimed and fired. The pistol bucked; the knot didn't even spit dust. He fired again,

again, until the chambers were empty. Not a hit.

He reloaded and tried again, and this time a shot connected. The next time was even better. Three slugs shattered the knot.

His ammunition low, McCan holstered the pistol and headed back into Deadwood. *Let Sturley show up now*, he thought. *I'll splinter his head like that pine knot*.

He rode down the center of the street and pretended to search for Sturley. He thought he saw him, and suddenly his last meal was at his throat, threatening an exit. *Better practice some more. Not ready yet.* Then he saw it wasn't Sturley at all, and felt ashamed, like all Deadwood could look through him and see the fear tapeworming through his insides.

The next day he went back to Webster's grave and practiced some more; he improved. He came back the next two days. Each was the same: shoot out more ammunition, gather a bit more skill, a little more confidence, and ride into Deadwood looking for Sturley—but not too hard. Finally he allowed himself to drop the pretense and admit he didn't really want to find Sturley at all. He admitted one thing more: it wasn't Sturley's escape from punishment that ate at him. It was that he himself had been so scared when Wyatt faced him that he probably would have taken a bullet had not Evan Bridger stepped in.

That was why he had come here and fired all those useless shots. It was a waste. He couldn't bring back Webster, nor atone for past fears by becoming a jury-rigged pistoleer well after the fact.

He spat a curse and fired off a quick shot at a blackbird on a pine stump. The bird flew into feathers and red spray, and McCan exclaimed at his accuracy; he hadn't even aimed.

"Now you're getting the hang of it, son," a voice

from behind him said. He wheeled. It was Evan Bridger.

"I been watching you shoot. You got the skill, but you try too hard, overaim. What you have to do is let that pistol become part of your hand. Point it like a finger. You'll hit your target nine times out of ten."

McCan was wordless. He felt strangely awed.

"Let me show you," Bridger said. He drew out his Remington, and five quick shots erupted. Two hundred feet away, a pear-sized rock became dust.

"Point and shoot natural, without the strain," he said. "And always keep one last round in your cylinder. A man who faces a gunfight with empty cylinders is asking to be killed."

McCan found his voice. "Luke McCan's my name," he said. "I want to tell you how grateful I am for what you did back in town." He paused. "Though I'm not sure why you did it."

"I'm not, either," Bridger said. "It seemed the thing to do at the time. I saw the darky buffalo that redtopped fellow in the afternoon, and it was about the funniest thing I ever did see. I guess I took a liking to him, and when old Red-Top shot him, I just jumped in."

"You probably saved my skin," McCan said. He lifted his Colt. "I'm not much good with this thing. I wasn't any good at all when my friend needed me to be."

"You do much shooting in your boyhood, son?"

"Nothing much with a pistol—mostly squirrel hunting. I always was a good marksman with a rifle."

"Loosen up and you'll be a good pistol man too." Bridger smiled, showing even teeth. "Being a good pistol man can be a good thing, or bad. Depends on how a man uses it."

McCan thought back to what had happened to

Caleb Black on the trail, and asked: "How do *you* use it, Mr. Bridger?"

"Any way I please," he said. "I see you know who I am."

"I asked."

Bridger mounted a big black gelding tied to a branch nearby. "I expect I'll see you around some more," he said, and rode away.

McCan suddenly felt a crazy urge to do two contradictory things: to warn Bridger of how Caleb Black had hinted at retribution for the trail attack, and to raise his Colt and put a slug through Bridger's brain. The first urge was the offspring of gratitude; the second came from some deeper source that one day McCan would identify as intuitive foreknowledge, but which now seemed mere insanity.

So he did not shout or shoot. He just watched Bridger ride away.

CHAPTER 7

McCan wondered why he remained in Deadwood at all. So far, he had made no attempt to become a miner. He suffered a general malaise, and when his money began running out, eaten up by meals and boarding-house rent, he began playing poker.

He was a good poker player, and Deadwood a good poker town, so he easily made enough money to sustain himself. But he refused to think of himself as a gambler—just as he always had all those previous times the cards had held him—and told himself he would begin mining the next day, or next week, or maybe the week after that. But every night he would sit up with stonefaced men, circling a table, staring at his hand through the smoke of his cigarette. When the gaming was done, he would stagger off to his room—usually several dollars richer—and sleep until midday. Then he would loiter away the afternoons out of town, still practicing with his Colt, but not knowing why. Sturley was a dead issue; the big coward probably had run back to Weaver and the wagon train and Pierre.

Secretly, McCan worried. He felt like a powder keg that might blow, or might just fizzle out. He had gone through something like this right after his parents had been killed, but it hadn't lasted. Webster's murder had brought it all back, though. He thought of writing his sister for advice—but not now. Later. When he was through gambling.

Bound for trouble, bound for crime. Such had been his own mother's prediction for him. He remembered it often now, and didn't deny it like he once had. His mother always had seen the worst in him, even when wanting the best for him. Maybe she was right, he mused. He'd think about it again, after the next poker game.

A rain came and went; McCan walked the muddy street. He stepped across a soaked drunk on the boardwalk, wrinkling his nose at the sewer-pit smell of the town, boosted now to a nearly intolerable level by the rain.

A man across the street caught his eye. He was dark, so much so that McCan first took him for a black man. On closer inspection, the man proved to be an imprecise mongrelization of Spanish and Anglo, with maybe some redskin thrown in. His mustache was wide and so thickly waxed it reflected the sun. His other facial hair was something between a neglected scruff and a true beard. A sombrero pulled low across his grimed forehead enhanced the Spanish look.

Noticeable as the man was, it was the one with him who drew McCan's interest: Caleb Black. Black spoke to the dark man, then glanced around the way men do at the doors of back-street brothels. Black and the man walked into an alley. Sun glinted on the butt of a pistol thrust into the stranger's belt. The man was a gunman. It might as well have been written on him.

* * *

His name was Morgan Hamm. McCan learned it when they brought him in, draped over the back of his horse. He had been shot three times in the chest, but not before being efficiently sliced up by a knife.

"Somebody tortured him bad," said a stranger who watched Hamm's corpse flopping past on the horse's rump. "Whoever did it didn't want him dead too quick."

"Why would they want him dead at all?" McCan asked.

"Hamm's a hired gunman. Kills for pay. Probably whoever did this was supposed to be his victim, but turned the tables. He probably got tortured so he would tell who hired him."

McCan thought about that a moment, then said, "Oh, no."

The stranger gave him an inquiring look. McCan ran for the livery.

Where was Caleb's brother's claim? Out toward Lead, Caleb had said. That was little help, but all he had. McCan had to get there now.

He galloped through the middle of the street, his mount's hooves splashing puddles, his reckless passing evoking a curse from a back-stepping man he nearly ran over. McCan sped past him and out of town.

McCan rode past claims where miners labored. He looked at their faces, but did not know them. They watched him with vague frowns, seeing urgency in his manner.

"Where is Walter Black's place?" he shouted at a trio of them. Two stared back in silence, but the third pointed and said, "Yonder, maybe half a mile. Cut left on the trail through the pines."

McCan spurred his tiring mount. He rounded a bend a quarter-mile ahead, then reined to a halt. A rider came toward him, lazily plodding along.

"Howdy," Evan Bridger said. He touched his hat. "Fine day, Mr. McCan."

McCan watched him round the bend. Then he dug rowels into horseflesh and plunged on, fearing he was too late.

Walter Black's claim was humble, a simple shed with a canvas roof provided his shelter. McCan dismounted in the yard of pounded dirt. Slowly, he approached the open door.

"Hello?"

No response. A bird called and the creek splashed, but that was all.

"Caleb?"

He pushed the door further open and stepped inside. Sunlight spilled in.

A man sat at the table, leaning back against the wall. McCan could scarcely make him out in the shadows.

"Hello? Caleb?"

The man said nothing, did not move. McCan stepped into the shadows himself, and understood why.

This was not Caleb Black. But a strong facial resemblance was there, and McCan knew he had found Walter Black. He had been eating bread with butter and drinking coffee when Bridger came in. The coffee was still steaming.

In Walter Black's forehead was a neat, round bullet hole. A thin trail of blood marked the space between his eyes and spread across his nose. McCan did not want to see more. He turned away, wondering where he would find Caleb's corpse.

He walked to the back of the shed and looked about the clearing, but saw no sign of Caleb.

McCan called Caleb's name and headed toward the woods. He walked through the spruces and pines, and heard a faint but identifiable sound: a man crying.

McCan followed the sound. He found Caleb Black hugging the base of a tree, crying, with his eyes squeezed shut.

"Are you wounded?"

Black shook his head.

"Walter is dead, Caleb."

Black's voice strained: "I know."

"Evan Bridger did it. I saw him riding away. He tortured your hired gunman into telling him you hired him. He probably thought Walter was you."

"I just hid," Black said. "Hid like a coward."

"Come on," McCan said. "We've got a grave to dig."

McCan helped Black to his feet, and together they walked to the clearing.

CHAPTER 8

After Walter Black was buried, Caleb Black stayed drunk three days, and on the fourth went looking for Evan Bridger. McCan, who had stayed at the Black claim after the murder, figured he would see Black no more. But only a day later he was back, sober, saying the talk was that Evan Bridger had left the Black Hills. Headed north.

"So what will you do, Caleb?" McCan asked.

Black rubbed his chin and looked around. "Mine this claim, I reckon. And I'd like you to help me. Put away the cards; a man who plays poker gets into trouble, and folks in trouble a lot of times get hurt."

You're a fine one to preach to anybody, McCan thought. But he knew Black was right.

"All right. I'll try it for a few days. But I don't know a thing about mining."

"I'll show you what I know."

That proved to be relatively little. Caleb Black had been at the job only a short time himself; he was nearly as green as McCan. But the work satisfied both of them. McCan ceased his trips to town and the poker tables. He missed the money at the beginning, but with time, their takes increased. McCan thought he had found his calling. He scribed out a letter to his sister in Missouri, telling her the good things that had happened, omitting the tragedies of Bob Webster and Walter Black.

Three months passed. McCan was convinced by then that Caleb Black had gotten over Walter's death. They never discussed it, and he no longer bore the haggard, haunted look that had marked him those first days.

Then, one night, McCan awoke and found Caleb's bunk empty. He went to the door and saw him out-side, walking around fast and nervous, pumping his arms up and down like a man about to explode. McCan knew then he had not gotten over the murder at all, maybe never could.

For almost six months they mined and redeemed their gold as usual—every day like the rest. Black still seemed happy, and there were no more restless nights. Then, one night in early spring, he left.

McCan found a note on the door: BRIDGER IN WYOMING—GONE TO FIND HIM. MAY BE BACK SOON OR IT MIGHT BE AWHILE. WHICHEVER, YOU KEEP ON AND THE GOLD IS YOURS. SHALL SEE YOU AGAIN, CALEB.

McCan kept on alone for a week. But without Caleb Black, it was dull work. One night, he slipped on his hat, pocketed his money, and rode into Deadwood. There he found a poker game, made a few dollars. The next night he went back. From then on, his course was set, and mining gradually gave way to poker.

Jack Parker was a big man with smallpox scars, a little talent for poker, and a propensity for big talk. He was new to Deadwood, his background unknown. McCan took a bit of his money over cards nightly for two weeks, but Parker never seemed to mind. He kept his big smile and guffawing laugh, and turned over his losses with unfading good humor.

"I like you, McCan," he said. "You've got a good look about you. The kind of man I like to work with."

"What line are you in?"

"High profits, son, high profits. We'll talk some more about it when the time is right."

McCan dismissed the vague talk and concentrated on his gambling. But then his luck went bad. For three consecutive nights he lost badly at the table. Parker came to him and threw a fleshy arm across his shoulder.

"Take a break from the game tomorrow night," he said. "Head out to the little house beside Tolbert's Gunwright Shop and wait for me. I want to talk something over with you. Business."

McCan would have said no any other time. But his luck was low—*he* was low. He nodded without much thought, and the next night went to the designated place.

The house was two rectangular rooms joined by a hallway; the roof was flat and leaky. McCan entered it. Flies swarmed through an atmosphere thick with the smell of Jack Parker's person, for he lived here. Tonight he waited by a window. When McCan came in, Parker scowled at him.

"You're late," he said.

"I don't even know why I'm here."

"It doesn't matter much now. They went ahead without you. I'd decided you weren't going to show."

McCan waved his hat at the flies. "Explain all this to me, would you?"

But Parker had stopped listening. He straightened

and looked into the dark street. "They're coming!"

"Who?"

Two riders came past the window and cut around the house. Parker rushed to a back door and opened it. McCan recognized two men who sometimes joined the poker games, but who more often loitered in the background, hanging around Parker. They dismounted and walked around to a packhorse they led.

"Did you get it?" Parker asked.

"Take a look," said one of the men. He and the other lifted a pack off the back of the third horse. It was heavy, for both grunted at the effort.

"Get it inside!" Parker said. "Did anybody see you?"

"We were careful."

Inside, they laid the pack on the floor. It made a loud, metallic clump on the floorboards. Parker closed the shutters and threw back the cloth pack cover. Underneath was a small but heavy strongbox.

"Oh, sweet thing, there's no woman finer than you," Parker said. He rubbed his hands together, then fiddled with the lock. "I can saw it off easiest," he said.

"What's going on here?" McCan asked.

"What's it look like?" one of them asked.

"Like robbery."

The man frowned and said to Parker: "Who is this, anyway? Why's he here?"

"He's a latecomer," Parker said. "He's fine. Just not filled in yet."

"I don't want any part of this," McCan said.

"There. See?" the first man said, waving his hand at McCan. "He don't even want to do it. Why you always dragging in extra baggage, Jack?"

Parker didn't answer, for he was working on the lock with a saw. Sweat beaded out on his red face, then began dripping on the strongbox. His well-greased locks swung back and forth across his forehead as he sawed.

"I'm leaving," McCan said. He turned toward the door.

One of the men made as if to draw his pistol, but McCan drew first and thrust his weapon against the man's chin. Just then, there was noise outside—a horse approached, then they heard voices.

"*Law!*" said one of the thieves.

"I thought you weren't followed," Parker said.

McCan holstered his pistol. "That's *law* out there? And me in here with—"

Parker swore. He had thrown open the box. Inside was a handful of change, just a few low-denomination bills.

The men outside came to the door. Parker leaped up, stuffing the money in his pocket. He ran out the back door, and the others followed. McCan was left alone in the house.

"Open this door!" somebody shouted from the front.

McCan almost obeyed, the response automatic. Then he thought again, and ran after the others out the back door.

Thank providence he had tethered his mount in the rear. He leaped astraddle and rode away, hearing yelling behind him as the front door was kicked in and the empty strongbox discovered. A shot popped flatly, and a slug sliced the air high above him. He bent lower and rode as hard as he could until he was out of Deadwood, and knew as he left he could not go back.

A week later, McCan sat by a campfire on the windswept prairie and wrote the following:

Mrs. Martha Hyatt
Independence, Missouri

My Dear Martha,

I'm thinking of you and home tonight because now I've got no home at all. My old partner, Caleb Black—about who I wrote you before—is gone, headed out to find a man who killed his brother, and probably will kill him before he is through, and that is a shame because Caleb is a good man but for his temper and his vengeful ways.

Since he has gone I have not done well, I am sorry to tell you. In your confidence I will be honest—without meaning to I've fallen in with common outlaws, and I guess am not much better than one myself. I listened to a man named Jack Parker and didn't recognize him for a thief and a scoundrel and that is my fault. We are on the run from the law, and all for about fifty dollars in bills and coins.

If you scorn me for this I do not blame you and expect no better. Our mother might have been right about me after all, though you always took my side with her, which I will always be grateful for. Anyway, I am out of Deadwood now and near the Powder River in the Montana Territory, writing this letter by the light of our campfire. I am still with Jack Parker, for I have nobody else to run with and he is at least some protection in the wilderness. There were two others with us, but they cut out and left three days ago.

I don't know what we will do or where we will go. I am sorry also to tell you I've been playing poker a lot more again and may have to keep it up to make some money, though like you always said, it takes a man's worth from him to live on gambled money.

Forgive my gloomy writing, but it makes me feel better to tell of it, even though I know you would want to hear better of me.

Mention me to old friends, but don't tell them what I'm about, nor your family, for I am ashamed of it. Say prayers for me, for I have forgot how and don't think I would be heard in any account. I hope you will hear better from me the next time I write you, and maybe even by the time you receive this my situation will be better, for I am nowhere near a post and cannot send this until I don't know when.

Your foolish but devoted brother,
Luke M.

CHAPTER 9

McCan was playing poker in a saloon at Rosebud when he encountered a man he had not expected to see again. He heard a voice, turned, and there he was. For a moment McCan remained frozen, then he thrust his hand to his gun and began to rise.

Parker rose first. "Roy Sturley! Why, I ain't seen you since we gigged frogs together back in Arkansas!"

Sturley smiled at Parker, then saw McCan; the smile vanished. Sturley went chalky white, but McCan, thrown off-balance by Parker's unexpected greeting of Sturley, did nothing. What went through his mind was this: *If I'm so low as to run with a fifty-dollar robber, I might as well go dishonorable all the way and just let Sturley off the hook.*

Feeling the sense of relief that comes with abandoned principles, McCan sank back into his seat and toyed with his cards. Sturley alternated between glancing at McCan with poorly hidden fear and flashing nervous grins at Parker.

After more bubbling about Arkansan boyhood

days—which, McCan gathered, involved an excessive amount of frog-gigging, petty theft, fornication, and arson—Parker turned to McCan and said, "Luke, I want you to meet the finest partner a man ever had. I grew up with this cuss. Roy Sturley, this here is Luke McCan."

Sturley looked as if he would gladly sacrifice a mouthful of teeth to be anywhere else. McCan smelled the fear in him. Without the support of a flared temper or a bellyful of alcohol, Sturley was as meek as he had been when Ben Weaver had knocked him back on the trail to Deadwood.

"We've already had the pleasure," McCan said. "Sturley and me have known each other since we were teamsters together. Right, Roy?"

Sturley nodded.

"Well, who'd a-thought it!" Parker exclaimed. "This is just mighty fine, all of us getting together by accident like this. Roy, sit down and let us deal you in."

"I'm broke," Sturley said.

"Your credit's good with us, Roy—right, Luke?"

"Well, I recall that I owe Roy a little something myself," McCan said. He said it to watch Sturley shudder, which he did.

They played two hours, and McCan won handily. He rarely cheated at cards—though he had the ability—but tonight he did cheat, just to drive Sturley deep into his debt. When the game was done, Sturley was humiliated, McCan satisfied.

The group retired to the prairie for the night. McCan spread his bedroll and lay down, but sleep eluded him. Through his mind played the scene of Bob Webster's death, and his own obsession shortly thereafter of making Sturley pay for his role in that injustice.

By the next morning, a new memory was lodged in McCan's brain: a memory of how he had risen in the dark after seeing Sturley do the same. Sturley had quietly taken his horse and crept off; McCan had followed. Out on the open land he had cut Sturley off, made him stop.

"I decided earlier I would forgive you for what you did," he told the frightened man. "Then I thought about it, and changed my mind."

McCan raised his pistol. "For Bob," he said as he squeezed the trigger.

McCan recalled it all with clarity—unusual for him, for he usually did not remember his dreams. Only one part had really happened: Sturley had, indeed, slipped away. McCan had not seen it, for sleep had finally come, bringing with it the dream of revenge McCan could never really have performed, but which gave a certain satisfaction nonetheless.

Parker was saddened and mystified by Sturley's nocturnal departure. "I can't figure it out," he said. "Why would he do it?"

"I guess we'll never know," McCan said.

"Well, he'll miss out on a good deal," Parker said. "We're heading for the Missouri Breaks, son. Good money to be made up that way."

"How so?"

"Rustling, my friend, rustling."

McCan immediately saw a clear image of himself swinging a couple of feet above the ground, neck stretched out nearly a foot long, head slumped to the side, eyes half shut, and tongue dangling out. It was enough to empty his stomach, but he only smiled and said, "Sounds mighty good to me."

From that moment on he looked for a chance to leave. None arose for a long time, not until days later, when they reached the Breaks and rode to an old cattle

station occupied by a coal-dirty Irishman named Todd
Feeney. Feeney knew Parker, and welcomed him, but
watched McCan warily.

McCan spent one night there, and the next day;
when darkness fell again, he took his horse and rode
fifteen miles through the night. He camped in a draw
at the bend of the Missouri, slept half the next day,
and waited out the rest. Just before sunset he rode
again.

Satisfied he had not been followed, he relaxed, let a
deep breath of relief flow out like a prayer, and put
his days of criminal association forever behind him.
Then he cut southward and rode toward the little settlement of Glendive, having no plan, no goal, and very
little money.

PART II

THE TIMBER CREEK
CATTLE ENTERPRISE

CHAPTER 10

——

In Glendive, McCan found a job as a clerk in a general store. He passed a spring and summer in relative comfort, but in the fall and winter, business grew lean. Cattlemen who came in complained of wolves and rustlers, and bought mostly on credit. The next spring the store closed when the owner abruptly decided to head back east.

McCan turned to the cattle industry. He found a job on a ranch near the Tongue River and learned the requisite skills from a one-toothed old Texan named Rufus Meuller. In the fall, he went on his first roundup.

That was a harder venture than being a teamster, and about equal to mining. He slept five or six hours at night—sometimes in the rain—and spent what seemed ten times that many in the saddle. On roundup, his standard meal was a concoction of lean beef, cattle heart, brains, guts, and hot sauce, all cooked together under the name son-of-a-bitch stew. "Eat it with gratitude, boy," Meuller would say. "Not only will it fill your belly, but it'll keep you dewormed."

After the roundup, he spent a winter in a line camp on Mizpah Creek, bored and reading the backs of soup cans to remain sane. His job was to keep the cattle of his home ranch within that spread's accepted range, and he did the task well, despite no cooperation from weather or cattle.

When spring came he moved on, looking for a larger spread. He bought a weary old horse and a good saddle and rode to the Timber Creek Cattle Enterprise near the Mountain Sheep Bluffs, about fifty miles west of Glendive and the same distance north of Milestown. There he sought out the ranch boss, Abe Hunt, and asked for work.

There were others there at the same time, also seeking jobs, and a dozen of them lined up in the shade of a lean-to, awaiting the verdict. Hunt would have made the decision alone and quickly under normal circumstances, but today a representative of the holding company that owned the ranch was present and wanted a hand in the hiring.

The company rep's name was Henry Sandy; he looked like a Bostonian and talked like an Iowan. He chose McCan and five others; Hunt sealed the choices with a nod. The new employees headed to the bunkhouse to deposit their possessions, but Hunt motioned McCan aside first.

"That horse of yours ain't worth poleaxing," he said. "Pack it in the corral and pick out a good one. We'll fill out the rest of your string later."

"He likes the look of you, neighbor," said a man at the corral. "He always gives first pick to them he likes."

McCan went to the bunkhouse. It smelled almost fishy from sweat, and McCan was further disheartened to see a grizzly of a man pick a louse from his beard and throw it to the dirt floor. McCan jumped and almost yelled when the man suddenly produced a pistol from beneath his blanket and shot the evicted parasite.

"A big one," the man said.

McCan drew his Colt and pumped two more slugs into the floor at the man's feet. "Sure was," he said. "You just winged it."

After dumping his goods, he walked out the door. At least three men had witnessed the incident. McCan figured he had just saved himself a lot of harrassment; the story would spread ranch-wide by nightfall, and the Timber Creek crew would know he was no greenhorn ripe for torment.

It was mid-April, and the plains turned green after the long winter. Snows on the western mountains' lower slopes melted, making rivers and creeks rise. The barrens became active again.

Out of the hidden valleys and ravines where they had passed the winter, cattle emerged to feed on the new grass. It soon would be time for the spring roundup, when the losses of the winter would be assessed, and new calves branded.

McCan was given the job of preparing the chuck wagon for roundup. Helping him was Stewart Biggs, the lice-shooter from the bunkhouse. Together they greased the wheels and axles and replaced a damaged sideboard. They cleaned mouse nests from the chuck box and strung a new tarpaulin beneath the wagon as a pocket for wood and chips. They worked under the guidance of John Weatherby, the Timber Creek cook— maker of the Montana Territory's finest raisin pudding.

As McCan expected, the louse story earned him respect. Biggs and Weatherby both seemed fond of McCan, and he was popular among the crew at large. A particular friend was Dan Tackett, nearly twenty years McCan's senior, and an old man among cowboys. Tackett had come up from Texas with the first Montana herds, and had worked ranches from Dakota to the Deer Lodge Valley. McCan learned that Tackett had once been married, and had lost a son to the Cheyenne—a boy who, Hunt told McCan, looked a lot like him, something McCan took as a partial explanation for Tackett's attachment.

Two days into May, the Timber Creek punchers rode into Milestown to begin the roundup. With them went punchers and reps from scores of other spreads over eastern Montana and western Dakota, even some from northern Wyoming. Cattle ranged far on the open land, despite efforts to contain them, and it was common to see reps from far-spread ranches in the roundup.

McCan rode beside Tackett as they slowly approached Milestown. The town looked sleepy and drab across the distance, but that was a mirage, conjured from the mist of the nearby Yellowstone. Milestown was no Deadwood, but it was a lively enough place, particularly when cowboys were in town.

Tackett bit off a chew of tobacco and settled it into his jaw, then lit a cigar. He was the most tobacco-permeated man McCan knew, seldom going to sleep without an unlit cheroot between his lips. "You're going to snore that thing down your gullet," Hunt would warn him repeatedly. But Tackett never did.

Tackett gestured toward the panorama of men, horses, and wagons.

"You'll see good times here today, Luke," he said. "Folks getting together after a long time apart like to whoop it up a little. I wonder if old Stanley Branch is here? He's with the Connors crew down on the Powder, I ain't seen him since last year."

Tackett was excited, and it rubbed off on McCan, for Tackett was not prone to easy enthusiasm. But today his eyes laughed and his shoulders were thrown back.

McCan dismounted at the circus of cowboys. It seemed all of them were talking, laughing, and cussing at the same time. To the right, five men played poker, the pot being pay the players would not receive until roundup was done. Elsewhere, a footrace was in progress, and beyond that, a horse race. Two men arm wrestled at McCan's left, and nearby, others huddled around a bottle, passed in violation of roundup rules. On the fringe of the group, someone with a harsh and supervisory expression tried to shoo off a wagon of prostitutes who had come over from the far side of town to advertise their inventory.

McCan wandered through the crowd, occasionally nodding at those he knew from previous ranch work. At length he saw a rope corral, in which a husky black man carefully approached a horse with a wild eye. Unlike the rest, the men at the corral were silent as gravediggers.

The man slowly twirled a rawhide rope as he eased up to the defiantly snorting horse. He was like a cat, moving silently, loop always twirling, until at last he cast it true over the horse's neck.

The animal contorted, reared, kicked, jerked its head to free itself. Two men moved in to help the buster keep hold of the rope, and finally looped it around a snubbing post set deep in the earth.

The horse braced and pulled until he threw himself over, and in a second the buster was on the animal, hobbling it with the rope now jerked free from the post. He whipped a bridle from his belt and secured it in place.

He let the horse up again, then approached with the blanket and saddle. After several tries, fifty pounds of leather and metal were cinched on the horse. Before the horse could respond, the buster twisted its ear enough to hurt and swung into the saddle.

The horse became an explosion of hide, dust, and lather. The buster was thrown high and hard, one arm flapping like a wing. As the horse tried to throw him, the men at the corral broke their silence: "Ride that thing, Bill!" "Don't let him throw you, son!"

On it went for several minutes, until the weary horse gave up. The buster dismounted, then mounted again, over and over until the horse was accustomed to the feel of it.

The man removed the saddle and bridle and gave the horse a rest. It wasn't fully broken, but its spirit was. Before long, it would be a good working horse.

Dusting off his gray breeches, the buster walked to the side of the corral. Appreciative pats drummed the sweat-ringed shoulders of his blue shirt.

McCan found him later, sipping coffee beside one of the chuck wagons. "You did a fine job on that bronc," McCan said.

"Thanks," the buster said. He looked up, and McCan drew in his breath.

Bob Webster!

"You all right, friend?"

"I don't know what to say—you're the image of a friend of mine who—I lost down in the Black Hills."

The man grew serious. "You knew Bob?"

"Bob Webster—right."

"He was my brother. I'm Bill Webster from the Lazy Arrow."

McCan smiled and stuck out his hand. "I'm proud

to meet you, Bill. I heard Bob speak of you. My name's Luke McCan."

This time it was Bill Webster who looked surprised. "McCan? You were with Bob when he died?"

"Yes, but how . . ."

"*He* told me." The black man pointed at an approaching figure. It was Hardin Crowley. McCan and Crowley saw each other at the same time—Crowley speeded to a near run, his hand already extended.

"Luke! Never figured to see you turn cowboy!"

"What about you, Hardin? I thought you'd still be in Deadwood, getting rich."

"Left two years ago. I see you done met Bill."

"Yeah. Thought I was seeing Bob's ghost for a second, Hardin, you haven't changed. But the times have, that's for sure. You're the first old face I've seen in quite a spell."

They talked several minutes, and Crowley said, "I saw your old partner awhile back, down in Bozeman."

"Caleb?"

"Yeah, but you'd hardly know him. All beard and grit and muscle. He's had a hard road to follow."

"What's he doing now?"

"What do you think? He's trailing Evan Bridger. And it's making him and Bridger both a little famous. There's a magazine back east that wrote about them. Called Bridger the badman with the ghost at his heels, the haunt that won't let him rest. Would you ever have thought such as that out of Caleb, huh?"

CHAPTER 11

After the first week on roundup, McCan quit counting the days. All was repetition, so there seemed no point in keeping up. Only the terrain varied.

Most days McCan worked closely with Dan Tackett, particularly when they entered the land around the Yellowstone. They worked hills and gullies, driving out calves with mothers bawling at their tails, rumbling down to the day herd that followed the chuck and bed wagons and the remuda.

Bill Webster, to McCan's pleasure, was rep on the same roundup team as he. They had little time to talk, but McCan enjoyed the company, for it was much like having Bob Webster back again.

The roundup team of which they were a part split two days into the roundup, one portion heading east, their own smaller one combing the west. They generally followed the contours of North Sunday Creek, moving across the Little Dry, over Crow Rock Creek and up Timber Creek, delving finally into the rugged lands near the Missouri. Here they were not far from

Wolf Point, and the area McCan had reached with Jack Parker.

They worked back along Crow Rock Creek through a series of knolls and gulches. Tackett and McCan had the worst of it today—following a narrow rivulet winding through hills, Tackett low and McCan high on the ridges, where he could scan coulees for strays. They did well, rousting out cattle like rabbits from a bush, and Tackett herded at least twenty before him now.

McCan saw the remuda and the wagons far out on the plains, the day herd spread peacefully beyond it. A thin cloud of dust showed him where some other cowboy was drawing together quite a herd of his own.

McCan galloped to the top of a ridge and looked down as Tackett rounded a bluff and entered a small, lush valley where several cattle grazed. Tackett waved up to indicate he saw them, and McCan sent his mount half-sliding, half-walking down the slope to him. An avalanche of gravel rolled ahead.

"Look at this," Tackett said.

They dismounted and walked to the little valley's gaplike mouth. The valley was really a box canyon, and across the entrance was a thin strand of barbed wire. McCan understood what it meant.

His eyes swept the little valley, and he pointed. "Look there. There's been a camp here awfully recent."

"Yep. And I'll bet if you check them cattle every one will have a brand that ain't on the record books yet. This is a running iron operation. Rustle mavericks, brand the yearlings, rebrand the others, hold them until you can register the brand, and have your own herd free and clear, nobody the wiser."

"Guess we ought to tell Abe," McCan said.

"Don't cut the fence or nothing," Tackett said.

"Abe will want to see this as it is." He shook his head. "Damn Missouri River's lined with thieves."

"I know," McCan said. "I was up there a little while."

Tackett looked at him with more interest than his old poker face had shown before, but he said nothing.

When they got back to the camp, Abe Hunt had not come in. They drank Arbuckle coffee and waited for him. When he arrived and heard their story, he looked disgusted, but not surprised. After a quick meal he rode with them to the valley.

Hunt clipped the barbed wire with cutters from his saddlebag. McCan wondered how many ranch and homestead fences had yielded to that tool, for Hunt was a wire-hating man.

The cattle spooked, but the men caught three yearlings. Hunt inspected the new brands on them.

"Running iron, no question," he said. "I've seen no brand like this one before."

"Think we'll find whoever did this?" McCan asked.

"I doubt it," Hunt answered. "They've probably cleared out for the Breaks."

But the next day, Tackett flushed from a coulee a couple of mavericks, a five-foot rattler, and a very scared man. Tackett brought the man into camp. The fellow claimed to be suffering from a blow to the head given to him by an unnamed partner, who had since ridden away.

Hunt watched the man with a grim, ominous expression. "Who are you?"

"My name is Terrence Brown. I'm from the XIT— at least, until a month ago, when I had to take off."

"Why'd you do that?"

"My old mammy took sick, and I had to get her to a doctor in Milestown. But she died."

"Why you out here alone?"

"I was on my way to Rosebud with a man named Ernest Smith. We had jobs lined up there. My horse hit a hole and snapped its leg and I had to shoot it. Then he just popped me with his gun butt and left me, Smith did. I don't know why."

"You say you worked for the XIT?"

"That's right."

"Until a month ago?"

Now Brown looked cautious. "Yes."

Hunt called to one of the men back at the chuck wagon, "Dillard! Come up here." A gangly fellow rubber-legged it over to him.

"Mr. Brown, Dillard here worked the XIT not three months back. He knows every man on the place. Dillard, do you know this man?"

"Never seen him before," Dillard said.

Brown looked scared.

"*I've* seen him," said someone behind McCan. It was Lester Tracey, a young man just shy of twenty. "I can't give all the details, but I was with a bunch of cattlemen who cleaned out a nest of cattle thieves here a few months back, and this here's one that slithered out."

Brown's eyes darted like those of a cornered cur. "If I'm being accused of a crime, I want a fair trial. A courtroom, with a real judge."

"We've got no need for such," Hunt said. He looked around. "That cottonwood should serve the purpose."

Someone found a rope and knotted it into a hangman's noose. As Brown watched in horror, Tackett threw the rope over the branch of the cottonwood.

Brown ran. Tackett stepped out, bounded in broad strides, and took him by the collar. Brown went down, and Tackett dropped his knee onto his belly, full-weight.

They dragged Brown, kicking and yelling, to the cottonwood, where they stood him atop a keg from the chuck wagon and tightened the noose around his neck. McCan's pulse raced as he watched; he was glad he had left the company of Jack Parker.

They pulled the rope tight. "I'm sorry there's not enough drop for a proper slack," Hunt said. "We'll just have to let you choke it out. Do you want a prayer from anyone?"

Brown only glared at him. Hunt shrugged. "Whatever you prefer. Good-bye, thief." He kicked away the stool.

Brown choked, his face red, eyes bulging, horrible sounds coming from inside him. McCan was about to turn away when Hunt drew his pistol and shot the rope in two. Brown dropped to the ground on his rump.

Hunt holstered his pistol. "I spared you because I'm a man who can hardly stand to kill a rattler, not because you deserve to live. Now I want something from you in return. You go to every rustler you know and tell them the territory is full of cattlemen who are about to go to war, and there'll be no mercy shown like you've gotten here. Tell them you were lucky, and the next man won't be. Go. Get out of here."

Brown worked himself to his feet. Hunt drew his knife and cut off most of the rope that trailed down his back. But he left the noose on his neck, and he used the cut-off rope to tie Brown's hands behind his back.

"You can't send me out like this!"

"Start walking."

"But there's no telling what will happen to me!"

"All right, then we can go ahead and hang you."

Brown cursed, but started walking. Tackett drew his pistol and put a slug into the dirt at his heel, and Brown ran.

CHAPTER 12

Among cowboys, Jonas Carrington was exceptional in two ways: he had a family—though only a daughter, for his wife was dead—and he had his own house, away from the ranch.

It was the latter distinction that was the most unusual, for several of the Timber Creek hands either had been married at one time or had fathered children without the formality of marriage. Several had kept company with squaws, primarily the handful who had come to Montana in the days of the Alder Gulch mining rush.

Carrington was employed by the Timber Creek Cattle Enterprise, but he worked irregularly, mostly during roundups. The rest of the time he spent raising sustenance crops for himself and his daughter, and that made him an exception in a third way: most cowboys hated any form of sodbusting and refused to do it. Carrington kept busy at it, and he also repaired wagons and did some occasional blacksmithing work.

His daughter, two decades old, was a dark-haired

beauty whose picture Carrington kept in a pillbox in his pocket. Like her father, she was a busy person. She taught piano lessons to the daughters of other ranchers, sometimes to cowboys who used the lessons as an excuse to be close to her. With relatively few women on the plains, the cowboys idolized Jonas Carrington's daughter, though few knew her personally. Jonas, it was rumored, was prone to run off at gunpoint any who came calling without meeting his approval first.

Carrington was shy and quiet by nature, but throughout the roundup had been even more reticent than usual. He stayed alone most of the time, and appeared thoughtful and somewhat troubled.

Near the end of the roundup, Carrington approached Abe Hunt.

"I've got to go home, Abe," he said.

"We will go, in about a week."

"Something's wrong back there. I've got a feeling. I have to go back now."

Abe Hunt pursed his lips, then nodded. "All right. Head on back and do what you need to. Come back here if there's time, and if not, I'll see you back at Timber Creek."

Carrington smiled, thin-lipped and tight. His face looked drawn. "Thank you, Abe." He walked away, rubbing his left arm as if it hurt.

The next morning, Hunt shook McCan awake just before dawn. Weatherby was putting on coffee to boil. Almost everyone else still slept.

"I want you to ride back home with Jonas," Hunt said. "I don't think everything is all right with him."

McCan rubbed his eyes, then nodded. "Whatever you want, Abe. Why's he going back?"

Hunt filled him in. "He's not too happy to have you along. He thinks I'm nursemaiding him."

Carrington was by the chuck wagon, wolfing day-old beans in a rush, too hurried to wait for breakfast. McCan did the same, figuring from Carrington's manner that they might not stop for food the rest of the day. He had barely filled his belly when it was time to go.

Each took an extra mount trailing behind. They rode southeast. When they were about a mile from camp, dawn broke, sending their shadows westward, so long they faded into the horizon.

Carrington said little to McCan. When he did speak, he wasn't unfriendly, but preoccupied. McCan did not ask what Carrington thought was wrong; indeed, he suspected Carrington himself did not know.

They rode until their mounts were lathered and puffing, then paused to give them rest. McCan ate some jerky from his saddlebag; Carrington refused it. They changed mounts and rode on.

McCan noticed Carrington favored his left arm, holding it awkwardly as he rode. McCan asked him about it.

"It's nothing. I strained it a couple of days ago throwing a calf."

In early afternoon, clouds rolled up over the hills, fed by the Missouri River waters many miles to the north. The clouds gathered in a black layer, spread across the sky. A moist wind arose, cool and tingling, and a rumble of thunder came from somewhere deep in the sky and rolled into silence.

Carrington and McCan dug ponchos from their packs and slipped them on. A minute later the clouds put forth drenching splatters too big to be raindrops, too small to be bucketloads. It was like riding ten feet too close to a waterfall. The horses pulled back their ears and trudged, heads down, as lightning slashed above. McCan's poncho turned away all the water it could, then gave up and let it pour through. Carrington said something about hoping the storm didn't stampede the cattle back at the roundup. Yet when a lightning bolt splintered a tree not a quarter-mile away, he didn't seem to notice.

Thunder made Carrington's spare horse skittish, and it pulled away. It ran into the murk, and they saw it no more. Carrington muttered something, but did not go after it.

After an hour the storm slowed into a steady, calmer rain. McCan was chilled and saddleweary, but on they plodded. At sunset the clouds opened, and red light streamed like blood through the gash.

Carrington rode to the top of a slope and halted. He rubbed his left arm again. McCan stopped beside him. Below lay a small cabin beside a creek that gushed rainwater. A light winked on in the cabin window and spilled out around the edges of the shutters.

"Everything looks fine, Jonas," McCan said.

Carrington clicked his tongue and dug rowels into his mount; the exhausted horse moved down the slope. McCan followed.

"She's cooking supper, I bet," McCan said. "I'd say she's a fine cook, huh?"

Carrington, still silent, dismounted about a hundred feet from the house.

"Maggie!" he called.

No answer came. Suddenly it was as if somebody had slipped a shard of ice down McCan's shirt. Carrington's apprehensions became his own, and he reached for his pistol as he dismounted.

"Maggie!"

Still no answer. Carrington drew his pistol and went to the door. With a kick he shattered the latch and the door burst open, revealing a dimly lighted room. In one corner stood Maggie Carrington, pale and scared. About ten feet from her was the rustler Terrence Brown, holding a rifle. He aimed it at Carrington. Brown's hands trembled. Rope burns were starkly visible on his neck. He fired; a slug sang past Carrington and McCan. Carrington moved to the center of the doorway, silhouetted against the light of the room. His pistol thundered and flashed orange fire.

Brown screamed and grasped his chest; the rifle clattered to the floor. Carrington fired twice more, filling the cabin with smoke and sound. When the shooting ended, McCan heard Maggie Carrington's screams.

Brown was dead, three wounds in his chest. Carrington walked to Brown's body, looked at it, then groped at his heart and slid slowly to the floor. He took one shuddering breath and died.

CHAPTER 13

It was his heart that killed him—Brown's shot hadn't even come close. But when news of Jonas Carrington's death got out, he was thought as much a victim of a cattle rustler as if he had been shot by Terrence Brown, rather than merely startled to death by him.

McCan and a neighboring rancher named Oren Marby buried Carrington. Marby, whose left leg was arthritic, stayed home during roundup. Despite his affliction, he dug with gusto when it was time to bury Terrence Brown. He and McCan scraped out a shallow hole, dumped the rustler's body in facedown, and then Marby spat on the corpse as McCan threw in dirt.

In the meantime, Marby's wife took in Maggie, who had become hysterical for only a few moments after her father's death. Then she had pulled herself upright, forced tears away from her eyes, and stilled the trembling of her lips. She rode beside McCan on Carrington's old buckboard, never crying, never speaking.

McCan slept a few hours before starting back to the

roundup. There, news of Carrington's passing was taken badly, particularly by Hunt, who blamed himself for not snuffing out Brown when he had the chance. When the roundup was done and the Timber Creek punchers were home again, several of them secretly sought out Brown's grave and, under the leadership of Stewart Biggs, performed some atrocities on the corpse. It was a useless bit of barbarity, but the only outlet for their rage, and no one complained.

McCan rode to the Marby spread to check on Maggie and found she had gone back home. The girl had vowed to live at her own place, regardless of the bad memories and the loneliness. That made McCan respect her; she was a young lady with grit.

He rode to her house and found her at the well. She was a pretty lady, there was no denying. Much more so even than the pillbox photograph showed. Slender, of medium height, her face oval and dusted with freckles, her shape utterly feminine—she looked like ladies McCan had seen in portraits in fancy parlors back in St. Louis.

He greeted her, and she smiled in return. "I wanted to see if you were making it all right," he said.

"You're kind. And I am all right."

"I was surprised to hear you came back here so fast."

"I've never run from memories, even bad ones," she said. "Mr. McCan, I owe you thanks for the help you were to me. I should have thanked you earlier, but the time wasn't right for saying anything. You understand."

"Of course." McCan looked at the cabin. He noticed a torn muslin window, flapping in the wind.

"While I'm here, I might as well help you out some more, if you'd not mind."

She didn't, so he repaired the window, restoring the

waxed muslin. They talked quietly as he worked. When he was done, he said good-bye and rode away.

When he was out of view, he reached into his pocket and pulled out Jonas Carrington's pillbox. He flipped it open and looked at the picture.

He shouldn't have done it—picking a dead man's pocket. But he wasn't sorry. He pocketed the box and spurred his horse across the prairie.

About a week later, McCan and Abe Hunt sat with coffee cups in hand and tobacco in their jaws.

"I hear you spent some time along the Missouri before you came to us," Hunt said.

"That's right."

Hunt took a slow swallow of coffee before he spoke cautiously. "No offense to you, but that's surely the haunt of thieves."

"No offense taken. That's true. It's why I left."

"You were running with somebody up there?"

"Wasn't there long enough to really run with them. But I kept company with one particular fellow for awhile before he started talking cattle rustling."

Another sip of coffee, another cautious, exploratory question from Hunt: "Are you a man who objects to naming names? 'Cause if you are, it don't . . ."

"Jack Parker. I got no reason to keep his name secret."

Hunt nodded. "I've heard of him. And a Feeney?"

"I met him."

"What about a father and two boys, last name of Bain?"

"Them I don't know."

Hunt nodded. He asked no more questions. But he did say: "Rustling problems are getting worse. Roundup showed it this year, and the winter isn't the only cause. Horses are dissappearing too. Some of the

ranchers are hiring range detectives and forming pro-
tective associations. There's been a lynching or two,
but it doesn't seem to stop the problem."

"You think things are going to get more . . . dras-
tic?"

"I do."

In the days that followed, McCan returned more
frequently to Maggie's home. He would work, they
would talk. She began fixing some of his meals.
McCan thought of her constantly; he spent a lot of
time looking at the pillbox portrait.

In September the Marby ranch hosted a dance, and
McCan escorted Maggie to it. It was their first public
appearance together, and it led to an association between them in the eyes of the locals.

But their involvement remained quiet, mostly private. And it remained, to McCan's disturbance, rather
cool. McCan always was aware of something in Maggie's eyes, in the tightness of her shoulders, that kept
her a little distant from him. He worried about it, laid
awake about it, but said nothing.

The unseen barrier was there when he left for fall
roundup, and there when he returned.

Hunt assigned McCan to line-camp duty, and he
knew he probably would see Maggie not at all through
the winter. The thought was a dull cramp inside him
that did not go away, even when Maggie gave him a
sack of books as a defense against the inevitable bore-
dom of the lonely winter camp. She was a cowboy's
daughter; she understood.

She waved at him until he was out of view across a
distant hill, riding toward the line camp with the bag
of books slung over his saddlehorn.

CHAPTER 14

—————

The snow hit quickly and hard.

McCan got the first hint while trying to determine if a steer that had fallen into a ravine was slightly or seriously injured. There was a sudden, subtle change in the atmosphere, and he anticipated snow by morning.

The steer was badly hurt, so he shot it. He carved out what meat he could handle and went back to the line camp, a low-roofed building of unbarked logs, a small woodshed behind, and a large lean-to shelter for the horses in bad weather. Beside the shelter was a corral fenced with cut saplings.

McCan reached the camp as the first flakes fell. He slung most of the meat into a sack hung from a jutting roof beam, counting on the cold weather to retard spoilage. He went inside and stirred the fire, then greased a skillet for a steak.

He missed Maggie terribly. The first days had been the worst. Now he was more used to the misery, the way a man with a bad back learns to ignore how badly he is hurting.

That night a blizzard came with awesome fury. Wind whistled around the cabin; hard-frozen snow drove against the shutters with a haillike rattle. Every crack in the chinking spewed cold air. McCan huddled beneath a buffalo robe and drank coffee.

He heard a noise outside. One of the horses? When he heard it again, he stood. It *was* a horse, but not one of his own. He had learned to distinguish their whinnies and trumpets from all others, for he heard them constantly through the wall.

McCan checked his pistol and slipped it into the waist of his trousers. He went to the window and partially opened a shutter. Biting wind struck him, and snow whipped in. Squinting against it, he peered out.

The darkness was heavy as a sodden blanket. He could see only six feet, and there was nothing out there but darkness and snow. Then he heard the neighing of a horse again, not more than a few yards away.

"Hello, the camp!"

The wind distorted and weakened the voice. McCan flung the shutter wide and shouted, "I hear you! Ride in!"

He wrapped the buffalo hide tightly around his shoulders and put on his hat. He threw open the heavy slab door and went out. Immediately, snow encrusted his brows and whiskers.

The rider approached on a horse that appeared ready to drop. Huddled in the saddle, the man looked like he was carved from an ice block; long icicles hung from his hat, and his eyes were frozen nearly shut.

He slumped from the saddle as McCan reached him. McCan struggled inside with him and put him on his grass tick bed. He threw a blanket over the man, then went outside and took the horse into shelter. He fed it hurriedly, then went back inside the cabin. He threw off his buffalo robe. In contrast to the bitterness outside, the cabin seemed warm and life-giving.

McCan knelt beside the pale man. He touched him; he felt like a corpse fresh from a mortician's ice room.

McCan took the right hand and slowly began rubbing the blue fingers, warming them, working out the stiffness. He warmed the left hand too, then the toes. The toes worried him. They were badly frostbitten; gangrene could set in.

But to his surprise, the toes warmed beneath his fingers. He felt the throb of a pulse, and glanced up at the face. Color was returning as the ice melted from whiskers and hair. The man breathed steadily, shallow gulps making his chest heave.

McCan worked his way up the arms. The man's breathing deepened; he was asleep. McCan looked again at the face, and pulled back as if a gun had fired near his ear.

Caleb Black!

He was bearded, much more weathered than before. The nearly five years that had passed since last he had seen him had left deep tracks, but this was, indeed, Caleb Black.

McCan pulled the blankets tighter around Black and put the buffalo hide on top of those. He went to the stove and rebuilt the fire, then drank some more coffee as he watched Caleb sleep.

An hour later, Black stirred. He moaned like a hung over man waking up; his eyes opened and he stared at the ceiling.

"How's it feel to be froze, Caleb?" McCan said.

Black's head turned slowly toward him, as if his joints needed oiling. He squinted. McCan raised his coffee cup in salute. Black tried to smile, but couldn't. He did manage a weak, ironic laugh. In a coarse whisper, he said, "I thought for a minute I was back in Deadwood."

"You might have suspected this was the heavenly gates, considering how froze up you got yourself."

"I got lost out there. I was on my way to Miles-town."

"You're a long way from it. And why did you come this way?"

"Give me some coffee and I'll tell you."

McCan gave him a cupful, and also cooked some thin slices of beef. Black ate and drank slowly, taking careful swallows that made him wince.

"I hear you still trail Evan Bridger," McCan said. "Is that why you're in these parts?"

"It is. But I came out here to find you. I heard you worked the Timber Creek spread, so while I was in the area, I had to look you up. They warned me about the snow—I should have listened."

"I can't believe you still chase Bridger. You can't bring back Walter."

"It's not just Walter anymore." Black's eyes turned brooding. "I got married, Luke. Annie was her name. And Bridger killed her—killed *them*, for she had a baby in her."

There was a long silence. "I don't know what to say, Caleb," McCan said.

"I met her over near Virginia City," Black said. "I had been chasing Bridger here and there, finding trails and losing them and finding them again. We had met up a few times, took shots at each other. Sometimes he trailed me, trying to kill me to get me off his back. Finally he got away from me, and I traced him to Virginia City. I never found him, but when I met Annie, Bridger didn't seem to matter anymore. I fell hard, Luke. You ever had a thing like that happen to you?"

McCan smiled, rather sadly, and nodded, but Black wasn't looking. He went on. "I married her and we settled down to start a family. I did this and that to

keep us alive—hunting, trapping, trading, whatever—
and we weren't rich by a long shot, but we were
happy. I all but forgot about Bridger.

"But he didn't forget me. He showed up one night
while I was gone, and he shot Annie. Shot her dead,
right there in our own home, and left a note pinned
to her body, telling me the things he had done before
he . . ." Black couldn't finish. His throat tightened,
squeezing off the words.

"Damn, Caleb," McCan whispered. "I had no idea
he had put you through that."

"It's what he put *her* through that eats at me. I
swear, Luke, I'll be on his trail until one of us is dead,
and if he kills me and it's possible to come back, I'll
be on his trail then too."

McCan nodded. "I understand." He rose and re-
filled Black's cup. "How long will you wait?"

"I'll leave as soon as the snow lets me."

The next morning a foot and a half of snow was
piled out across the prairie. Drifts were saddlehorn-
high in places.

Black waited out the day and one more night, and
then was ready to go. "I'll see you again, Luke," he
said.

McCan nodded. He watched Black ride away until
he was a spot on the field of white. "Caleb!" he yelled.

Black stopped and turned in the saddle.

"You get him—hear?"

Black nodded and waved, then turned away and disappeared into the vast whiteness.

That night it snowed again, hard as before. McCan
prayed for Black, wondering if the heavens heard
prayers for a man who lived for the death of another,
even one as evil as Evan Bridger.

For another day terrible cold lingered, spread like
ice out across the plains. It was weather to freeze a

man's fingers to the reins before dropping his horse from beneath him. There was no way, McCan feared, Black could have made it.

But the next day the cold broke. A period of unusual warmth melted the snow down to the dirt, leaving only patches in shaded recesses, piled up against the north side of rocks and trees and the line-camp cabin.

On a bright Tuesday morning during that lull, Dan Tackett, Abe Hunt, and a blond man McCan didn't know rode out to the camp.

CHAPTER 15

—◆—

The stranger's name was Jephthah Avery—"Call me Jeff"—and until recently he had been a woodhawk along the Missouri, supplying wood to fuel the steamboats. Now he was a range detective.

Hunt, as usual, took the lead, and with few preliminaries explained why the group had come.

"All over the territory, cattlemen are responding to rustling," he said. "But things just keep getting worse. There's no sign they will improve if we let things go as they have.

"Back years ago, the worst kind of scum was running loose in Virginia City and Bannack, and it took outright vigilante activity to take care of them. We're hoping to stop short of doing all that those regulators did, and our aim is to be peaceful and law-abiding—but it's obvious we need to increase our aggression against the thieves who are robbing us blind.

"This spring, a group of us will ride north to the Breaks of the Missouri and clean out the core of rustlers. Jeff here is familiar with the area, and knows the whereabouts of the main troublemakers. We hope to bring them back alive, if possible, dead if need be. Either way, they'll become an example that might make the more fainthearted among them think again before rustling any more stock."

Hunt rolled a cigarette as he talked; now he twisted it, set it on his lip, and fired it with a sulphur match. He looked squarely at McCan.

"We want you to be part of that group, Luke. It's specially selected, handpicked, secret. You're a man we can trust, and you can take care of yourself. Plus, you know the region firsthand—at least a little—and you know the kind of people we'll be facing. It could be dangerous, but I'm asking you just the same: will you ride with us?"

Before McCan could answer, Avery said, "And can you keep your mouth shut about it?"

The words riled McCan, but before he could answer, Hunt spoke again. "Jeff talks a little too straight sometimes, Luke, but he's got a point. This gets out, it would ruin it. Maybe cost some lives. Now, what's your answer?"

He tried not to show it, but McCan was flattered he had been asked. He accepted solemnly, and the others looked pleased, except for Avery, who seemed indifferent. Tackett and Hunt shook McCan's hand, but Avery didn't extend his. He was a droopy-eyed, sneering fellow McCan found inherently repulsive.

Hunt turned to more mundane talk. He quizzed McCan about his work, the condition of the cattle, the adequacy of the grass and water. McCan gave a report, then asked about news from Timber Creek. He was thinking of Maggie, but did not mention her.

"We got us a new town getting started right there," Tackett said.

McCan expressed amazement, but Tackett nodded

and went on, "A man name of Rodney Upchurch has come up from Milestown, and once the winter breaks, he's putting up a big store. Upchurch's Emporium, he'll call it, just like the one in Milestown. Figures he can make a pile off the ranchers and get some other folks to start up businesses, move some houses in, start up a new community. The word is he'd like to have it named after himself. One thing I'll say, he's a real character, sort of a city type, all bouncy and starry-eyed. He'll have to prove himself to me."

Hunt smiled. "Dan's a skeptic. But this fellow is onto something, I think. Run a few supplies in from Milestown by freight wagon, and people will be glad to take them off his hands."

"Where will it be?" McCan asked.

"Within view of Maggie's house," Hunt said.

"How is Maggie?"

"Fine. Doing fine." Hunt smiled quickly, a forced effort. He averted his eyes and put on his hat. "We got to be going."

"Wait a minute," McCan said. "Is something wrong with Maggie?"

Hunt and Tackett exchanged glances. Hunt said, "No. She's fine, like I said. And we really do need to go. If we don't get back out to you before spring, just come on in when it looks like the snow is done."

They went out the door and mounted. McCan, knowing he had not been told all, went to Hunt and asked again about Maggie. Hunt paused, looked him in the eye, and said, "Rodney Upchurch is courting her. Has been since he came. And that's about all there is to it."

McCan looked at him silently, then nodded. He felt something like a pig of hot iron doing a slow roll in his stomach.

The three rode off, Hunt and Tackett together, Avery slightly behind, spine bent and shoulders slumped as blue cigarette smoke trailed after him, puffed out steady as the belches of a train stack.

For the rest of the winter McCan did not see another human being. He was glad of it.

Upchurch had wasted no time. As McCan rode home, the last real snow a memory of two weeks back, the framework of a large building stood starkly against the sky. It stood on a rise about a half-mile from Maggie's cabin, and swarmed with workmen.

McCan admired one thing about Upchurch, even though he had not met him—a venture like this took grit. The store was miles from the nearest town, lonely and isolated in the middle of cattle range. Yet the notion was sensible. Many who lived here made it to Milestown maybe once or twice a year. A closer outpost would be a luxury. Upchurch might just succeed.

Too bad.

Something drew McCan's gaze northward. Standing there, in brand-new riding clothes, was Maggie. McCan's fingers tightened on the reins; he suddenly was aware of his unshaven face and dirty, smelly clothes.

But he rode to her. She saw him, and her eyes grew wide, but it did not seem a look of pleasure.

McCan dismounted and walked to her. "Hello, Maggie."

"Luke. How have you been?"

He wanted very badly to take her in his arms, but he couldn't. "Cold, mostly. Mighty cold."

"Did you read the books I gave you?"

"About two times each. It made a lot of difference."
Here I am, talking to Maggie, and it's like I'm chatting with a stranger in a tea parlor.

She smiled at him. A distant smile, almost formal.

"There's a store being built here," she said.

"I heard. Why are you out here, Maggie?"

Her smile became tighter, more artificial. "Waiting for someone."

A buggy clattered up behind McCan. He turned and saw a slender young man in a derby and a tailored brown suit expertly brake the rig. The man jumped lithely from his seat and trotted toward McCan, hand already extended. He was all teeth and sparkling eyes and the scent of bay rum.

"Rodney Upchurch, sir," the newcomer said. He pumped McCan's hand firmly. "Have you come looking for work?"

A burst of fury struck McCan. His fist clenched, began to go back. But Maggie's presence stopped him.

Upchurch finally dropped his hand, but kept the smile. He turned to Maggie and took her hand. *Moves like a nervous rooster*, McCan thought.

"Hello, dear," Upchurch said. He bent stiffly from the waist and kissed her cheek. She dropped her eyes.

"Thank you for waiting, dear," Upchurch said. "We'd best be getting on before it's any later." He tugged at her hand and pulled her toward the buggy. He flashed his smile at McCan again. "I'm sorry you didn't come earlier, when there was still work to be had," he said. "If you'll tell me your name, I'll be glad to keep you in mind."

What came into McCan's mind could not be vented in front of Maggie Carrington. He turned away and went to his horse. He rode toward Timber Creek, and did not look back as he heard the buggy rattle away in the opposite direction.

CHAPTER 16

For the next three weeks, McCan stayed to himself. He volunteered for jobs that took him away from the ranch, away from other people, and when he was not gone, he remained aloof. At times he reminded himself of Ben Weaver, back on the Deadwood freight run.

He saw Maggie only at deliberately great distances. The thought of her stabbed him every morning and stole his rest at night. He began gambling again, slipping off to poker games in back rooms or organizing his own in the bunkhouse. But his work did not suffer. Pain only concentrated his efforts at whatever he did, and he worked with great intensity.

Meanwhile, the courtship of Maggie and Upchurch progressed. So also did the work on the Emporium. Behind it, Upchurch built a house; not a log or rough-lumber hut, but a real, solid home built of high-grade finished lumber, and with a metal roof.

Upchurch moved into the house when it was nearly completed. He lived in a single room at first, with a large window that faced west, and he developed a habit of watching the sunset through that window. About a week after he moved in, he noted a rider on the hill, looking down at him. The next night he was there again, then the next, and the next. And one night he was gone.

Upchurch heard a pounding at his door. *Maggie*. He went to the door and flung it open.

Luke McCan—drunk—walked in, pulled back his fist, and left Upchurch on the floor, mouth bloodied.

"Next time, I'll carve you like a dead beef," he said.

Upchurch didn't get up until he was gone.

McCan returned the next day and apologized. Upchurch just looked at him, then had him arrested.

McCan lay in a cell in Milestown and watched a spider busily wrapping a fly in his web in the corner. A cigarette burned unheeded on his lip until the heat made him spit it out. He then saw Abe Hunt at the cell door, looking grimly at him.

"I'd invite you in, Abe, but the door seems to be jammed shut," McCan said.

"I've got a key," Hunt said. He turned the lock and entered. "If you want to trounce me and take it, go ahead. I hear you're good at trouncing men unexpected."

"If you've come to fire me, do it and spare the sermon," McCan said.

"I ain't come to fire you, though I should. I've come to get you out."

"Out? How?"

"Upchurch has decided not to hold it against you. He's not taking it to court."

"Why?"

"It seems somebody talked to him, made him decide to go easy on you."

Maggie. The thought just made it worse.

"Let's go, then," McCan said. He took his hat and pushed past Hunt and out the cell door.

Hunt had brought McCan's horse. As they rode, Hunt said, "Remember what we talked about in the line camp?"

McCan nodded.

"In a few days, there will be a few men riding in, one and two at a time, to that old line camp at the bluffs. You know the place. They'll come that way to avoid attention, and they'll come quietly. You'll be one of them."

"Who else?"

"You'll know them when you see them. I'll be there."

"And then?"

"And then I wish I knew. Maybe an easy time. Maybe something a lot rougher."

They reached a hill nearby Upchurch's Emporium. They had ridden all day, and were tired. McCan halted his mount. Sunset gilded the land, the nearly completed store building, and Upchurch's house behind it. Down a new road, a line of freight wagons rolled in. The creaking of their wheels sounded mouselike across the distance.

"Looks like Upchurch's stock is arriving," Hunt said.

"Yeah." The sight brought memories to McCan: the roll into Deadwood; the death of Bob Webster, then Walter Black; the departure of Caleb Black for a vengeance hunt that had only brought him greater loss.

A door opened and closed below. In the dying daylight Upchurch emerged, a lantern in his hand, Maggie beside him. Upchurch waved the lantern at the incoming freighters, a glowing pendulum of light etching a line through the dusk.

"That little lady down there—she's your problem, huh?"

It was a more perceptive judgment than McCan would have expected from Abe Hunt. "I think it's me that's the problem," he said. "Let's go home."

They spurred their mounts toward Timber Creek.

Maggie Carrington awoke the next morning to the sound of someone approaching outside. She dressed quickly, combed her hair, and went to the door.

It was Luke McCan. She threw a shawl about her shoulders and pulled it tight, then stepped outside and waited for him.

"Maggie," he said. He touched his hat.

"Luke." There was ice in her voice.

"You heard about what I did to Upchurch?"

Her silence was colder than her voice had been.

"It was a fool thing. I'm sorry about it. I tried to tell him that, but he wouldn't listen. I'll go and try again."

"Don't," she said. "For God's sake, just leave him alone."

"Whatever you want."

She pulled the shawl tighter, seeming to shrink within it. Her face was very white.

Luke said, "There are things I wanted to be different. Maybe I was the only one who did. But it makes no difference. I'll be leaving here soon."

"Where will you go?"

"Does that matter?"

She seemed again to withdraw from him. It made him feel like a leper.

"No, I suppose it doesn't," she said.

McCan studied her white face, trying to remember how she had looked to him before, but he couldn't. "Good-bye," he said, and rode away.

She called after him, "I'm going to marry him, Luke."

McCan would not look back. He rode until she was far behind, out of view; then he stopped. He looked eastward, considering very seriously just riding until he was lost somewhere in Dakota. Riding off and never coming back. But no—he had promised to do a job for Abe Hunt.

Do it he would. When it was done, he would be free. He thought about that for a time, waiting for it to make him feel better, until finally he was weary of waiting.

PART III

MISSOURI BREAKS
MASSACRE

CHAPTER 17

McCan rode alone, wondering what was coming and why he had agreed to take part. Really, he knew why: because Abe Hunt had asked him. And because he really had nothing else better to do with his life at the moment.

Funny thing, he mused. Not that many years ago he had been a green tinhorn fumbling with a new Colt pistol in Deadwood, clumsy and unable to protect himself and his friend from a cheap bumbler who was hardly a better marksman than he. He never would have thought, in those days, that he would ever ride into a vigilante effort, one that could be quite dangerous.

Vigilantism was on the rise at the moment. A lot of whispers, a lot of talk that drew public frowns from the cattle barons, but private smiles—McCan hadn't been so preoccupied as to miss that. Of late, bodies had been found swinging from cottonwoods by the Missouri, and bands of riders had been seen in the night.

McCan rode to the rim of a valley. It stretched out like a wide basin, rising into reddish bluffs on the far side, dotted throughout with scraggly brush. Below was the old line camp that was his goal. It was a particularly crude one and seldom used, built of the roughest logs, some with branches intact and groping wildly from its walls. There was a log corral nearby; three horses were in it.

McCan began his descent, wondering who waited below. He felt eyes on him.

When he was within three hundred feet of the camp, a husky black man appeared in the doorway. It was Bill Webster. McCan felt a burst of relief. If Bill, clearheaded as he was, had agreed to become involved in this, maybe everything was square. Then he realized that Bill might be just as lacking in information as he was.

"Have a hard ride?" Bill Webster asked.

"No problems."

McCan peered into the cabin and saw the shadowed form of Jeff Avery. *Lizard in a hole*, McCan thought. There were others with him, but McCan could not recognize them.

He dismounted and led his horse to the corral. He gave it water, removed the saddle and bridle. He hung the latter on one of the branches jutting from the cabin, and the former over the fence with the others.

The cabin smelled earthen, and was cool. A pungent scent of strong tobacco hung inside. Avery's cigarette butts lay by the dozens amid amber splatters of spittle on the floor. Avery reclined on a bunk that hung on rusted chains angled over to the log wall. He eyed McCan, who greeted him. Avery blinked back.

"Luke, this is Jed Strout, boss of the Lazy Arrow. And Solomon Smith and J. W. Anderson, same spread," Bill said. "This is Luke McCan, a good friend."

Hands went out, were shaken. There was tension here, palpable nervousness that exhibited itself in fingers a bit too stiff, grips too tight, nods of greeting too quick. Only Avery seemed calm and detached, his eyes in their usual droop, his lip in its usual snarl, defying anyone to move or impress him.

McCan sat in a corner and rolled a smoke. By now the sun was bloody in the sky, the cool night descending.

Abe Hunt arrived the next day, and with him was Tackett. McCan was glad to see them; their mere presence gave comfort and a promise of restraint in the conduct of the mission.

Hunt addressed them all. "Thank you for coming. You did it quiet, like we asked, and that's good. This is a serious business, maybe a dangerous one. But we're no lynch mob—not unless we're forced to be. We've been doing a lot these past months to trace down the points from where the worst of the rustlers operate, and we plan to move into those points quietly and quickly, taking prisoners. If they resist, we shoot them down. If they don't, we take them alive. That's the rule we'll abide by.

"Jeff Avery has done the background work, locating points for our raids and such as that. Listen to him, and he'll guide you well.

"There could be trouble, but you're men who can handle that. Otherwise you wouldn't have been chosen. But if anybody doesn't want to come along, now is the time to leave. It won't be held against you."

He paused. No one moved. The leather-faced ranch boss smiled. "Good."

Avery began talking, laying out details, background, plans. He was a vulgar man, obscene in speech and manner, and talked in ways that hinted at something other than the peaceful venture Hunt envisioned. Nothing overt—just hints, words and phrases that drew sharp glances from Hunt. Avery softened his words in response, until finally Hunt seemed satisfied again.

But Bill Webster leaned over and whispered to McCan, "There's a man with a personal grudge."

At noon they rode out, taking it slow, moving in a line toward the Missouri. Avery led them, cutting through gullies and behind hills so their course was hidden. But the farther they rode, the more unsettled McCan felt.

Don't turn coward, he told himself. But it wasn't cowardice. More like intuition, forewarning.

That night they bedded down in a grove, the men taking turns at watch. McCan awoke when Bill Webster bolted up, pushing back his blanket.

"What is it, Bill?"

"Oh, Lord," Bill said. "It was just a dream. Thank God."

"What was it?"

"That we was dead. All of us, bloody and dead."

McCan lay back down. "Oh."

CHAPTER 18

There had been a cabin here once, but it was now, for the most part, a relic. The roof had collapsed and its wood had been used for fires, and two runs of upper logs had been cannibalized in the same manner. Now only canvas covered the top, but the cabin obviously was occupied, just as Avery had said.

"Good spot for rustlers," he said to Hunt as they watched the gaping door of the building. "Hidden away, and nobody even knows it's being lived in."

"Which are these?" Hunt asked.

"Leroy Bain and his boys. Small-time stuff before, but now they're tied in with bigger operators. They've led upwards of twenty rustled herds across the border into Canada."

Across the clearing from the cabin was a small stable and a corral. The remnants of a haystack were scattered up against the cabin wall.

At Avery's direction, the men divided into two groups and crept down separately, drawing closer to the cabin. McCan, Hunt, Bill, and Tackett comprised one group; Avery and the rest the other. They moved quickly but quietly, then crouched and watched the cabin from both sides.

A man came out. He wore filthy long underwear with a missing backflap. His hair was matted from sleep. He was rolling a cigarette in one hand and using the other to open the fly of his underwear and relieve himself just outside the door.

"Now there's a trick for you," Tackett whispered.

Avery shouted, "Leroy!"

Cigarette makings and spray went everywhere. Hunt smiled; Avery had obviously timed his yell for just that effect. But the man in the long underwear didn't remain flustered for long; he vanished into the dark cabin, and a moment later a rifle muzzle slid out the front window.

"Who are you?" he shouted.

"Get out of the cabin—there's thirty of us out here!" Avery yelled back. "Six of us are deputy marshals, ten are soldiers, and the rest kill for fun."

"I recognize your voice, Jephthah Avery!" Leroy Bain shouted. McCan glanced at Hunt; the ranch boss's eyes narrowed at the realization of Avery's familiarity with Bain. "I never figured you'd have the guts to come 'round here no more!" Bain continued.

"Why does he know him?" McCan asked, but Hunt waved off the question.

"Bring out your boys and drop your guns, or we'll roast you alive in there," Avery said.

Bain fired, the shot ripping the cottonwoods and sending the raiders ducking. But it was a symbolic shot; Bain obviously could not see his targets.

Suddenly another shot jolted out, this one fired by Jeff Avery. The slug shattered part of the frame of the window from which Bain had fired.

Hunt swore and said. "Why'd he do that?" Then

he shouted, "Give it up, Bain, and there'll be no more shooting." Hunt glared across the distance at Avery.

Suddenly the canvas roof was in motion; it bulged upward, then down again. Somebody had slipped over the back wall, hidden between the top run of logs and the edge of the canvas sheet. McCan saw a man dart into the rocks and brush behind the cabin.

"One's gone!" Strout shouted.

Leroy Bain fired again, this time with better aim. Dirt kicked up near Strout, who was crouched near Avery. Reacting, Strout lost his balance and fell back on his rump. Bain fired again, and Strout grabbed his shoulder.

"Oh, no," Hunt said. He raised his rifle and fired at Bain.

McCan and the others did the same, and McCan knew what Hunt was thinking even as they did so: the peaceable intent of the venture was now moot. With the first spray of lead, a tone had been set. Now there was only one thing to do: fight the best fight they could.

They fired again and again toward the cabin, joining slugs in a volley that threw out chinking and rattled against rotting logs. The canvas bulged again—another one going over the back wall—but this time Avery fired. The bulge jerked and disappeared as the climber fell back inside the cabin.

Bain's voice called out: "You've hit my boy! We're giving up! Coming out!"

Bain's rifle flew out of the window a moment later.

"Thank God," Hunt breathed.

Bain came to the door, hands upraised. "You shot my boy," he said again. "He's bleeding bad."

Jephthah Avery raised his rifle and fired. Leroy Bain fell dead with a bullet through his heart.

Avery stood and rushed across the clearing. As the

others watched, stunned, Avery stepped over Bain's body and entered the cabin. There was a muffled yell, then another shot.

Avery emerged from the cabin with a grin on his face and his rifle raised triumphantly in the air.

Jed Strout, whose wound was superficial, sat in the corner of the cabin and stared at the blood where the youngest Bain had died. Strout was a quiet man, gentle by nature, and it was obvious to McCan he was trying hard not to cry. McCan didn't blame him.

"Do you know what you've done?" Hunt boomed at Avery. "You know that you've violated everything we set out to do? Turned this into a mission of murder?"

"It wasn't just *me* shooting at Leroy," Avery said. "Besides, he shot at us first."

"He was *surrendering*, Jeff! Nobody but you shot at him then. He had no gun. And it was worse, what you did to the boy—shooting a dying young fellow you had no call to kill."

"It was mercy," Avery said. "He was suffering and I spared him."

"Seems to me this Leroy Bain knew you right well," Tackett cut in. "You wouldn't have killed him to shut him up, would you?"

Avery's expression darkened. "I don't like your tone, fat man. If you're accusing me of—"

"Of murder. You're worse than the rustlers you're hired to take care of."

"I'll kill you for that," Avery said.

"When? When I'm unarmed somewhere, or lying on a floor bleeding to death? That's the way you kill, ain't it, Avery? You take me on man-to-man, and I'll feed you your own privates."

Avery lunged at Tackett, who seemed to expand to

bear-size, arms stretching out toward his attacker. But Hunt put himself between the men, pushing Avery back to his seat. McCan jumped in to restrain Tackett. Strout bowed his head and lost the battle against tears.

Bill Webster came through the door. "They're buried. What now?"

"I don't know," Hunt said.

"I never wanted to be part of no killing party, Mr. Hunt," Bill said.

"None of us did. Or maybe *one* did—Avery, was this your plan from the start? Kill off those you had a personal grudge against?"

"I'm a range detective, and a good one," Avery said. "I don't know why you're worked up. I know you've lynched rustlers yourself, Abe!"

"When we knew a man was guilty, and when there was no other way to do justice," Hunt said.

Bill Webster said, "Maybe we ought to turn back and just keep quiet."

"You're forgetting one thing," McCan said. "The first Bain boy got away. And he heard his father call Avery's name."

Avery went white. "We got to track him down and kill him."

"Want to murder another one?" Tackett said.

"You don't understand," Avery said, talking scared. "Bain had friends, men who follow the law of the feud. They'll come after me."

Rain began pelting the canvas above. It grew dark outside, and soon water fell in sweeping sheets across the prairie. It blew through the door on the back of a cold wind.

"We're stuck here awhile," Hunt said. "This could last the rest of the day."

The conversation waned. Hunt brooded, his lip curled. The others huddled in corners and along the walls. Avery paced about, fidgety and stripped of his normal cocky sneer.

The rain did not stop until night. Thick clouds blew gouts of water all day and brought the darkness early. Avery stopped pacing and sank into a sullen heap among the others. Hunt chewed slowly on a piece of jerked beef.

"There's only one thing to do," Hunt said at last. "Just what Bill said—go home and keep quiet. It's our best bet."

"I can't do that, Abe," Avery said. "Them that Bain was friends with, they'll come after me."

"That's your problem, then," Hunt said.

Avery's face went grim. "I'll name every mother's son of you to them," he said.

Tackett stood, a looming form in the little cabin. "I can snap his neck right here, Abe," he said. "Just give the word."

"Sit down, Dan," Hunt said. "Just sit down and let a man think."

They passed the night on the cabin floor, not sleeping. Morning broke, moist and golden, and Bill Webster was first to rise. He stepped out the door and stretched, and then he froze.

He went back inside. "Luke, Abe—look at this."

They went to the door. On the hillside, backed by the rising sun, was a long line of riders. Stock-still, side by side, and they were armed.

CHAPTER 19

From the shadows of the cabin the group watched the silent, unmoving riders. There were fifteen of them, most with rifles resting butt-down against their thighs, and all their intended victims knew why they brandished the weapons: to let fear get a firmer choke hold, for frightened men died with greater suffering.

"The Bain boy's out there," Avery said. "I never would have figured him to get such a group so quick."

Tackett said flatly, "When this is over, if both of us are alive, Avery, I'm going to kill you."

"He won't be alive to kill," Hunt said. "He'll be the first one they go after."

Avery made a tight, gulping noise in his throat. Tackett said, "Send him out, then. Feed him to them, and maybe that will satisfy them."

Hunt shook his head. "Not as long as I'm leading this affair. I don't do such as that to no man."

Jed Strout stood, took a deep breath. "Well, I'm not going to sit and wait for them. I'm riding out of here."

"They'll nail you dead first thing," Hunt said.

"They might. But if I stay, I'll be no better off. Maybe all they want is Avery. They might let me through."

Hunt slowly nodded. "They might at that."

"I don't think so," McCan said. "They'll be after all of us. Every one of us fired on this cabin, and the one that got away probably doesn't even know who killed his father and his brother."

"You can argue if you want," Strout said, "but I'm riding out. Sol, are you with me?"

Solomon Smith said, "If you ride, I ride."

"Anyone else?"

Nobody moved, and Strout nodded. "Sol, it's you and me." Decision seemed to have brought him courage—no tears now.

Strout and Smith walked to the door and held their rifles high, then laid them down in the doorway. Together they walked toward the little stable. In a few minutes they were riding slowly toward the line of horsemen.

The riders did not react in any visible way across the distance. Smith and Strout drew nearer, riding stiffly. McCan thought his heart would burst from his chest, and tension took his breath.

"They've reached the line," Hunt said.

Strout and Smith stopped, and for a time no one on the slope moved. It was evident they were talking, but nothing could be heard. Then, amazingly, the line of riders parted, and Smith and Strout passed through. The horsemen shifted position and watched them ride away—and when Bill Webster saw none of them looking at the cabin, he said, "I'm going over the wall to get the horses saddled. We can get out, maybe. Ride away."

He grabbed a chair, placed it against the wall, and slid up and out, just as the first Bain boy had done earlier. Behind the cabin, he slipped into the brush and crept to the stable.

McCan saw one of the riders signal. He thought for a moment that Bill had been spotted. But the signal had a different meaning. Two riders raised rifles and fired in the direction Smith and Strout had gone. Two shots, and that was all.

"God rest them, and thanks be they had no wives," Hunt said.

On the hill, the rider signaled again and the group divided. They moved in opposite directions along a line parallel to the cabin front, then each line cut toward the cabin through the protecting cottonwoods.

"It's starting," Hunt said. "Dividing for the kill."

As he spoke, a shot roared and a slug smacked the wall behind him. Every man in the cabin dropped and began searching for fighting position.

It was hard to find in the cramped quarters, for only the doorway and window afforded outlets. Gunfire pelted the cabin. Bullets whizzed through the doorway, the window, dug up the dirt floor, kicked out wood chips from the rear wall.

One slug tore out a line of chinking on the front wall, leaving a space about three feet from the floor—wide enough to accommodate a rifle barrel. McCan thrust out his Winchester and fired. One of the riders gripped his stomach and fell; his horse ran wildly back up the slope.

Several of the attackers dismounted, tied their horses in the most protected spots available, and worked down through brush and cottonwoods, still divided into two uneven lines. They peppered fire onto the cabin, making the canvas roof dance. With every tear, more light streamed in, its shafts dimmed by the gunsmoke and dust polluting the cabin's hot atmosphere.

McCan thought of Bill and darted to the southern wall. He pushed out chinking with his rifle butt and looked toward the stable.

Bill was in there, a vague shadow moving among the frightened horses. McCan saw him slide a saddle onto one of the mounts. Little gunfire struck the stable; the attackers apparently did not know it had a human occupant, and likely were hoping to preserve the horses for booty or trade.

But now a man slipped toward the stable through the grove. McCan strained his eyes, burning from gunsmoke and dust, and recognized Todd Feeney. He thrust his rifle barrel through the crack, took careful aim, and Feeney fell, with his side pierced. He kicked twice, fired a shot into the air, and lay still.

Meanwhile, Bill had saddled another horse. If the defenders could buy him enough time, perhaps he could ready enough mounts to give them a chance for escape—*if* they could vault the back wall or race across from the front without being shot down and safely make it to the stable.

Hunt and Tackett were busy at the front window. They took turns rising and firing, ducking down alternately to give the other his chance. They were an effective team—three bodies sprawled outside attested. Tackett breathed heavily, choking in the grit and smoke. But Hunt was utterly calm, moving up and down like a machine, aiming, firing, levering his rifle as he came down again.

Avery was at the front door, left side, J. W. Anderson at the right. They worked independently and connected on fewer shots than did Hunt and Tackett. Still, Avery had killed one man, and Anderson had wounded another.

The original attacking force of fifteen had been reduced to nine, one of them wounded. Still, those in the cabin were outgunned, and Bill was too busy in the stable to fight. McCan saw another man creeping toward the stable and he fired; dirt spat up at the man's feet, and he jumped behind a mound of rock for cover.

Avery yelled, "I got Bain!" McCan turned. Avery crouched beside the door, grinning broadly; then suddenly the top of his head was gone, and his body pitched across the room. The grin remained, now ghastly in death.

"Never a better deserved slug through the brain," Tackett said.

"But one less man for us," Hunt responded.

Anderson shouted, "They've got fire!"

A flare arced across the background of the cottonwood tops, and something thumped onto the canvas above. A smoldering spot appeared where the torch lay, a little seep of smoke came through the underside, and then the canvas began to catch.

McCan grabbed the chair from which Bill had vaulted the back wall and moved it to the center of the room. He climbed onto it, but suddenly his leg went numb and he fell. Blood ran down his trousers— a slug had cut a clean notch just above his knee. Wincing, he forced himself up again and grabbed at the torch through the smoldering hole left by the flame.

He hoped enough moisture remained from last night's rain to keep the fire from spreading, but the sun had dried the old and brittle canvas. What was worse, the torch was drenched in coal oil that spilled, flaming, across the cloth. McCan got the torch and tossed it to the floor, but the canvas was in flames. Then came two more arcs of fire, two more thumps on the cloth above. Finally, a whiskey bottle filled with coal oil, a flaming wick in the neck, landed on the canvas. A slug shattered it, and fire was everywhere.

McCan leaped down just as a bullet cut one of the chair legs in half. He spilled awkwardly to the side and then across Anderson. He rolled off and bounded up, and Anderson recovered as quickly. Anderson drew a careful bead on a figure outside, fired, and dropped him; then a bullet pierced his neck and he fell back on the fallen torch, his hands at his throat and his back smothering out the flame. He did not move again.

By now the cabin was filled with a thick, black, choking smoke—and the canvas above raged with fire.

"Over the back!" Tackett shouted. He leaped toward the back wall and hung his hands on the top run, but the flaming canvas dropped on him and he fell back, two bullets piercing him before he struck the ground.

CHAPTER 20

―

"Dan!" McCan shouted.

He pushed aside the big piece of flaming canvas with his rifle and uncovered Tackett. The big man still breathed, but his eyes were glazed, and blood gushed from the two holes in him.

Behind McCan, Abe Hunt screamed. It was a grossly unnatural sound. McCan turned and saw Hunt beating at flames that crept up his trousers, then ignited his shirt. McCan ran to him and also beat at the fire, but it was too late. Hunt lost his head and ran out the door, where multiple shots felled him. He dropped to his knees; a final shot ended his suffering.

"Luke!" McCan heard Bill's voice from the southern side of the clearing. A sudden burst of gunshots came from the corral, a fusillade that seemed unending.

McCan returned to Tackett, and with strength he did not realize he had, hefted the bulky, limp body to the top of the back wall. The canvas was gone now, so Tackett's body rested a moment in full view of the attackers. McCan, too, was exposed. Bullets pounded the logs around him as he pushed Tackett across and behind the wall.

A slug tore at McCan's arm, creasing the skin. McCan fired at a man who had reached the doorway and aimed at him with a pistol. The man took the shot in the chest, dropped the pistol, and fell.

McCan yelled as he vaulted and grabbed the top of the wall. He clambered clumsily upward, losing his rifle in the process, and reached the top. From there he leaped over and landed beyond Tackett.

Bill Webster, who had just fought his way across the corral with two horses strung behind him, came to him and said, "Mount up!"

McCan did, moving in a surreal daze. He leaned across the saddle horn, then coaxed his horse across the corral, with no idea where to go from there. His horse overran another gunman who met him at the corner; the hooves pounded his body into the dirt. McCan galloped the horse across the open space and jumped the fence.

He faced three men there, all aiming weapons at him. He crouched low and went for his own pistol. They fired, he fired, and suddenly he was through, un-hit. Whether he had wounded or killed any of the three he did not know, and he did not turn to see. He spurred his mount into a run.

He had no sense of time or distance. His horse ran on; wind rushed by his face. He kept low in the saddle, hurting now, blood dripping down his leg.

He felt the wind of a slug at his ear. He looked across his shoulder and saw three riders coming fast after him. One was far closer than the other two.

McCan triggered off an unaimed shot over his shoulder. The report deafened him, and smoke prickled his face.

He could not see Bill or Tackett. He fired another shot, and the man behind him yelled and fell from his horse. The others fired as a unit toward McCan; one bullet clipped off part of his hair, the other sliced through his shoulder and made him scream.

Ahead was a jumble of bare rock. He guided his horse through it, scrambling up a narrow passage as more bullets spanged around him. His horse was getting winded, but he pushed it hard. At the top, as the riders reached the base of the rocky knoll, McCan's mount stepped into a crevice and went down, trumpeting in pain. McCan pitched across to land facedown behind a boulder.

He reached for his pistol—*gone!* He saw it in the dust near his fallen horse. He went for it, stumbling on his wounded leg.

Before he could reach it, one of the riders topped the rocks. McCan saw his grin as he leveled down, ready to fire. McCan dropped behind his horse; the slug went into it rather than him. The horse shuddered and died.

McCan could not reach his pistol, but he found a fist-sized rock. He stood and heaved it, hard as he could, as the gunman fed a new cartridge into his rifle chamber. The stone crushed the man's nose, and he fell back over the rump of his horse. McCan reached his pistol as the man pushed upward and went for his own. McCan put a bullet through the man's chest.

Then the second rider was up the slope. McCan aimed at him, squeezed the trigger, and heard an empty click. He tossed the pistol aside and went for the dropped rifle of the first rider. He almost had it when the second rider's horse reared and threw him. The man, though big, hit the ground on his feet, for he leaped when he saw he could not retain his seat.

Then he shouted and threw himself atop McCan. McCan went down, breath driven from him.

The man was heavy, and he drove sledgelike fists against McCan's kidneys. McCan's face ground against gravel and grit; his mouth filled with sand and blood. With a painful twist, he pushed the man off and himself up.

A boot caught him in the chest and he fell back. He saw then his attacker was Jack Parker.

He took the first blow but dodged the second, and Parker's fist cracked against rock. Parker yelled and grasped his damaged fingers. McCan said, "Jack, don't you know me?" and Parker started shouting curses. He reached for his side arm, and McCan rolled over a boulder and out of view.

Here the rocks leveled into a kind of small plateau, and farther on dipped up again into a stone ridge, jagged as a rusted knife. McCan ran for those rocks. A bullet thumped just behind his foot, and a second ricocheted off just ahead. Parker shot too fast and carelessly to connect; McCan made it to the rocks.

He was so tired he almost blacked out. He fell into a recess and panted; his lungs burned and his throat was raw. He found a stick, about four feet long and with good heft. It was a pitiful weapon against a six-gun, but he kept it, hoping maybe he could get behind or above Parker and clout his skull with it.

McCan rose to run, but the rocks were crumpled like wadded paper, and he had to clamber slowly among them. Another bullet smacked too close to him, and he hurried on over the boulders to a gradual upward slope of flat rock.

He ran, but saw a rider approaching from the right. Nowhere to go, no way to protect himself. He waited for the death shot, and then saw the rider was Bill

Webster. Riding double with him, amazingly, was a badly bleeding Dan Tackett.

McCan pointed toward the rock spine he had crossed. Parker climbed over it at the same time and triggered off another round. McCan's leg was shot from beneath him.

Bill drew his pistol and shot at Parker, but missed. However, Parker did turn and throw himself behind cover, buying McCan a few moments.

"Hide—I'll come back!" Bill yelled, and rode off with Tackett swaying behind.

McCan didn't blame him; Bill could do little else until Tackett was safely stashed somewhere. McCan tried to run on his wounded leg, but it was numb, and he did well to stand.

Parker came up and shot again, missed again, and when he pulled the trigger next, the gun was empty. He went after his pistol, but he had tied it down too tightly and had to fumble with the strap. McCan stumbled, rolled, half-walked, half-tumbled down the slope and threw his club into Parker's face. Parker still had not freed his pistol.

McCan used his good leg to lunge against Parker, and together they fell against abrading stone that took off skin. McCan clung to Parker, then pushed him back and started hitting.

He pounded Parker's face three times, and the big man pulled away, grabbing his nose. McCan kicked his belly by clumsily swinging his numb leg, and though he could not feel the impact, it must have been significant; Parker doubled over, and McCan brought his fists down on the back of his neck.

Parker did not get up. McCan took the dropped rifle and cracked the stock into Parker's skull. He looked around and saw Bill coming back, Tackett no longer mounted.

"Good to see you," McCan said as he hefted himself onto the horse's rump. When he was mounted, Bill guided the horse back the way he had come. From the corner of his eye, McCan saw Parker rise.

McCan shouted a warning into Bill's ear, but Bill did not understand. Parker freed his pistol from its holster—McCan cursed himself for not thinking to take it—and then McCan reached up and drew Bill's side arm.

He twisted in the saddle and fired at Parker as Parker fired at him.

Parker's shot missed McCan but struck Bill in the side. McCan's shot ripped through Parker's abdomen. Parker fell, and Bill slumped over the saddle horn. Too late, McCan saw they had reached the edge of a bluff about thirty feet high. Bill's shifted weight caused the horse to lose its footing, and it plunged with its two riders over the edge.

McCan blacked out, but came to moments later. He had not fallen to the bottom, but had lodged on a rock outcrop about halfway down. About half of him dangled over emptiness; the other half teetered in an uneasy balance on the rock. Below, he saw Bill's body sprawled beside that of the dead horse.

Something dripped onto him from above, splattering on his hand. Blood. McCan looked up. Jack Parker stood at the rim, pistol in hand, wavering like a drunk. He aimed and fired. McCan felt a hot poker ram through his shoulder as Parker died on his feet and toppled over on top of him.

McCan was dislodged and plunged with Parker's corpse to the rocks below. He landed on top of Parker, and that saved him.

Something moved nearby. He rolled over, the effort sending spasms of pain through him.

A man on a gray horse aimed a Spencer at him. It was Evan Bridger. McCan noted it dispassionately. The image of Bridger shimmered and danced away like a heat devil as McCan gave in to the darkness.

CHAPTER 21

Coming to was a slow rise through muddy water, a steady lightening, a murky disorientation and sense of disbalance. McCan stared upward at the underside of a brown peak of canvas, felt the breeze, and knew he was alive. He might have cried, but his eyes were crusted and tearless, and when he moved, the pain erased thoughts of all but itself.

A man's blurred face looked into his. "Hello, Luke."

McCan forced his eyes to focus. "Hello, Caleb."

McCan had whispered, but the effort tired him as if he had tried to shout. His body ached so badly he could hardly tell one limb from another.

"You're going to be fine, Luke. Just rest."

McCan slept and dreamed he was back in Deadwood. He woke up in darkness and asked for water. Black brought him a cup of it, and he sipped it slowly, washing the grit from his throat, the acid sourness from his tongue.

"I saw Evan Bridger," McCan said.

Black nodded, a suspicion confirmed. "I thought he was here. I'd have got to him if I'd moved a little faster."

Always the chase, McCan thought. *He'll chase Bridger right into hell.*

Rain whispered on the canvas. It cooled the air and soothed McCan. He lay with eyes shut and listened, not sleeping, not really awake. Caleb Black hunched over on the other side of the little tent, smoking a pipe and sometimes humming softly an old mountain melody.

Strength came slowly, but it came. Caleb Black took care of McCan with the devotion of a nurse, and a surprising gentleness for a powerful man whose once-smooth face now looked like a desert map, parched and windburned, lined from weathering and something that cut deeper even than that.

Luke McCan surmised as best he could what had happened after his pitch over the bluff, but mysteries remained.

"Did you find a black man at the bottom?" he asked Caleb.

"No. Only a big fellow, white, lying right under you."

"Jack Parker. There should have been a black man too. Bill Webster—Bob's brother. You remember Bob?"

"I do. The one the redheaded gunfighter killed."

"Jimmy Wyatt. And then Evan Bridger killed him."

Black merely nodded at the mention of his old foe. He bit the end from a cheap cigar and lit the smoke.

"Maybe Bill survived," McCan said. "What about a hefty fellow, even bigger than the one under me, probably shot two or three times. He would have been hid out somewhere close by."

"Nope. Just you and the dead one."

McCan was solemn. "So he's dead then. Probably died alone, wherever Bill left him."

That night they ate roasted rabbit and drank coffee. Black threw in a pinch of salt, just like he did back in Deadwood, and the taste, as familiar tastes and scents will, brought back vivid memories of those times. McCan realized he missed them, and said as much to Black.

"I know," Black said. "I think about those days myself. We've gone many a mile since then. Sometimes I wonder when it all will stop."

"When Bridger's dead. Or you."

"I reckon."

"Is it worth that much to you, Caleb?"

Black smiled. A pinched tightness at the edge of his lips made him look old: "No. Not really. But hate is a funny thing. It has a sweetness all its own. It's a deep spring to drink from, and when you do, you're thirsty for more."

McCan said, "I don't blame you, really. I'd do the same in your shoes. But this life is aging you fast. It'll kill you if keep on. I can see that."

"So you're a preacher now? When did you get the call?"

"Not preaching. Just common sense." McCan's wounds hurt again, and his voice grew tight. "Why didn't Bridger kill me, Caleb? I was in his sights when I passed out."

"Why does he do anything? He lives on impulses, whatever strikes at the moment. Why did he kill Jimmy Wyatt? Why did he murder a woman and an unborn baby who never did him no harm?" Suddenly Black's jaw trembled, his eyes brimmed. "If I could put a bullet through my brain and know it would kill him too, I'd do it. Without a thought."

There was silence. Black puffed his cigar furiously. McCan closed his eyes and tried to will away his hurting.

"Maybe when I'm all healed up and you've finished with Bridger, we can become partners again," McCan said.

"Doing what?"

"Anything. Running a store. Being ranchers. Sodbusters. Sheepherders. Selling bloomers to the females."

Black laughed. It was the first real laugh McCan had heard from him since the Deadwood days. It was good to hear, and made him laugh too, even though it hurt.

After a time, McCan quit numbering the days. He grew stronger as the pain went away. But he was in no hurry to return to Timber Creek, and one realization made him consider not returning at all.

Everyone back there certainly thought him dead by now. That gave a strange feeling of freedom. He could ride away, forget the ranch and Maggie and everything else, and start over again in some other place.

McCan thought of that, but he thought of it very little. Mostly he rested, ate, talked to Caleb, enjoyed the refuge and the quiet.

It was good to be here. Good to hide, good even to be dead in the eyes of the world.

That existence went on for several weeks, until one day, Caleb said it was time to go looking for Evan Bridger again.

CHAPTER 22

"You'll go back to Timber Creek?" Black asked.

McCan said, "I don't know. It depends on if you're willing to let me ride with you instead."

Black smiled thinly. "It's a hard road I travel, but suit yourself."

McCan's wounds were healed, but tender. He ached from the inside out, muscles stiff from lack of use. Black had found McCan a fine bay roaming near the battle site, but just saddling the horse winded McCan.

"Where will we go?" he asked.

"The Missouri Breaks. I know somebody who can put me on Bridger's trail, though he won't want to."

"What if he won't talk?"

"I'll persuade him."

They rode north to the river, then turned west along its course.

Four men played cards and drank whiskey in a low, wide cabin. Sunset flung magnificent purple-scarlet rays through the open westfacing door. Something blocked the light, and the men turned.

"Evening, gentlemen," Caleb Black said.

One of them stood and turned slightly to make sure Black saw the Texas Dragoon in his belt. "Who are you?"

"My name is Caleb Black." The man looked past Black to McCan, who was still mounted outside. Black said, "That's a friend of mine who's no concern to you."

"What do you want?"

"Not what—who. I'm looking for Cyrus Keye."

Another man stood. He was a six-footer, broad and muscled. His black beard swept halfway down his chest and ended in a gray flourish. "I'm Keye," he said.

"Well, Keye, you've got two options. The first is to give me some information."

"Or?"

"The second is to oblige me to drag your corpse to a ranch I know that pays good bounties for dead cattle thieves."

Keye filtered a smile through his drooping mustache. His black eyes flickered over the others; the other men stood.

"You're right entertaining, Mr. Black. But you got no call to talk so to good Christian folk."

"Which option, Keye?"

"You're wearing thin, Mr. Black," Keye said. "But I'm curious. What information do you want?"

"I'm looking for Evan Bridger."

Keye's brows lifted and lowered. "Why should I know where he is?"

"You're a knowing kind of man."

Keye nodded. "That I am. And I know you. You must be one hell of a crazy man to tail Evan Bridger all these years."

Black smiled. "That's right. I'm crazy enough to call

down four men at once too." He looked calmly from man to man. "It really ain't much of a challenge. Only two of you have half a chance, and that ain't enough. The other two have none at all."

Cyrus Keye laughed—big, booming guffaws. "Mr. Black, I kind of like you. You're as loco and reckless as I am. But I can't tell you nothing about Evan Bridger."

"Can't, or won't?"

"It's all the same."

"Then I'll have to kill you," Black said. Keye leaned back and laughed again. The man with the Dragoon drew; Black put a slug through his neck. Keye quit laughing, went for his pistol, and Black shot him to death. The other two toyed with the idea of drawing only a half-second, then forgot it.

Black waved his pistol at them. "Bridger?"

"He was here two days ago. He headed for Wolf Point."

"What else?"

"That's all I know."

Black thumbed the hammer; the men paled. "I swear it," one said. "We don't know nothing else."

"Then you're no use to me except bounty," Black said.

The first man spoke, "The only other thing was he looked like he was feeling poor. All washed-out and trembling."

"Where at Wolf Point was he going?"

"He runs with Crandal Booth. He's a woodhawk and a whiskey trader."

Black indicated the dead men. "Drag them out and put them over their horses."

The men obeyed, obviously very scared. McCan wondered what Black would do with them. He was stunned by the calm way he had dispatched the other two. Hard to believe this cold pistol fighter was the Minnesota wheat farmer who had dropped his tools on the boardwalk in Pierre.

When the men were finished, Black made them lie down and told Luke to guard them. Then Black found a rope and slung it over a jutting roof beam at the corner of the cabin. One of the men whimpered.

"Shut up—I ain't going to lynch you," Black said.

Two minutes later, the men dangled back-to-back from the beam, hanging by their wrists with their feet eight inches off the ground.

"You're going to leave us like this?" one said.

"Yep."

"It could be days before somebody comes along!"

"I suggest you try yelling—and hope whoever hears you ain't a cattleman."

Black and McCan rode toward the river, two dead bodies bouncing on the horses trailing them. When they were a few hundred yards from the cabin, the dangling men yelled. Their cries echoed off the bluffs across the river.

"What will happen to them?" McCan asked.

"They'll wiggle out after awhile. It'll probably cause me trouble later. I should've shot them, but I'm just too softhearted. And a soft heart ain't nothing but a headache."

CHAPTER 23

—➤

They took the dead men to a ranch house four miles eastward, and there a squint-eyed cattleman inspected the corpses and handed Black a wad of bills. Black pocketed the money and they rode away.

"That's the first bounty I've seen paid," McCan said.

"Bounty, lynching, shooting, burning, stock detectives—cattlemen use it all. But thieves don't stop. As long as there's cattle, there'll be rustlers."

They rode along the knobs and slopes bordering the Missouri. Cottonwoods grew thick over long stretches, gave way to barren dirt at others. As they progressed, the land inclined and the river banks steepened, pushing them farther inland. They saw no one except a distant raftsman, and heard nothing but the flowing of the water and the chop of a woodhawk's ax somewhere on the far bank.

In a thick grove of cottonwoods and poplars, they camped for the night, tired and dirty from the trail.

* * *

Something stirred on the border of McCan's dreams. Something rustled in the forest. He heard the whisper of stealthy footsteps and awoke. It was dark, the sky covered with clouds no starlight could penetrate. The fire was just a coal bed spitting up sparks when the breeze gusted.

McCan slid his hand to the rifle beside his bedroll. He listened, unmoving. Wind stirred the cottonwoods; branches creaked. Through slitted eyes, McCan scanned the forest as he pretended to sleep.

A shadow moved beyond the tree line.

McCan slid the cover back and rose. More movement—a vague shifting. He slid through the trees, levering the Winchester.

A figure whirled to face him. Eyes locked in the darkness.

"Lucky I didn't kill you," Black said.

"Don't flatter yourself."

Black lifted a finger to signal silence. Like McCan, he had a rifle. He crouched; McCan knelt beside him.

They peered into the empty campsite. A whirlwind, moist with river mist, swirled across the little clearing and sent embers spiraling. In that faintest of glows, they saw dark forms on the opposite side.

"Shoot?" McCan suggested in a whisper.

"Not yet."

The forms came closer, to the very rim of the clearing. Fireglow glinted on a shotgun barrel.

The shotgun blasted, lighting the camp like a lightning flash. McCan's bedroll took the charge, dancing up like a wraith.

Black raised his rifle and fired.

The shotgun roared again in return. McCan flattened on the damp earth; pellets scattered above him. He rose and darted to the right. Unseen branches slapped him.

McCan dropped behind a rock. Something moved several yards from him. He raised his rifle, but did not fire, for he realized Black was no longer with him. That might be him in his sights.

Gunfire slashed through the cottonwoods; McCan saw the disembodied flares. In them he picked out Black's shape, and two others near him. McCan aimed, but the forms shifted and he did not know friend from assailant.

Someone cursed; a rifle fired. The figures in the forest moved away from him. McCan pushed upward, over the rock, but his foot slid on the damp ground and he crashed down hard. His head struck something, night closed in, and he was out.

He came to moments, maybe an hour later. His head was bloody and throbbed. He struggled for perspective. He pushed up on his forearms and looked across the campsite, and suddenly his view was blocked by what appeared to be twin tree trunks. Focusing, he saw they were legs. His eyes lifted—a rifle butt descended toward his face.

He rolled to the side. The rifle butt struck rock; sparks jumped off the metal buttplate. McCan reached for his own rifle but did not find it. His attacker brought down his weapon again. Once more McCan rolled, then came to his feet. He ran, toward the river, and the man followed.

Weaponless, McCan felt like a declawed bear chased by hounds. Gravel tore like dull razors at his bare feet. He bit his lip and ran harder.

His toe stumped rock and he pitched forward, rolling onto his back as his attacker fired. The slug thunked into the ground beside his ear.

McCan leaped up as the man levered. He grabbed the rifle and pushed it aside, and with his right hand pounded first the man's stomach, then his mouth. The man grunted at each connection, then pulled the rifle free and swung it; the front sight ripped a cut across McCan's lip.

A pure anger, simultaneously primitive and righteous, filled McCan. He grasped the rifle and wrenched it away. Fighting with emotion rather than logic, he tossed it into the river, then drove his knee into the man's crotch.

He buckled; McCan joined his fists and brought them down on the back of the man's neck. Then McCan's old injuries flared, with new ones, in a burst of pain that took his consciousness. He fell beside the senseless form of his opponent.

He came to after several minutes, feeling sick. He pushed nearly upright. His assailant still lay unconscious near him.

McCan rolled him over; it was one of the men he and Black had left hanging back at the cabin. "Finally got mad enough to be brave," he said aloud. Then he rose and returned to the camp. Black was not there.

He went into the woodland and hid until morning, listening for Caleb, hearing nothing.

In the light of dawn he looked for his partner. Back at the river, the man he had fought was gone; McCan had not heard him rise and creep away.

McCan wanted to yell for Caleb, but could not risk it. So he walked silently until he found blood on the ground. It made a crooked trail to the river.

On the bank was a pink pool of bloodied water. Someone had knelt here to wash a wound. McCan examined the ground; there was a wide smudge in the thin mud. Maybe the mark left by a body that had collapsed into the water.

There was no body there now. The current must have carried it away.

Don't let it be you, Caleb. But McCan knew Black would have found him by now if he was able. He shook his head, and hot tears skimmed his eyes. He turned back to the camp in the cottonwood grove.

CHAPTER 24

———

McCan rode to Timber Creek in the night, but the moon was bright and lit his trail. The sleeping ranch was eerily beautiful beneath the vast sky. McCan had thought seriously of not returning here, but now that he saw it again, he was glad he had.

He rode to the corral and dismounted, then carried his saddle and gear to the stable. He walked to the bunkhouse, but did not enter. Instead, he sat by the door to wait for dawn. Entering now would bring only confusion, maybe fear, among those who thought him dead.

A few moments later, however, Stewart Biggs came to the bunkhouse door. He wore long underwear and looked like some gray ghost in the darkness. Biggs looked blankly at McCan, rubbed his eyes, and looked again.

"Thank God," Biggs said. "We had no hope for you."

"Sorry I roused you, Stewart. I planned to wait it out until morning."

"How did you make it through alive? Bill Webster said—"

"Bill? *Alive?*"

"Yes." Biggs spoke solemnly. "But things are bad for him. And for Dan Tackett, it's worse."

"Tackett is alive too?"

"Yes, but . . ." He stopped. McCan prompted him, but he said only, "Let me get my clothes. I'll take you to them."

McCan waited until Biggs reemerged, clothed and boots in hand. He sat on the ground and pulled them on. "I didn't wake up anybody. No point in stirring them just yet."

They rode east. "How *did* you survive, Luke?" Biggs asked.

"It's a long story I'll tell you sometime. Right now, I want to know about Bill and Dan."

"The short of it is, Dan lost his job—and more. You remember the little Iowan who hired you? He fired Dan. 'No vigilante works in my hire,' he says. Cuts him loose, and Dan in the shape he is."

"What do you mean?"

"We're here. See for yourself."

They came to a dark little hut, starkly outlined on the barren land. Biggs dismounted and knocked on the door. "Bill! It's Stewart. I've got somebody you'll want to see."

Bill Webster came to the door, eyes half-shut from sleep, expression confused. Biggs smiled and pointed to McCan. Bill looked at him a few moments silently. McCan dismounted, came to him, and thrust out his hand. Bill took it, his shoulders heaved, and he threw his burly arm around McCan.

"I didn't think you lived through it, Bill," McCan said.

"We hardly did. Tackett saved me. He dragged himself out from where I had put him, found me all battered up, and somehow put together a litter and rounded up a stray horse and got me home. And him half-dead himself. But he paid a price for it: his leg is gone. Got putrified, and they sawed it off soon as he got here."

Inside, they awakened Tackett, and McCan forced a smile despite the shock of the realization: Dan Tackett was dying. McCan knew it as soon as the lamplight played across the old cowboy's face. He was wan, losing weight, eyes sunken. There was an empty place beneath the covers where his left leg should have been.

"It's a miracle," Tackett said. "An answered prayer. I figured you for dead."

"I figured the same for you," McCan said.

"God was with us."

"I'm sorry about your leg, Dan."

"It don't matter. Soon I won't need this old body no more. He'll take me home with him."

He's turned religious, McCan thought. *Knows he's dying*.

"The ranch turned Dan away, I hear," McCan said to Bill when they had left Tackett. "How are you living?"

"I had to leave the Lazy Arrow to take care of Dan. We're living on pure charity. The Timber Creek boys slip out here and give a hand. John Weatherby brings us food. Even this house is on loan from Stewart—it was his brother's before he died. I'd look for work around here, but I'm all torn up inside, and Dan takes a lot of caring for. I got to be with him all the time."

McCan nodded. "I'll find a way to help. Count on it."

When McCan and Biggs returned to the ranch, McCan was greeted with awe and a few cheers. Disheartened though he was by the plight of Tackett and Bill Webster, McCan was overcome by the welcome.

He told how Caleb Black had saved him, and then apparently been killed at the river. Most of the men had heard of Black; his pursuit of Bridger had made him part of the folklore of the Territory.

When word reached the main house of McCan's return, he was sent for. He knew what to expect.

Henry Sandy awaited, a fop with spectacles on his narrow nose. He looked at McCan through the bottoms of the lenses, like a museum manager examining a butterfly on a pin.

"You are Luke McCan?"

"I am."

"You participated in the vigilantism to the north?"

"I did."

"You realize, then, that I must dismiss you at once."

"Well, I know you fired Dan Tackett. I don't expect better for myself."

"The Timber Creek Cattle Enterprise does not sponsor vigilante activity, and it does not take up arms against lawless men. That is the job of the law. This is a nation and a territory of laws."

"It's a territory of cattle thieves," McCan said. "And what do you mean, Timber Creek doesn't sponsor vigilantism? I took part at the request of Abe Hunt, *for* Timber Creek."

"Mr. Hunt went beyond his authority. Had he lived, I would have fired him first."

"Do your superiors back east know what you're doing?"

"I'm now the manager of this ranch. They don't need to know every move."

"Well, ranch manager, you can bet Abe Hunt wouldn't have done anything like what we did without the approval of the highest officers of the company. You'd best check to see whose side you're playing up to."

Sandy gave a sniffing little laugh. "You obviously don't comprehend the operation of this cattle company."

"Maybe not. But I understand cattlemen, and know you're not one. You're just a dried-up Iowa jackass who'll run this company broke before your bosses know you're doing it. Abe Hunt was the best cattleman on any spread within five hundred miles, and he did everything he could to keep that mission peaceful and law-abiding. It was a range detective carrying some old grudge who turned it into a war. You don't need to fire me. I wouldn't work for a gut-worm like you anyway."

Sandy's little black eyes glittered through his spectacles. "You're quite the speechmaker, Mr. McCan. But I think you need to leave now."

McCan suddenly thrust out his hand. Surprised, Sandy took it. McCan noted the softness of Sandy's hand, like a woman's.

"Apart from the fact you turn my stomach, there's no hard feelings on my part," McCan said. "But this is for Dan."

He drove his fist into Sandy's nose. The spectacles split at the nosepiece and lenses flew east and west. Henry Sandy flipped backwards over his desk and sprawled on the floor. McCan strode out of the room, whistling.

Mrs. Martha Hyatt
Independence, Missouri

Dear Martha,

You've heard I am dead, so they tell me, so I suppose it would be appreciated by you to hear

I'm not. I don't know what all you were told about the circumstances of my supposed passing away, but I'll just tell you the basic facts—I came mighty close to dying, and some men with me did die. We were on a chase after some no-accounts and thieves, so I was on the right side of the law at least. I've done worse in the past as you well know.

I'm without any work right now and not sure just where I'll be going. I'm living with two friends, both good men who got hurt, just like me, and came close to not making it back, just like me again. There's one that will die yet, I think, and that's why I'm staying around for now. There is another tie holding me here too, but that is one of a different sort and her I don't want to discuss.

I will do well in some way or another and will let you know just as soon as I am settled differently. It may be I will come to see you soon but as of now I'm inclined to remain away until my times are better. Write me a letter so I can hear what your own circumstances are.

Your brother still living,
Luke

CHAPTER 25

―⁓―

Dan Tackett sang a hymn just before he died, clutching a Bible they left in his hand when they buried him.

McCan, never prone to cry, cried now. It was more than grief for Tackett alone. He mourned for Abe Hunt, for Caleb Black, for Maggie—all of them lost to him.

When it was over, McCan asked Bill, "Where will you go now?"

"Looking for work wherever I can find it."

"Need a partner?"

"Be proud to have one."

"Good. But there's something I need to do before we go."

They rode to Upchurch's Emporium. The store thrived; people, buggies, horses, wagons were everywhere. A blacksmith shop—new—operated nearby, plus a barber shop and tack store and horse trading pen. Three houses were under construction within view.

"Looks like there really *will* be a town here," McCan said.

They tethered their horses to the hitching post outside the Emporium. They walked inside and swept off their hats. An organic, marvelous smell filled the place—a mixed scent of leather, cloth bolts, candy, tobacco, spices, flour, gun oil.

Rodney Upchurch tended a customer in the back. McCan walked there and waited until Upchurch was finished. Bill wandered off in the meantime to inspect a shotgun he had admired a long time but never could buy.

Upchurch finished his business and saw McCan. His smile disappeared. McCan could not read his expression.

"Well," Upchurch said. "I see the stories *are* true. A man really can come back from the dead."

"I'd like to talk to you, Upchurch."

"Step into my office."

"No. Outside. If your buggy's handy, we'll take it."

Upchurch looked irritated but curious. He made a show of removing his apron, slapping it to the counter, and striding out the front door. McCan followed him. A few minutes later the two men were bouncing down the dirt road in Upchurch's leather-dashed buggy.

"What do you want from me?" Upchurch asked.

"First, I wanted to tell you again I'm sorry I attacked you. It was wrong."

"That's already forgotten. I didn't run you through court, did I?"

"I appreciate that too."

"This isn't what you came to talk about, McCan. You came to talk about Maggie."

"Yes."

Upchurch chuckled bitterly. "You know, I didn't even know you and Maggie had had a relationship until just a few weeks ago. When word came you were dead."

"How did you find out?"

"From Maggie. She . . . cried. I started asking questions."

"Cried." McCan shook his head and smiled sardonically. "Well, I'm capable of stirring something in her, at least." It was a private thought spoken out loud, and Upchurch didn't appear to appreciate it.

"Just what do you want from me?" he said.

"I'm not sure. Just to hear me out, maybe. I loved Maggie, you see. I *still* love her. But I'm not a fool. You've won her, which makes me the loser. But I want you to know this: if I could take her from you right now, I'd do it. And there's a part of me that will always resent you because that won't ever happen. It should have been me, not you." He paused. "I just needed to tell you that. Does that make any sense to you?"

Upchurch said, "Yes. More than you might think." He was silent awhile, then said, "I might be a fool for this, but—in two days, Maggie and I will be getting married. It will be an outdoor wedding, at the Emporium, and you're welcome to attend."

McCan nodded. Neither man spoke again until they were back at the store. McCan rejoined Bill. "We'll be staying on another day or two," he said. Bill started to ask a question, but noticed McCan's expression and held his peace.

It was more than a wedding. Typical of Upchurch's style, it was a three-fiddle party that drew people from fifty miles around. First came the ceremony, short but elegant by frontier standards. McCan stared at Maggie throughout, watching her being stolen from him while he stood helpless. When it was done, he turned away and went searching for spiked punch.

The party began. It was a fine setting: tables spread with white cloths and laden with washtubs of cold punch, heaps of roast beef, boiled potatoes, thick biscuits, hot ears of yellow corn, pies, cakes, gallons of steaming coffee, beer, jellies, big hunks of mold-pressed butter, puddings, sausages, and wild fowl.

The fiddlers sawed away. As darkness spread over the sky, out came paper lanterns. Dozens of couples danced—girls in their finest dresses, the ones they kept wrapped in muslin; men with new haircuts that raised their hairlines an inch above their ears and made them look like peeled onions. Their trousers were washed and pressed, their small-collared shirts with baggy sleeves starched and snow-white.

The scene was colorful, whirling, lit by the flaring lanterns. Children ran about. Boys wrestled on the fringes of the gathering, as others stood guard at the tables, charged with defense against dogs and flies.

McCan approached Bill Webster, his fourth glass of punch in hand. "Nothing at all to hold me here now," he said. "That was my last tie to Timber Creek."

"You're lucky and don't know it," Bill said. "Just like me. I came close to getting caught, but I didn't."

"What happened?"

"She decided she liked my brother Bob better than me, and she was after him like jaybird on a squirrel. That's why Bob run off to be a freighter. He never told you?"

McCan laughed and shook his head.

"It's the truth. After he was gone, she had no use for me. Took a cap-and-ball pistol and shot off half my little toe, and that's no lie."

"I'm glad you survived your love life, Bill."

The party went on. Upchurch and Maggie stood on

the store porch as a line of people greeted them. McCan had never seen her look as beautiful as she did now. Salt rubbed on a wounded heart.

McCan tossed down his final mouthful of punch. "Might as well give the couple our regards," he said.

Maggie smiled and took his hand when he came to her. "I'm so glad it wasn't true—about you being dead."

"I'm right pleased about that myself. Good luck to you, Maggie. I wish you happiness."

"I wish you the same," she said, and then she kissed him.

He wandered off alone to the south end of the store building, musing. The day was almost gone, only the faintest memory of daylight remaining. McCan heard a noise. Far down the road he saw a bobbing glow—a lantern held by a rider, it appeared. As it came closer he saw a wagon too. Both the rider and the wagon driver were rushing. McCan walked toward them and met them before they reached the party.

The rider with the lantern had a badge on his shirt. "What's happening here?" he asked.

"A wedding party."

"Anyone there a doctor?"

"None for miles."

"That's too bad. I got a sick man in the wagon." He waved the lantern back across the wagon, and light spilled across the bed and a man lying in it. McCan drew in his breath.

It was Evan Bridger.

PART IV

THE LAST DAYS

CHAPTER 26

———

"My name is Taylor Longhurst," the man with the badge said to the huddle of people who gathered around Bridger's unconscious form. "I'm a U.S. deputy marshal out of Fort Maginnis. That man is Evan Bridger. He's my prisoner."

"Bridger?" someone said. "I've heard of him. Old highwayman and stock rustler."

"That and more," Longhurst said. "He also was the thief once of an army payroll, which makes him of interest to the federal government. That's why I've got him."

McCan asked, "What's wrong with him?"

"I think a recurrence of malaria. I'd bet this old bird came across the isthmus in '49 or so."

Bridger had been found, Longhurst said, passed out in the back of a one-room saloon at a one-horse settlement to the southwest. The saloon owner saw Longhurst's badge and called him in. Longhurst recognized Bridger, and for a day had been seeking medical help for him.

"We've got no doctor," Upchurch said, "but I'll send to Milestown for one right now. There's a small apartment in the back of the store, and you can keep him there."

"No jail?"

"We're a new community."

"The store it is, then. I'm obliged."

They placed Bridger on a cot. When the others were gone, McCan lingered to talk to Longhurst.

"I know Bridger," he said. "At least, I've had encounters with him going back several years. I met him first in Deadwood, down in Dakota."

"Where did you see him last?"

McCan paused, then decided to tell the truth. "At a shooting match between some cattlemen and rustlers. I was with the former, and him the latter."

"I see." Longhurst looked like he knew more than he was saying. "Vigilantism isn't legal, you know. But it isn't easily stopped." He smiled vaguely. "Sometimes it isn't a thing we see much need to interfere in."

McCan relaxed. "This time it turned into something it wasn't supposed to be."

"So I heard. And Bridger was there, Mister . . ."

"McCan. Call me Luke. Yes, he was there."

Longhurst took out a snuff tin and delicately placed a pinch of the powdered tobacco on his thumb. He snorted it up his long nose with a satisfied wince. He offered some to McCan, who declined.

"Can't live without the stuff myself," Longhurst said. "Listen, I could use some sleep. I like the look of you. Are you needing a job?"

"It so happens . . ."

"You got one. Consider yourself deputized. You guard Bridger, and I'll see you get good compensation for it. It should be easy. He ain't going anywhere, sick as he is."

Longhurst gave McCan a shotgun with sawed-off barrels and put him in a chair by the door of the little apartment. The lawman went to the other side of the store, threw together a pile of empty feed sacks, tossed a blanket over them, and went to sleep.

McCan studied Bridger. The outlaw looked terrible, almost dead. *Looks like you may get that justice you always wanted yet, Caleb*, McCan thought.

An hour later Upchurch came in. He approached and looked at Bridger a few moments.

"I figured you'd be off on your wedding trip," McCan said.

"No trip for now. Too much work. And now this outlaw's here, there's even more reason to stay."

"Shouldn't you be with your bride?"

"She's who sent me in here. The thought of this man scares her. I think maybe it reminds her of the night her father died. Have you heard that story? A man like this one broke into her home. Her father and another cowboy came and—"

"I've heard," McCan said. He felt sullen; Maggie obviously had never told Upchurch who that other cowboy had been.

"Why are *you* here?" Upchurch asked.

"I'm deputized."

"I see." Upchurch turned away. "Well, I'll leave you to your work." He headed for the door.

"Upchurch."

"Yes?"

"Congratulations. Take good care of her."

"Thank you. I will." He went out the door and locked it behind him.

After a time, McCan became sleepy, so he went to the wood stove in the middle of the store, built a fire, and made coffee. He drank cup after cup of it until dawn. Longhurst stirred awake, stretched, and went for a cup himself. He came back with it and leaned against the apartment doorframe, his hair disheveled and face whiskered.

"How's our prisoner?" he said.

"Didn't move all night."

"This old bird's going to kick, I believe." Longhurst took a sip of coffee and made a face. "Tastes like a horse peed in this."

"I did my best. I'm worn out. Can I take off now?"

"Go ahead," the lawman said. "Get some rest and come back about supper time. I'll be needing a night guard until he's ready to ride. Or dead."

"I got a friend who could use a job too . . ."

"Is he reliable?"

"Absolutely."

"I got me a day guard then. Send him on."

As McCan left, Longhurst went through a snort-and-sniff routine with his snuff. McCan rode out to the little house, found Bill, and told him about the job.

"I don't know," Bill said. "Bridger killed my brother's murderer. I owe him a debt for that."

But finally he relented, for he needed the job badly. He rode to the Emporium, and McCan crawled into bed.

When McCan returned to the store about dusk, Bill was there with the shotgun in his lap. Longhurst sat on a cracker barrel, eating pickles and drinking warm beer.

"Did that doctor get in?" McCan asked.

"Nope. But we found an old Union medic who checked him out. Bridger's going to be sick for days."

McCan went to Bill. "You been sitting all day?"

"Yep."

"Doesn't Longhurst do any guarding himself?"

"Nope." He smiled.

"Lazy lawman, huh?"

Longhurst called, "You two are doing a good job. Proud of you." He drew more snuff up his nose, then expelled it in a loud sneeze.

At the sound, Bridger opened his eyes. He focused on McCan, then was out again.

CHAPTER 27

Over the next several days, Bridger became first an attraction for visitors, then a fixture that drew little attention. Awareness came slowly to him, strength even slower. He recognized McCan, and was amused their paths had crossed yet again.

"You and me seem bound to run into each other," Bridger said. "By the way, I almost blew off your head at the Breaks before I recognized you."

"I'm obliged you didn't."

"Then let me go."

"I can't do that."

Bridger laughed. "A man can do whatever he wants. Once you figure that out, it frees you up considerable."

"You're not very free right now."

"Freer than men who spend their lives with codes and rules. I never could tolerate that."

"So you don't believe in rules?"

"I don't believe in good or bad, right or wrong, God above or devil below. I believe in Evan Bridger."

"So what kept you from killing me?"

"I didn't feel the urge. Maybe I like your face."

"What do you think of me now, guarding you with a shotgun?"

Bridger shrugged. "You're doing a job. Nothing personal."

McCan leaned back in his chair. "You're right about one thing—we have had a bunch of encounters through the years. Same with me and Caleb Black. He just turns up. Or used to. I think he's dead. You can rest easier now, I reckon."

Bridger looked at the ceiling, mulling over the information. "Why do you think he's dead?"

"I was with him this year when we got jumped in camp. There was shooting. I got away, but we got separated. I never found him, but there was sign he had died."

Bridger smiled. "So, old Caleb's killed! I wish it could have been me that done it."

McCan's temper flared. "Caleb was my friend. God knows it would have been better for a lousy child-killer like you to have died instead of him."

Bridger's smile vanished. "What did you call me?"

McCan was silent.

"I never killed no child."

"You just don't know you did."

Bridger's smile slowly returned. "You're joshing with me. Trying to get me riled."

"I don't know why being called a child-killer would rile a man who doesn't believe in right or wrong."

"You don't think too highly of me, do you?" Bridger said. "How much do you know about me, about who I really am?"

"Not much."

"Let me give you some history. I was born in Baltimore, in an alley by a church where folks in fancy clothes sang hymns while drunks froze to death at the back door. I never knew my father, nor my mother, except that she was a whore who left me in a pile of rags at a stable door. I never had even the first suck at her breast. A policeman found me. I was raised in an orphanage six years, fighting and scrapping with the others, and never crying my first tear. I ain't cried it yet.

"They finally shipped me off to a preacher, who kept me for nine hard years. He preached at me, screamed at me, beat me, told me the meek would inherit the earth and I'd better get meek, by God. But I knew about his drinking, and the way he beat his woman and run around on her with a darky girl across town. I hated that man. When I ran off, I left his house burning, and I hope it cooked him.

"I stole, rolled drunks and such to live, and worked my way west to Kansas. When I was full-grown, I married a gal and ran a little farm, until she died having a baby. I buried them both. Killed a man the next night in a card game—he cheated, but it was really out of grief that I done it.

"I went to California during the rush—picked up this sickness on the way—and mined until I figured out it was easier to steal gold than grub it. Since then, I've been most everywhere, doing what I want. That's the way it'll be with me until I'm dead—doing what I want. If that's good or bad, I don't give a damn. That, son, is who Evan Bridger is: a man who just don't give a damn."

Bridger stopped talking. McCan said, "I'm grateful to you for helping me in Deadwood, and for not killing me up on the Missouri Breaks. But the fact is, the world will be a better place the day you go in the ground, and the air will be a little cleaner the day you quit breathing it."

Bridger laughed. He was tired, and closed his eyes. For several minutes he seemed to be asleep, but then he looked again at McCan and asked, "Why did you call me a child-killer?"

"Caleb Black's wife was pregnant when you killed her. Not that you give a damn."

Bridger's lip twitched almost imperceptibly. "Yeah," he said, and closed his eyes again.

McCan stood guard the next night, and this time Bridger did not talk. He was worse, his fever higher, his eyes sunken deeper.

In the silence, McCan dozed, the shotgun across his lap. Something made him wake up an hour later. He looked groggily at a figure before him in the flaring lamplight.

"Good to see you, Luke."

McCan blinked to be sure he was awake—he was. "Good to see you too Caleb. I thought you were dead."

"I thought *you* were dead. How'd you get away?"

"I knocked out the one after me and hid out in the woods until morning. How about you?"

"Me and the other took a shot from each other. His was worse. I passed out in the woods for about a day. I think he died by the river and fell in."

Black turned to Bridger, who was asleep. "Would he have lived?"

"What do you mean, 'would'?"

"I mean, would he have lived if I hadn't showed up, because I'm going to kill him right here."

McCan raised his shotgun. Black looked at him like he was insane.

"What are you doing?" Black demanded.

"Stopping you, it appears."

"*Why?*"

"I don't know. It's my job."

Black glared disbelievingly at him. "I ought to shoot *you*."

"You'd shoot me just to get him?"

"You turned saint or something, Luke?"

"Not saint. Just deputy."

In Black's mind, a game of balancing, debating, option-shifting went on. It evidenced itself in subtle movements of his fingers near his side arm. Black was coiled tight, ready to be sprung with a breath. But, after several tense moments, he relaxed. The fingers went still.

"I'll get my chance," he said. "They'll never get him to no prison. I'll get to him first."

"I don't doubt it. It just won't be tonight."

"Maybe we'll run across each other again, Luke."

"I don't doubt that, either."

Black walked out. Bridger moaned and stirred. He sweated profusely. McCan gripped his shotgun so tightly his fingers were numb. He, too, sweated.

The door of the Emporium, its lock ruined by Caleb's entry, banged shut. Black was gone. All was silent except Bridger's labored breathing, which rattled like a tinker's wagon, and the buzzing of a fly trapped in a web in some dark corner of the store.

CHAPTER 28

�019

When Bill Webster relieved McCan the next morning, he came in late and noticeably happier than before.

"I got a new job," he announced. "Over at the LU Bar, starting as soon as I can get there."

"Good," McCan said. "Are you healed up enough to do it?"

"These bones ache a bit, but a man can't let that stop him."

"Nope." He slapped Bill's shoulder. "When will you go?"

"Tomorrow morning. Maybe Longhurst can find somebody else to sit day guard."

McCan went to the porch of the store and rolled a cigarette. Upchurch came around the corner as Longhurst rode in from the north. He had abandoned his feed-sack bed in the store for a real one in a spare room at a ranch three miles away. McCan nodded his usual silent greeting at Upchurch and waited until Longhurst had dismounted.

"Looks like you'll have to do some guarding yourself," he said. "Bill Webster won't be around starting tomorrow."

Upchurch, who saw the damaged lock on the door, turned to McCan. "What happened to this?"

McCan debated: tell the truth? He decided against it. "I caught somebody trying to get in last night," he said. "I ran them off, but they already had busted the lock."

Upchurch looked worried. "Thieves!" he exclaimed, as if the thought was novel. "Thank you for running them off. Did you see their faces?"

"Too dark."

Longhurst asked, "Why is Bill leaving?"

McCan told him about the new job. "I'll just take his place myself, then," Longhurst said, looking glum.

"No," Upchurch said. "I'll do it."

McCan was surprised. "But you've got a store to run!"

"If my store is threatened by thieves, I want people to become used to seeing me with a shotgun in my lap. That might deter any other attempts like this one."

Have mercy, McCan thought. *Rodney Upchurch, deputy. The daisy-plucker of law enforcement.*

Longhurst, seeing a chance to preserve his cherished idleness, immediately accepted Upchurch's offer. "Excellent suggestion," he said. "Do you have any experience with shotguns?"

"None beyond selling them."

Longhurst took the shotgun from McCan and dug extra shells from his saddlebag. "Come on. I'll give you some lessons."

McCan went back to his chair at Bridger's door to stand guard until they were through. Moments later, the shotgun boomed off behind the building. Bridger jerked up with a choked cry in the back of his throat.

"Don't worry," McCan said. "Nobody's shooting at you. Yet."

Upchurch apparently enjoyed guard duty. As Bridger improved again over the next few days, Upchurch befriended him. Whenever McCan came to relieve Upchurch, merchant and outlaw were always deep in conversation.

But Bridger had little to say to McCan anymore. When McCan was with him, he either slept or just stared at the ceiling. If McCan asked a question, Bridger merely shrugged or muttered something vague in response.

Still, Bridger's health was obviously returning, Longhurst often came in to evaluate his prisoner, and at length told McCan he would be well enough for travel soon. "I want you to go with me," Longhurst said. "An extra guard would be helpful."

The day before they were to leave for Fort Maginnis, McCan passed the shotgun to Upchurch, as usual, and went off to bed. He was restless today, though, and spent most of the morning puttering about. Finally, about noon, he went back to his bunk and fell asleep.

He awoke later than usual. Darkness was heavy. He intuitively felt something was wrong back at the Emporium.

He rode to it at a gallop, throat tight, a sheen of dampness on his forehead, though the night was cool. At the store, all was in commotion—men moving about, more lights than usual, a jumble of loud voices.

He dismounted and hitched his horse. "What happened?" he asked a man standing nearby.

"Mr. Upchurch has been shot," the man said.

McCan pushed through the crowd into the store.

Longhurst was there, his usual half-cocky smile gone, his face gray as coal ash.

"How'd it happen?"

"Bridger somehow just got the shotgun and used it," Longhurst said. "Shot Upchurch in the side, and him unarmed."

"Is he dead?"

"No. But he's bad—his side looks like chewed meat."

Maggie. McCan had to see her.

He circled the store to the house behind it; even more people were there. He entered the main room.

The bedroom door stood ajar. Upchurch lay in there, bloodied and pale, his eyes squeezed shut, his breathing spasmodic. Somebody worked on him, digging out pellets from his mangled side.

McCan looked for Maggie but did not see her. He left the house.

He found her around back, crying. He said nothing, just stood holding his hat and wondering if he should slip away and leave her alone. But suddenly she became aware of him. She came into his arms and wept against his shoulder. When the crying was finished, she looked into his face.

"Find that man, Luke. Find him and bring him back—or kill him. He's taken my husband from me."

"I will, Maggie. And your husband will be all right. A lot of good folks here are taking care of him."

He led Maggie to the back step and made her sit, then went inside and got coffee. "Drink this," he said. "It will help."

McCan sought out Longhurst again. "When do we ride?"

"First light. Bridger stole a horse, and he'll have a good lead. I figure he'll steal another one as soon as he can. I just hope nobody else gets shot."

"Will you organize a full posse?"

"No. Just you and me. It will be quieter and quicker that way. We'll catch that bird. We'll bring him back for trial."

Not if I make the choice, McCan thought. *If it's up to me, we'll bring him back dead.*

CHAPTER 29

Standing before his hovel of a house, a skinny man old and shriveled from sun—wiped his hands across his mouth and said, "He was here, all right. Came riding in all a-lather and aimed a shotgun at my belly. 'Give me a horse,' he says, and I did. He was a ghastly soul, all pasty and sweaty. I done like he said."

"You did right," Longhurst said. "He would have killed you if you hadn't, and you're lucky he didn't anyway. Which way did he go?"

"West. And that's a funny thing—he said where he was going, and to make sure whoever followed him knew."

"Trying to bluff us off his trail, probably," Longhurst said. "What did he say?"

"Garrison's, over on Froze To Death Creek."

McCan said, "I know the place. Just a lonely old outpost."

Longhurst crossed his arms on his saddle horn and looked thoughtful. "The odds are he was lying, but we've got little chance to catch him at any rate. Maybe we ought to follow the only clue we've got."

"What are you suggesting?"

"Take Bridger at his word. Go to Garrison's."

They tipped hats to the old man and rode away, heading due west. McCan was amazed to see Longhurst successfully take a double load of snuff while riding in a good breeze and not lose a grain.

"How long you been snorting that stuff?" McCan asked.

"Since I was six. I got only one regret about it, and that's that I didn't start when I was five."

They rode steadily, following a trail here, a wagon road there. Each had brought an extra horse, and they changed periodically to keep the animals fresh.

To McCan, there was something ironic in the situation: here he was, tracking the outlaw Caleb Black had sought for years, one who had brought pain to a lady he cared about, one who deserved death if any man did. And this after McCan had protected that same outlaw from his deserved fate only shortly before.

He couldn't forget that if he had let Black kill Bridger there in the Emporium, Maggie would not be in the torment she now was.

They pushed steadily and ate up another twenty-five miles before dark. Longhurst built a fire, cooked beans and bacon, and brewed coffee. McCan was on his second cup when Longhurst grinned.

"That Arbuckle has a special ingredient."

"No."

"Yes."

Longhurst laughed, lay down, and almost immediately began snoring. McCan shook his head. Probably the laziest, most devil-may-care deputy in the hire of the government, yet he had to like him. He even liked the snuff-tainted coffee he brewed.

The next day they cut southwest and marked off thirty hard miles, camping near Great Porcupine Creek. McCan was bone-weary and rump-sore from the saddle. Manhunting was as hard on a man as roundup. Harder, for there was a gnawing uncertainty about what would happen at the end.

The next day they rose before dawn and ate a quick breakfast of jerky strips. They rode hard, for today they would reach the trading post where Bridger had said he would go.

McCan and Longhurst sat mounted at the base of a slate-colored slope, looking up through a forest of pine and elder, studying the nondescript trading post called Garrison's.

"Think he's there?" McCan asked.

"Depends on how sick he was when he relieved that old man of his horse. He might not have been clear-headed enough to lie."

"Well, let's ride in and see."

They tied their mounts at a water trough at the front of the post, unbooted their rifles, and walked into the largest of the three log buildings comprising Garrison's. The air was close inside, very dank, smelling of rot and other foul things. At a long bar of puncheon boards laid out on stumps was a fortyish man with one ear. He was, McCan assumed, the barkeep, but, from the look of him, might be a whiskey-runner or Indian trader.

There were others too. Three men shoveled beans into their mouths at a corner table. Another sat alone in the back, drinking. His face was turned to the wall; for a moment, McCan thought it was Bridger, but it wasn't.

Longhurst went to the bar and ordered two glasses of whiskey. McCan sipped his; it tasted like a mix of brimstone and alcohol. He made a face. "Don't drop an ash into this, Longhurst. It would flare in your face."

He did not notice the movement of one of the men at the table at his mention of the deputy's name.

Longhurst did notice. He watched the man out of the corner of his eye as he drained the liquor in one swallow. He smacked his lips and shook his head. "Sweet as candy." He clicked his glass against the bar for a refill, and shifted position to allow a casual but more direct look at the bean-eaters. He took a snort of snuff as he eyed them.

McCan realized what was happening, and also that Longhurst had left his badge on his shirt. He wished he had taken it off.

Longhurst sipped his second glassful rather than gulped it. One of the men at the table stood and walked toward him and McCan.

Longhurst grinned. "Well, howdy, Grunt! Long time no see. How's that hand?"

McCan pieced it together quickly. This man apparently was one of Longhurst's old captures. The reference to the hand he interpreted after a glance at the man's mangled right extremity. Something had pulverized it long ago—a sawed-off shotgun, maybe?

"I wondered when I'd see you again, Longhurst."

"When did they let you out, Grunt? I thought you'd be in a lot longer than this."

"Things have a way of working out." The man smiled, revealing teeth moldier than a swamp log.

Longhurst took another sip. "Can I buy you a drink? You'd like this stuff, Grunt—tastes like it was drained out of a hell-pit. A man's drink for sure."

"Why are you here, lawman?"

"Just out doing my job. Grunt, it's coming back to me—seems I heard you escaped."

"What do you plan to do about it?"

"Well, I'm in a good humor. I'd like to cut a deal. I won't arrest you if you'll give me some information about the man I'm looking for."

"Arrest?" Grunt laughed. "Hear that, boys? He said he'd not *arrest* me. Longhurst, I got grave doubts you'll ever arrest anybody again!"

This time Longhurst laughed. He nudged McCan. "Hear that, Luke? He said *grave*."

Something in the air snapped. Grunt lunged for his pistol, but Longhurst was ready. He drew easily and fired twice. Grunt's ugly face twisted and he fell back, screaming. Blood spurted from what had been his unmangled left hand—now missing a thumb and forefinger.

One of the men with Grunt ran out the front door, arms outstretched, body careening. The second looked momentarily as if he might join the fight, but Longhurst turned his pistol on him and the man slipped sideways, then bolted for the door. Grunt, still yelling and gripping his bloody hand with the shotgun-mangled paw that was his other, quickly followed.

"That boy'll have to quit messing with me, or eventually he won't even be able to pick his nose," Longhurst said.

Suddenly the deputy screamed. He had rested his left arm on the bartop, and now he pulled it around in front of him. Blood dripped from it. Behind Longhurst, the barkeep drew up the Bowie he had used to gash the arm. It came arcing down, and McCan yelled and threw out his own arm to block it.

That saved Longhurst from taking a full-blade stab in the back, but the knife went in four inches at least, and Longhurst screamed once more.

McCan went for his pistol, but the lone man who had been drinking in the back made that unnecessary.

The man rose, turned, adeptly fired. The barkeep gave a thoroughly canine bark and fell sideways to the floor. He grasped his wounded left arm, and the knife fell from his hand. McCan kicked it away.

"Oh lordy, oh lordy, oh lordy," Longhurst said, over and over again, falling on his knees so the chant became a strange parody of prayer. "Oh lordy, oh lordy, oh lordy."

McCan turned from him to the man in the back, then slumped against the bar, shaking his head.

"I should have guessed I'd run into you, Caleb."

Caleb Black smiled. "Why not? We're two hounds chasing the same rabbit."

He crossed the room and shook McCan's hand. Longhurst quit his chant and started moaning, and the wounded barkeep did too. It made an eerie barnyard harmony: the barkeep howling like a kicked beagle, the lawman whining like a cat.

CHAPTER 30

McCan went to the writhing barkeep and knelt to touch the man's injured arm. The barkeep rolled onto his back and looked at McCan, who only now recognized him.

"You don't hold a grudge, do you, Luke? You don't hold a grudge after all these years?" the man whined.

McCan was momentarily too surprised to speak. The barkeep took that for a bad sign and howled out again, a sort of coward's deathsong.

"Oh, shut up, Sturley," McCan said. "I don't figure to kill you, though it'd be a loss to nobody if I did."

Roy Sturley hushed. "Thank you, Luke. God bless you, son. I always thought the highest of you, I really did."

"How'd you lose that ear?"

"It was bit off in a fight."

"Good for whoever. You know there was a time I was set on killing you, Roy?"

"I ain't surprised, Luke. I didn't always do right by you, but we're friends now—huh?"

"You'll never be that, but I'm letting you off just the same. Now tell me why you cut my partner."

"I seen he was a lawman, and that he was with you, and thought maybe he was after me. I'm sorry, honest I am."

Longhurst was angry. He stood and wheeled toward the prone man. "Give me a reason I shouldn't gut you like a hog right here!"

Sturley scooted away on his back until he was against the wall, anticipating his own slaughter.

"Leave him be, Longhurst. He might help us," McCan said. To Sturley he said, "You remember the night Jimmy Wyatt got killed? The man who did it was Evan Bridger. We're looking for him. Have you seen him here?"

Sturley said, "There was a man on a lame horse, wanting a trade. I didn't have nothing for him, so he went on. It might have been Evan Bridger, but I don't know for sure because I wasn't there to see who shot Jimmy."

"That's right—you ran off. You were as big a coward then as now," McCan said.

"This fellow, what did he look like?" Black asked.

"Tall, pepper-haired, skin kind of loose—like he'd lost weight—and he looked sickly."

"And he's on a lame horse?"

"That's right, sir."

"He'll have stole or traded for another by now," Longhurst said. He thrust his hand out to Black. "Taylor Longhurst. Thanks for your help."

"I'm Caleb Black." The men shook. "Luke's an old friend of mine. We've got a way of running into each other every now and then."

"Seems I've heard about a Caleb Black who trails Evan Bridger."

"I'm the man," Black said. "Though I'm no ghost, despite what a few say."

"I thought you were a story somebody made up."

"Bridger wishes I was."

McCan shook Sturley by the shoulder. Sturley's face screwed up like a crumpled mask. "What else do you know?" McCan demanded.

"A letter. He left a letter and said, give it to any lawman who came after him."

"A *letter?* Where?"

Sturley pointed to a folded piece of paper sticking out from a crevice in the wall behind the bar. Black took it, opened it, and read.

"It's just a note," he said. "It says, 'To you on my trail, find C. Black and tell him the game is over and it is time to settle and he'll know the place if he is savvy. E. Bridger.'" Black refolded the paper, frowning.

"What does *that* mean?" McCan asked.

"I don't know," Black said. "It's mighty strange. He's never done nothing like this before."

McCan looked again at Sturley. "Did he say where he was going?"

"Billings. He said to be sure and tell he was going straight to Billings."

"First time I've ever had a criminal tell me where I could catch him," Longhurst said, his voice stressed from pain.

McCan looked at Sturley's wound. "I'll bind that up for you," he said. "The bullet went clean through, so you'll be all right. Which proves there's no justice: you live, and Bob Webster died."

When McCan was finished, Sturley struggled to his feet, slid in his own blood, and fell. He scrambled up again and rushed out the door.

"I'm hurting bad," Longhurst said. "That blade was hot as a brand."

"I'm no doc, but Luke can tell you I'm a fair nurse-maid when I got to be," Black said. "Let me see what I can do for you."

Longhurst took off his shirt and sat on a bench. Black poured whiskey across his bleeding back, and onto the sliced arm. Longhurst yelled and almost passed out.

"Give me some of that," he said. He grabbed the bottle and took a long swallow. Then he snorted a pile of snuff into his sinuses and seemed to feel better.

"Let's get out of here," McCan said. "This blood is drawing flies. Taylor, I take it that Grunt fellow was an old friend of yours."

"One of many," the deputy said.

Longhurst became sick that night. His pain worsened, and he threw up his supper right after he ate it. He lay on his bedroll somewhere between wakefulness and stupor.

"He can't go on," McCan said to Black.

"That's no good," Black said. "We're so close to Bridger I can smell him."

"We won't lose him," McCan said. "He's marked his trail from the beginning. I don't understand it, but it's like he wants to be caught."

"Something's different, that's for sure. The letter alone proves that." Black borrowed McCan's makings and rolled a smoke. "All right," he said. "I'll help you find a place to let the lawman heal a little. But after that, I'm going on, with or without you."

Five miles beyond Muggins Creek the next day, they found a humble spread wedged into a shallow valley. It was small, poorly built, impoverished. Some cowpoke's attempt to build a cattle operation of his own, McCan guessed. If so, his success was meager. A few scrawny cattle ranged within view, along with a couple of horses and a yardful of chickens. Only a vegetable patch appeared to be thriving.

"Let's go in," McCan said. He rode toward the house. Behind him, Longhurst trailed along, his face flushed and wet. Black rode in the rear, looking about thoughtfully.

"Hello, the house!" McCan shouted. "Anybody here?"

No one answered. Only the chickens responded, clucking and bustling away. McCan dismounted some distance from the house and walked in.

"Hello!" he shouted again. He went to the door and knocked.

Something moved inside. He rapped again, gave another hello, then stepped back. A moment later the latch moved, and the door opened about halfway. A boy appeared, his brows and mouth quirked downward in a scowl. He held an ancient percussion cap revolver.

"Oh," McCan said. "I didn't mean to trespass."

"What's your business, mister?" Illogically, the voice surprised McCan. The dark little face could have been that of an old man, but the voice was merely the elfin squeak of a very scared boy.

"My name is McCan. I've got a friend out here, a deputy territorial marshal, who was hurt by a criminal. He was stabbed and he's sick. We hoped you'd let us lay him up here for a bit."

At mention of the lawman, the boy looked confused. The expression, though, evolved quickly into one of resolute inapproachability. "We got no place here," the boy said. "You can ride on."

"All right then. Where's the next spread?"

"Twenty miles west. Or you can get to Junction City, due south. It's closer."

"Thank you. I'm leaving, and I'd appreciate you being real careful with that hogleg." McCan returned to the horses, shrugging.

"I can't believe it," Black said. "It ain't typical of these parts to turn somebody away needing help."

"I wasn't about to push him, not with that pistol in his hand. We'd best head for Junction City."

They turned mounts and rode away, but Caleb Black raised his hand and they stopped. "Look yonder," he said. He pointed toward the horses grazing nearby. One was a scrawny black mare. But the other was a gray gelding with a bad leg.

McCan didn't grasp the significance at first, but suddenly he remembered: Sturley had said Bridger was on a lame horse.

"Just keep calm and ride off like nothing's happened," Black instructed. "Once we clear the ridge, we'll cut around and wait for dark. Then we can slip in. Taylor, you can rest it out on your bedroll."

A few minutes later they stopped, hidden beyond the rise. Longhurst found a shady spot and laid down, complaining about dizziness and pain.

"No wonder the boy acted so funny, if Bridger really is in there," McCan said. "I had a peculiar feeling the whole time I was at that door."

Black checked his pistol. "I'm bellying up to where I can see the house. If he slips out, I want to know it."

McCan went with him, and they laid on their stomachs and watched the little building. No one emerged for a long time, and when finally the door opened, only the boy came out. He went to a shed, came back with a hoe, and went to work in the vegetable patch.

When it was nearly dark, the boy went back inside. McCan and Black slid, silent as the moonlight, across the clearing to the door. They drew their pistols and readied themselves on either side of the doorway; then Black wheeled and kicked the door open.

He and McCan rushed in and leveled their pistols on the occupants.

There were only two of them. The boy, gaping, and a lady, who had once been pretty but now looked faded—somehow eroded. Evan Bridger was not there.

The lady cried out and rushed to her boy. She hugged him close, protectively. McCan saw the broad swell of her belly. She was pregnant.

Black lowered his pistol and thumbed down the hammer. His face was deathly pale. "My god," he murmured. "I almost shot her."

For a moment, McCan thought Black was going to pass out.

CHAPTER 31

~

Her name was Jerusha Harpe, and for more than eight months she had lived with one child struggling to survive inside her, another struggling to survive without. She tried at first to make the intruders believe her husband would quickly be home, but it was soon evident she was lying. When her fright faded and reassurance came after they brought in Taylor Longhurst and showed his badge, she admitted her husband was dead.

"We're sorry," McCan said. "About that, and how we busted in here. We thought a very dangerous man was in here with you."

"There *was* a man here," she said. "But he was gone long before you came. He said men were after him, and there was someplace he had to go, where—what was it he said, George?"

"Where it all could end," the boy said. His face no longer tight with fear, he looked like a child again.

"Yes. Where it all could end. I didn't understand what that meant. He was strange. Like he was losing his sanity."

"I can believe it," Black said.

"But he was tender, in one way," she continued. "Particularly toward me, even though he held his pistol in his hand the whole time he was here—maybe six or seven hours. Most of what he said made no sense. And he just kept staring at my—" She became embarrassed. She glanced down and touched her protruding belly.

Black said, "Something's happening to him. Messages to us, him asking for me to be brought into the search—I don't understand this."

"I was afraid when you came," Jerusha said. "That's why I had George stand you off at the door. I didn't know who you were, or if you might not be just as dangerous as that man was. You know, he never said his name."

"His name is Evan Bridger," McCan said. "Have you heard of him?"

Jerusha shook her head, but the boy nodded excitedly. "I know—he's an outlaw. A robber and a killer. And he's haunted by a ghost that stays on his trail and tries to kill *him*."

"Don't talk nonsense, George," Jerusha scolded. "People tell all kinds of silly stories."

McCan looked at Black, who seemed not to have heard. He was thinking, apparently very seriously. And he, like Bridger had done, stared at Jerusha's pregnant belly.

"That story's *true*, Ma!" George said. "Everybody tells it. I wish Pa could know I'd met a real outlaw!"

Jerusha frowned; the lines around her eyes became more evident. "If your pa was here, this outlaw never would have come in on us. And besides that, your pa wouldn't have thought much of you being pleased to have met such an evil man. If this Evan Bridger is evil, then I can tell you it's no ghost that haunts him, but something else. You remember what I've read to you about the wicked?"

George Harpe twisted his mouth and plucked a scripture verse from his memory: " 'The wicked flee when no man pursueth.' "

"That's right," Jerusha said. "What chases them? Their own conscience. Knowledge of their own evil."

McCan stood, digging for his makings. "Not in Bridger's case, ma'am. The man's got no conscience. He doesn't believe in good or bad—told me so himself. There is no evil as far as he's concerned."

Jerusha gave McCan a stern look, and he saw she did not appreciate being contradicted in front of her son. "There is not a man who has walked this earth who doesn't have to face his own evil at some point. There's not a man who can deny it forever," she said.

McCan was sheepish. "Yes, ma'am. I'm sorry. I'll just step out for a smoke now."

He went outside and lit up. The rich smoke kicked pleasantly against the back of his throat. He walked around the little spread and wondered how a pregnant widow and a twelve-year-old boy managed to survive here.

Inside, Caleb Black was still lost in thought. He didn't notice when Jerusha Harpe rose heavily from her chair and walked stiff-legged to the stove. She brewed coffee and brought a cup to Black. She thrust it before his eyes, and he looked up and smiled at her.

In the corner, Taylor Longhurst moaned and twisted on a cot.

"God have mercy on a knife-stuck sinner," he said.

George Harpe bounded to his side. "Are you hurting, mister?"

"Yes. And out of snuff. Be a good boy and head to the shed where my saddlebags are. There's some inside there."

The boy ran out the door, proud of his assignment. He darted past McCan, into the shed, and came out again with Longhurst's snuff in hand. McCan touched his shoulder and stopped him.

"How long until your mother's to give birth, George?"

"Any day now. That's what the granny woman says."

"Where does the granny woman live?"

"Down toward Junction City. About five miles from here."

McCan nodded and blew smoke through his nostrils. "Maybe it's providential we came by when we did, then. Your ma might need help real soon."

A peal of thunder grumbled across the sky. McCan breathed deeply and tasted a hint of distant rain.

"We're in for a storm," he said.

McCan's predictions were correct. The rain came at dark, the baby at midnight.

McCan rode off with directions from George, hoping he could find the midwife's house, praying he could get back with her in time. He left Caleb Black with Jerusha, Caleb's hands scrubbed clean and his shirt stripped off, ready to do what he could if the child came quickly.

The storm whipped McCan without mercy. Rain slapped him like hail, stinging his face and lips. Lightning ripped jagged tears through the night, spooking his horse, but also providing the only light by which he could keep to the road.

The wind blew against him, and progress was slow. By the time he reached the dirt-roofed hovel where the midwife lived, he feared he was too late. Jerusha's labor had come swiftly and hard, and by now the baby surely had been born. Or lost.

The midwife was old, but moved nimbly. She wrapped a heavy shawl around her shoulders and mounted behind McCan, her fat-dangling arms around his waist. McCan spurred his tired mount back the way it had come.

The storm abated when they were halfway home, and when they reached the Harpe cabin, the sky was clear. McCan slid down and helped the midwife descend, then whipped his still-saddled mount into the corral. He trotted to the house, threw open the door, and went to the bedroom.

He stopped, overwhelmed by what he saw.

Caleb stood beside Jerusha's bed, his skin slicked with sweat and golden in the lamplight. He beamed, face upturned, as he lifted a tiny, red, squalling girl who barely filled his broad hands.

The infant, shining with its mother's water and blood, cried in hoarse, steady bursts. Caleb Black laughed at the sound, and when he laid the child into the upheld arms of its mother, Jerusha laughed too.

CHAPTER 32

Days passed, and Caleb said nothing about going after Bridger. Instead, he took care of the new mother, and when Caleb—big, gruff, bearded—cradled the child in his burly forearms, it reminded McCan of a pink baby robin nested in an ancient, battered oak. The man and child played a delightful counterpoint to each other.

Jerusha named the girl Lucy, after her grandmother. Lucy was a scrappy, healthy infant who thrived at her mother's breast, and it was clear she was deeply loved by the man who had first held her.

Longhurst, meanwhile, recovered from his wounds, fighting off an infection that had set into his arm. He grew restless to move on. McCan, too, knew that the longer they waited, the less likely they were to catch Bridger.

Bridger had indicated he was going to Billings, but that had been days ago. They needed to ride at once. Ironically, it was Black who was the least concerned. He was preoccupied with Jerusha and Lucy and George.

Longhurst called aside his two partners and said, "It's time to go. We need to ride out at first light tomorrow."

McCan nodded, but Black looked displeased. "We owe it to Jerusha to make sure she's in fit shape before we leave," he said.

"She's in fine shape already, and we've paid our obligation to her a dozen times over—you especially, Caleb. Now, I'm going on tomorrow, and if you want to come, you're welcome. If not, it'll just be me and Luke—or maybe just me." He looked inquiringly at McCan.

"I'll be along," McCan said.

Black fidgeted, but finally he nodded. "First light, then."

George waved them out of sight the next morning. Black would not look back at him. McCan watched his old partner thoughtfully, and while Longhurst was ahead, came to Black's side.

"You think highly of this family."

Black smiled. "I've surprised myself, Luke. It's the first time in years I haven't been jumping to go after Bridger. That's been my whole life up until now."

"And now?"

"Now I just don't know. Nothing makes sense. When I caught that baby, it was like it would have been if Annie hadn't been killed and things had gone on like they should. I got a glimpse of what it would be to really have a life again."

McCan said, "Have all these years of chasing an outlaw and living on the trail been a waste then?"

Black thought a few moments before he answered. "For a man to waste his life, he's got to have one to waste. I never did. Not after Bridger killed Annie. What was left after that was existence, not life."

"Well, you've got more than that now, Caleb. I saw

you with that baby in your hands. It's a sight I won't forget."

Black spurred on ahead of McCan, ending the conversation. McCan fell back to a comfortable distance and rolled a smoke.

They reached Billings, a little cluster of buildings near the Yellowstone, a few miles above its juncture with Clark Fork. Here they questioned several people, but found no remembrance of Bridger's presence, no clues like those he had left up until now.

"That ends it," Longhurst said. "If he ever was here, he's not now. And there's no way to know where he might have gone. He might even have doubled back on us, or passed us on the other side of a hill."

McCan looked at Black. "Caleb?"

Caleb Black nodded. He was glum, but not furious, as McCan normally would expect. "We've lost his trail," Black said. "And I sure can't guess where he was going."

"He said a place where it could end—a place you would know," McCan said. "That doesn't help?"

Black only shook his head.

Longhurst ingested some snuff and presented his hand. "Gentlemen, it's been fine. I'm sorry we have to end on a failure, but I'm marking this one up to Bridger and heading back to Fort Maginnis. If either of you make it to the South Judith Mountains, I'll expect to see you there."

They shook hands and said their good-byes. McCan and Black watched the deputy ride away whistling, his easy and reckless air utterly undisturbed by the fact that he had lost his prisoner.

"There goes a man who wouldn't care if the sun fizzled out," Black said.

"He'd just figure it a good reason to sleep late," McCan said. "Well, Caleb, what now?"

"I been thinking about a hot bath, in a real tub. A few good cigars, some decent grub—what do you say?"

McCan was agreeable, and the pair checked into a hotel and located a bathhouse. At the latter, they basked in hot, suds-slick water, kept steaming by a fat man with no shirt and no shoes.

McCan said nothing of it, but he detected great levity in Black. He was happy. He joked, smiled— McCan had seen little of that behavior in all the time he had known the man, for from the beginning, Black had struggled with problems ultimately connected to Evan Bridger and his own stubborn pride.

If you had just let it go when Bridger attacked you on the Deadwood Trail, your life would have been a very different one, McCan thought. *But you had to salvage your pride.*

In a little restaurant, they ate fried steak and drank tea. "What's next, Caleb?" McCan asked around the rim of his cup.

"I'm going back to Jerusha and George and Lucy. They could use the help of a man. They're a fine bunch, Luke. I can't stop thinking about them."

"Jerusha in particular?"

Black glanced up, smiling vaguely. "You ain't no cupid, so put away your bow."

"Just talking, that's all."

They ate some more. McCan smoked a cigarette. "What about Bridger?"

"Hell with him."

"You're going to *forget* him?"

"I'm going to try."

McCan slept lightly that night. He listened to Black's snores for two hours before finally falling asleep. Later, he awoke. No snores came from the trundle bed across the room. Black sat on the windowsill, looking at the moon.

"Caleb?"

"Go back to sleep, Luke."

"What's wrong?"

Black shook his head. "I think I know where Bridger went."

"Where?"

"Let's don't talk about it, huh?"

McCan put his hands behind his head. "Will you go back to Jerusha tomorrow?"

There was a long pause. "No. Bridger was right. It's time to end this thing. How could I live with Jerusha, knowing he might show up like he did before, and—" He broke off. "I couldn't stand that again. And I won't put them to the risk."

"I'm going with you."

"No need. It's my fight."

"Not anymore. I made a promise to someone. I plan to keep it."

CHAPTER 33

When McCan awoke in the morning, Black was already up. Whether he had slept or stayed at the window all night, McCan did not know.

McCan splashed water on his face at the basin. "How long until we get there?"

"A few days, pushing hard," Black said.

"Can you tell me where?"

"I don't feel like talking about it. Come along, if you got to."

Black stayed almost completely silent from the time they left Billings. McCan tried to talk to him some, but gave it up, limiting conversation to what was essential and no more. Black was heavyhearted, grim.

The weather cooled dramatically. A heavy breeze whipped down from the western ridges, rustling the conifer groves and making the bunch grass dance. They rode ploddingly, Black always in the lead, but riding as if in no hurry. That, like Black's silence and his unwillingness to talk, puzzled and slightly angered McCan.

They followed the old Bozeman Trail, a cattle route. They went through Bozeman with hardly a pause, following the trail's sharp southward curve toward the Madison River.

As he rode, McCan recalled the night he rode with Jonas Carrington to the house where first he saw Maggie. The memory fit in well with the grimness of the mission and the sense of oppression that exuded from the silent, slumped form of Caleb Black.

They reached Virginia City about noon and stopped for a meal. Black ordered food, then refused to touch it. He stared into a corner while McCan ate and drank and wondered how close they were to the end of it all.

After the meal, they mounted and rode southwest, into the mountains. The air was cool, and in the sky, clouds congealed into a dull spread of flat gray. They rode more than an hour, and at last topped a ridge. There Black stopped, and McCan rode up beside him.

Before them lay a valley, beautiful even in the gloom of this day. A long spine of jagged mountains stretched off to the southwest, rocky and barren at the peaks, dotted with evergreens at the bases. Rich, golden grass grew along the valley bottom where a stream splashed over mossy stones. Willows and elms lined its banks.

Two hundred yards from the stream's widest point, about halfway down the valley, stood a house. It was unpainted, its front built with sawed timbers, its rear with unhewn logs. The front porch roof, supported with cedar poles, sagged in the middle. The door was crumbled and splintered. All about grass, scrub trees, and saplings grew abundantly.

Now McCan understood. "This is your old place, Caleb?"

Black nodded. "Where he killed them."

A roan wandered lazily from the other side of the

house. McCan felt a chill. Bridger *was* here.

"Let's go," Black said.

They rode down slowly, splashing across the stream. A few dozen yards from the house, they dismounted and tied the horses to a sapling.

The door swung open on silent leather hinges, and Bridger stepped onto the porch. The door closed behind him.

Bridger was changed. For one thing, he was drunk—but the change went far beyond that.

He's old, McCan thought. *Ten years older than when I saw him last.*

Bridger wore a Colt. He must have picked it up at Garrison's, maybe even stolen it from Upchurch's Emporium the night he escaped.

"Hello, gentlemen," Bridger slurred. "I've been waiting for you. I didn't know if you'd be savvy enough to trail me here or not." He swept bleary eyes over his old foe. "We've dogged-and-catted it a long time, Caleb."

Black said, "Don't call my name. I don't want it fouled by you."

Bridger laughed. "We ain't led much of a life, either one of us, have we?"

Caleb Black did not respond. His nostrils flared like those of a wild mustang ready to bolt.

Bridger smiled at Black like an old man smiles at a grandson. Slowly, his face went lax, and the smile disappeared. The impression of age became even more stark.

"It's high time it ended. High time."

McCan said something he had not expected to: "We have him outgunned, Caleb. We can take him alive." But there was no clue from either that he even had been heard.

McCan stepped to the side. Caleb was right; this

was *his* fight. McCan's promise to Maggie couldn't overrule Black's years of obsession. McCan felt peculiarly out of place, like a stranger who has entered a room where lovers embrace. He looked at Black's face: unreadable. He looked at Bridger: what he saw was—surprisingly—relief, and something like satisfaction.

Bridger smiled again, that same, old-man smile.

"Let's do it," he said.

"Let's do it," Black repeated.

Both dropped into a tense stance, legs slightly bent, arms flexed, fingers curved and ready. Bridger's smile vanished and was replaced by a look of determination. McCan heard his own heartbeat, the movement of the horses, the splashing of the creek.

Like blackbirds that move together in answer to a silent signal, both men put their hands to the butts of their pistols.

Black drew and leveled his gun before Bridger cleared the holster. Black clicked back the hammer, his finger tensed on the trigger, and everything stopped, as if in a photograph.

Black aimed his pistol at Bridger's heart, ready to fire, but not firing. Bridger held his own gun pointed to the ground.

"You've done it!" Bridger said. "You outdrew me! *Do it!*"

Black's hand trembled; he bit his lip. He did not fire. McCan stood to the side, confused.

"*Do it*, damn you!" Bridger shouted. "Isn't this what you've waited for? Think what happened here all those years ago—what I did in this cabin! Think of the mother and the baby I killed! *Why don't you fire?*"

Caleb Black slowly lowered his pistol. "No," he said.

Bridger stood unbelieving. He cursed and raised his pistol.

McCan never remembered drawing and aiming. His shots struck Bridger in the chest, driving him backward through the rotting door, which shattered into splinters as he fell faceup inside the cabin.

McCan went to the outlaw's side. He cradled the old man's head in his hands. Caleb slowly walked up and also knelt beside him.

Bridger was alive, but barely. Weakly, he opened his eyes, locking them on Caleb, then McCan. He smiled, and a thin rivulet of blood escaped the corner of his mouth.

To McCan he said, "You finally learned it. Aim like it's part of your hand. Point like it's your finger."

Then he looked at Black. "It really was high time, Caleb. High time."

Something changed in Evan Bridger's eyes, and he died, his breath a final, slow hiss.

McCan looked at Caleb Black, but Black looked no longer at Bridger. Instead, he gazed at the back wall of the cabin, and McCan followed his stare.

It is a funny thing, McCan later reflected, *what guilt does to a man—how it eats at him even when he denies it, and fills him until he has to let it out however he can.* McCan knew now that Evan Bridger's long-denied guilt at last had found its outlet.

All over the wall hung papers scrawled with pictures, crude as a child's, of women with large eyes and sad faces, and infants clutched in their arms.

Black rose and walked to the horses. He stood there, leaning against the saddle, and McCan thought he saw him cry.

Gently, McCan lowered Bridger's head to the floor and closed the eyes with his fingers. He saw the outlaw's Colt on the floor beside his relaxed hand. He picked it up and checked it. It was empty.

Evan Bridger had engineered his own death as surely as if he had put a bullet into his own brain.

CHAPTER 34

McCan found a board, scratched out the sides of a wash, and buried Evan Bridger as best he could. He pieced together two more boards into a cross, wrote the name of the outlaw on it, and planted it at the head of the grave.

He went to Caleb Black, who still stood at his mount. McCan untethered and slid into the saddle.

"Well?" he said.

"Let's go," Black said.

They left the valley behind and rode into Virginia City. They found a hotel and rented rooms—separate this time, for both men wanted to be alone.

"I'm going to bed early," Black said. "I want an early start back to Jerusha tomorrow."

Inside his room, McCan sat on his bed. It began raining, pelting the roof and driving in through the open window. McCan did not care.

He lit a lamp and dug from his pocket the little pillbox portrait of Maggie. He looked at it, thinking about the truth he had been able to accept only gradually.

Maggie was not his, and never had been, even in those days when she shared his company. Furthermore, whatever happened to Rodney Upchurch, she never *would* be his. It was Upchurch she loved, live or die. There was just no place for Luke McCan.

He smiled at the irony, then rose and walked to the window. He held the pillbox in his fist, squeezed it, and threw it out into the rain and darkness. Then he found a pad of paper and wrote two notes.

One was to Caleb Black. It said:

Caleb, I cannot stay even the night. I am going back to Timber Creek to report what happened to Evan Bridger and to see if Rodney Upchurch is alive or dead, and then I will be gone. Somewhere else, but I don't know for sure just where. I have my horses, guns, and poker, so I can live. You will see me again, and I wish you well in the marriage you will have.

Luke.

The other was to his sister in Missouri. It said:

Martha—I am somewhat free and have missed you and I think I will see you soon. Just a visit, but one I look forward to. I shall sleep in the barn and be no bother.

Love, Luke.

He folded the letters and put them in envelopes. Then he gathered his hat and saddle bags and walked into the hall. Caleb's note he hung on the latch of Black's room. The other he marked and posted downstairs, and left with the clerk for mailing.

He walked into the downpour to the livery. He saddled his horse and rode away, not looking back, and thus not seeing Caleb Black standing at the window of his room, watching him go.

Black watched until McCan was lost in the rain and darkness. "Good-bye, my old friend," he said. He went to his bed, slid beneath the covers, and in moments was asleep.

*Near the Chickasaw Bluffs of the Mississippi River,
just after the turn of the 19th century*

Bush flicked his knife one more time on the piece of
cane, held the cane to his eye, and looked down it.
Good and straight, and cut just below the joint so the
bottom of the cane section was enclosed. Perfect. He
laid the cane section, about a foot in length, aside, and
picked up a straight piece of hardwood already partially whittled into the shape of a pestle, or plunger.

Bush glanced up and around, wondering where Cephas was. He'd been gone too long, already over an
hour beyond their rendezvous time. Bush wondered if
he'd made a mistake and come to the wrong rendezvous point. He thought hard. No. This was the right
place. He and Cephas Frank had rendezvoused at this
same point along the river many a time over the past
six years.

Six years. Hard to believe that much time had gone
by since the dismal, rainy evening they first met at the

burned-out cabin where Bush had dug for the bones of his sister, to no avail. Six years of searching, of question-asking, praying, and hoping, and he was no closer to learning whether Marie Underhill was living or dead.

He whittled on the hardwood plunger a little more, then test-fitted it to the piece of cane. It fit in, sliding all the way to the enclosed bottom, not too loose, not too tight. Perfect so far.

Noise near the river made him look, wondering if Cephas was arriving at last. No, just a possum prowling around lazily. Bush looked around and wondered again what had become of his partner.

Old Cephas. A rather peculiar stranger to him that first day, and now one of the closest friends Bush had ever known, every bit as close as Jim Lusk had been. Bush and Cephas had much in common, despite their different races and backgrounds, and Bush had always thought that was what made them get along with one another so well. Neither fit well into the dominating society around them. Both were far more comfortable in the wilderness than in towns and society, both were capable, natural woodsmen, and both appreciated the privilege of freedom more than most.

And both had lost sisters. That more than anything seemed their strongest common bond. Cephas's sister had died during the raid on the Simpkins cabin and lay buried beneath it. Bush's sister, who could say? Perhaps some of those bones under the cabin had belonged to her. Maybe the raiders who struck the cabin had hauled Marie away. Or perhaps she had already gone from the Simpkins house, on her own or with someone else, before their arrival.

Bush was tired of not knowing, and though he hadn't said anything of it to Cephas, he was beginning to think of giving up. He'd hoped against hope that they'd somehow pick up some bit of Marie's trail, but so far years of effort and countless miles of travel had failed to turn up a thing. And for Bush, hope was beginning to wear thin.

He picked up some hemp fibers he'd gathered and prepared, and began wrapping them tightly around the large end of the plunger he made. What he was up to was something of an experiment, dreamed up years ago by Jean-Yves Freneau, who never had a chance to try it, because his life was cut short by the raid on Coldwater. Bush always wanted to carry out the experiment himself, but only now got around to it.

He looked about for Cephas again. The day was waning. If Cephas didn't come in soon, he probably wouldn't see him this day at all, and Bush would spend the night worrying. They often separated to go on individual hunts and explorations many, but never before had Cephas failed to show up at the designated time and place.

I'm getting to be like an old woman, Bush thought. *Cephas can take care of himself.*

Bush wrapped the pestle until it fit so snugly into the cane section he couldn't muscle it in farther. Good. He popped it out again, then from one of his pouches produced a little wooden container filled with grease. He smeared the grease liberally over the tightly wrapped fibers on the end of the plunger. Then to that end, he attached a little ball of charred tinder. He placed the plunger against the open end of the cane section and pushed it in. Lubricated by the grease, it went in more easily this time, but the fit was airtight.

"Well, let's give your idea a try, Father," Bush said to the spirit of the man who raised him.

He rapidly pushed the plunger into the cane section, giving it a lot of force. Pulling it back up again, but not quite out of the cane section, he rammed it down one more time. Again and again he pushed and withdrew the piston-like plunger, compressing and decompressing the air inside the cane section.

The cane began to grow hot in Bush's hand. It was working!

When his instinct told him to, Bush pulled the piston out of the cane section with a loud popping sound, and to his delight found the tinder glowing and sparking. Jean-Yves Freneau, with that philosophic and scientific mind of his, had been right! Through the compression of air alone, a man could generate enough heat to build a fire.

Bush blew the tinder into a flame and applied it to yet more tinder piled and waiting beside him. As the fire caught, he added kindling sticks, then gradually, larger pieces of wood. The fire burned nicely, a fire created by nothing more than muscle-power and air.

Bush grinned as the flames rose. Jean-Yves Freneau would have been proud to see this.

Above and around, shadows descended. The sun was edging westward over the river. Pleased as Bush was with his successful experiment—and the fact that he now possessed a very practical new fire-making tool—he was still preoccupied with concern for Cephas Frank.

He surely hoped everything was all right.

Three miles downriver, Cephas Frank crouched in the brush on a high bank and looked down on a scene playing out on a roughly made flatboat moored below him. Though this craft, hardly more than a raft with a low-ceilinged, flat-topped shed built in its center, seemed hardly worthy of any kind of name, someone had given it one: *The George Washington* was painted onto the side of the shed.

Three men on the flatboat were talking with a fourth; occasionally some of their conversation would be loud enough for Cephas to hear. What he heard troubled him. As best he could tell, the three men were striking some sort of bargain with the fourth, and the object of the deal was a dark-haired, pretty woman who stood at the door of the shelter. Cephas looked closely at her. Her face was sad. One of the saddest he ever seen.

She turned slightly. Cephas peered more closely at her, and whispered, "Sweet mother of—"

"Well!" a man's voice behind him said. "What've we got here?"

As Cephas began to rise and turn to face two men, who'd come up unheard behind him, the second said, "Looks to me like we got us a nigger poking about where he got no business."

Cephas had laid his rifle on the ground beside him while he watched the flatboat, but picked it up as he rose. He shifted it just a little, ready to bring it up for use if need be.

"Is he right, nigger? You been watching our boat? Or maybe you been eyeing that white woman down there! Ain't right, you know, a darky looking at a white woman. What's your name, darky?"

"I go by Cephas."

"Got you a last name, or are you just one of them one-name slave darkies?"

"He's a runaway. Sure as hell."

"I'm no runaway."

"We supposed to take your word? There might be a reward for you, nigger. You're coming back to the boat with us, and then you can explain why you been up here watching us. And maybe we'll make you pay for staring at our woman. She don't come for free, you know."

Silence. Followed by a sudden charge in the air. One of the intruders cursed and moved at Cephas, who raised his rifle. His position and close quarters in the brush worked against him, though, and he was unable to get the rifle raised before the second man moved in, much faster than the first, and got his hand around the barrel, pushing it away, making it impossible for Cephas to aim.

The first man brought up his arm; there was something in his hand. The arm flashed down, and Cephas felt a jolting, painful thud against the side of his head. He staggered, losing his strength and his grip on the rifle, which was pulled away from him.

He stumbled backward, fighting not to pass out. He saw the glitter of a shiv's blade. His opponents moved toward him.

Cephas put up his arms to fight as the world danced and moved before his unfocused eyes, and a dark numbness began to descend upon him. He went down, and even before he fully passed out, they were upon him, cursing, the shiv rising and then falling, once, twice, three times.

Something's wrong, Bush thought. *Cephas should be here by now. Something's surely wrong.*

He rose and put out the fire he so cleverly built, hefted up his weapons, and set out for Cephas. When they'd split up, Cephas had headed south and he north, so now Bush turned southward.

The farther he traveled the more unsettled he felt. It was just an intuitive feeling, but Bush couldn't shake it off. He searched, called Cephas's name, though not too loudly. Along the river, one never knew who was within earshot, or what kind of response one would receive.

The sun was almost to the horizon. Bush pressed his

search all the harder. Another hour, and he would have to give up and go back to the rendezvous point in hopes that Cephas was merely late.

Ten minutes later, he found the first evidence that something was amiss. A wooden powder horn plug, lying on the ground in a clearing, proof of recent human presence. Bush picked it up and examined it. Cephas's powder horn plug, no question of it. The plug had a distinctive shape and a chip off one side.

Bush examined the clearing and detected that there had been some significant activity here. Branches were bent and broken, grass and young tree sprouts mashed to the ground. A scuffle, maybe.

Soon Bush located evidence that something heavy had been dragged through the brush. There was blood.

Hurrying along in the waning light, following the sign, Bush soon found him. Cephas was on his belly, having dragged himself nearly a quarter of a mile from the clearing where Bush had found the powder horn plug.

"Cephas . . . Lord, Cephas, what's happened to you?"

Bush dropped to his knees beside his partner and carefully rolled him onto his back. The moment he saw Cephas's puffed, bruised face, he knew it was bad. There was blood coming out his nostrils and crusting around his mouth.

"Bush . . . Bush . . . listen to me . . ."

"You shouldn't try to talk, Cephas."

"Listen . . . George   Washington . . . flatboat . . . saw them . . . saw them there, and I saw—" He cut off, blood coming up his throat in a great gush, filling his mouth, choking him.

Bush turned Cephas's head to one side, letting the

blood clear from his throat. "Lie still, Cephas. I got to find us help."

Cephas would not lie still. He pulled his head back to its previous position. "Got to . . . listen . . . brothers . . . it was them . . . saw her, Bush. On the boat . . . George Washington . . . woman . . . saw her . . . the mark . . . I could see it, clear . . . knew she was . . . she had to be . . ."

Cephas was almost unconscious, his words coming harder, making less and less sense. George Washington? What could that mean? Bush was sure his partner was babbling because his mind was failing him as his life drained away.

Bush pulled open Cephas's shirt and winced. Puncture wounds, small and deep, like those a riverman's shiv would inflict. They'd bled much, but were now closed and crusted. Most likely the story was quite different deep inside Cephas, though.

"Cephas, don't die. Don't die." Bush didn't want to weep, but tears came.

"Bush . . . two of them . . . hit me, cut me . . . and they, they . . . she was . . . they was . . ." A new gush of blood came up from inside, cutting his voice off, filling his mouth, spilling over. Cephas's head rolled slowly to the side and his eyes went glassy.

Bush knelt over him and wept like a child. Cephas Frank was dead. Another friend and partner lost, as he had lost Jim Lusk.

Bush buried his partner where he had died, and for all the next day, lingered in the vicinity, numb with grief at the loss of a friend, angry at the world for its unfairness and cruelty, and sorrowful for Cephas Frank himself, his life cut short.

He thought over Cephas's final babblings, trying to

make sense of them. Much of what Cephas had said Bush already forgot—he'd been in such shock at Cephas's condition that most of it had sailed right past him—but some of it, maybe, made sense.

Cephas had probably been trying to tell Bush who hurt him. The "George Washington" reference Bush could make no sense of, but there'd been something about a flatboat, and brothers. "It was them," he'd said. Them. The ones who'd hurt him, he must have meant. Men from a flatboat. A couple of brothers, Cephas's words indicated.

Standing by Cephas's grave, Bush collected his thoughts, then spoke to his departed friend. "I'll not let this pass, Cephas. Somehow I'll find whoever did this to you. I'll see they receive their due punishment, if only from me." Bush's throat grew tighter, emotion filling him. "For three years you and me have roamed, hunting, trapping, fishing, working the river. For three years you've kept my hopes up about Marie when I was ready to give up. You've told me time and again that I should never think her dead until I know she's dead, and that if me and you had switched places, and it was your sister who maybe was still alive out there, somewhere, you'd hunt for her long as you lived." Bush rubbed his eyes. "Well, Cephas, I appreciate all of that, you keeping me going, keeping me thinking that maybe I can find her someday. But three years is a long time, time enough to drain a lot of the hope and spirit out of a man. And now that you're gone, I don't know I've got any spirit left at all, nor any will to keep trying. So I'm going to give up looking for Marie for now. Maybe for good. I'm too weary of it to keep up, and tired of having my hopes rise only to get pulled down again. I'm letting Marie go, Cephas. From now on, the looking I'll do is for the ones who did this to you. And that's one quest I won't fail in. I promise you. I promise."

He took up his rifle and packs, looked for a last time at the grave of another friend and partner, and turned his steps southward.

It was easy now for Bush to understand what had overtaken Jim Lusk in the last days of his life.

Lusk had lost a wife, a greater loss, Bush knew, than that of a friend and partner, but the grief was similar. And with the passing of Cephas went his sole source of encouragement to keep up the seemingly vain search for Marie Underhill, Bush felt a double bereavement.

As he watched himself over passing weeks, he began to wonder if the soul of Jim Lusk had mystically replaced his own.

Bush found he simply wasn't the man he was. He began making mistakes, losing the edge of perfection that always marked his woodcraft. His mind wandered; at times he became lost in areas he'd traveled a score of times with Cephas Frank.

It was just like Lusk had done.

One new thing entered Bush's life that hadn't entered Lusk's in his last days. Bush began to drink, much more than he ever had. He'd never really had much fondness for liquor, drinking it minimally, never getting drunk, and many times taking a simple glass of cold water in honest preference over stronger drinks others clamored for. It was different now. He left the woods behind, began haunting the dives of riverside communities, drinking, brawling, acting and even looking so different from his prior self that he sometimes went initially unrecognized by men he'd met on the river years before.

Bush forgot much of himself as days passed, even stopped thinking about Marie, who'd occupied at least some back corner of his attention almost constantly since that day at Nickajack when he'd pledged to find her, no matter what. But he never forgot what happened to Cephas Frank, and his vow to find and punish his killers.

Bush got it in mind to go to Natchez. There, in the hellholes and dens of infamous Natchez-under-the-hill, he would have a better chance of finding the sort of river trash who would murder a man such as Cephas.

He continued working his way southward, living on what he could kill, and twice, to his astonishment, on what he could steal. These thefts were not large, just a loaf of bread in one case and half a pie in another, but they were atypical of Bushrod Underhill, who'd had honesty drilled into his soul by Jean-Yves Freneau in his earliest days, and reinforced by Jim Lusk and others since.

Bush was half-drunk one late afternoon on a saloon barge that had pulled to shore about halfway between the Chickasaw Bluffs and Natchez, when he found what he was looking for. He'd been seated on a keg at the edge of the barge, looking out across the water and drinking from a dirty pewter cup, when a flatboat came into view up the river. He watched it idly as it drifted along at the speed of the current.

A friendly young boy, son of the owner of the saloon barge, came over to Bush and sat down crosslegged beside him. "Look yonder at them clouds sweeping up," the boy said. "There's going to be a devil of a storm this evening."

"Believe so," Bush said, taking another swallow.

The boy said no more for a while, watching the rising storm, then turning his attention to the same flatboat that Bush had been casually observing.

"George Washington," the boy said.

Bush, frowning, looked down at him. "What'd you say?"

"George Washington. See? It's writ there on the side of that flatboat. I read it off myself." The boy smiled, proud of his literacy in a day when many an older soul than he couldn't read a word.

Bush came to his feet, dropping his cup, staring at the flat-boat. "Lord . . ."

With both heart and mind racing, Bush stared at the flatboat as it neared, wondering if it might swing toward the bank so those aboard it could take advantage of the saloon barge. The boy's father, hoping to stir more business, went to the side of his barge and called across the water, encouraging the flat boatmen to stop in for "fine libation."

A call came back, carrying loud over the water: "Not today, friend! 'Nother time!"

Bush turned to the boy and grabbed his shoulders a little too roughly. The youngster's eyes went wide. "Son, I need a canoe, something I can use to get over to that flatboat."

"Only canoe we got is right yonder, but that belongs to—hey!"

Bush, releasing the boy, had already gone for the

canoe, which sat on one end of the barge, tied upside down. He loosened the ropes and prepared to put it into the water.

The barge owner approached. "You, there! What the deuce are you doing? That's my canoe!"

Bush wheeled, knife in hand, and held it toward the man. "I got to borrow it. I'll bring it back."

"That canoe ain't available for loan."

"Then I'll rent it, damn it! Now you stand aside. Boy, go fetch my rifle and such over yonder. Bring it to me, easy and careful, and don't think of trying any tricks with it."

The boy turned. "Ain't no rifle."

Bush looked. The boy was right—his rifle and packs, left near the place he'd been seated, had disappeared. Some other patron of this floating establishment had made off with them while he was drunkenly unaware.

Taken aback, momentarily unsure of what to do, Bush watched *The George Washington* moving on past in the river. Men stood on the deck. He saw a woman there, too, dimly. One of the men turned to her and pointed at the shelter on the middle of the flatboat. She entered it and Bush saw her no more. One man who had ordered her inside took up a spyglass and looked through it at the people on the shore.

"If my rifle's gone, then it's gone," Bush said. "Mr. Saloon Man, just consider this canoe my compensation for what was stole from me while I was at your fine establishment here." Bush put the canoe into the water and took up the paddle.

A burly fellow with a flintlock pistol beneath his belt came up and said to the barge owner, "You want me to stop him?"

"No," the man said. "This fellow's a madman. Just let him go. Ain't much of a canoe anyway."

Bush pushed away from the barge, turned the canoe in the water, and began paddling toward the flatboat, adding the speed of his own muscle to that of the current, gradually closing in on *The George Washington* as the men on its deck watched him coming.

Bushrod Underhill usually would never have been so reckless as to single-handedly attack a flatboat with no more than a canoe and knife. But it wasn't Bushrod Underhill as he had been. This was Bushrod Underhill transformed and maybe ruined. Bushrod Underhill transformed into something utterly different from the man he'd been before.

The canoe came within talking distance of the flatboat. A tall man, dark-haired, with a clean-shaven face, called out to him: "Who are you, pilgrim?"

"What? Don't you know me?" he grinned harmlessly, knowing he had to get on the boat, and that it would be almost impossible to do so without permission.

"I can't say I do."

Bush cast his eyes skyward, saying, "It astonishes a man how quick his old friends forget him!"

"We don't know you."

Bush looked heavenward again, the image of an exasperated man, and said, "Surely you recall old Jim!"

Another man, much younger than the prior two, said, "I can't say I do."

Bush shook his head. "Gents, my feelings are nigh to getting hurt. I can't believe you can't remember old Jim Lusk!" He looked back at the nearing storm, clouds whipping in low and close, lightning beginning to flash in the distance. "Can I come aboard?" He glanced left to right, and grinned wickedly. "Got me some money . . . and I hear you got something to sell."

The attitude of the men instantly changed. "Jim!

Now I recall you! Come on up and join us."

Aided by the youngest of the flatboatmen, Bush got the canoe up against the boat and climbed aboard. There were five men aboard besides him, and the unseen woman inside the shelter. All the men appeared to be brothers, their features and coloring quite similar.

It came to Bush's mind that he might not leave this flatboat alive. If he determined that these men, or some of them, had killed Cephas, he intended to do all the damage he could with his knife. He was a good fighter, but five against one was five against one.

A moment of doubt—then he was past it. Tuckaseh had told him once that it's too late to think of dry land once one has already jumped in to swim. And there was some biblical quotation Jean-Yves had been fond of, about not looking back once you've put your hand to the plow.

He grinned and nodded at those around him, trying to look a little drunker than he really was. Best to seem a bit of a buffoon just now, rather than a threat.

"You fellers are all looking healthy."

The one Bush had pegged as the eldest spoke. "Let's end the bilge. We don't know you, though maybe you do know us. We meet a lot of men on this river. We're in business, you see. And if I heard you right, I believe it's business you got in mind?"

Bush stepped back one pace and covertly put his hand on the handle of his knife. "The truth is, I came because I believe I owe a debt to you gentlemen."

"What debt?"

Bush looked from face to face. "The debt I owe at least two of you for killing my partner on back up the river. He was a black man, beat and stabbed to death . . . but before he died, he told me the pair who killed him seemed to be brothers, and he called the name 'George Washington.' "

The older men stared stonily, but the face of the youngest told the story, and a moment later it wouldn't have matter if it hadn't, because he chuckled nervously and said, "That nigger. He's talking about that nigger."

The eldest one swore at the youngest, telling him to keep his mouth shut.

So now it was confirmed. Bush pulled out the knife. "Cephas Frank was my friend and my partner, and I swore above his grave that I'd make the men who killed him pay, no matter what the cost."

The eldest brother produced a pistol and leveled it at Bush. "That cost is going to be quite high for you, sir."

"No," the youngest said, pulling a long knife from beneath his waistcoat. "Don't shoot him. This one's acting like a knife-fighter. Let *me* have him."

The eldest glanced at the others, shrugged, and put away the pistol. "As you please."

With a grin, the young man edged to the low, flat-roofed shelter, which wasn't high enough for anyone above a child's height to stand in. Bush thought of the woman within it. Lying down or sitting, no doubt. Probably watching out a knothole.

If so, she was going to have the privilege of witnessing a death, he thought morbidly. Maybe his own.

"Up on top," the young one said, nodding at the shelter. "Good fighting platform."

"You first."

The challenger put one hand on the shelter top, heaved himself up lithely, and was on the shelter so quickly Bush didn't quite see how he did it. "You next."

Bush, wishing he hadn't drunk so much earlier, gave

it a try, and to his pleasure succeeded. On the shelter, with the storm now almost over them and the river moving faster because of heavy rains that had already fallen to the north, Bush confronted his foe, and readied himself to die.

The young flatboatman made the first lunge. Bush jumped back, then forward, slashing. His blade caught his enemy on the side of the face and laid open a shallow cut.

At first the young man, who obviously considered himself a fine knife fighter, looked shocked. He wiped the blood from his face and backed away. He regained his composure quickly, though, a grin spreading across his face. His teeth were perfect and white, which for some reason made him look all the more dangerous.

He lunged and slashed. Bush dodged back, almost too far, nearly dumping himself over the edge of the flatboat platform to the lower deck. He caught himself just in time. The boatmen whooped and hooted and urged on the knife-flourishing combatants on the platform, which was actually the roof of a shed built in the middle of the big raft-like cargo vessel.

"What's the matter with you, my dear and blooming peavine?" the younger fighter mocked from behind those pearly teeth. "Are you looking for a coward's haven to run to? You'll find naught on this boat! You've bit into the flesh of Beelzebub when you met me! I'm the mud hen of hell's darkest thicket! I'm the very child who put the fork in the serpent's tongue! Waaaauuugh! I'm a screamer! I'm damnation and redemption! I'm brimstone! I'm a gouger! Whoooop! Run from me, coward, while you can!"

"I run from no one," Bush said. "You're nothing but the murderer of a fine man, not fit to boast of anything. As for me, I don't brag. Any boasting to be done my blade does for me."

The pair circled and lunged and feinted and snarled, though neither made contact with the other. Lightning flashed and thunder pealed. On the farthermost shore, trees whipped wildly in the wind and birds cawed and called; dogs barked faintly in the distance. The air was wet and crisp, almost crackling with the energy of the approaching storm. Darkness was falling fast, the river flowing faster.

"I'm seeing some prime dancing, sweethearts, but can you fight?" someone bellowed.

"Cut his gullet!" another yelled. "Show him who's the true Orleans fire-belcher!"

The young man barked like a mastiff and slashed, and Bush danced back suddenly with a red line across his bare chest. The cut was not deep or even painful, but sufficient to make the momentum of the fight shift away from Bush.

For five minutes they danced and dodged and slashed, neither gaining much advantage over the other. If the flatboatman had thought he would have an easy opponent, he learned otherwise. Bush Underhill wasn't easy to kill.

But Bush was worried. Even if he prevailed over this one, there were four others. Short of a miracle, he was a doomed man.

The storm caught up with the flatboat, hard rain gushing down all at once, lightning striking somewhere beyond the far bank. Two more lightning flashes came in fast succession. The first splintered a tree on the closer shore, beside a cabin on the very brink of a badly eroded bank. The second struck farther away, but illuminated a sight that made both combatants break their gaze from one another and look landward: the bank beneath the cabin gave way, sliding with a dull roar into the river, carrying the cabin and dumping it into the water.

Lightning ripped through the sky just as Bush looked back at his opponent. His heart jumped throatward as a monstrous and impossible vision appeared before the flatboat and behind the younger man: a gigantic hand. The great claw reached up from the river, bending down toward the deck and crew, ready to snatch as many men as possible into the river.

The boat jolted hard against something. Timbers moaned and cracked, the boat turned completely about, tilting slightly. The great hand knocked several men to the deck, and suddenly the flatboat tilted the opposite direction.

It wasn't really a hand, Bush realized after the initial shock, but a gigantic tree, broken loose and floating free in the water. It had chanced to reach an unseen sandbar at the same moment as the flatboat. The tree was wedged against the underwater obstruction. Its trunk wrenched in the current so that long branches grappled out across the boat while it slammed hard against the spit of sand.

Bush's opponent unexpectedly screamed. A new flash of lightning revealed to all that the young knife-fighter had just been impaled on a sharp branch of the tree. It poked into his back and out of his belly, crimson and wet, some of his stomach pushed out on its end. The force of the racing flatboat had driven the branch completely through him from behind.

The boat twisted on the sandbar and moved forward again. The knife-fighter's bloody form, lodged on the branch, came at Bush and went past him. Something closed around Bush's middle, picking him up. He yelled and scrambled madly but could find no footing.

The boat moved out from beneath him and the tree

that held him twisted down, turning him sideways and plunging him beneath the dark and cold water.

Bush, caught in the limb of the same tree that had killed his opponent, struggled underwater for a moment, then broke free. He had no idea whether he was upside down or right side up, so he merely flailed and kicked. Moments later, he broke through the surface of the water. He'd somehow washed right over the sandbar and now was free in the river, being pushed helplessly along in the current.

As he turned and twisted, struggling to gain control, he caught intermittent glimpses of the flatboat being wrenched about on the sandbar. Voices cried out frantically; receding, barely-visible figures grappled about on the deck. Then, miraculously, the boat came free of the bar and bumped around it. Twisting back into the main current and down the river, it kept pace with Bush as he washed along—though far off to one side of him—then steadily outpaced him and drifted toward the opposite bank.

The miracle he'd needed had come; he was out of reach of those on the flatboat. But the river was just as likely to kill him.

A branch brushed against him and he grabbed it, but it was far too small to float him. He let it go and swam some more. The flatboat had gone out of sight, though he heard the occasional snatch of a voice carried to him like a wind-borne zephyr.

Bush struggled in the water as his feet and hands went numb and his body began to feel heavy. Muscles cramped all over his body, wracking him with pain.

He knew he was going to die in this river. Dead and gone in his mid-twenties, a life cut short before he even had time to figure out what it was all about.

A log bumped his shoulder and pushed him beneath

the surface. He twisted, kicked, and came up again. The log had already passed by, but, working with the current, he managed to catch up with it and get a hand around a stub where a branch had been. His fingers slipped away and again the log went out of reach, but with another great effort Bush managed to reach it and, this time, hold on.

Pulling himself forward, he hooked his other arm around the log and dragged himself slowly up over it. He relaxed as much as possible, letting the log keep him above water.

Now, he thought, he would just float, loosen his muscles and after a few minutes, see if he could kick to the nearer bank.

The log began to turn beneath him, almost throwing him back into the water. He held on tighter, then looked up just in time to see a big sawyer poking out of the water right at him.

He tried to maneuver the floating log around the sawyer, but he had seen it too late. One log bumped another, and Bush was thrown free, back in the water again.

Despair swept him in. He knew his strength would never last, unless he could reach the bank.

Something made Bush turn his head and look behind him.

Floating at him through the storm was something huge, black, and heavy, rolling like a big wheel in the water, moving too swiftly and taking up far too much river on each side for him to hope to escape it.

He surrendered. No hope now. Whatever this was, it would be on him in a moment, slamming him senseless and pushing him under the water.

He closed his eyes and waited to die.

* * *

Moments later, Bush was thinking: This thing must have a mouth, whatever it is, for I swear I believe it's just swallowed me!

He opened his eyes as his body was thrown up against something rough and hard. He rolled over, splashing into water, then bumped against another hard surface. Debris rushed around him. Then it felt, as sure as the world, as if someone had slapped his face. Not particularly hard, just a flat, wet slap, palm and fingers.

Bush found a handhold and pulled himself farther up onto the hard surface, out of the water. The thing he was in steadied and stopped rolling, floating now at a cock-eyed but steady angle. Looking around in nearly pitch blackness, broken sporadically by lightning flashes, Bush suddenly made sense of it all.

He was inside that cabin he'd seen fall off the bluff. The deuced thing had floated down the river, and somehow he'd gotten inside of it!

As best he could guess, the cabin must have rolled over him in just the right way to draw him in through a door or window. He laughed at the absurd luck of it—moments from death, and he was rescued by a floating cabin!

The cabin twisted sideways and something hit him hard on the side of the head. He caught it—a three-legged stool. He saw it drop, in the brief white moment of a lightning flash, into the water below him, and float about, trapped like Bush himself inside the cabin walls. A stout cabin, this one. Obviously spiked together instead of merely notched.

Bush scooted up farther; he was somewhere at the top of an inside wall, just under the edge of the roof. He bettered his handhold, tried to wedge himself as securely as he could, and hoped the house wouldn't roll over again.

It did. The wall to which he clung suddenly pitched downward, dipping into the water and pulling him with it. Then he was out, looking down at the water again, losing his handhold, and falling into the murky wet.

Something fleshy and soft was next to him. He pushed the thing away as the cabin rolled over yet again, then resettled.

Bush was half in, half out of the water. Lightning flared, and he found himself looking into the face of a man who stared back at him but did not see him, for he was dead, the back of his head crushed like a dropped egg. For a moment Bush thought maybe this was the knife-fighter, washed free of the stabbing branch, but it wasn't. The face was different.

Bush pushed the corpse away, disgusted, and scrambled back up the wall again.

The house moved along, rolling no more, though it did twist continually. Bush kept an eye out for the corpse, as if by its own power it could climb up the wall and slap him again like before.

The cabin leveled somewhat as it moved down the river and Bush was able to position himself more steadily. He noticed, however, that the cabin was also riding lower in the water. Before long it would sink, and take him down with it.

At length the cabin angled up enough to bring its puncheon floor, which was spiked to the base logs of the wall, mostly out of the water. Several puncheons were missing; through the gaps he saw the sky go white with each lightning flash. He would work his way out through that opening, climb atop the cabin, and keep his eye open for some alternative support, before the cabin went fully under.

Bush began to climb. He made slow but steady progress, then slipped on the wet wall logs and slid into the water again.

Solidity gave way beneath him and he went down, falling out a submerged window into the cold river below. For a few moments he was wedged in the window, competing for space with something else—the corpse! Then he was through, but found himself under the cabin, and stuck.

He struggled to find a way out from under, but part of his clothing was stuck on some protrusion from the cabin, keeping him below water level. He ached for air, struggled for freedom, and at the last possible moment before the surrounding blackness became unending, the cabin rolled again, pulling him up and out of the water and freeing him from whatever had trapped him.

He gasped, and sucked in huge, welcome breaths. Suddenly, he was tossed into the water again. But as he fell it seemed to him that the eastern bank was not nearly as far away as before. Blindly, he began to swim, realized he was going the wrong way, then turned in the current and pulled himself in the other direction. He swept downriver much more swiftly than he managed to move across it.

Farther ahead in the river, the cabin gave one more roll, wrenched into pieces at last, and vanished. He kept swimming. The bank seemed no closer. He was growing very, very tired.

Bush walked in darkness through a light rain that had begun in the wake of the storm, with no clear memory of having made it to the bank. He was weak, sore, lost, and very disoriented.

He was also weaponless and shoeless; his footwear had come off sometime during his river ordeal. Staring across the river, he looked for the flatboat he had fallen from, but saw nothing. Too dark. Eventually, the rain stopped, the clouds opened to let through the moon, and the broad river shimmered with reflected light. Still no flatboat visible, just assorted floating trash and refuse discarded by the storm.

As bad luck would have it, Bush had washed onto an unpopulated area. Not a cabin was in sight, not a distant glimmer of a settlement or camp—nothing but black Mississippi forest.

Finally Bush quit walking, realizing he'd best wait until daylight and hope for aid from some passing boat. He'd build a fire on the shore, see if he could snare a fish or roust up some other game come morning, and make his way downriver however he could. He'd not gone more than twenty feet when he caught a glimmer of light coming from deeper in the woods. He peered closely. A campfire? It appeared so.

Stepping gingerly because he was barefooted, Bush began moving toward the light, pushing aside branches and brambles, wincing when his foot trod on a stone or burr. The light grew brighter and bigger and soon he began to smell the delicious scent of cooking meat. He listened for voices but heard none. Either the campers were not talking, or there was only one.

Bush stopped, panting. His strength was nearly gone. Whoever started the fire, he hoped they were friendly, and wouldn't be overly startled to see a battered, half-clothed figure such as himself appear.

When the campfire was close enough that its smoke stung his eyes and the smell of the cooking meat made his stomach rumble, Bush cleared his throat and called, "Hello, the camp! Hello! I want to come in, if I may."

No reply came. Bush cleared his throat again and repeated himself, only louder.

Still nothing. Could the fire have been started by lightning, with no one about at all? It didn't seem likely. Not a confined, controlled blaze like that one. Then he sniffed the cooking meat again and knew that the fire had to be man-made. Lightning didn't spit-cook squirrels.

A burst of light-headedness caused Bush to stagger. He leaned against a tree and decided he would have to take his chances and go on in even without permission.

"I'm coming in . . ." His voice was weaker. "I'm a friend . . . I'm coming in."

He advanced, reaching the edge of the woods and

the small clearing where the fire burned. Pausing, he looked about for whoever was camped here, and saw no one.

A mystery indeed, but Bush wouldn't try to solve it. Feeling he might pass out at any time, he walked into the clearing and slumped down near the fire. He was intensely weary, almost too tired even to eat. The scent of the meat was too rich to be ignored, however, and he took the squirrels from the fire, waited until the meat was cool enough to eat, and took a bite.

When he was sated, he tossed the remnants aside and lay out flat on the ground, drifting quickly into a deep slumber.

What awoke him he could not say. His eyes opened; he was facing the fire, but it had mostly burned down. Red embers, spewing smoke and sparks.

Bush was not alone. He felt it.

Sitting up, he sucked in his breath, a reaction to an army of pains that marched up and down his battered body in a short span. Slowly he twisted his head and looked into the darkness just outside the glow of the fire.

Somebody out there. Watching.

Bush rolled over slowly and sat straight up, then came to his feet unsteadily.

"Your camp, I reckon," he said into the darkness.

No response.

"I ate the meat you'd roasted. I'm sorry."

Still nothing.

"I'm hurt . . . got knocked off a flatboat in the storm, and nearly drowned."

Nothing. Silence.

"Is there anybody there?"

The darkness itself seemed alive and ominous.

"If there's somebody there, I'd sure be obliged if

you'd show yourself. I'm unarmed. I'm no threat."

The darkness moved; a piece of it advanced. Not quite fully into the light, but just into the fringes of it. A ghostly, black figure, hard to discern.

"Howdy," Bush said, honestly wondering if it was, in fact, a ghost he was seeing.

The figure held its silence. Bush squinted and tried to see him better. Or was it a man at all? So vague was the image that Bush could not even discern the sex.

"My name's Underhill," Bush said. "Bushrod Underhill. Most just call me Bush for short."

No answer.

"Please, friend, I'd like to ask you to come more into the light if you would. I can't see you well enough to tell a thing about you."

The figure did not move for a moment, but then stepped forward.

Bush stared at the strangest human being he'd seen, either in the world of white men or red. Tall, gaunt, the man had black hair that hung thickly around his narrow face and past his shoulders, as unkempt and uncut as Samson's. The beard was just as long, reaching to the middle of his chest, and black as the river depths by night.

His nose was narrow and protruding, his eyes intensely dark and indefinably strange. Almost unblinking—yes, that was the strangeness of them. They hardly blinked, just gazed ceaselessly.

The clothing was as black as the hair and beard. Loose, dirty trousers, a bulky black coat over an equally colorless waistcoat, and if the shirt had ever been white, it was now dirtied to an indistinct buff.

"Sir, I tell you again that I'm sorry I ate your meat."

The man did not speak.

"I'll be glad to pay you for it, sir, as soon as I can

get my hands on money. I've lost all my possessions, you see. They're still on the flatboat I had the misfortune to be knocked off of, and the boat is no doubt long down the river by now."

The figure moved to one side and slowly bent over until he was seated on his haunches. An uncomfortable looking position, but it didn't seem to bother the stranger.

"Sir, do you speak English?"

The man, who, with his long coat draping past his knees, seemed to be floating on air, still said nothing.

Bush asked him his name in French, to no avail, then dug fragmented German out of the dustiest memories of his days with Jean-Yves Freneau, and repeated his question. Bush even asked in Cherokee. Still no reply.

Bush sat down again, watching the man mistrustfully, thinking him surely the oddest living being on the river. Why did he not answer? Was he deaf?

Bush shifted his position so that he could keep the man in the corner of his eye without staring openly at him, but within minutes the man rose and moved around to face Bush again, with no look of apology about doing so. Bush grinned at him, hoping to earn one in return. He didn't.

The remainder of the night seemed longer than two. Bush didn't dare sleep with this stranger watching him endlessly, saying nothing, looking malevolent with those dark and probing eyes. The pair of them remained as they were, each watching the other in silence. Bush, thinking he must have roused up a forest demon of some sort, scanned through all the Cherokee legends he could recall to see if he could find a match. Nothing quite did. He maintained the fire and made sure he always kept the stranger in sight.

By the pitch-black minutes of pre-dawn, Bush was

mentally exhausted by the extended staring game, and thought it might be better if he abandoned the safety of firelight and heat to take his chances in the forest alone. But with daylight so close, he had developed a superstitious curiosity about what would happen to this vampirish creature come sunrise. Would he vanish like smoke? Retreat into some cavern or hollow tree?

Bush had actually dozed off when the first rays of morning came streaming over the horizon. The stranger, who had been seated on the ground on the opposite side of the fire, suddenly came to his feet, walked to the edge of the clearing, and faced the rising sun. Bush, startled awake, watched him closely.

The man raised his hand skyward, lifted his face toward the clouds, and bellowed, "I thank you, oh Father, for the morning, and I thank you, oh Father, for life and sun and survival through the night. And I thank you, oh Father, for my new companion Mr. Underhill, who you have sent to me for his good and mine. All praise to Father, Son, and Holy Ghost. Amen."

The man turned so quickly that Bush jumped to his feet, expecting to see a pistol come out from under his coat. But the man was empty-handed, and extended those empty hands his way. "Mr. Underhill, I welcome you to my camp. And there is no need to apologize for having eaten my meat. What I have is given me not to hoard but to share. And I'm very sorry about my rude silence. I'd vowed to the Lord that I'd be silent until day, you see, and was simply fulfilling what I'd promised."

Bush was so taken aback to hear a voice coming out of the raven-like man that he hardly knew how to reply. "Sir, who are you?"

"My name is Moses Zane."

"Zane . . . I've heard that name before, sir. You're

a preacher, I think, one my late partner, a free black man name of Cephas Frank, told me of. You're the man folks say can—"

"Can summon up the devil himself and by the power of God make him dance at my command? Or so people say. Yes, I'm that same Moses Zane." He smiled, and seemed a little less odd for it. "And now, Mr. Underhill, how about you and I enjoy a bit of breakfast?"

From behind a tree Zane produced a large leather pouch, and from it pulled half a loaf of hardened but unmolded bread, a hunk of cheese, some nuts, jerked beef, and even a small jug of cider. To Bush it looked like a king's feast.

Zane fished out two crockery cups, scratched and lacking handles. He uncorked the cider and poured some into each cup.

"You do enjoy cider, Mr. Underhill?"

"Yes sir."

"Good, for I have no other beverage to offer you, unless you want to try to find some pure water after such a terrible storm as the mighty Lord sent us last night. I don't think you'll have much success if you do, as much mud as was stirred up." He took a small sip of his own cider while handing Bush the other cup.

"What kind of preacher are you, Mr. Zane?"

"My confession, do you mean? I'm Methodist by doctrine, though at the moment I'm not a part of any official circuit or under the authority of any church structure other than the one true and universal church of Almighty God." He sipped his cider again. "In short, Mr. Underhill, I've been put out of the ministerial fold and must make my way as an independent. Are you hungry, Mr. Underhill?"

"I could eat the very grease off a wagon axle."

"Well, I hope you'll find my fare, such as it is, better than that." Zane distributed the food. A very different man he seemed now from the silent, looming vampire he had been in the darkness. "I normally eat rabbits and squirrels and other small game, saving this food for those times I enjoy the pleasure of human companionship."

"You're alone a lot?"

"Never. My God is always with me. But in the sense in which you meant the question, yes. I'm alone quite often."

"May I ask why you'd told the Lord you would hold silent until morning?"

"Certainly. In my prayers yesterday, I implored the Lord to see to my aid in my time of distress and give me guidance. There came to me at sundown the strongest impression that I should remain silent until sunrise, and during that silence I would find the help I needed. So I made my promise to my Father, and was bound to keep it until the sun came up." Zane ate a handful of nuts.

"What 'time of distress' are you talking about?"

"I was put off here, Mr. Underhill. A crew of keelboatmen found my company to be intolerable. They were not agreeable to hearing the truth that changes souls."

"So you prayed for help. No offense, preacher, but I don't see the Lord has answered your prayer."

"Of course He has! You've come."

"I just fell off a flatboat, sir." Zane needed to know no more than that. "I rode some distance down the water in a cabin that'd come off the bank and was floating down the river with a corpse in it. That cabin rolled right over me in the water and swallowed me like that Jonah fellow with his big fish. I don't know quite how I got out without drowning."

"You were protected in order to be sent to me. And now we must decide what to do now that you've come."

"I know what I have to do," Bush said. "I have to move down the river and look for somebody." He didn't intend for the men who'd killed Cephas Frank to escape him.

"And so we can see providence at work! It happens I need to head downriver myself."

"You may not have noticed, Reverend, but I got no boat. I'm afoot just like you. I ain't even got shoes! I lost my boots in the river."

"I have an extra pair of boots in my pouch. They pinch my feet, but may do better for you."

Indeed they did. Moments later Bush was admiring a pair of boots finer than those he had lost, fitted nicely over his feet. If Zane was peculiar, he was also generous.

Zane said, "I have a proposition for you, Mr. Underhill. You and I will remain together for now and see if we can't find some good passage down the river. Your company and protection will be welcome to me."

It was absurd. Bush couldn't be hampered by company as he tried to track down Cephas's killers, but the preacher had him hooked as a partner for now simply because Bush felt indebted to him for the boots, and he certainly had no money to pay for them. So he heard himself saying, "Well, I reckon we can travel together—for a time."

"Good! Then let's be off, shall we?"

"Where to?"

"Down to the river. Providence has already sent you to me by way of the river. Let's see what else might come floating along."

* * *

As they broke camp, Bush made the pleasing discovery that Moses Zane owned a good flintlock rifle, an almost equally good pistol, two fine knives, and a hatchet. They had been out of sight before, tucked away behind the same tree that had concealed the leather supply bag.

"Please, take the weapons with my blessing," Zane told him. "I make them a gift to you. I hate the cursed things. I rarely use them except to occasionally kill small game, such as those squirrels you found on my fire. Most of what I eat is either fish I catch, food good people along the way give me, or rabbits and such I snare."

Bush was astonished that a man would give away such fine weaponry to a near stranger. "Sir, I don't think I can take such a gift as this."

"Nonsense! It's my pleasure to give you the guns, and it should be yours to take them. You lost what you had in the river, I'd be willing to wager—though don't take that literally. I don't favor wagering."

After they had hiked about two miles, the preacher pointed to something Bush had just spotted himself—something caught in tangled brush on the bank. Bush trotted over and found a dugout canoe trapped there. Just the right size for two men.

"God provides!" Zane declared.

Bush reached into the canoe and pulled out an odd item: a dented old hunting horn. Putting it to his lips, he tested it, sending a piercing blast across the water. "Has an unusual sound to it. Clearer and louder than most. Wonder how it came to be in there?" he mused aloud, examining the instrument.

"For a reason, I'm sure. Maybe it will prove to be something I can make use of in some way." Zane looked at the horn and rubbed his chin. "You know,

I think perhaps there is a good use for this instrument. I can use it to sound the call for my meetings. Here, let me try a blow on that."

Bush handed the horn to Zane, who drew in his breath and blew, with pathetic results. With greater effort, he tried again, doing a little better this time.

Suddenly Zane changed. His eyes bulged, his face reddened, and his mouth fell open. The horn dropped from his fingers. Bush went to Zane's side as the man began to collapse slowly to the ground, hand on his chest as he gasped for air.

"Preacher, what's wrong with you?"

"Back . . . away from . . . the river . . ." He collapsed.

Bush swept the man up in his arms and ran.

Zane sat slumped on a rock beneath a spreading, moss-draped tree, looking at the ground and breathing deeply. "Thank God," he whispered. "That time I didn't know if I would make it through."

"What happened?" Bush asked.

"My lungs," Zane replied softly. "Since my boyhood I've struggled with it. My wind sometimes is cut off, my lungs seem to close, and I struggle to draw my breath. An attack of Satan, who always tries to silence me."

Bush looked up and down the preacher's gaunt frame, studying the sallow, narrow face. He looked like someone who had known weakness and sickness all his life. It was no surprise that he was asthmatic.

Zane lifted his gaze and looked gratefully at Bushrod. "Had you not been there, my friend, I might have never breathed again."

"I didn't do a thing," Bush said. "You commenced breathing again on your own."

"Because you carried me away from the river,"

Zane said. "There seem to be times and places that cause it to happen. Excitement, sorrow, fear can all bring it on. And being near rivers can do it as well, though not all the time. Generally, I'm quite able to function normally, or at the very least to have only minor difficulties. This one was . . . different." He shuddered and looked down again. Despite the preacher's apparent tendency toward religious bravado, it was evident to Bush that this man was thoroughly shaken by what happened.

"Reverend, has it crossed your mind that maybe you ought to find some place other than the river country to do your preaching? There's some folks who can't do well for their health in certain places, certain kinds of air. I knew a man once who'd break out in red patches every time he'd walk through a copse of maples, and get wheezy in the chest if ever he breathed air from a cave."

"It's here I belong, Mr. Underhill. Nowhere else. And I've never suffered such an attack while preaching. I believe I'm protected then."

"I wish you'd call me Bushrod instead of 'Mr. Underhill.' "

"Very well, Bushrod. And you may call me Moses." And he went straight into another asthmatic attack. Bush hustled him farther away from the river until his breathing again settled.

Bush grinned at the preacher when he was well again, but he wasn't happy at the moment. He ached to continue his pursuit of *The George Washington* and its murderous crew, but suddenly this puny preacher was, as it were, tossed into his lap, giving gifts and making Bush feel obliged to him. He had no impression that Zane was trying to manipulate him—but he'd hooked him all the same. He couldn't abandon a man who might smother to death at any given moment.

It appeared that, for the short term, he had himself a traveling companion.

The fire was strong, and in its warm glow Zane didn't look nearly as weak and pale as he had in the white, color-stealing light of morning.

"So, Bushrod, where are you from?"

Bush didn't really want to enter that rather complicated history. "A lot of places. I was born near what's now Nashville, in Tennessee."

"I see. I've never been there. What profession do you follow?"

"I've been a lot of things. Mostly now I hunt, work the river some, flatboating and all. And live off the land."

"I see. Sounds, in some ways, like my life. Much wandering."

"Yes, there's that."

"Do you have family?"

"No wife. My parents are dead. I have a sister—had a sister."

"She's dead?"

Bush paused, looked down. "Yes."

"I'm sorry. Was she a Christian?"

"I never had the chance to know her much, preacher. We were separated early on in life."

"You've had some sorrows, my friend."

"I have."

"How did you become separated?"

Bush was just opening his mouth to respond when the brush on the far side of the camp clearing opened, and a man stepped out of the woods with a rifle raised, aiming it squarely at Moses Zane's head.

HANGING BY A THREAD . . .

Outside the mob was growing louder, rowdier. They were a pack of dogs who had tasted blood and were thirsty for more. In the tangle of words pouring from them I heard eager talk of hanging.

I rolled over and groaned. Right then I could have killed Fiddler Smith with my own hands, for this was his fault entirely.

Part of me wanted to pound on the shed door and shout out that the man who really deserved to hang was Fiddler Smith, not me. It was Fiddler who had actually done the deed, Fiddler who had left me helpless, to be found and charged the price of a crime that had not been mine.

A fierce defiance sparked in me. No. I wouldn't stand by, waiting for a gaggle of drunks to end my life. I would fight to the end—no, until the end was avoided . . .

RENEGADE LAWMEN

(previously published as
Fiddler and McCan)

CAMERON JUDD

St. Martin's Paperbacks

TIMBER CREEK / RENEGADE LAWMEN

Timber Creek copyright © 1989 by Cameron Judd.
Excerpt from *The Glory River* copyright © 1998 by Cameron Judd.
Renegade Lawmen copyright © 1992 by Cameron Judd.
Previously published under the title *Fiddler and McCan*.

All rights reserved.

For information address St. Martin's Press, 175 Fifth Avenue, New York, NY 10010.

ISBN: 0-312-94556-6
EAN: 978-0-312-94556-5

Printed in the United States of America

Timber Creek Bantam edition / May 1989
St. Martin's Paperbacks edition / November 1998

Renegade Lawmen Bantam Domain edition / December 1992
St. Martin's Paperbacks edition / March 1999

St. Martin's Paperbacks are published by St. Martin's Press, 175 Fifth Avenue, New York, NY 10010.

10 9 8 7 6 5 4 3 2 1

For Joan, who kept asking:
"Whatever happened to
Luke McCan?"

RENEGADE LAWMEN

PART ONE

WALDEN CITY

Chapter 1

It was hard to know who to side with: the skinny fiddle player with the missing ear or the hefty trail bum with the harelip. The former was taking some fierce punishment from the latter, but then, he had brought it on himself by his heartless teasing. I am a man with little sympathy for anyone who taunts another because of his looks, for there's not a one of us who can control what nature gives us, or fails to.

Of course, I couldn't stand by and see a small man beaten to death by a big one, either, no matter what the circumstances. That made my decision for me. I hefted up a big cuspidor, advanced, and brought it down as hard as I could on the back of the bigger man's head. It made for quite a messy explosion.

I had hoped it would drop him. It didn't. He turned and glared at me in disbelief, stinking cuspidor muck running all down both sides of his wide head. He had eyes that drilled like augers. His nose was wide and flat, like his face; his whiskers were as coarse as wool and thirstily soaking up the foul stuff I had just baptized him with.

The whiskers hid his mouth deformity fairly well, but his speech betrayed it. I couldn't make out all he said—mostly just catch cusswords that came out with their edges rounded off. His general point came through even if his words didn't, that being that I had been mighty foolish to cut into his business in so rude a manner.

His partner had been holding the fiddler from behind during the beating. He gave me the ugliest, most threatening grin I had ever received. He was a shrimpy man with a beard worthy of Elijah; his eyes were bright with the prophecy of my impending doomsday.

The fiddler was the only one who welcomed my intrusion. He took advantage of the distraction to wriggle free and dance off, very spritely, to the corner. From there he poked fun at his interrupted tormentors, obviously having gained no wisdom from suffering.

I felt surges of both anger and fear. I had butted into this situation only because I had thought that the fiddle player was about to be killed, for he had howled pitifully at every blow he took. Yet now it seemed he hadn't been hurt at all—in other words, I had endangered myself for darn little reason. That accounted for my anger. The fact that the harelipped man was big enough to single-handedly separate me from my limbs accounted for my fear.

"Have yourself some tobacco, rabbit-mouth, have yourself a chew!" the fiddle player chortled from his safe distance. His fiddle and bow lay at his feet, kicked into the corner earlier by the two hardcases. The fiddler stooped and snatched them up. The rosiny bow dragged across the strings and made a high, scratchy drone that melted into music. The fiddler's voice rang out, shouting more than singing in raucous jubilee—"Well, I went down in Helltown, to see that devil chain down . . ."

Now I knew how the Romans felt as Nero fiddled while their world crumbled to ash around them.

The hardcases advanced and I backed up, promising myself that if I lived to get out of this place I'd never lend a hand to any more one-eared fiddlers for the rest of my days.

"Here now, let's have no more trouble!" pleaded the wiry barkeep from behind his protecting counter. He had been yelping and begging for peace throughout the whole thing.

The harelipped man said something to me that I couldn't understand. Elijah the Prophet interpreted: "Peahead says he's going to pluck out them curls of yours like the feathers of a roasting hen."

Meanwhile, the exuberant fiddler was scratching and shouting away, ". . . Johnny, won't you ramble? Hoe, hoe, hoe . . ."

I wanted to ramble myself, not that there was any way with these two between me and the door. If the side window had been open I would have made a dive out of it, but it wasn't open, for outside the February cold still crawled over the western Nebraska landscape.

"Listen, friend, you've got my apology," I said placatingly. "I thought you were getting a little rough on the fiddler, that's all."

Another muffled statement, another interpretation: "Peahead says the fiddler made fun of his mouth. Peahead don't stand for nobody making fun of his mouth."

"I don't blame you, Peahead, I don't blame you at all," I replied. "He had no right to tease you. Listen, I'm mighty sorry about the cuspidor. I'll pay right out of my own pocket for a bath for you, I promise."

The white-bearded one shook his head. "You shouldn't have called him Peahead. Peahead don't like nobody but his friends calling him that."

"Peahead!" yelled the fiddler at once, having heard the last statement. His fiddle droned up high like an excited bee. "Well, I went down in Hell-town, to see old Peahead chain down! Peahead, won't you ramble, hoe, hoe, harelip!"

"Here now, don't do that," the barkeep said fee-bly.

The fiddler's mockery proved helpful to me this time, for it snatched the attention of Peahead and his partner away from me for a moment. In that moment I balled up my fists and lunged forward, striking two blows in tandem, the first pounding into Peahead, the second into his companion.

The effort jolted me worse than my victims. These fellows were solid, even the little one. My attack did no more than draw their attention back my way.

"Fiddle man!" I yelled, backing up again, wish-ing my gunbelt was hanging around me, not that wall peg behind the bar. "Fiddle man, this is your fight, not mine! Get over here and help me!"

". . . Peahead, won't you ramble? Hoe, hoe, hoe!" He was so caught up in his mocking music that I'm not sure he even heard me.

They fell upon me then and the world became a confusing whirl of grit, muscle, motion, and the stink of the tobacco spittle that dripped from Peahead. Then came pain, the dull pain of repeated blows that pounded me like spikehammers and made me sink toward a floor that was beginning to spin beneath me. I tried to fight, but there can be no fighting when your main foe weighs twice what you do and doesn't mind using it to full advantage. How long this went on I did not know; time had come to a halt.

I heard my voice yelling for help, calling out to the fiddle player, the barkeep, anyone at all, to give me aid, but aid did not come. A fist struck my jaw and I called out no more. I felt tremendous weight atop me, felt the floor hard as an undertaker's slab beneath my back. My eyes, already swelling, opened enough to let me see the fearsome faces above, the massive fists that went up and down like shafts on a locomotive—and then a bare blade, glittering and sharp, that sliced open my shirt and exposed my chest. For some reason I noticed right then that the fiddle music had stopped.

I didn't hear Peahead speak, but he must have, because his partner said, "He says he's going to carve his initials on your chest for you to recollect him by."

I was near passing out when the knife pricked my chest. Writhing, I tried to pull free, but couldn't. The blade was cold and stinging. My eyes began to flutter shut and the images above me were almost gone when a third figure appeared behind the two that leaned over me. A heavy chair hovered, descended, crashed against the rocklike skull of Peahead. My last light dwindled and everything turned black. All I could hear as I sank away was the voice of the barkeep saying here now, don't do that, here now, don't do that, over and over.

The face that slowly put itself together before my blurry eyes was slender and brown and wore a mean expression. I groaned and swiped a hand across my eyes. When I looked again, the face was in sharper focus, and glittering somewhere below it was a badge on a blue shirt.

"What's your name?" the man with the badge demanded.

"McCan . . . Luke McCan," I answered in a whisper.

"Luke McCan, you think I need your ilk drifting through our town and stirring fights with the locals?"

"I . . . didn't stir any fight . . . just tried to help out . . ."

"You've helped yourself into a cell, that's what you've done. The barkeep says you lit into Peahead Jones with a spittoon, then fisticuffed with him and his brother before they raised a hand against you. Is that true?"

"The fiddler . . . they were slapping that fiddler . . ."

I pushed up a little and groaned. Somebody had put me on a bed in a small room. It might have been a spare bedroom in somebody's house, or maybe the sickroom of a doctor's office.

"It was to help out the fiddler that I got into it," I reaffirmed. I found a window to my right and looked out it. The sun was edging down.

"Well, this fiddler was gone when I got there, and the barkeep seems to hold you most at fault," the man with the badge said.

"He's a coward, then. Blaming it on me because he's afraid the other two will come back on him if he tells the truth."

"You can argue about it with the judge, Mr. McCan. You're under arrest on a charge of brawling, city ordinance number fifteen. However, if you'll make restitution for the saloon damages, I'll drop the charges and let you go. Fair enough?"

"Restitution? I'll pay no restitution for a fight I didn't start."

"Have it your way, then. If you won't do the responsible thing on your own, we'll let the city judge make the decision for you." The lawman reached over to a chest of drawers and fiddled with a pile of bills and change lying atop it. I recognized the prior contents of my pockets. "Let's see—three dollars and seven cents, a folding knife, and a handkerchief. Not a lot, but the cash I'll take to be applied toward your fine and the knife I'll take as a potential weapon. The handkerchief you can keep."

"Thanks very much. You're too kind." My attention was somewhat diverted from the lawman at the moment because I was examining my chest to see if there were any initials carved onto it. There weren't. The fiddler had brought that chair down on my attackers in time to save me a slicing.

"Old Doc says he wants you to stay here a few more hours so he can keep an eye on those bumps and bruises. I'm going to chain one of your ankles to the bed, in case you think you might like to run away. Tomorrow morning I'll move you to a cell, unless you've had more cooperative thoughts about paying that damage bill. Do you own a horse and saddle?"

"No." It wasn't really a lie, because the horse and saddle I possessed technically were property of my brother-in-law. In a way, you might say, I had stolen them from him, but not really, for he was dead when I took them. And he would have gladly given the horse and saddle to me, anyway, had he been alive. We got along well, my brother-in-law and I.

Without more talk the lawman produced a chain and linked me up firmly to the metal footboard. "That will do, and that's all for now. Good evening, Mr. McCan."

I gave an ill-tempered grunt in response, and closed my eyes. Every inch of me hurt, and from the feel of my face I knew I was probably no beautiful sight. But at least I was alive and uncut.

A little later a boy brought me supper on a tray. It must have been provided by the doctor, whom I had yet to talk to, rather than the jail, because this was better food than any jail would put up for a small-time prisoner like me. It was hard to chew the chicken because the left side of my jaw hurt every time I moved it. As I ate I wondered what had become of my pistol and gunbelt, which I had left hanging on the peg in the saloon. The lawman had not listed them among my personal effects, which must mean he was unaware of them. After supper I dozed off.

A pecking on the window beside the bed awakened me. I sat up. There was a face looking back in at me. It was lean, battered, familiar . . . the fiddler. He pecked lightly on the window again and made motions to indicate I should be careful and quiet.

The window was stuck, my muscles sore, and my ankle chained to the footboard; sliding up the lower window section proved difficult. With help of the fiddler outside I finally got the job done.

"Come on—I got your horse out here—we can ride out of this sorry town!"

"Not with me chained to a bed, I don't reckon."

He looked in over the sill, saw my situation, and swore beneath his breath. He clambered in through the window, making too much noise even though his thin, Lincolnesque form moved with the lightness of a wind-blown feather.

There proved to be strength as well as suppleness in those long limbs. He squatted at the end of the bed, wrapped a hand around the picketlike metal post I was chained to, and with a few grunts and twists worked it out of the footboard top-piece. My ankle chain slid off. The fiddle player stood and grinned.

"The name's J. W. Smith, but call me Fiddler," he said in a low voice. "You're . . ."

"McCan. Luke McCan."

"Pleased to know you, McCan, and thanks for your help today. This here's my way of repaying the favor."

"What's going on in there?" came a gruff voice from the other side of the door. The knob began to turn.

Fiddler Smith turned and dived headlong out the open window. Without a moment's hesitation I followed, hitting the ground with a grunt as the wind was knocked from me. I rose and ran, ankle chain jingling, struggling for breath that would not come, as behind me I heard the exclamation at discovery of empty room and open window. It gave me a joyful feeling, and as soon as breath returned, I laughed.

Chapter 2

We rode like wind blowing through a narrow mountain gap. For an hour we did not speak to each other, and we looked behind us often to see if there was sign of pursuit. There was none, and at last we slowed our pace to a lope, then a walk. Fiddler Smith's violin bounced on the side of his horse, hanging from the saddle horn in a large flour sack.

"Reckon I'm not enough of a criminal to merit a chase," I commented.

Fiddler Smith grinned. "Reckon not." He dug into his pocket and pulled out a twist of hot tobacco. Carving off a chew with his knife, he shoved the twist at me. I declined.

"Thanks for helping me out," I said.

"No, sir, it's me who owes thanks to you. Them two in that saloon might have done me in if you hadn't stepped in."

"You didn't look much scared, not with the way you kept on teasing that Peahead gent."

"I never had much sense, I admit. Once somebody pushes me, I push the other way. He gave me a hard time about my fiddling, so I gigged him about the lip." He grinned again. "Right mean of me. A man can improve his fiddling, but he can't change a harelip."

I reached down and touched the butt of my pistol, finding it reassuring to have it there again. "You must have took my gunbelt off the peg," I said. "I didn't figure I'd have it again."

"A man needs his weapons. Hey, that is your own horse I gave you, ain't it? It was the only one tied out front of the saloon. I figured it for yours."

"It's mine. Thanks for fetching it."

We rode a while longer, me sizing up Fiddler. He was an interesting-looking man and as ragged a one as I had ever seen. He wore nankeen trousers that had gone out of fashion a decade and a half back, a shirt that once had been yellow and now had faded to a sickly tan and white, and a dark broadcloth coat that hadn't been sponged down for a year or more. His hat was a battered derby greased from much handling. It fit his head as perfectly as a cartridge case around a slug.

We made camp in a grove beside a little stream. Fiddler gathered wood and built a roaring fire. I commented that maybe the fire was a bad idea, in that followers were still a possibility. Fiddler just shook his head.

"Never could abide to camp without a big fire," he said. "A man needs the comfort of light and heat out in the wilderness."

Fiddler had several cans of beans in his saddlebags and broke out two of them. I was glad to see them, being down to dried-up biscuits and a bag of jerky. My plan had been to resupply myself in town, a plan ruined by the row in the saloon.

After we had food under our belts, we fell to talking. Fiddler Smith spoke cheerfully—he seemed one of those types who are always cheerful—and told of a most unillustrious past.

"The mountains of West Virginia's where I come from—that'll always be home to me, though I doubt I'll ever again live in them. Never had a thing as a boy except two good parents. But they died young and left me alone, and that's how it's been for me ever since. My daddy left me nothing but that old fiddle yonder. My two sisters are dead these six and seven years, and the only brother I've got lives up in Powderville, Montana. I ain't seen him in twelve years.

"I took to roaming when I was sixteen. Even though I'm a slender fellow, I was a lot stouter in my younger days, and I've always been strong. The only two things I've ever known how to do is fight and fiddle, and that's how I've made my living. I'd fiddle in saloons, and toss out drunks who got too rowdy and such. Every now and again I'd serve as deputy or policeman in this or that town back east. Mostly I roamed through the cities, doing whatever I had to do to keep body and soul together. I was in Colorado awhile, too, at a little mining camp called Craig City. You might have heard of it."

"I think I have."

"McCan, I'll tell you, I ain't seen a bright prospect in a long time, not until now. Back when I was living in Chicago, I got myself fired from a saloon over a bit of trouble. Well, right after that into town comes this fellow named Walden, Ike Walden, a big white-haired man who called himself a 'freethinker for temperance and health.' He lived in a big house and had some sort of bee in his bonnet about closing down this saloon that had fired me—he claimed it was destroying the community or something like that.

"He held a big rally to close the place down and drew the biggest bunch of old women and teetotalers you ever saw. I was at the rally because of the food they were handing out. Things got hotter and wilder and before you know it, here goes Ike Walden and an army of these ax-carrying liquor-haters down to bust up the saloon. I went along, hoping to see the fellow who fired me get his come-uppance. Things got still hotter and before you know it, Ike Walden was staring down the barrel of a pistol. He decided to fight and was just about to get his brains blown out when I jumped up and wrestled my old boss to the ground and took the gun. To this day I ain't sure why I did it.

"Ike Walden declared me the finest fellow he had run across. He gave me a job doing general work around his place for almost a year. I got restless then and left for the West, but he told me to keep in touch with him and I did.

"Well, about two weeks ago I got a message from him, offering me new work. He's in Colorado now, and built himself a town about forty miles west of Fort Collins."

"What's the new work?"

Fiddler beamed with pride. "Town marshal. Town marshal of Walden City, Colorado mining town. Bound to be the best durn job I've run across."

"Can you handle it by yourself?"

Fiddler cocked his head and looked closely at

me. "Don't know. That's a good question. I'll tell you this—Walden's not allowing saloons or gambling in the town. He says that draws 'undesirable' folks. It seems to me that marshaling in a town without saloons and gambling halls ought to be a right easy job."

"Sounds like it."

Fiddler loaded and fired a corncob pipe. "Well, that's my story. Let's hear yours. You got family, McCan?"

There's no way Fiddler Smith could know the stab of pain that question brought to me. I doubt it showed on my face, for pain had been a constant companion of mine for months now, and I had grown accustomed to hiding it. I didn't want to answer his question, but given his openness with me, I felt obliged.

"I had family," I replied. "No wife, just a sister and her husband. And there would have been a wife by now, except . . ." My will failed me.

He gave a perceptive look. "She's dead?"

I nodded. "Not only her. My sister, too, and her husband. They were together on a train in Chatsworth, Illinois. It was last August when it happened. A railroad bridge caught fire and collapsed beneath the train. More than a hundred people died." I paused, my voice growing tight as it always did when I talked of this. "I was going to go with them at first, but at the last minute I had to stay behind. I was running a hardware store in Independence with my brother-in-law, you see, and our clerk quit on us just in time to knock me out of the trip. It saved my life, but when I think of what that accident took from me, I swear that sometimes I wish I had been on that train, too. Life without Cynthia hasn't been much of a life.''

"I'm sorry," Fiddler said.

"Me, too. Me, too.''

"So what brought you out here in the midst of this godforsaken territory?''

I rolled a smoke as I talked. "I wasn't brought out here. I was driven. Loneliness, mostly, and bad memories. After Cynthia, I didn't want to stay in Independence. The business didn't matter to me anymore, even though it passed to me after the ... tragedy. I sold out, tucked some of the money into the bank to draw on as I needed, then took out roaming. Just like I did during my younger years. Roaming, working here and there. Mostly gambling. I gamble a lot. Too much. I had given it up for Cynthia, but after she was gone, it kind of reached out and took hold of me again.''

"You tell a sad story, McCan. Too sad to have happened to a fellow young as you. You can't be out of your twenties.''

"I'm well into the thirties now, Fiddler. I've always looked boyish, everybody tells me.''

"Losing a woman is hard for a man of any age. Look at it this way, McCan, there'll be other women. Odds are the next one you won't lose.''

"I've already lost two in my time.''

"Two?''

"Yes. Before Cynthia, there was a girl in Montana. Maggie Carrington was her name.''

"She died, too?''

"No, but as far as cutting herself off from me, she might as well have died. She married another man, name of Rodney Upchurch. Your talk about this Ike Walden and town-founding put me in mind of Upchurch. He set up the Upchurch community near Timber Creek.''

"You talked about roaming in your younger days. Was that in Montana?''

"Mostly. I started out in Dakota. I freighted into Deadwood from Pierre during the big boom and stayed on to mine for a time with a man named Caleb Black.''

"Caleb Black . . . sounds familiar.'' Fiddler drew on his pipe and his eyes suddenly lit up. "Wasn't it a Caleb Black who trailed the outlaw Evan Bridger for so many years?''

"One and the same.''

"No! You mined with him? Well, I'll be, I'll be!''

"More than mined with him. We rode together up in Montana. I worked for the Timber Creek Cattle Enterprise, then finally just drifted out of the business and went back to Independence. That's tended to be my way, just drifting in and out of things, never settling down. Kind of funny, in a way. I thought when I met Cynthia that my wandering days were over. Now here I am, drifting again, shiftless as ever. I've already gambled away half of what I got from selling off the store.''

"Montana,'' Fiddler said thoughtfully. "Sure got to get up to Montana myself one of these days, and see that brother of mine. Lord knows he might even be dead by now.''

Fiddler sat quiet with his thoughts and eyed me through his pipesmoke for a while, then got up, stretched, and pulled his fiddle from its flour sack. He sat by the fire and played a couple of slow tunes, real strange and pretty, then laid down his bow and put the fiddle across his lap. I had gone to work on the ankle chain with a file from Fiddler's saddlebag. When at last the chain fell free, we both grinned. I rubbed my ankle in relief.

"Think you might want to cut out the drifting for a while and settle into some steady work?"

I shrugged. Fiddler must have found more yes than no in it, for he spread his easy grin again.

"In that case, why don't you stick with me and go to Walden City? Town marshaling might be too hard a job for one man, after all. I could use a deputy."

He surprised me with that one, I admit. "I don't know, Fiddler . . . this Ike Walden might not have in mind to hire more than you."

"Why, he feels he owes me. I can talk him into it or I ain't Fiddler Smith. What do you say, McCan? I like your company. You're good folks— I can spot it right off."

"Well . . . I got no other offers pending."

"That a yes?"

"Just a maybe. I can ride in with you and see how the place feels, and what this Ike Walden has to say."

Fiddler grinned all the broader. Picking up his fiddle again, he sawed out a new tune, this one lively and bright. I lit up my cigarette and lay back, smoking and watching the sky and wondering what kind of place Walden City would be, and whether I would stay there for any length of time.

A little later Fiddler brought out a bottle and took a long swallow. He waved the bottle at me but I turned it down.

"What's a champion of temperance like Ike Walden going to think of a town marshal who pulls on a flask on the side?" I asked him.

"Why, Ike Walden don't have to know everything," he replied. "And I don't have to be no angel of teetotalism to safeguard a town—at least as long as everybody else stays sober."

I chuckled, but the incident gave me my first pause as to the likelihood of Fiddler's success as a town marshal. Surely Ike Walden wouldn't put up with an enforcer who broke his own rules, not if he really was the authoritative type that Fiddler painted him.

We slept a little while and rode out with the dawn, crossing into Colorado just south of the South Platte. It would take some long traveling to reach Fort Collins, especially in that Fiddler planned to get there by way of Denver. Clearly he was in no real hurry to claim his new job, even though he seemed to be looking forward to it.

The longer we rode together, the better I got to know Fiddler Smith, and the greater my doubts about his ability to perform his awaited job became. He drank too much, usually not to the point of full drunkenness, but enough to become tipsy by sundown. "Don't worry," he reassured me. "I can hide it. Anyway, maybe a town without saloons will give me the nudge to throw the bottle away once and for all."

"Maybe so," I said. "And maybe a town without gambling halls will break me of my card habit."

Hours rolled into days and miles stretched behind us. We reached Denver and remained there three days, then rode north to Fort Collins and west into the rugged mountains, following the narrow trails that led to the new mining town of Walden City.

Chapter 3

Picture a trainload of new lumber hammered together into two rows of nondescript buildings, spread a wide street of mud between them, throw in abundant swinging shingles and windows with painted-on business signs, almost all incorporating the name "Walden," and you have a good image of what Walden City, Colorado, looked like the midmorning that Fiddler Smith and I finally rode in. There had been rain since dawn, and it had only just stopped, so the Walden City we saw was a wet one.

It was a typical new mountain town in most ways, built along the contours of the narrow valley in which it sat. The main street had a slight curve that was mandated by the rocky bluffs bumping up almost against the backsides of the row of buildings facing north. The opposite row wasn't so pressured and therefore in most mining camps would have been built straight, but here it curved right along with the other row, keeping the street a uniform width. I didn't understand the reason for that until I got to know Ike Walden. Then I knew: Walden wasn't the kind of man who would put up with irregular streets in any town bearing his name. Everything in Ike Walden's world was orderly, rigid, militarily precise. He permeated his town like the smell of fresh-cut pine lumber.

"She's a beaut, ain't she?" Fiddler Smith said as we slogged down the muddy street. He bent to the side and shot an amber dollop of tobacco juice into the mud. "This here town's going to be dancing to Fiddler and McCan's tune before long. We've come into our own, son, into our own."

Truth be told, though I was glad to be here, I wasn't nearly as excited as Fiddler. Maybe it was because I wasn't being awaited here, like he was, and so didn't feel the town was quite so much mine. Or maybe there was more to it. Maybe it was that beneath the town's facade of commonality with every other mining community, there was something remarkably different.

It took me a few minutes to realize what that was, and I chided myself for having been surprised by what I should have been expecting, considering Fiddler's earlier talk. The difference about Walden City was that among its plethora of buildings and businesses, there was not a single saloon. In most towns like this, a saloon was the first place built, before people got around to throwing up the less-important enterprises, such as hardware stores, restaurants, and livery stables. Niceties such as schools, churches, and doctors' offices usually came much later.

I scanned the buildings and picked out what looked like a brand-new schoolhouse still in the works. There was even a four-roomed hospital already open for business; a young medical-looking fellow stood leaning in its doorway, watching the bustle outside. I wondered if he would make much of a living in Walden City, given its lack of saloons and, presumably, knife-and gun-happy drunks.

"This Walden must be quite a powerful man, if he can dominate a whole town," I said to Fiddler.

"Dominate? Durn, he owns it!" Fiddler replied. "Most every one of these businesses here, he owns. Them he don't he leases out the buildings for. Even that there hospital belongs to him."

"How the devil did he manage to set up such a place?"

"Friends in high places, as the phrase goes. He worked out some special grant of land up here, some deal there ain't nobody else got. He even controls all the mineral rights—gold, silver, everything. I don't understand it all that much, but suffice it to say, this here town is Ike Walden's all the way, and anything you get you get only because he deals it out to you. There may not be kings and such in this country of ours, but there sure as Sally is a king in Walden City."

We turned down what would eventually become a side street but which was now only a short, rutted thoroughfare with a handful of small houses and huts along it. Our horses splashed through a deep puddle of brown water, beyond which the fledgling street became a lane, then a mere trail that threaded into the trees.

"Where we going?" I asked.

"Open your eyes, McCan! Were you so smit with that muddy town that you didn't look up on the hillside?"

I looked now; through a gap in the trees I saw a house, painted a neat white, perched on a plateau above the western end of the town. From its front window you could look right down the center of the street. It wasn't all that big a house—just a typical two-story that would have looked modest in an Eastern city neighborhood—but it had a pretentious round tower and was set high up enough that it seemed bigger than it was. As I studied it, a shaft of sunlight cut through the clouds and gleamed off the white clapboards, making the house stand out against the mountains like a diamond among pebbles.

"That's got to be Walden's house," I said.

"Reckon so. His letter described the place right well. 'The Walden Palace,' he calls it."

. "Palace, huh? Well, it's got a tower, but it falls pretty far short of a palace."

"Don't get picky about Ike Walden or his things. He's not a man who likes pickiness in other folk. He figures that being picky is his job."

We circled up the trail and onto the big flat on which the house stood. We approached it from the side. Glancing up the tower, I saw a figure standing in the big window row that curved all the way around the top. I couldn't make out much about him other than that he was portly but tall and had a gray topknot and long hair that stuck out wide on both sides of his head. It made him look from here like some wild-eyed Puritan expositor from long ago.

Fiddler threw up his arm and waved eagerly at the figure, smiling brightly. The man in the tower stood up straight and waved back, very dignified and haughty. So far my impressions of Ike Walden were falling out just as I expected they would.

We dismounted beside the house and were about to tether our horses to a tree when out of the house came two black servants, both wearing uniforms that made them look like railroad-station baggage carriers. "We'll be happy to take your horses, gentlemen sirs," one of them said. "If one of you gentlemen sirs is Mr. J. W. Smith, Mr. Walden is waiting to see you."

"I'm Smith," Fiddler said. "This here's my partner, Luke McCan. You want we should just walk in?"

"I'll show you in, Mr. Smith, sir," the servant said. He had a beaten-down look in his eye, and you could tell at once that being handservant to the king of Walden City was a draining job. I felt sorry for him.

He led us into the house, which was as spanking new as the rest of the town but more finished. I figured Walden had seen to the completion of his "palace" before anything else. The interior was fancy, though again only in comparison to the rest of the town. In any other setting it would have been nice but nothing to gape at. There was carpet and wainscoting and a shiny ceiling, but a close look revealed seams and gaps that showed the place was rather hastily built.

The servant took us over to a big oak door that was still awaiting a sanding down and a coat of paint. It creaked open to reveal a circular staircase, made of rough lumber, leading to the tower.

"You sirs will need to take care 'cause there ain't yet no banister," the servant said. He began plodding up the stairs. We followed, making one full circle around the tower before we reached the landing at the top and faced another oak door.

The servant knocked, then opened a little metal slide three quarters of the way up the door and through it said, "Mr. Walden, sir, Mr. J. W. Smith and his partner Mr. McCan are come to see you."

"Bring them in, then, Bob," came a booming voice. I was thinking how peculiarly formalized this process was, given that Walden had already seen us through his window and we had seen him. I suppose a "king" has to maintain some sort of protocol when he gives audience to his subjects.

As the door swung open, I was already thinking to myself that I wasn't going to like Ike Walden much, not if such airs as this were common to him. Ever since I had had trouble with a pompous little Iowa-born snoot named Henry Sandy back at the Timber Creek ranch in Montana, arrogance had set poorly with me.

Walden was a broadcloth expanse of belly, vest, and watch fob, peaked off with a wide and somewhat pasty face. What I had from a distance taken for long hair hanging down either side of his head actually were big stiff sideburns that ran down almost to his deeply dimpled chin. He had no mustache, but needed one: the space between his mouth and the bottom of his little nose seemed overly wide and could have used some filling in.

"J. W., it's good to see you," he said to Fiddler, thrusting out his delicate hand. "I can't tell you how thrilled I am that you've accepted the job."

"I've been slow to get here, Mr. Walden," Fiddler said. "I hope that ain't given you no problems."

"None at all, sir. We have peaceful folk in this town." He glanced at me. "Mr. McCan—isn't that the name you gave?"

"Luke McCan. Pleased to meet you, Mr. Walden." His handshake was soft and moist, the kind that leaves you conscious of your own palm and makes you want to wipe it on your pants leg, which of course you can't do.

"I'm glad to know you, sir, but I admit to being at a loss. I had expected only Mr. Smith."

Fiddler stepped forward. "Mr. Walden, McCan here is a longtime partner of mine. We've known each other for years, and he's a fine man with peace-officer experience. He and me served together under Masterson back in my early days at Dodge City."

I fired a shocked glance at Fiddler, who was lying through his tobacco-coated teeth. He had laid out his life fairly thoroughly to me by now, and had never mentioned being a deputy in Dodge—and I sure as heck knew I had never been. Obviously Fiddler had greatly inflated his credentials to Walden even before now, for the Dodge City reference had been given in the easy manner of a mutually familiar subject.

"Well, I'm impressed, then," Walden said. "Am I to presume you wish Mr. McCan to assist you in the job?"

"Well, sir, I had hoped you'd consider it."

Walden scratched the deep cleft in his chin and looked at me in a way to make me feel like I was on an auction block. His brows came down in an evaluative frown, then he shook his head.

"I have nothing in the budget for an assistant, even one who looks as fit and promising as this young man," he said, making me feel flattered even in rejection.

"Oh, he'll work for free," Fiddler promptly replied. "All he requires is room and board."

I didn't even try to hide my glare of shock, but

Walden had gone into a coughing fit and was looking down, hacking into his fist, and didn't see it.

When he had cleared his throat, he begged our
pardon and picked up where Fiddler had left off,
"Labor in return for only room and board? Are you
really willing to do that, Mr. McCan?"

"Well, actually I—"

"McCan is a former hardware-store man out of
Independence, Missouri," Fiddler chirpily interrupted. "He sold out his business and is fairly well
off, and might set up in trade right here, if he likes
the place." I could only listen in amazement as
Fiddler revealed to Walden plans and dreams even
I didn't know I had. "Free room and board in return for some part-time marshaling would set him
ahead just enough to make this town a mighty appealing place for him—and I could surely use his
help from time to time."

Walden seemed impressed. I started to speak
up to burst the bubble of illusion Fiddler was
blowing—then I decided abruptly not to. Making
Fiddler out for the liar he was might cost him the
job he had come for, and I didn't want that to happen. Besides, it would be fun to see what Walden
would say.

"Well . . . well . . . all right, then. There's a
small house set aside for you behind the jail, Mr.
Smith. With only a little effort and expense I can
quickly add another room . . . if Mr. McCan is serious in this offer."

I opened my mouth, honestly not knowing what
I was going to say. What came out was, "I'm serious." What the devil, I was thinking. I've got
nowhere else to go, I've got to stay somewhere,
and a free room is better than one with a price tag.

"Fine, then, fine," Walden said. Suddenly he faced me and spoke in a surprisingly forceful tone. "You understand, I hope, that in Walden City I tolerate no drunkards or opium fiends, no gamblers, sluggards, harlots, or any such ilk?"

"I understand. Fiddler . . . Mr. Smith, I mean, has told me all about it."

"Good. And no preachers, either. Purveyors of unscientific superstition have no place in Walden City. We are overshadowed not by steeples but by reason, by intelligence and rationality. If anyone waves a Bible on a street corner in this town, you may summarily escort them past our borders, gentlemen."

"Seems to me a good preacher or two might help you keep out the gamblers and drunkards you despise so."

Walden's eyes seemed to pop in their sockets. He stepped forward, suddenly a foot taller than before. "I am a freethinker, Mr. McCan, unfettered by belief in some bearded overseer on a heavenly throne. This is my town. It will operate in accordance with my lights, not yours. If you work for me, you must understand that."

I said nothing. He stared at me a moment or two, then his harshness faded and he smiled. "You understand me, I can see. I like you, McCan. You have a healthful look about you—the kind of man who can serve as a good example for the people of this town." He looked at Fiddler. "And I must confess, Mr. Smith, that I detect in your eyes the tracks left by the beast alcohol. I do hope you'll not fail to live up to the standards I require."

"No fear of that, Mr. Walden. I know what you expect."

"Good. Very good. Now, if you gentlemen will return downstairs, I'll join you in a moment and show you your new office and quarters."

While we were waiting below, I commented, "Strange character."

"No doubt of that. But once you get used to him he ain't bad."

"I'm talking about you, not him. What was all that Dodge City nonsense, and when did I tell you I was willing to work just for lodging?"

"Well, you took the bargain, didn't you? Shows I was right."

A door across the room opened and in walked a woman who was obviously barely into her twenties. She was rather plump but very pretty, even though her eyes were red as if she had been recently crying. She stopped short when she saw us, stared at me for a couple of moments, then withdrew quickly back into the door from which she had come.

"Who was that?" I asked.

"Vera Ann Walden, Ike's daughter. He's a widower, you see. Pretty thing, ain't she!"

"Easy enough on the eyes, I suppose." I felt prideful over the way she had looked at me. "Did you notice how she—"

"How she looked at me?" Fiddler cut in. "You bet I did. Reckon I must be a handsomer gent than I had thought."

I stood with my mouth half-open, on the verge of correcting his obvious misperception. No—it wasn't worth it. "You are a fine-looking specimen of a man, now that I notice it," I said.

"Wish I could say the same for you."

"You can. All you got to do is lie about it like

I did. Ought to be no difficulty for you. I've had occasion to notice today that you're adept with the falsehoods.''

He just grinned. That was a good thing about Fiddler Smith: You could gig him and he'd take it without a flinch . . . most of the time.

Chapter 4

We had thought it would be an easy job. No saloons, no faro halls, no houses of prostitution— yet the people of Walden City proved to be the most ill-tempered, fight-mongering, downright sorry gaggle I had ever had the misfortune to run across. I commented to Fiddler that Walden City was like Deadwood in its early days, minus the vice. That's the very problem, Fiddler responded. Folks here don't have any way to let the steam off their boilers.

It took me less than a week to realize that Ike Walden's grand experiment in "rational temperance," as he called his civic philosophy, was doomed to fail. A lot of the people of Walden City were devoted followers of Walden and had migrated here with him, determined to make his dream a reality. But as many were followers in name only, their chief lure being the silver mines. Sure, they signed their names on Walden's line, as required to stake a claim in his territory. They agreed to use no liquor or opium, to follow his list of rules to the letter, and to make no attempts to form any religious or political bodies. Even so, before our first three weeks were behind us, Fiddler and I had busted up three illegal stills, run a wagon-load of prostitutes out of town, broken up an on-going faro operation, and given warning to two street-corner preachers. The last duty I had left to Fiddler alone; even though those times long preceded my church-going days, I didn't think it right to interfere with folks' religion. And from a strictly practical viewpoint, such bullying never worked, anyway. You can turn a people against you by denying them their righteousness just as quick as by denying them their sin, and Walden was doing both.

I made such observations to Fiddler late one evening after a particularly hard day. He responded by picking up his fiddle and scratching out an accompaniment as he sang a funny old cowboy tune about a freethinker in a cattle camp whose mouthing against religion earned him an opinion-changing whipping from a big brawling cowpoke who declared he wouldn't hear his mother's religion disparaged. As I pen this narrative all these years later, I can still hear Fiddler's coarse but pleasant voice stringing out that last line: "... and the spread of infideliteeeeee ... was checked in camp that day." Then came the fiddle's final flourish, done in a characteristic and indescribable style I had never heard any other string-sawer employ.

Fiddler Smith, I had already learned, gave his thoughts in his music as much as in his spoken word. In the brief time I had known him, I had come to like the man a lot. He was an entertaining, easygoing companion with whom I could be at ease.

But he had another side, one that didn't put me

at ease at all. Just as I had feared, he did not put aside his drinking after coming to the "town of scientific temperance." Where he got his bottles I never knew, but he always had one. Walden City had some underground liquor market that didn't run dry. It was more evidence that "King Ike" Walden, as some snickeringly called him, didn't exercise the deep control he thought he did.

King Ike, nonetheless, was for the time being firmly ensconced as the fountainhead of law in Walden City. He served as city judge and head of the town board, comprised entirely of his staunchest followers. Fiddler and I sat in on one of its meetings two days after our arrival; we were there primarily to be introduced. It was the most peculiar meeting I had ever attended. Little real town business was discussed. Mostly the event consisted of Ike Walden talking about his views, which he wrapped up in scholarly sounding jargon and dubbed the "new scientific gospel of human welfare." I didn't understand much of it, maybe because of my lack of education at that time, or maybe because there really wasn't much there to understand in the first place.

Walden's court, like his town board meetings, was equally a platform for his expositions. The courthouse, on the outside a plain plank building, was much fancier inside. It was almost churchlike, with pews lined up facing a raised stage on which a big desk sat beside a humble witness box. On the desk was Walden's motto: "Science, Temperance, and Freedom from Superstition." I witnessed many of the "trials" he conducted with his selected jury, and though I knew little of law, it was clear even to me that there was nothing legal about these farcical hearings. Walden's "criminals" ranged from merchants who failed to pay sufficient city sales taxes to drunks and gamblers. All were found guilty; all were evicted from the town by the pompous self-declared judge.

"This can't last," I told Fiddler after one of these sessions. "A real lawyer could take Walden to a real court and burst his bubble with one prod."

"You'll notice," Fiddler replied, "that there ain't no real lawyers in this town."

He was right, and that was another peculiarity of Walden City. Most mining towns swarmed with attorneys, both good and bad, but there were only two law offices in Walden City, both occupied by Walden-appointed men. For all I knew, neither one had any valid legal training.

It didn't take me long to decide that my days in Walden City were to be short. Not long could I continue to play a part in Walden's ridiculous drama and live with my conscience. At the end of the first month I told Fiddler I was thinking of leaving and urged him to do the same. He seemed dismayed, and begged me to reconsider.

"Why?" I asked. "Walden's bound to be brought down before a year goes by. I figure we can get out with our pride, or get tossed out looking as foolish as he is."

"Hell, you don't know he's going to go down, McCan," Fiddler replied. "This here's a remote town; ain't nobody much on the outside who even knows how it runs."

"Let Walden keep running people off and pretty soon the word will spread," I replied.

"Well, when that happens it'll be time to go. As it is, we got us a good situation until then. This is the first good-paying job I've ever had, McCan, but I can't do it without help. Dang, you've got a free place to stay and run of the whole city—why not stay on while it lasts?"

It had always been one of my flaws that I was too easily talked into things that my common sense told me were mistakes. Fiddler's hangdog plea hit me in a soft spot. Sighing, I said, "All right. I'll stay for now, though I can't see what you find so all-fired great about scraping for King Ike."

Fiddler grinned. "It ain't the king that holds me—it's the princess." With that he turned away, went into his room, and closed the door. In a moment fiddle music came wafting through, broken by short pauses that I knew marked pulls from another hidden bottle.

The princess . . . he had to mean Vera Ann Walden. It was the first hint I had received that he had been seeing Walden's plumpish daughter on the sneak. Before long the hints would grow stronger.

Fiddler Smith and Vera Ann Walden. The combination smelled of trouble from the beginning, for by now I had seen enough to know that King Ike's heavy hand lay heaviest on his own single child. He guarded her like a treasure, and I doubted any man who tried to take that treasure away would be spared Walden's wrath.

I should have gotten out then. Should have, but didn't.

The next day Ike Walden called me up to his house. This is it, I figured. He's heard something bad on me and I'm about to be gone . . . which might be the best thing to happen, come to think of it.

But Walden surprised me. He called me into his

tower sanctum, handed me a long cigar, and told me he had authorized a salary for me almost equal to Fiddler Smith's. I was so surprised I dropped the cigar and scorched his rug. Walden didn't even seem to mind.

"I like you, McCan," he said. "You inspire confidence in a way that—I must speak frankly—your superior doesn't. You're fit, strong, young, reliable. Marshal Smith, on the other hand, seems to have lived an unhealthy life. I suspect he doesn't hold to the principles on which this town is built. Tell me, have you any knowledge as to whether Marshal Smith might be drinking liquor in secret?"

My surprise over being given a salary faded into a suspicion that I was being plied. Walden wanted to use me as a source of damning information about Fiddler. I wondered if Fiddler's drinking was the only reason Walden was turning against the man he had specifically sought out for the marshal's post.

"If you don't mind me saying, Mr. Walden, if you have personal questions about Marshal Smith, maybe you ought to put them to him, not me."

Walden's expression soured and for half a second it looked like he might get mad. Whatever he was about to say he swallowed down, though, and drummed his fingers on his desk as he said, "Perhaps you're right, Mr. McCan. My reason for coming to you first is that I would hate to confront Marshal Smith on so important a matter if I've misinterpreted his situation. He'd have justification for being angry about that."

"I suppose he would, but I think he'd be more likely to be angry if he found out you'd been asking behind his back. That's my opinion, at least."

Walden nodded briskly, his lips tightly shut. It crossed my mind that it was a good thing he'd already promised me the salary, for now that I wasn't cooperating with him like he wanted, he didn't seem quite as happy with me.

And maybe he wasn't, but he still had another surprise for me anyway. He obviously saw it as a positive one. My own feelings were different.

"There's a special favor I'd like to ask of you, Mr. McCan," he said. "My daughter, Vera, wants to go into town to buy a couple of dresses. I'd like you to accompany her."

"Beg pardon?"

"I said I'd like you to accompany her. Look out for her, you know."

I was confused. "Is Miss Walden in some sort of danger?"

"No, no, not specifically . . . well, not danger as such." He licked his lips and looked uncomfortable. "Mr. McCan, let me tell you something in confidence. My daughter has fallen victim to some sorry rumors—damnable things, slurs against her character. I won't dignify them by repetition. Let me assure you, they are unjustified. My Vera Ann is a staunch, upright, dignified young woman. I've raised her free of superstition but have given her a strong moral base. Yet there are those who like to spread lies. I'll ferret them out and rid this town of them soon enough, let me assure you.

"But in the meantime, I hate for her to be on the streets alone, where she might be humiliated by some loose-tongued scoundrel. I want her with someone I can trust. That's you, McCan." He cleared his throat. "I can trust you, can't I?"

Indeed he could, where Vera Ann was concerned. She was as appealing to me as a feeder pig in skirts. Vera Ann was the Lord's positive answer to the prayer "Lead us not into temptation." It was Fiddler Smith's chime she rang, not mine.

And that was one reason I didn't want to have to become her escort. I wanted nothing to do with the lady whose secret relationship with Fiddler Smith was bound to get back to her father's ears. Nor did I relish the thought of walking around Walden City with a lady folks were whispering about.

None of it made a difference. There was no way to turn down Walden's request, not after he had just handed me a big salary and a potful of praise. "I'll do whatever I can to see to her safety, Mr. Walden," I glumly replied.

He smiled now. "Thank you, Mr. McCan. I don't forget those who display a willing and helpful attitude—you'll see that."

He reached over to his desk and picked up a bell. Its jingle brought Bob, the servant, to the office door.

"Tell Vera Ann that Mr. McCan will be waiting for her below," he said. "Tell her not to make him have to dawdle around overlong."

"No hurry," I said. "I'll just finish smoking this cigar while I wait."

The cigar was long gone by the time Vera Ann finally came down the stairs. She smiled brightly at me with that pretty-but-plump face, and I found myself seeing things in that smile that I might just be imagining but probably wasn't. I dreaded this. Before nightfall half of Walden City would have seen me walking around with King Ike's ill-reputed daughter and I'd probably never hear the end of it.

"Thank you so much for escorting me, Mr.

McCan,'' she said, slipping her arm under mine.
She smelled strongly of perfume and powder.
''Daddy worries a lot for me ever since my . . .
trouble began.''

''I'll try to make sure you're in good hands,'' I
said as we went out the door. At once I realized
what a poor choice of words that was.

But Vera Ann apparently did not. She leaned
over to me and whispered into my ear: ''I wouldn't
mind that, I don't think.''

I couldn't find a single thing to say. I pretended
to go into a sneezing fit so I could pull myself free
of her as I dug my rag of a bandanna out of my
pocket. The ploy only worked for a moment, for
her arm slid right back into place. Together we
walked down the curving path that led down from
Ike Walden's ''palace'' to the town, me feeling
Walden's gaze on us from his big tower window
all the way.

Chapter 5

Vera Ann's expression combined sympathy and admiration as she dabbed at my bleeding lip with a lacy handkerchief pulled from her purse.

"Oh, you poor thing," she said, standing too close as she tended me. "Bless your heart, you've hurt yourself fighting over me."

"It's not that much," I said. "Just a split lip— you needn't do any more, thanks." I pulled away.

Her face was tear-streaked and red. "Oh, Luke— can I call you Luke?—you don't know what it means to me that you defended me against that, that . . . insulting scoundrel."

The time was exactly one hour after I left Walden's house with Vera Ann hanging on my arm. And a more uncomfortable hour I couldn't recall. Vera Ann had walked beside me like she was pasted to my hip, keeping such perfect beat with my stride that we must have looked like a two-headed, two-gendered monster stumping down the boardwalk. It felt like every eye in Walden City was on us; many were the grins and nudges I noted in the corner of my eye as I stared straight ahead.

Vera Ann had steered me into a dress shop,

where she poked around among the most expensive frocks and made agonizingly slow selections. I muttered something about going out onto the porch for a smoke and escaped after about ten minutes.

A glitter-eyed fellow with an aggravating grin slid up beside me. "What's your boss man going to think about you running 'round with Vera Ann, huh?" he asked smirkingly.

I figured at first that he was talking about Ike Walden and replied that it was my "boss man" himself who had sent me out with her. His eyes widened.

"Fiddler Smith sent you out with his own woman?" he asked disbelievingly.

"Not Fiddler—Ike Walden."

"Oh! Fiddler won't like that much, I bet." He grinned again and started to go away.

"Wait a minute—just what do you know about Fiddler and Vera Ann?"

"Same thing everybody else in the dang town knows. Them two have been sparking like two hot coals right under King Ike's nose." He winked. "Old King Ike don't look kindly on it, either, from what I hear."

The man walked away, leaving me feeling uncomfortable and unhappy. Fiddler's relationship with Vera Ann was between him and her, and, I supposed, between them and Ike Walden. I didn't like being thrown into the mix just because Ike didn't like his daughter keeping company with my immediate superior.

Three cigarettes later, Vera Ann came out with her new dresses wrapped in brown paper parcels. Though I didn't feel particularly gentlemanly at the moment, I took them from her. "I'll carry these back up to the house for you."

She took my arm and squeezed it. "Oh, let's not go back yet," she said. "I'd sure like to have a piece of pie and some coffee first."

I was tempted to sigh in displeasure but politely held it in. "All right. Lead on."

She led me across one of the wide walkways laid across the muddy street, and toward a little cafe. That was where it happened.

A big bearded miner stepped forward. "Howdy, there, Vera Ann," he said, grinning at her and acting as if I wasn't even there. "How about you and me having a little fun this evening?"

Vera Ann pulled back and closer to me. She looked offended and scared. I stepped between her and the man.

"I don't like your tone, friend," I said.

"I don't recall talking to you, curly," he replied coldly.

"My name's McCan. I'm the assistant marshal here, and I suggest you go on about your business elsewhere."

He was twice as big as me and looked tough enough to eat horseshoes for breakfast. "I don't care if you're the president's first cousin," he said. "My business is with Vera Ann." He leered in a way that raised my hackles. "And I hear tell she likes the kind of business I got in mind."

The rest you can easily picture for yourself. By the time our row was finished, the big fellow was too busy tending his broken nose to care about "business" anymore, and I was striding with Vera Ann back across the street, my split lip putting the taste of blood on my tongue. I could have arrested the man, but I felt too disgusted and mad to bother with it.

For half the distance back to Walden's home I didn't say a word to Vera Ann. People stared at us all the way. At last she managed to squelch her tears, pulled out her handkerchief, and began tending to my lip and talking to me as described before.

"Vera Ann," I said, "do you want me to tell your father what happened?"

She looked at me with horror. "No! Please don't! He wouldn't . . . understand."

I had my doubts about that. Probably he would understand, maybe already did. His daughter obviously had the reputation in Walden City of being a loose woman.

"All right," I said. "I'll say nothing. But let me tell you this, you obviously need to be careful about the way you . . ."

Her tears threatened to come again. "About what? What are you trying to say?"

"Nothing. Never mind. Let's just get you home."

This time Ike wasn't in his big window, to my relief. At the door Vera Ann surprised me with a hug. "You're a wonderful man, Luke McCan," she said. "I feel safe when I'm with you. I like that."

I mumbled something vague.

"Maybe we can do this again," she said, seemingly having forgotten already what a humiliating experience this had been for both of us. "Please come back . . . I like you a lot." Suddenly she became intense. "This town is no place for you, any more than it is for me. Let's leave. Together."

"What?"

"I've got to get away from here, away from Father. Soon."

"You're talking to the wrong man, Vera Ann."

"No, I'm not. You're the rightest man I ever met." She hugged me again. "Think about it—but don't think too long."

Never before was I as glad to get away from a place and a person as I was when I plodded back down the hill to town. My lip was starting to throb and swell now, and I headed home to see how bad the damage was.

It was nothing serious, just a little cut from my own tooth. I slapped some of Fiddler's whiskey on it to clean it, then lay down on my bunk to calm down. I wound up falling asleep.

When I woke up, Fiddler was there, slumped in his chair at the table, looking at me sternly.

"Who lit into you?" he asked.

"Does the lip look that bad?"

"Puffed up like a riled cat."

"It's nothing. I had a little go-around with a rude fellow on the street."

Fiddler was filling a pipe. "Yeah. I heard about it. Everybody in town's talking about it."

"Wouldn't you know it."

He fired the tobacco. "What were you doing out with Vera Ann?"

"Ike put me to it. He asked me to go with her to buy some dresses. Apparently he's got the idea that people in this town have funny ideas about his little girl." I touched my sore lip. "It seems he's right."

Fiddler sat up straight. "What's that supposed to mean?"

"I doubt I need to explain it."

He puffed the pipe vigorously, and fumed more than it did. "I don't like you catting around with Vera Ann."

"It wasn't my choice. Like I said, Ike Walden put me to it. I was just doing my job." I paused, wondering whether to go on. "He's picked up some rumors about you and her, Fiddler."

He said nothing, just sat smoking until the pipe went out. "I'm hungry," he said. "Think I'll open us a can of beans."

For the rest of the evening, we had little to say to each other.

I found them together the next evening when I came home unexpectedly to fetch a new sack of tobacco. Fiddler was in his long johns and Vera Ann in her petticoat. She screeched and hid on the other side of Fiddler's bed when I came through the door.

"McCan, what the devil are you doing here?" Fiddler bellowed.

"I might ask you the same—except I can figure out the answer for myself."

"A man can't have no privacy, it appears," he said angrily.

"It's my place, too. If I had known, I'd have stayed away."

Vera Ann began to cry. "Don't tell my father, please!"

"Don't fret. I'm a man who minds my own business."

"You could at least have the decency to turn your head," Fiddler growled.

I did turn away, digging into my trunk for the tobacco. When I turned again Vera Ann had her dress back on and Fiddler was in his trousers.

"I'm leaving," I said. "And I'll knock the next time I come in." I glanced at Vera Ann and noticed her face was very white. "Are you all right?"

Her answer was to stumble back to the other side of the bed again and get sick on the floor. Fiddler made a face, then looked worried.

"Honey, I didn't know you were sick! What's wrong?"

"Nothing," she said weakly, straightening. "I want to go home."

"I'll take you," Fiddler said.

"No, no, Father's there. He'll see you."

"Well, I can't let you go alone, not with you sick."

"I'm not sick. Really I'm not." She turned a pleading face to me. Her color was starting to return. "Luke can take me."

Fiddler didn't appear to like that idea any more than I did. Under the circumstances, though, he could say nothing.

Along the way she hugged close to me like before. "Have you thought about it?" she asked.

"Listen, Vera Ann," I said. "I can't take you away from here. It just wouldn't be the thing to do."

She pulled away. "Why? Do you believe all the bad things people say about me?"

"What I believe doesn't matter. It just wouldn't work. I'm not looking for female company right now. I was going to be married not long ago, and I lost her. She died. It'll be a long time before I can get past that."

She looked at me in silence. "Then I'll just have to get Fiddler to take me away."

"Why do you want to go so bad? You've got a good life here, a good home . . ."

"There's nothing good here, and it's going to get worse. A lot worse." She looked like she might cry again. This was the most emotional young woman I had ever met, so much so that I began to wonder if there was something wrong with her, if maybe she really was sick.

And then it came to me. I understood.

"Why are you staring at me like that?" she asked.

"Never mind," I said. "Come on, let's get you home."

I left her at the door, happy that there was no light up in Walden's tower office. I had escaped being seen by him.

Fiddler was drunk and playing his fiddle when I got back later that night. Once again I had been left to patrol Walden City on my own.

"You been funning around town with my woman again?" he asked.

"Nope. I've been out doing my job—our job, if you'd take more part in it."

"I reckon I do what I should. How I handle my job is between me and Ike Walden."

"That's not all that's going to be between you, once he figures out the truth."

"Truth about what?"

"About Vera Ann. It looks pretty clear to me. Her getting sick, her all fired up to get out of Walden City as soon as she can . . ."

"How do you know about that?"

"She talks about it. That girl has got something to hide from her father that she won't be able to hide much longer."

"Talk straight, man!"

"Can't you see it, Fiddler? Vera Ann's pregnant."

He didn't say a thing, but slowly went as white as Vera Ann had been earlier. He spun around in his chair, turning his back to me, picked up his bottle, and took a long, bubbling swallow.

Chapter 6

If Ike Walden had thought his influence was broad enough to keep vice away from his part of the world, he quickly learned otherwise. Shortly after I found Vera Ann and Fiddler together, a saloon began going about a mile east of town. In what had been an empty mountain meadow a pile of lumber appeared one day, and by the next afternoon most of the shell of a large building stood there, with word spreading that this was to be a full-fledged saloon.

King Ike was infuriated to see this moral incursion at the border of his kingdom. Fiddler came in grinning the night after the board siding went up on the building, saying Ike and he had ridden out to the site so Ike could voice his formal protest. The answer had been a sawed-off shotgun fired into the sky by one of the handful of men working on the building. King Ike had hauled his royal self back to Walden City as fast as his horse could carry him, Fiddler chortled.

Out on the streets, the new saloon was the talk of everyone. Lots of people began riding out to the site, watching the building go up and wondering when the liquor would be freighted in. A few of Walden's sincere followers seemed distressed by this development. Most others were openly delighted. Clearly, Ike Walden's hatred of demon rum was not going to staunch its flow outside his jurisdiction, nor would he be able to halt the flow of his people from town to tavern.

Walden called Fiddler and me into his tower office for a conference about the saloon. As he paced the floor, smoking one of his big cigars and shaking ashes all over the place, he raged and declared that any Walden Citian who came into the city drunk from the saloon would face the most severe punishment, either jail time or banishment, whichever they chose.

"You're likely to deplete your population, then," Fiddler declared. "You can't ride herd on everything folks want to do."

Walden turned a fierce gaze on his marshal. "That's a particularly interesting comment, coming from you," he said. He didn't explain what he was getting at. He didn't need to.

I confess that I was among those who were glad to see the saloon going up. My Walden City days were one of several low times I've had in my life, the loss of my beloved one being still fresh. The call of the long-missed gambling table was strong. With my own eyes I witnessed a roulette wheel and faro table being unloaded at the saloon; the effect on me was like that of a finely roasted steak laid out before a starving man. The gambling fever took hold and I knew that at first chance I would be in that saloon, scratching the familiar old itch.

The day I saw the gambling equipment unloaded was the day I first saw the big Indian. When I say big, I mean big. He towered over every other man there by a good six inches, was as broad as a wagon, and sleekly muscled like a puma. Beyond that there was nothing sleek about him; he was grizzled and harsh and ragged-edged. Across the middle of his face ran a harsh scar that mangled his nose to gristle—and most remarkable of all, he had a missing ear. Just like Fiddler.

I watched him from a distance, and saw from his manner and motions that he was a man of some authority. He himself worked hard, hefting around big stacks of planks as if they weighed nothing, but also directed other laborers.

"See the redskin?" came a voice from behind me. I turned in my saddle and saw a blond-haired miner riding up beside me. "That's one of the proprietors of this fine new establishment."

"That right?"

"Yes sir. His name's Jim. Big Jim the Scarnose. He's a Sioux, or at least mostly Sioux. Likely he's been a bit mongrelized along the way."

I stuck out my hand. "McCan's the name."

We shook. "I'm Baker. Tate Baker. Don't even think about calling me Tater."

"I wouldn't. How do you know so much about the saloon yonder?"

"Why, I just rode up yesterday and asked. I'm looking forward to seeing it opened, I don't mind telling you."

"You don't sound like one of Ike Walden's devoted."

"I ain't. Walden's crazy, in my book." Tate Baker suddenly gave me a shocked look. "Say, ain't you the marshal?"

"Assistant marshal."

He cast up his eyes. "Lord, Tate, you've gone and done it now!" he said. Then to me: "Look, please forget what I said. Don't go tattling back to Walden about me coming out here. I don't want to lose my claim."

"Don't worry. I work for Walden, but I'll be danged if I'm going to be his eyes and ears."

Tate grinned slyly. "Walden City's assistant marshal ain't too happy in his job, I take it?"

"You take it right. And as far as I'm concerned, you can take the job, too. I don't aim to hold it much longer."

"I don't blame you. It's rough just living in Walden's town. It's got to be even rougher working for him."

"It's got its pressures, let's put it that way. And there's a hot situation that's likely to explode soon." I looked wistfully across the clearing. "Still, it seems an odd time to think of leaving, now that a saloon is coming in. I like to gamble."

Tate chuckled. "What do you know! Ike Walden's lawman's going to sneak off on the side to flirt with vice!"

The comment made me think about Fiddler and Vera Ann—the explosive situation I had subtly mentioned. Walden's control of his "kingdom" was breaking down, just as I had expected. It wouldn't be pleasant to work under him as it all crumbled. The time to get out was now.

But as I left Baker and rode back to town, I was thinking I wouldn't get out, not yet. For getting out would only mean roaming again, without purpose or friends, homeless and lonely. In Walden City I at least had a job and saw faces to which I could attach names.

And so I stayed on. If I had known how much trouble staying on was going to bring me, I wouldn't have done it.

Big Jim was even uglier up close than he had been at a distance. But there was nothing ugly about the way he handled a deck of cards. Those big fingers bent and flexed with the limber beauty of snakes, making the cards move and shuffle with the precision of soldiers.

The game was faro, my weakest weakness. Too bad for me, because a skilled dealer, the sole handler of the cards in this particular game, could clean out a faro player's purse quicker than a London pickpocket. And Big Jim the Scarnose had every appearance of being a skilled dealer.

Or maybe I was just edgy, sitting there in the crowded saloon, violating one of the fundamental rules of my employment because I didn't have the fortitude to say no. I was no better than Fiddler Smith, when it came down to it. The only difference was our weaknesses, his being whiskey and Vera Ann Walden, mine being the gaming table.

The outcome of faro is staked on the order of appearance of certain cards, and my prognostication skills obviously were no match for Big Jim's dealing. "I'm out," I said in disgust after losing yet again. Standing, I pushed back my chair.

"Hey," Big Jim said. "You—somebody said you were law in Walden City."

"Who said that?" I demanded, acting offended. I didn't want this man to learn the truth.

"Don't matter. Are you law?"

"I don't believe a good man of Ike Walden's

kind of law would be playing faro in a saloon, do you?''

He didn't answer me. Those dark eyes cut another couple of holes through me and then lowered to the cards again. I pushed my way through the crowd, heading for the door and fresh air. The stench of tobacco and unwashed miners made it hard to breathe the saloon air for too long at a stretch.

Outside the air was much cleaner. I rolled a smoke and grinned up at the sign above the big front door. Big Jim's partner, a weasly little British scrapper who sported arm garters and the mouth-filling name of Alphonzo M. Swallows-Beasley, had tauntingly named the establishment King Ike's. Ike Walden was reportedly appropriately furious.

"Nice-looking sign, don't you think?"

It was Tate Baker, a beer in his hand and grin on his face. "You have a way of coming up unexpected on a man," I commented.

"I find being lightfooted is a valuable trait to cultivate, particularly when one has to beat a hasty departure."

"You have much experience with hasty departures, Baker?"

"The question is whether you have, McCan." He became just a touch more serious. "The proprietors here don't much like you hanging around. They think you're in here spying for Ike Walden."

I laughed at that one. "If Walden knew I was here, he'd have my backside."

"He's bound to find out—folks know you."

"Let him find out. I don't care."

"You talk just like your fiddle-playing boss."

"When did you talk to Fiddler?"

"Earlier this evening. He was right over there putting away whiskey like it was water. He's not too friendly a sort, is he?"

That didn't sound like the Fiddler I knew. "Usually he's as friendly as they come."

"That right? Well, he must have something on his mind, then. He was cussing everything and everybody when I was around him. Mostly he was cussing Ike Walden, and talking about getting shut of him." Baker leaned over a little, dropping his voice. "You know what folks say? They say that Fiddler Smith and Ike Walden's girl have something going. Not that that would be any big surprise. That Vera Ann Walden is a bit too free with the menfolk."

Obviously Baker hadn't seen me during my little forced outing with Vera Ann; otherwise he wouldn't have dared speak so freely about her.

"So Fiddler Smith isn't her first . . . conquest?"

"Not by a long shot. No sir."

"That's interesting," I said thoughtfully. "Mighty interesting."

Fiddler was scraping out a slowed-down Irish reel on his rosin-caked fiddle when I came in later that night. He looked somewhat ashen and wasn't his usual jubilant self.

"You feeling all right, Fiddler?"

He put down his fiddle and stared at the scroll of it, lightly plucking at the E string with his forefinger. "You're looking at a man with a lot to mull," he said.

"Vera Ann?"

He nodded.

"Is she . . ."

"Yes. She's pregnant." He let out a loud sigh. "I ain't never fathered a baby before. Didn't aim to now."

I cleared my throat. What I had to say might not be taken well. "You might not be the father, Fiddler."

He looked up at me curiously, that expression giving way to one of anger as he understood my implication. "You watch what you say about my woman, McCan!"

"It ain't what I say, it's what others tell me. Apparently Vera Ann has a . . . history, if you follow me. Look now, Fiddler, don't get mad—this is just what I hear on the streets."

"In the gutters is more like it!"

"Hear me out—you owe it to yourself to listen. Fiddler, I think Vera Ann may have already been pregnant before she ever took up with you. She's looking for a way out of Walden City before her father catches on to her condition." I paused. "She even tried to talk me into taking her away myself."

He rose and came at me, his fiddle falling from his lap to the floor. I deflected his fist and got a grip on his arm. He was too drunk to put up any kind of fight.

"Dang it, Fiddler, calm down! I'm saying what I'm saying because I owe it to you as a friend."

"Friend? What kind of friend spreads such truck about a man's woman?"

"I'm sorry. I just don't want you to get bumfuzzled into something you'll regret later. You got to consider the strong possibility that Vera Ann is just looking for somebody to take care of her and get her away from that lead-weight father of hers."

Fiddler was getting green around the edges now

and staggered away from me, trying to hold down the contents of his stomach. A minute or two later he seemed back in control of both his belly and his emotions.

"I'll overlook what you said, McCan, because I like you. But I don't believe you. Vera Ann says I'm the father of that baby, and I don't think she's a liar."

He sat down again and checked his fiddle to make sure it hadn't been damaged when it fell. Satisfied, he took it to his bed and put it into its flour sack.

"I'm taking her away from here, right after I get paid," he said. "That means the law job will be yours to do alone. Maybe Walden will let you hire you some help."

"Maybe. If I stay around."

"You thinking of leaving? You could go off with Vera Ann and me—long as you watch your mouth. We're going up to your old stomping grounds, Montana. I want Vera Ann to meet that brother of mine in Powderville."

"Thanks, but no thanks. I'll go . . . somewhere. Don't know where. Don't know when, either. Since the saloon opened the place is a bit more interesting."

"Ain't that the truth. I been in there myself, you know."

"So I heard. Hey, did you see the Indian?"

Fiddler looked at me quizzically. "No—what Indian?"

"One of the proprietors. Big and ugly and scarred, and he's missing an ear, just like you. Except he doesn't cover his with a patch. Tonight he dealt faro and I . . . Fiddler, what's wrong?"

He looked sick again, worse than before. He staggered back to his bed and sat down, hand on stomach.

"What's wrong with you?"

He shook his head. "Too much to drink, that's all." Rising, he lurched past me and out the door.

Chapter 7

I dreamed of Cynthia, alive and married to me. It was early morning of a bright spring day, the smell of frying bacon filled our house, and she was delicate and beautiful as she walked in and touched me to wake me and tell me breakfast was waiting . . .

Except Cynthia would never have shaken me this roughly. Nor would she have reeked of whiskey and pipe smoke. I sat up, my wonderful dream giving way to the dull reality of the Walden City hut, and Fiddler Smith's unshaven face hovering above me.

"Get up, McCan," he said tersely. "We got a job to do."

I blinked, fumbling for lamp and matches. "A job? What time is it?"

"Three o'clock the morning after payday, that's what," he said. "Now get up—Walden's give us a job."

"At this time of night? What kind of job is it?"

"Just get up and shut up. I've already got the horses saddled and waiting."

My mind was so bleary I wondered if this was

nothing but a dream after all. Maybe the earlier part about marriage to Cynthia was the reality and this was the fantasy, the nightmare.

If only it could really be like that.

Fiddler had two jugs tied together and slung over the back of his horse. I asked what they were, but he didn't answer. His manner was intense, determined, unspeaking. A very bad feeling began to come over me.

We rode through the sleeping town—in liquorless, cardless Walden City, there was nothing to keep most people up late—and out onto the new but well-beaten trail toward the saloon. The farther we rode the more my feeling of disquiet grew.

"Fiddler, just what are we about to do?"

"Shut up and ride. Don't make noise."

"What the devil are we doing?"

"A job for Walden—that's all you need to know."

The saloon was open. There were several horses and wagons outside it even at this hour.

"I don't like this, Fiddler. What are we up to?"

Fiddler was breathing loudly through his nostrils, his lips clamped tightly shut. I hadn't seen him like this before. He led us to a thicket near the saloon and dismounted. I remained in the saddle for a few moments, considering whether I should turn and ride away. Everything about Fiddler's manner smacked of trouble.

"Get down off that horse, McCan," he said gruffly.

Had I disobeyed him at that point and gotten away from there, it would have been the wisest thing. That's hindsight, though, and as you know, hindsight usually finds itself looking back on mistakes. I dismounted as instructed.

Fiddler pulled the twin jugs off his saddle. He moved quickly, fiercely. I swear I could almost hear the pounding of his heart from where I stood. Or maybe it was mine.

"Seems a peculiar time to be taking a drink," I said.

He popped the cork. A breeze wafted across us, carrying the smell of the bottle's contents. Kerosene.

Fiddler's intentions needed no explaining now. He had come here, and dragged me with him, to burn down a saloon. A saloon with patrons still inside. Ike Walden obviously had concluded his problem required a radical solution.

But it was a solution I would be no part of.

"No, Fiddler," I said. "This is loco—we can't set fire to a building, I don't care who ordered it! Walden's a crazy man. In the name of heaven, Fiddler, somebody might die in there!"

"Hell, they'll get out—there's a big door, ain't there? You turning yellow all at once, McCan? Scared to do your job? You damn sure ain't backed down on Walden's orders before! You've kissed his feet, trying to climb up over me so he'd favor you! I know he's took to paying you near as much as me. Trying to get my job, that's what you've been up to!"

I couldn't believe what I was hearing. Was this the same man who had told me he was handing over his job to me, without me even asking for it, so he could run off with his woman? I saw now that Fiddler had been secretly jealous of me, probably stemming from the way I had risen in Ike

Walden's eyes even as he had declined. That's a funny thing about some people: they care deeply about what others think of them, even those they despise.

"I'm not after your job, Fiddler. I don't want your job. God only knows why I've been fool enough to keep my own this long. I'm through—I'll have nothing to do with torching a building."

I guess it was the whiskey and anger mixing together inside him that made him lose his control and swing the jug at me. It was made of heavy crockery and hit my skull like rock. I went down, groped upward through the stars and rockets that exploded and flared a foot above me, then passed out cold.

Cold water splashed my face and washed the blackness away. My eyes opened and were confused by a yellow-orange glow that bathed the tall figures above me. I seemed to be in the bottom of a grave, looking up at the mourners who surrounded me, grief on their torchlit faces.

Then understanding began to return. I lay not in a grave, but on the ground. The men gathered around me were not mourners; what I had seen as expressions of grief were actually looks of deep anger. And the yellow glow was not torchlight. It came from the flaming saloon.

"Oh, no," I murmured. "He went and did it."

"What'd he say?" one of the men above me asked. A face descended, drawing near mine. It was Swallows-Beasley, the Britisher.

"What do you have to say for yourself, you bloody arsonist!" his crisply accented voice said.

"Fiddler . . ."

"Eh? What's that?"

"Fiddler . . . where's Fiddler?"

One of the others said, "He's talking about Fiddler Smith, Ike Walden's marshal. Now I know this bird—his name's McCan. He's a marshal, too, or a deputy."

"Do tell! Well, soon he'll be nothing but a corpse on the end of a rope." He leaned even closer. His breath stunk in my nostrils. "Talk to me, McCan. Did Ike Walden order my saloon burned?"

"Get . . . out of my face . . ."

He struck me, sending up stars again. This time I remained conscious. "Don't talk smart with me, McCan. You can make this a lot easier on yourself by speaking up—or else I'll turn you over to my red-skinned partner for his own brand of persuasion."

My eyes shifted; now I saw the wide, scarred face of Big Jim glaring down at me. Satan himself couldn't have been uglier.

"I didn't burn your saloon," I said weakly.

"No? So it sparked up all of itself, then? You expect me to believe that?" Swallows-Beasley said.

I forced myself to think—I had to find some way out of a lynchman's noose. "I didn't burn your saloon," I reaffirmed. "But I saw the man who did . . . he hit me when I came after him."

"Is that so? And why, pray tell, would a peace officer with no authority outside Walden City be prowling about all the way out here in the middle of the night?"

"I was coming for a drink. I've been here before."

"That's true," someone said. "I seen him at the faro table. You dealt his game, Big Jim."

The Indian said something that reached me only as a bearish growl.

"I don't believe you, McCan," Swallows-Beasley said. "You smell too strong of kerosene for me to buy that bill of goods."

Kerosene . . . indeed I did smell it hanging about me. I remembered the crockery jug. Probably it had cracked when it struck my skull. Some of its contents must have spilled on me.

Fiddler . . . where was he? Why had he abandoned me here to be found by these men? It was equivalent to leaving me to die.

Anger surged and gave me strength. My fist came up and pounded Swallows-Beasley, making him grunt and jerk back. I rose, but found the world spinning around me. Something encircled my neck—an arm, a massive arm. Big Jim the Scarnose had me firmly in his grasp. I gasped for air that would not come.

"No, not that way!" Swallows-Beasley said, rubbing his chin. "We'll swing him properly— with Ike Walden right beside him."

The statement drew a roar of assent from the saloon's former patrons. Fiddler's firing of the saloon had roused a lynch-mob fury among these men, many of whom were on the outs with the oppressive Walden anyway. The destruction of the saloon was to them a justification for counteraction.

They hustled me toward a rude toolshed that had been nailed together during the saloon's construction and not yet torn down. There was nothing in it now but trash and scraps of wood. Big Jim heaved me inside like I was no heavier than a feather pillow. My head struck the wall when I fell to the dirt floor, and I sank down, not unconscious but slightly stunned. Light from the burning saloon probed through cracks and knotholes in the board walls.

Outside the mob was growing louder, rowdier. They were a pack of dogs who had tasted blood and were thirsty for more. In the tangle of words pouring from them I heard eager talk of hanging Ike Walden. The level of tension and anger in the atmosphere was too high to let me believe the threat was idle. In minutes this mob would move through the night to Walden City, and bring back Ike Walden with them. I doubted anyone would dare try to stop them. Walden would hang with me right beside him.

I rolled over and groaned. Right then I could have killed Fiddler Smith with my own hands, for this was his fault entirely.

Part of me wanted to pound on the shed door and shout out that the man who really deserved to hang was Fiddler Smith, not me. It was Fiddler who had actually done the deed, Fiddler who had left me helpless, to be found and charged the price of a crime that had not been mine.

But I didn't do it. Maybe it was because I was too honorable. Or maybe just too stunned.

Chapter 8

Through a knothole I watched the mob recede toward Walden City. To my dismay, though not to my surprise, they left two men to guard me, figuring, I guess, that I might be able to pound my way out of so crude a shed if left alone.

I sat alone in the dark little shack, my face pressed against the knothole, wildly searching for a plan to get me out of here. My two guards were drunk, and after the mob went out of sight, they turned their attention to watching the spectacular destruction of the saloon. The fire was at its peak now, pouring enough light through the cracks of my shed to let me see fairly well. The heat of the blaze was tremendous, even as far from it as I was.

Heaven above, how my head hurt! I rubbed it gently, rolling my neck in a vain attempt to lessen the throbbing. In a few moments I gave it up. What would it matter how my head felt when they put that noose around my neck?

A fierce defiance sparked in me. No. I wouldn't stand by, waiting for a gaggle of drunks to end my life. I would fight to the end—no, until the end was avoided. There in that shed I learned something

about myself: Despite all my despair at the loss of
Cynthia, despite my foolish and self-destructive
gambling and drifting, despite my occasional as-
sertions to myself that life didn't matter anymore
. . . despite all these things, I wanted to live. I
wanted to see the morning and breathe the air and
know what it was like to grow old, even if I grew
old alone.

Surely there was something here to use as a
weapon. If I was to escape, it must be soon, before
the mob returned. Against two men I stood a slim
chance; against a full mob I stood none.

Dropping to my knees, I felt about the shed
floor. Nothing. Papers, bent nails, empty boxes.
Despair began to mount. Then one of the walls of
the burning saloon crashed in, sending up an explosion of sparks and intensified light that spilled
through the shed walls and revealed something
standing in the corner. An ax.

I leaped up and grabbed it. My heart sank. This
wasn't an ax, just an ax handle, and broken at that.
What could I do with this? I noted the broken end
was splintered to a point. A man could gore another
man with that—but not with a wall dividing them.

I had to get out of the shed somehow. Setting
the ax handle aside for a moment, I began examining the walls. They were rough, splintered, hap-
hazard, but strong. I did not find a single board
loose enough for me to kick away, not without raising a major ruckus.

Well, maybe that's what I would just have to do.
If I made enough trouble, the two guards would
have to open the door to come in and stop me. A
well-timed thrust or two with the splintered ax handle might, just might, be enough to get me past

them. Then I could run into the forest as far as I could and escape them. Yes sir, if I could only get to the forest, escape I would. I'd run all the way to Mexico if I had to.

Locating what looked like the weakest wall-board, I raised my foot to pound at it. Before I could, one of the men outside shouted to the other, who apparently had wandered off some distance, "Hey, Big Jim's coming back!"

That stopped me. I went back to my knothole at once. Sure enough, the hulking Indian was riding back into the wide circle of firelight. My guards stepped forward to meet him. Fortunately, they came together while still within my earshot.

"You forget something, Big Jim?"

"No. Swallows-Beasley sent me back. Change of plans. I came back to get this McCan. We'll take him into Walden City and hang him there with Walden. We don't want to have to drag Walden all the way back here before we lynch him."

"Well, that makes sense," one of them said. "Let's hurry—I don't want to miss seeing Walden hang."

Big Jim dismounted and strode toward the shed. I took a dry swallow, picked up my ax handle, and readied myself for the opening of the door.

The Indian let out a yell when the sharp point probed into his broad midsection. It didn't poke deep, but splintered off and remained stuck into him an inch or so. I bounded right over him, leap-frogging like I had done with friends back in my Missouri boyhood. The two surprised guards let out a shout and came at me, tugging at pistols. I yelled right back, like the Rebel soldiers used to do, and came at the nearest one with the ax handle extended. He ducked to the side and missed the thrust. It didn't help him much, because I brought the ax handle down like a club and caught him on the back of the head. He fell with a loud grunt.

The other guard had his pistol out by now but was too unnerved to fire. I ran straight at him and hit him on the side of the head. He fell to his knees. I grabbed his pistol.

Now there was more than just hope. I had a weapon.

Big Jim's horse stood where he had left it, and I ran straight for it and leaped into the saddle from behind like the finest dime-novel hero you ever read about. I had tried to do that sometimes, just fooling around back in my earlier cowpoke days, and had never achieved it nearly so well as now. I felt proud of myself.

The feeling was short-lived. Big hands came up from the side and grabbed my clothes. I was pulled from the saddle before I knew what was happening.

It was Big Jim, of course. He threw me aside; I hit the ground and rolled. To my good fortune I kept hold of the pistol, which I swung up and fired, twice. Both shots went high. I squeezed the trigger a third time and nothing happened. The gun had been loaded with only two cartridges.

Big Jim grinned and bore down on me. I scrambled to my feet and tried to dart away, but he had me. I fell and he was there, leaning over me with that fierce grin burning down from his ugly face.

"Now, McCan, you talk to me! They said you called the name Fiddler before I came up close enough to hear. They tell me this Fiddler is the marshal of Walden City, and you help him. You tell me: Does he have only one ear, like me?"

"Yes," I said. "Yes . . . one ear."

His face was even uglier after that. Another wall of the saloon crashed in and sent up more sparks, light, and heat. Big Jim shook me, knocking the back of my head against the ground.

"Fiddler Smith! Fiddler Smith is here?"

I remembered now how Fiddler had gone pale the time I mentioned the big, one-eared Indian who ran the saloon. These two must have had more in common than missing ears. They had histories that overlapped, and apparently not pleasantly.

"I'll kill him!" he said in a fierce and triumphant tone. "At last I'll kill him, kill him dead!"

It came to me that I still had the pistol in my hand. It was empty but heavy. I brought up my arm as hard as I could and let the blue steel barrel say a firm hello to the side of Big Jim's head.

What happened next was so rushed and confused that I can't fully describe it. Somehow I was up again, Big Jim grappling at me. One of the men who had guarded me joined him, but tripped up and wound up getting in Big Jim's way instead of helping. At the same time, the lynch mob came riding back in, drawn back by the sound of my two earlier gunshots. I ran, they pursued. The woods loomed dark before me, then swallowed me. I dodged through brush and clambered across rocks and ravines.

They could not ride here, and so came on foot. Their voices were loud behind me, and too close. My head hurt worse than ever. The land tilted up before me and I climbed, straining for breath. I reached the top of a ridge, but my foot caught on a root. With an involuntary yell I fell, tumbling into a ravine. At the bottom I lay still, unable to rise. I was on my back, looking up at the sky.

They were close now; their voices were louder by the moment and rising toward the crest from which I had fallen. Groaning, I tried to rise again and managed only to push up onto my elbows. Maybe they would pass me by. Maybe they wouldn't see the ravine . . .

Then a face appeared, looking down over the edge of the ravine. It was dark and I could see no features, just the outline of the shape. I froze in place, hoping that the night shadows would hide me. A moment later a light flared; the man had struck a match.

The matchlight flashed onto the face of Tate Baker. None of it, as I could tell, spilled down on me. The flame held for only a moment before the wind snuffed it.

"Find something, Tate?" someone asked.

There was only the briefest pause before he answered. "Not a thing. He didn't come this way, that's for sure."

After that the voices began to recede. I was alone and alive, and the prayer of thanks I sent up toward the black heavens was surely the most sincere ever voiced by any member of our mortal race.

How long I lay there I'm not sure, but it couldn't have been long. Though I had momentarily escaped the noose, danger still threatened Ike Walden. I expected that the lynch mob, having given up on me, would now return its attention to finding Walden. He had to be warned, had to know that his order to burn the saloon that mocked his name and his philosophy was about to cost him dear.

I climbed out of the ravine and headed down

through the forest, aiming for the trail to Walden City. It felt as if a great weight rested on my shoulders, the combined result of injury, weariness, and the need to reach Walden before the lynch mob did. I reached the trail to Walden City and discovered, from hearing their noise beyond me, that the lynchmen had already passed. I could not hope to make it to Walden City before them—unless I could take a shorter route by leaving the trail.

Such a thing was possible, for the trail curved and followed the easiest portions of the terrain. As the crow flies, the distance to Walden's ''palace'' was much shorter. Too bad I wasn't a crow.

If I couldn't fly, at least I could attempt to maneuver a more direct route by land. The effort seemed doomed, but if following the trail was obviously hopeless, what harm could come from trying the only alternative?

So into the forest on the other side of the trail I went. I knew the general direction toward Walden's house and tried to keep on that line as closely as possible. The darkness was thick here and had me groping like a blind man. I had almost given up the effort as failed when I emerged into the clearing on the hillside where Walden's big house stood.

Pausing, panting for breath, I listened. Distantly I heard the sound of the mob. They would be here within minutes.

No time to waste. As quickly as I could, I half-ran, half-staggered around to the front of Walden's house. I pounded the door and shouted for entry. A few moments later the door opened slowly.

Ike Walden, lamp in hand, faced me. His face was white and his hair mussed, his clothing disheveled.

He looked so bad that for a couple of seconds I forgot the urgent matter that had led me here.

"Mr. Walden, are you sick?"

He looked at me with lusterless eyes. "Vera Ann is gone," he said. "She's gotten herself pregnant and made me give her money and now she's gone, run off with her man."

"Her man?"

"Yes . . . she's run off with Fiddler Smith."

Chapter 9

Walden slumped back toward a chair that sat beside an end table in his front parlor and plopped heavily into it. The lamp he sat on the floor beside his bare feet. He stared into a corner like he was drugged. My eyes flicked over to the little table and saw a bottle and glass. Now I really was amazed. Ike Walden, champion of temperance, was drinking.

"Mr. Walden, you've got to get away from here," I said. "There's a mob coming from the saloon—they plan to hang you for ordering the place burned."

He looked up dully at me. "Burned? I didn't order anything burned."

I let that sink in for a second. "Then it was Fiddler, acting on his own . . . because of Big Jim, no doubt."

None of that made sense to Walden. He lifted the glass and took a swallow of liquor. You would think that a man unaccustomed to alcohol would flinch to swallow as much as Walden did, Walden didn't flinch. Clearly he, like Fiddler Smith, had been drinking on the sneak a long time. It was one of the most ironic revelations of my life.

"Coming to hang me," he repeated calmly. For some reason he chuckled. "Coming to hang me."

"They would have hung me, too, if I hadn't got loose," I said. "Come on, Mr. Walden, let's get you out of here."

He said and did nothing for several seconds. Off in the distance I heard disturbing sounds. I could feel the mob's approach even without seeing it. Suddenly Ike Walden violently swept his arm across the table, upsetting it, spilling the bottle and glass across the carpet. He stood, wobbling a little.

"Coming to hang me, are they? Hell, I'll be ready for 'em!"

He stomped over to a cabinet, pulled open the door, and brought out a long old shotgun. This he loaded clumsily with shells from a box up on a shelf. "Let 'em come," he kept repeating over and over. "Let 'em come."

"This is insane, Mr. Walden," I said. "You can't hold off a mob with a shotgun. We get you away from here and give this thing time to cool down. That's the thing to do."

"Let 'em come—I'll blow their skulls open. Then it'll be Fiddler Smith's turn."

What a time for Ike Walden to get liquored up and loco! It was all I could do to keep my feet, for I ached and throbbed from my own ordeal and scramble through the forest. I was in no shape at the moment to physically force Ike Walden to come with me—and it appeared that physical force would be the only thing that would break his resolution.

I stepped forward. "Mr. Walden, I insist that

you come with me. Listen—can you hear them coming?''

He turned a cold gaze on me. ''You're my employee, McCan—you do what I tell you, not the other way around.''

''You're in no condition to make decisions, Mr. Walden. You're drunk.''

You should have seen how his eyes fired at that. A more fierce face you wouldn't expect to find under an executioner's cowl. ''You're accusing me of drunkenness?'' he bellowed. ''You're accusing *me*?''

''Calm down, Mr. Walden . . .''

''There's a rifle in the cabinet—get it and ready it, McCan.''

''Mr. Walden, if you don't come with me I'll have to use force.''

''I told you to ready that rifle, McCan! We have a fight ahead!''

''No—no fight. We've got to get away from here.''

''You're a coward, McCan. I despise cowards.'' And with that he swung up the shotgun and brought the butt of it arcing around toward my head. Under normal circumstances I could have ducked it, but in the shape I was then my reflexes were rusty. The hard buttplate struck my skull and drove me down. Unconsciousness came immediately.

The smell of smoke was choking and acrid when I came to. This wasn't the hot smoke of a blazing fire but the searing, thick kind that pours from something smoldering. I sat up, groaning, and found myself still in Walden's front parlor. The house was filled with smoke. Coughing, I stood.

"Mr. Walden!" I yelled as best my smoke-tightened throat would allow. "Mr. Walden, where are you?"

I found the source of the smoke—a pile of rags and such in the sitting room. Somebody had set the things afire, but they hadn't fully caught. Certainly someone in the saloon mob had done it—and it chilled me to know they surely had known I was lying unconscious in the very house they had set out to burn. I suppose it was my anticipated death by burning that had saved me from lynching.

"Mr. Walden!" I yelled again. No answer in the house . . . but I became conscious of frightening and distant sounds outside. I went to a window.

Walden City was burning. Not the whole town, but at least half of it, with the rest bound to catch. In the streets, lit now by the several blazes, I saw riders and runners all about, torches waving, guns firing into the sky. The saloon mob was avenging itself brutally against Walden's perceived attack. I prayed no innocent townsman had died in the tumult.

"Fiddler Smith, this is on your head," I said aloud in the dark room.

In all my life there were few, if any, times that I felt as helpless as at that moment. Down below me a town I had been hired to protect was being ravaged. Yet what could I, a lone man, do about it?

I had to do something, had to try. Heading back to the cabinet, I found the rifle, a Winchester, that Walden had mentioned, and two boxes of ammunition. I loaded the rifle, pocketed the rest of the cartridges, and headed out.

I didn't make it down the hill to the edge of

town before I found Walden. He lay on the muddy road, face down, a wide puddle of red beneath him. Touching his back, I found no movement of heart or breath. His shotgun was still gripped in his hand. Both barrels had been emptied.

I had never felt any affection for Walden, but right then I could have cried for him. The pompous man with his big ideas and big utopian dreams had come to a sad and ignoble end, his town being destroyed before him, his pride-and-joy daughter run off with a man who had betrayed Walden's trust and encouraged his daughter to betray him, too.

Finding Walden's body drained me of my impulse to respond to the carnage in the streets below. I turned and plodded back up the hill and around to Walden's little stable. There I took a horse and saddle, mounted, and rode off. The night was nearly spent; in an hour the sun would rise and spill its light onto the smoking shell of Ike Walden's dear departed dream. And when that happened, I didn't plan to be around to see it.

The sun, run by those universal clockwork gears that keep working in peaceful ignorance of the doings of the wicked creature, man, lit the Colorado landscape, but not my spirits. I had put three miles between me and Walden City before I finally reined to a halt and twisted in my saddle to look behind. Smoke billowed into the morning sky. I sighed, turned the horse, and began plodding back.

I wasn't sure why I felt compelled to return. Maybe it was duty. Maybe it was curiosity, having to know what the outcome of the Walden City attack had been. Or maybe it was the need to make firm my own case against Fiddler Smith and Vera

Ann Walden, whose combined irresponsibility was the spark that had fired this tragedy.

What was left of Walden City wasn't much to look at. The fire had spread since I had left and even now was finishing off several sheds and outbuildings. Most of the main buildings had been destroyed. Only a handful of sizable structures had been saved.

I rode down the center of the street. The people of Walden City stood, stared, paced, murmured. There was a tangible feeling of general disbelief. And well there should be. How many of these people even yet knew what had caused the mob to destroy their town? The average Walden City resident knew nothing of the saloon-burning that had led to this.

An armed man, followed by three others, strode up to me. I stopped my horse and stared down at him. He was Joe Gamble, a dry-goods merchant of good reputation in the town. I glanced past him to where his store had stood. It was a smoking ruin of black lumber.

"Mr. McCan, I strongly suggest you turn that horse around and get out of this town right away," Gamble said.

I lifted my left brow. "I gather I'm not held in high esteem here, eh?"

Gamble apparently thought I was trying to make a joke, and it made him mad. "Damn it, McCan, we could string you up right here on the street and be within our rights to do it. This is your fault, yours and that worthless superior of yours."

"Fiddler Smith's fault, yes. Mine, no."

"You're trying to say you didn't help torch that saloon?"

"So you've found out about that, huh? No, I didn't. In fact, I objected and got myself knocked cold by Fiddler Smith for my trouble. I near got myself hung, too. Not that you're going to believe a word I say."

"Was it Walden who ordered the saloon burned?"

"That's what Fiddler said, though Walden denied it. I believe Walden."

Gamble snorted. "Walden will get his chance to explain himself."

"He's unavailable. Off meeting the maker he didn't believe in."

Gamble cocked his head. "Are you saying he's dead?"

"Yep—up on the track to his house. Shot to death. I found him before dawn."

Gamble stared up at me as if he was considering gunning me right out of my saddle. I could hardly blame him. Fiddler had left me in a bad situation.

"I'd like to ride out of here," I said to Gamble.

He thought about it a couple of moments, then nodded tersely. I turned the horse and plodded away, heading for the edge of town. I knew I would never again return to Walden City, but I didn't have even the slightest impulse to look back.

Chapter 10

After three hours of riding, weariness caught up with me and I began to think about stopping to sleep. I kept putting it off, though; the more distance between me and Walden City, the better. Fort Collins was my destination—it was about the only place I could handily reach from Walden City. Where I was going after Fort Collins I didn't know; all that mattered was going, and putting behind me all the bad things that had come of taking up with Fiddler Smith.

I thought about Fiddler as my horse loped along, and the more I thought the madder I got. He had been trouble from the first moment I laid eyes on him in that Nebraska saloon. Thanks to him I had taken a trouncing there, and now, again thanks to him, I had barely escaped being lynched first by a saloon mob, then by the very townspeople I had tried to help. Yes sir, I owed Fiddler Smith quite a lot.

The most maddening thing of all was that he had left me there at that burning saloon—left me, senseless and defenseless, to take the blame for what he had done. Could that have been his very reason for taking me there in the first place—to be his scapegoat? Maybe it was jealousy over Vera Ann's interest in me. I didn't like to think of Fiddler as so low a sort . . . but maybe he was.

I thought about trying to track him down and settle my accounts with him . . . but no. It really wasn't worth it. I would just count myself lucky to be alive and put my association with Fiddler down to bad experience. Bad—but interesting. That much I had to admit.

Ahead of me on the trail I saw a rider. His tracks had been clear on the earth before me since I had crossed the Walden City limit. I had crossed the first person abandoning the town. Likely I wouldn't be the last, either. Lots of folks would decline to hang around after such a tragedy. And when the town rebuilt, it would probably be a far different place than when Ike Walden governed it. Without his strong personality in charge, all his "scientific" moralisms would die away. Whatever new Walden City phoenixed out of the old one's ashes would surely include saloons and faro parlors and houses of ill repute. Churches, too. All the things Ike Walden wanted to avoid. The town would thrive and shine and attract both those wanting a foothold and those wanting to be footloose, and eventually it would die and rot away into the Colorado mountain soil. Such was the way of so many mining camps of the day.

At length I caught up with the rider ahead of me, and found it was Tate Baker. The realization was startling, for Baker had been among the saloon mob who chased me up into the forest. I decided a quiet retreat was in order.

Too late. Baker, who was sitting under a tree

eating beans from a can, looked up and saw me.
He stood quickly—too quickly. The rifle I had
taken from Walden's was slung by a cord over the
saddle horn; I grabbed it and swung it free and
upward, leveling it on Baker.

"Luke McCan, is that any way to treat the man
who saved your neck from the noose?" he said,
lifting his hands.

I lowered the rifle a little. "You mean you saw
me in that gully?"

"Sure did. And if you'll recall, it was me who
turned them off in the wrong direction so you could
stay alive. Dang, McCan, the only reason I went
after you with that rabble was to try to save your
skin!"

He was sincere and his story rang true. I decided
to believe him and rebooted the rifle. "All right.
You'll pardon me for being uncertain."

"Sure I will. I'd be jumpy, too, in your boots.
Come on over here and have some beans with me.
Man, you look a sight!"

"Rough night."

"Don't I know it."

He pulled another can of beans from his pack,
opened it, and handed it to me, along with a rusty
spoon. Because of how busy and tense the past several hours had been, I had overlooked my own hunger. The beans disappeared rapidly and left me
scraping the juices from the bottom of the can.

Baker talked as I ate. He was leaving Walden
City, like I was, largely in disgust. He had been
ready to go at any point, anyway; all the trouble of
the previous night had been the final nudge. He had
simply mounted and ridden out before dawn.

His talk turned back to the beginning of the

night's trouble. He had been in the saloon, he said, when it was first torched. One wall was well ablaze before anyone inside realized it; all efforts to save it failed.

Baker described his own mounting fears as the realization spread among the saloon patrons that the fire had been deliberately set. "They all blamed Ike Walden," he said. "No one doubted for a minute that he had been the one behind it. When they started talking about lynching, I decided to get out—and then they found you. I stayed around, figuring you would need some help getting out of that particular jam."

Once I was locked up in the shed, Baker told me, he had gone on with the mob toward Walden City, hoping he could cut ahead and give warning to Walden, then rally help in saving me. He had changed that plan when he saw Big Jim turn and ride back toward where I was held; Baker had quietly followed. Then, shortly after, the gunshots had sounded and the entire lynch mob had returned, figuring I was making a break.

"When you headed up into the woods, I hoped to high heaven that I would find you before somebody else did. I'm glad I did, and sorry for all the scare you had."

"All's well that ends well, as they say," I replied. "For a while there I thought Big Jim was going to have my hide."

"Well, tell me straight, McCan, did you help torch the saloon?"

"No. It was Fiddler Smith all the way. And Ike Walden didn't order it, either; Fiddler did it on his own. I think it was because of this Big Jim character."

"What do you mean?"

"Big Jim knows Fiddler somehow, and vice versa. There's no love lost between them. When Big Jim left that mob to come back to me, it was Fiddler he asked about. He wanted him, bad."

"Now, that's a strange thing," Baker said. "And this ain't the first I've heard of it. I'd picked up word already that Big Jim was acquainted with our good town marshal. I'd sure like to know the story behind it." He lit a cigar stub he dug from a pocket. "Like to know it, but don't. I can tell you some more about Big Jim, though. I picked up some on him since we last talked."

"Like what?"

"Like how he lost that ear. It was back in '79, in the North Park area. You ever heard of the Independent Army?"

I had and told him so. The Independent Army was the overgrandiose name given to what amounted to a band of cutthroats hired by the leaders of the Craig City mining town in Colorado's North Park area back in 1879. Led by a fortyish Georgia ruffian named J. D. Reed, a veteran of the Third Georgia Rifles, the Independent Army was established to spook off any troublesome Indians about Craig City. The way they did it was vicious: the Craig Park leadership provided the Independent Army a base pay, supplemented by a bonus for every pair of Cheyenne or Sioux ears turned in. Reed would receive twenty-five dollars for every pair; a like amount would go to whatever Independent Army member actually removed the ears from the victim.

That, at least, was the version of the story I had heard. The end of the story was no prettier than the beginning. After Reed's "army" began preying on innocent Indians, including children, a party of Sioux decided to settle the problem on their own terms. The bulk of the Independent Army was massacred and their bodies axed to pieces. Reed suffered badly before his own end; when the Craig City leadership found him, he was nailed alive to a tree, with his eyes missing. The Sioux had left him like that. He was shot to death by his finders to end his misery. It was a terrible end for the Independent Army. Terrible, though not undeserved, in my opinion.

"So Big Jim lost that ear to the Independent Army?" I asked. "I wonder how he managed to keep the other one?"

"And how he kept his life, too? The only thing I can figure is he managed to escape whoever sliced him."

I sat down my empty bean can, thinking. "You know, Fiddler talked about being at Craig City. I wonder if he might have been part of the Independent Army. It could explain him and Big Jim knowing and despising each other."

"It's a funny coincidence, Fiddler and Big Jim both shy one ear," Baker said.

"That it is, Tate," I replied. "It's like you said, wouldn't I like to know the story behind that one."

"So why don't you go find Fiddler Smith and get that story?"

I shook my head. "It ain't worth it. Let Fiddler Smith go his way and I'll go mine. I'm through with him."

"That's the attitude to have, I reckon. I can tell you one that don't share it, though, and that's Big Jim."

"What do you mean?"

"Last night, during all the rampaging and burning, that Big Jim spent the whole dang time looking for Fiddler Smith. Whatever them two got between them, it ain't sweet. I don't think Big Jim's going to be content to let Fiddler get away with this one."

"Why do you say that?"

"That Englisher partner of his says Big Jim's declared he wants to go after Fiddler and square things up with him."

I whistled. "I wouldn't envy Fiddler having a devil like Big Jim on his tail."

"Maybe it won't come to that. The Englisher wants to just let Fiddler go. Said it wasn't worth the trouble to go after him. I don't know who won the argument. That was the time I was mounting up to leave town."

We rode together the rest of the day and made a common camp that night. It was beans for supper again.

"So where you bound?" Baker asked me.

"That's a better question than I can answer," I replied. "What about you?"

"Texas. I heard there's always good opportunities in Texas."

"Had your fill of mining?"

"It don't take me long to get my fill of most things. Except beans and beer and saloon sweethearts."

"The beans and beer I can take. Right now the sweethearts don't have much appeal to me." I told him about Cynthia, about how her face was the first thing I pictured when I awakened every morning, the image that stayed with me all day, and haunted me when I blew out the lamp at night. Maybe he didn't want to hear it, but I had to talk.

He proved as good a listener as he was a talker. When I was done he told me he was sorry, then offered his advice. "Find yourself another woman, McCan. There's good ones out there; I've come near marrying a couple of them myself. I skittered free at the last minute both times. Don't know if I was lucky." He chuckled. "Likely they were."

I grinned. "You're not a bad sort of fellow, Tate Baker. You remind me of an old friend I had up in Montana. He was a territorial marshal, name of Taylor Longhurst."

"Marshal, huh? Marshals give me the willies."

"Taylor wouldn't. You and him are biscuits from the same pan."

When I turned in that night, I thought about Longhurst. I hadn't seen him in years, not since the Montana days. But I had heard news of him while I was still in Missouri. He had left Montana and headed to Cheyenne, where he reportedly had joined the town marshal's force.

The next morning I knew where I was bound. Cheyenne lay to the north, an easy ride from Fort Collins. I would go there and look up Taylor Longhurst.

Baker and I reached Fort Collins and stayed there a couple of days until my bruises were better and he felt eager to make for Texas. We parted with a handshake and I set out for Wyoming.

Chapter 11

The rooming house stood on a Cheyenne street that was hardly more than an alley. Running it was a slender little woman with gray hair piled high atop her head and held in place with a pearl clip. She had a gentle face that must have been pretty in her youth; now it was lined and weathered, the corners of the narrow mouth stained with snuff. She granted me the privilege of renting from her because I looked like "an upstanding young man," then warned me not to come in drinking or in any way disturb the other borders, most of whom were elderly.

I made my promises and foresaw no trouble in keeping them. There had been a time when I wouldn't have been so confident, a time when liquor held a grip on me almost as strong as that of gambling. With much effort I had wrestled substantially free of alcohol's hold. Gambling was another story. That demon still held me fast.

That was why that within a day of arriving in Cheyenne, I had already located three good gambling halls. I made a trip to the local bank to arrange to draw on some of my dwindling funds on deposit back in Missouri, then set out to see if I could increase my holdings at the tables. As I pen this narrative from the perspective gained over passing years, I'm ashamed to admit my foolishness of those days. The gaming halls have ruined many a good man, and they almost ruined me.

I strode through the dark streets toward the largest of the gambling houses, my appetite whetted for faro. I ended up with poker instead, following an impulse, and as hours rolled by I had much good luck. About midnight I cashed in my chips and headed back toward my room, cheerful and thinking about looking up Taylor Longhurst the next morning. And in fact I would see him, though under circumstances far different than I had planned.

By the time I reached the street fronting the rooming house, I knew I was being followed. Shadowy figures had slipped out of the gambling hall and now crept in the night shadows behind me, drawing steadily nearer. The rooming-house door was inviting, an entrance to refuge. All I had to do was enter and close it behind me, and my followers would fade back into the night.

I didn't enter it. Out of pride, the couple of beers I had drunk, or maybe simple recklessness I decided to face them down. At the door of the rooming house I spun and saw them emerging. Seeing their prey about to disappear had made them reckless, too.

"Evening, gentlemen," I said. "Is there something I can do for you."

The first one drew near. He was tall and broad and had a voice that growled. "You know what we want. Hand it over and there'll be no trouble for you."

"What I won is mine," I replied. "You want it, you'll have to come and get it."

They did come, both at once. I bore no weapon except a folding knife that I slipped from my pocket as I turned. As they advanced I opened it, waved it—then the foolishness of what I was doing struck me and I wished I had just gone inside.

The thought came too late. My knife didn't frighten either man, for they had knives of their own, and bigger. The big one advanced and I slashed at him but missed. His aim was better, cutting a gash on the back of my hand and making me drop my own weapon.

I ducked the next lunge of the knife and by fortune found a brick that had been kicked loose from the flowerbed border in front of the rooming house. It made a wonderful hammer, and the bigger attacker fell back with a curse and a bruised forehead.

The other ducked and lunged, striking me in the middle and doubling me over. He grabbed my brick and threw it aside. For the next minute I was engaged in a fierce wrestling match with the man; his bigger partner still was out of action, swearing and gingerly holding his bashed forehead.

The door behind me opened. One of the elderly residents had heard the scuffling and had come to investigate, carrying an ancient cap-and-ball pistol. He picked a bad time to open the door, for my foe and I were in the process of falling back against it when he did. As a result we fell atop him, knocking him down. He howled; the pistol went off and shattered a chandelier above the long table in the adjacent dining room.

The fight continued only a few moments more,

and resulted in little damage to either me or my enemy. The furniture wasn't as lucky. By the time my attacker relented and darted out the door, a chair was broken and a shelf laden with glassware and china was overturned. I stood panting, sweating, dripping blood from my cut hand onto the Oriental carpet. The old woman who ran the boardinghouse was at the top of the stairs in a flannel nightgown, screaming out her fury.

"Sorry about the damage," I said. "I'll pay for it."

"Yes sir, you will," she replied. "You'll pay dear indeed."

This deputy might have been a brother to the one who gave me such a hard time back in Nebraska after that saloon brawl in which I defended Fiddler Smith. Same build, same expression, same attitude. He had not a trace of sympathy in him.

My hand was swaddled in a bandage ripped from a bedsheet. Blood was already soaking through. I sat in the twin of the chair I had destroyed, sullenly listening to the deputy deride me as a criminal while the boardinghouse woman walked around the room, making a list of everything broken and a few things that weren't. When the deputy referred to her as Aunt Harriet, I knew I was in big trouble.

"Am I going to jail?" I asked.

"He ought to," muttered the old man with the pistol. He and all the other aging boarders were standing around looking at me like I was worse trash than Jesse James.

"Well, sir, that just depends on you. Depends on your attitude, Mr. McCan." The deputy was haughtier than Ike Walden had ever thought of being. He said my name like it was a swear word.

"What attitude should I have? I was only defending myself."

"We may just have to let the judge decide that, Mr. McCan."

"Look, if you're asking me to pay for the damages, I've already agreed to that."

"Well, that's the right spirit, Mr. McCan. Pay you will, yes sir." He turned. "Aunt Harriet, how much you figure?"

The old woman, eyes spitting lightning, walked over and plopped down her list in front of me. It featured a long column of figures all added up to a total that bugged my eyes.

"I'm not paying that!" I bellowed. "That's ridiculous!"

"Bad attitude, Mr. McCan," the nephew with the badge said.

"Send him to jail!" the old man with the pistol urged. "Teach him what's what!"

I stood, dug my poker winnings from my pocket, and plopped the roll onto the table. "I think that ought to be plenty to pay for anything damaged."

The deputy picked up the bills, counted them, then handed them to his aunt. "That's short by half," he said. "You got more available?"

I did, considering my bank money back in Missouri, but I wasn't about to tell him about it, much less turn it over. "Like I said, I think that's plenty to cover what I broke."

The old woman picked up a shattered pitcher. "This was my mother's," she said eyes reddening. "It meant so much to me."

Now I was getting too mad for my own good.

"Glue the lousy thing back together, then."

The old woman burst into tears and the deputy turned red. "That's it. Come with me, Mr. McCan."

"I want to see Taylor Longhurst."

He didn't seem to know what to make of me calling the name of a fellow lawman. "You'll meet him, I reckon. He comes on duty in the morning."

"You're locking me up?"

"Indeed I am. Follow me, Mr. McCan, and don't try anything."

"You better hope I don't," I said. "I could bounce your head like a blown-up hog bladder if I had a mind to."

I must have sounded mighty dangerous, because he kept his pistol poked into my back all the way to jail. The old folks followed us out as far as the street and watched us tread off until we were out of sight. I figure I had given them the best entertainment that night that they had seen in years.

The rattling of the cell door awakened me the next morning. I sat up as a lean figure in loose-fitting blue trousers strode in with a food-laden tray. I winced at the sunlight that spread through the single narrow window and into my sleepy eyes.

"Lord, don't you look dangerous!" the tray-bearer said. "Maybe I ought to keep you covered with a shotgun in case you try to trounce me with this china plate. I hear you're murder on china plates and such."

Shaking my head to clear it, I finger-combed my hair and rubbed my face. "Shut up, Longhurst," I grumbled. "The last thing I need is smart-mouthing from you."

Taylor Longhurst sat the tray onto my hard bunk and smirked. "Luke McCan. I always knew I'd run into you again. I didn't figure it being in a cell, though. Since when did you turn desperado? Why, they'll be writing you up in them dime novels before long: 'Luke McCan, Terror of the Boardinghouse.'"

The comment didn't strike me all that funny. "It don't seem very nice, making fun of a man who's rode this far just to see an old friend."

"You came to see me? Why, I'm flattered, Luke McCan." He stuck out his hand, putting banter aside. "Good to see you, McCan. I've thought on you a lot these past years."

We shook hands and I managed a smile. "Good to see you, too, Longhurst. How's the deputy business suiting you?"

"I'm giving it up. Two weeks. That's all I got left."

"No fooling?" I picked up my coffee cup and took a welcome sip. Not bad for jail coffee.

"That's right. I'll tell you about it later, after we go."

"You mean I'm a free man? I figured old Aunt Harriet would be pressing to have me put away for life."

"Forget about her—she's satisfied now that she's been paid up."

"Paid up? Last night they told me I was half short on what I gave her."

"You were. I paid the rest."

I laid down the forkful of eggs I had just picked up. "I can't let you do that, Longhurst. Heck, I'll pay the rest. I'm not so mad now."

"Forget about it. I got lots of money now. Inheritance. The proverbial old rich uncle. He built up a good pile and then headed across Jordan and left it all to me not a week ago. I just got word on Monday. My notice went in the same day.''

''So you're taking up a life of ease, huh?''

''Not exactly. I'm going to be a cattleman. From now on I'm wrangling cows instead of criminal types like you.''

''You say the nicest things, Longhurst.''

''Finish that breakfast, McCan, then get out of here and see if you can stay out of trouble until this evening. I'll be through working about six o'clock. I'll buy you a meal. A real one, not this jail victual stuff.'' He turned and left the cell. This time the door stayed open.

''It is good to see you, McCan. Brings back the old Montana days. I'm looking forward to hearing what's happened with you since I seen you last. Six o'clock, hear?''

''Six o'clock.''

He grinned and headed toward the front office.

''Longhurst.''

''Yeah?''

''Thanks.''

He grinned again and strode away, whistling ''Soldier's Joy.'' The sun sliced in through the window while I finished my meal, and ten minutes after that I was on the street again, broke, without lodging, but happy. I had a friend again. A real friend, not a betrayer like Fiddler Smith had proven to be. It had been a long time, and it felt good.

Chapter 12

We sat in a little cafe and exchanged stories. Longhurst's was simple: He had wearied of the travel and constant vigil required by his work for the government in Montana and had tossed it aside for the smaller-scale task of Cheyenne peace officer. In that job he had been happy until lately, when the urge for an even greater change of pace came upon him. Then word of his uncle's death arrived, and Taylor Longhurst suddenly had bright new prospects. Montana was calling to him; the idea of becoming a cattleman was growing stronger by the day.

Longhurst listened intently to the story of all that had happened to me since our last parting in Montana, back in my days about Timber Creek. At that time we had been riding together, tracking the outlaw Evan Bridger, Longhurst acting on professional motivations, me on personal ones. There had been a third man with us, too: Caleb Black, my old Deadwood mining partner and a man whose ghost-like pursuit of Bridger, the outlaw who had taken the life of his wife and unborn baby, had even then become legend far beyond the Montana Territory.

Longhurst finally gave up the search for Bridger and returned to Fort Maginnis, leaving me and Black to go on after the outlaw alone. We found him, in the end, and there was gunplay . . . and Evan Bridger died with my bullet in him.

If I had desired notoriety I could have had it. I could have been known across the nation as the man who killed Evan Bridger. But it wouldn't have been true. I never took public credit for Bridger's killing, for I knew that it was Evan Bridger who brought about his own death, who orchestrated it with grim cleverness because no matter how hard he denied his own guilt, the guilt wouldn't quit haunting him.

My Montana days came back clearly as I talked to Taylor Longhurst. I was taken in memory back to the Montana countryside, the Timber Creek Cattle Enterprise, the little community of Upchurch, the big Upchurch Emporium—and to Maggie. Maggie Carrington, cowboy's daughter, child of the high plains, and a woman I had once thought would be my own, until Rodney Upchurch came along and took her away.

Maggie. The name was still magic to me.

I told Longhurst about my homecoming to Missouri, my engagement, bereavement, and return to roaming. I admitted the gambling, the lack of purpose, the waste of my money and time. Longhurst listened and did not judge. He had never been a judgmental man. That was part of the reason I liked him so much. As a lawman he knew better than most that human beings were human beings and no more. He demanded no perfection of them, or of himself. In other words, he was comfortable.

When my story turned to Fiddler Smith and

Walden City, Longhurst's interest doubled. The idea of me as a town deputy seemed to strike him as funny. And he was fascinated by the peculiar characters I had been moving among: Ike Walden, Fiddler, Vera Ann . . . and especially Big Jim the Scarnose Sioux, and his British partner Swallows-Beasley.

"Once you cross the Mississippi, you find all kinds crawling across these plains and mountains," Longhurst said. "I think that's half of what makes this wild country so fine for me, and why I became a peace officer. A man of the law meets more than his share of your interesting types."

"Think you'll be able to abide putting all those interesting types aside to wrangle cattle?"

"You bet. I've put in too many years behind the badge already. Before long the averages are bound to catch up with me. Some drunk will pull a pistol on the sneak, and old Taylor Longhurst will have snorted his last snuff."

Taylor was living in a small rented house on a back lot. It had only two rooms in it with hardly enough space in either for a man to squeeze in among the roaches. There was no question of me sharing that meager space with him . . . but there was a shed out back occupied only by emptiness and a big gray rat Longhurst had taken to calling Fred.

"Tell you what, I'll shoot Fred and you can have the shed for free up until I vacate for Montana . . . if you don't mind rough shelter," he said.

"Best deal I expect to get," I replied.

"Better than Fred's part, at least. It'll be good to have you about, McCan. Fred makes for sorry company."

*   *   *

Over the next few days I kept thinking about Montana. Talking to Taylor again had awakened a pining in me for familiar places and faces. As rough as times had occasionally been for me up about Timber Creek, there had also been lots of good times. Going back might be pleasant . . . uncomfortable, too, but on the whole pleasant.

I decided to ask Longhurst about it as his final day as Cheyenne deputy approached. In the meantime, I had to find something to do with myself, so I went out looking for temporary work. All I could find was penny-ante duty as a dishwasher and stove-stoker at that same cafe where Longhurst and I had exchanged stories. It wasn't much of a job, but it put a little new money in my pocket and kept me off the streets . . . and out of the gambling houses.

One evening, as I left the restaurant, Longhurst came pounding up to me, out of breath and rather worked up. I was surprised, for he was normally the most easygoing of men.

"McCan, I hoped I'd catch you here. Come back with me to the jail. There's somebody there I want you to see."

"Why?"

"Because he won't give us his name, and I think you know him. He's a British-sounding gent who's jailed for trying to stab a fellow who was with him. The fellow got away—but they say he was a big one-eared Indian. Just like the one you described."

I raised my brows. "I'll be darned. Big Jim and Swallows-Beasley here in Cheyenne! Couldn't be any others."

"My thoughts exactly."

Sure enough, it was Swallows-Beasley in the cell. He looked mighty ragged around the edges, mostly because he was drunk. He looked at me but didn't seem to remember me. I suppose he thought I was just another deputy. Longhurst questioned him in my presence.

"Is your name Swallows-Beasley?" he asked him straight out.

Swallows-Beasley looked very surprised. "How did you—" He cut off, but it was too late. He had already confirmed the identification.

"Never mind how. This partner you had a row with, does he go by the name of Big Jim?"

Swallows-Beasley looked surprised again. He nodded compliantly, probably wondering if Longhurst was a mind reader.

"Well, Mr. Swallows-Beasley, I suggest you start opening your mouth and talking. I happen to know that a little English squirt and a big one-eared redskin are said to have led a mob that burned a mining town down west of Fort Collins not long ago. I expect the Colorado authorities would be very interested in getting their hands on either of those two."

Swallows-Beasley looked scared. A thin trail of drool escaped the corner of his mouth; he wiped it on the back of a shaky hand. You could smell the liquor on him from five feet away.

"What do you want to know?" he asked Longhurst.

"Why you tried to knife this Big Jim character, to start with."

"We argued," Swallows-Beasley replied. "We always argue a lot. This time it was worse than usual."

"What did you argue about?"

"About where to go. We had been down near Walden City, operating a saloon, you see. It was burned down—Big Jim was sure it was an old enemy of his who did it. A man named Smith, Fiddler Smith. He was the law in Walden City at the time the saloon burned. Big Jim got wind that Fiddler Smith had left Walden City with a woman. He got hot to follow them and even up his score with Smith. I went along with Big Jim—I've always tried to go along with him more than he had a right to expect, truth be told. We figured they would head this way. We sniffed around, asked questions, finally picked up their trail. It brought us to Cheyenne.

"By the time we got here, I was ready to forget about Fiddler Smith. I wanted to go to Nebraska. Big Jim wouldn't hear of it; he's got it inside his thick head again that Fiddler Smith has to die. Big Jim was acting just like he did the last time."

"The last time? What do you mean?" Longhurst asked.

"I mean the time once before that Big Jim was hot to kill Fiddler Smith. Over in Kansas. Big Jim stumbled across Fiddler Smith in a saloon; they went it at tooth and claw. Smith got away, though he did leave an ear behind."

"So *that*'s how he lost that ear," I commented. Swallows-Beasley glanced over at me and studied me. He was beginning to recognize me, I thought.

"So Big Jim and this Fiddler Smith are old enemies and from time to time get it in their heads to try to kill each other. Is that what you're saying?" Longhurst asked.

"That's the long and short of it, yes sir," Swallows-Beasley answered.

"Why do they hate each other?"

"Because of Craig City. The Independent Army of 1879. You know of that?"

"I do," Longhurst said. "How do Big Jim and Fiddler Smith fit in?"

"All I know is what Big Jim has told me. Those days were long before we took up together. Big Jim says that Fiddler Smith was in the Independent Army. He says Fiddler Smith killed his family and tried to kill him to turn in his ears for bounty. He didn't kill him, and he only managed to get one ear. Big Jim has hated him ever since."

"That's understandable," Longhurst said. "Now let's get back to the present situation. What happened after you and Big Jim tracked Fiddler and this female to Cheyenne?"

"We lost their trail. And that was fine with me; as I told you, I was ready to let Fiddler Smith go anyway. After a time, a man grows weary of chasing someone else's enemy. But Big Jim wouldn't let it go. He asked questions all around town, until at last he found a saloon-keeper who had been posting bills about a horse for sale. He finally sold the horse, he told Big Jim, to a one-eared man who was traveling with a woman, and needed a mount strong enough to carry the woman at least as far as Powderville, Montana."

"That's Fiddler, sure as the world," I said. "He was bound for Powderville after Walden City. He has a brother there."

Swallows-Beasley flashed me another suspicious look, but as of yet had not placed who I was.

"So what happened next?" Longhurst asked.

"Big Jim was ready to ride up to Powderville and try to catch Fiddler Smith. I told him no, I had already had my fill of tracking and chasing—I was ready to go to Nebraska and make some new money. Big Jim wouldn't listen; he was determined to head for Montana. We argued, I pulled out my knife, and lo and behold, here I am in your jail."

"And Big Jim?"

"Bound for Montana alone, and may he go to the devil, if the devil will have him."

Swallows-Beasley looked at me again. Recognition lit his eyes.

"*You!*" he declared.

"Yes indeed," I replied.

Swallows-Beasley waved toward me. "Deputy, this man is the very one who helped Fiddler Smith burn down my saloon! You must arrest him!"

"Out of my jurisdiction," Longhurst said. "Besides, you're going to be too busy explaining to the Colorado law why you burned Walden City to worry over one little saloon. Good day to you, Mr. Swallows-Beasley. God save the king."

We ate our suppers from cans that night, seated in Longhurst's little rented shack. I was about to bring up my wish to accompany him when he went to Montana, when he turned the situation around and brought it up first.

"McCan, I been thinking—you're at loose ends right now. Why not go with me up to Montana?"

I grinned. "I've been thinking along the same lines myself."

"Good to hear it. Bet there's a lot of folks you'd like to look up, huh?"

"There are. Likely as not I'll find some of them

moved off and others dead . . . but it hasn't been all that long. There's bound to be lots of familiar faces around the Timber Creek ranch.''

''And the Upchurch Emporium, too.'' He looked at me with a twinkle in his eye. Though Longhurst and I had first met only after Maggie had already married Rodney Upchurch—we met the very day of her wedding, in fact—he knew of my prior relationship with her.

''If you're talking about Maggie, I admit I'd like to see her. Not that it can do me any good with her still married to Upchurch.''

''Maybe she's not married anymore.''

''Why do you say that?''

''Didn't I tell you? A couple of months ago I got a letter from one of my old fellow Montana lawmen. Monroe Starr. Monroe is the kind to keep up with everybody's news. He was over about the Upchurch area, and everybody was talking about how Rodney Upchurch had taken bad sick in his lungs and was likely to pass on soon. You know how he'd been bedridden for a long time anyway.''

I did know. I remembered clearly the night that Evan Bridger shot Upchurch, prompting that final pursuit that ended in Bridger's death. Upchurch hadn't been expected to survive at all, but survive he had, though in a pitiable condition.

''So Maggie might already be a widow,'' I said, mostly to myself.

''That she might.''

I stood and walked over to the door. Opening it, I stared out toward the north. It made me feel ghoulish to take the report of Upchurch's likely death as good news—but I meant no harm by the feeling, and couldn't help how I felt anyway.

Maggie . . . free again, marriageable. What a thought!

Long ago I gave up any hope that she would ever be mine. When I met Cynthia, I put all thoughts of Maggie behind. But now Cynthia was dead. My circumstances were much changed, and maybe Maggie's, too.

"Yes sir, Longhurst," I said. "I do believe Montana is exactly where I need to go."

"Then, go you will. Of course, you got to consider one thing. There'll be more than just Maggie Upchurch up in Montana. There'll be Fiddler Smith and Big Jim, too."

"Maybe, if they make it that far before one finds and kills the other. And even if they do, what does it matter? Montana's a big place. I doubt I'll lay eyes again on either one of them."

Part Two

BACK TO MONTANA

Chapter 13

It was good to travel with a friend again, good to be on the open trail, good to be riding toward the place where lived a lady I had loved and perhaps would love again. Twice in my life I had known what it was to love a fine woman and see that woman taken from me. Perhaps now it would be different. My dreams were big ones again.

The trail we followed northward was an old cattleman's-route. To the west rose the high Rockies, sun-glinting and magnificent; to the east lay the vast plains, stretching across Nebraska, Iowa, reaching over into Illinois. Days passed quickly, miles trailed off behind us. Now Cheyenne was distant, Walden City even more so. That unpleasant interlude in my life seemed dead and gone. A new time had come. Montana had until recently symbolized a finished interlude as well; now it symbolized the future. I hoped that there I would find the peaceful, settled life that had always eluded me.

From time to time I would think of Fiddler Smith and Vera Ann. Probably they had come this way—with Big Jim following. The more I thought about it, the more a sense of distress overtook my happiness. I had reason enough to be angry at Fiddler, given his abandonment of me the night he burned Big Jim's saloon. And, if Fiddler had in fact murdered Big Jim's family back in the Independent Army days, he was a more evil man than I would have ever thought. If Big Jim caught up with him, Fiddler would deserve any punishment that resulted.

Vera Ann Walden, however, was another story. She was no angel, as her illegitimate pregnancy sufficed to show, but beyond her promiscuity I knew of no fault in her. There was the distressing thing: If Big Jim caught up with Fiddler, he would also catch up with Vera Ann. And the odds were, she would fall victim to him right along with her unfortunately chosen partner.

I expressed this fear to Longhurst the day after we crossed the North Platte. He frowned, thoughtfully sniffed a pinch of snuff up his nose, and shook his head. "I got no answer for that one, McCan. It is a worrisome thought. But take heart—this here's a vast country. I'm betting that Big Jim will never find them."

"But he knows they're bound for Powderville," I replied. "If nothing else he'll probably find them there."

Longhurst shrugged. I could tell the thought of a pregnant woman being harmed, maybe killed, by a hardcase like Big Jim troubled him, but Longhurst tended not to worry long about what he couldn't control. I lacked that enviable trait; I tended to worry over everything. In silence I sent up a prayer for the safety of Vera Ann Walden, wondering if I would ever know its answer. It seemed unlikely that I would ever see that troubled woman again.

We crossed into the Montana country and headed toward Miles City. Some miles over the line, a couple of things happened that diverted our plans. First, Longhurst began to get sick. He had complained for the last two days of sore joints and a queasy stomach. Now he began vomiting everything he ate and drank, and he rode leaning over his saddle like a wounded man.

"You're in no shape to make Miles City," I said.

"I can make it," he answered. "Just keep riding."

So we rode, until the second obstacle met us the next morning, when Longhurst's horse threw a shoe after we crossed the Powder River.

"Got anything to fix it with?" I asked him.

"Nope. I appear to be a jinx, eh?"

I sighed. "Well, there's a town fifteen, twenty miles off. We'll just have to go there."

"What town is it?"

"You'd never guess."

He thought a moment, looked back at the river, then put on an expression of irony. "Powderville?"

"That's right."

He chuckled weakly. "Well, McCan, it looks like you might meet up with Fiddler Smith again after all."

"If he made it this far," I said. "Come on, let's go."

I let Longhurst ride my horse, since he was sick. As I led his limping mount, I wondered if in fact we would see Fiddler and Vera Ann in Powderville. Perhaps all this was intended to happen.

Maybe I would see them and be able to warn them about Big Jim—if he hadn't already caught up with them. After all, he left Cheyenne well before we did.

Longhurst was feeling much better by the time we reached Powderville. The sun had just edged down. The little settlement was well-lighted, a welcome sight for two weary travelers. I pointed out a little cafe that was sending out enticing smells of frying beef and baking biscuits.

Longhurst's appetite was back in a big way. We ordered a hearty meal and Longhurst ate like a starved refugee. I wasn't as hungry. Being in Powderville made me edgy; all I could think about was whether Fiddler and Vera Ann had made it here.

Across the dirt street a little saloon was doing middling business. I peered out the window, sipping my coffee as Longhurst put away a second round of biscuits and honey. Just as I drained off my last swallow, the wind shifted and carried noise from the saloon to my ears. I perked up when I heard the clear strains of fiddle music.

Longhurst heard it, too, and looked at me meaningfully. "You reckon?"

"It could be," I said, setting down the cup. "Guess I ought to go see, huh?"

"Guess so."

We paid, left, and walked across the street. The fiddle music was clearer now. So distinctive was its style that I knew even before entering the saloon that I had indeed found my old Walden City companion.

Fiddler stood in the corner, beside a broken-down piano, sawing the strings with vigor and sending up puffs of rosin dust that mixed with the smoke of his cigarette.

We went to the bar and ordered beers. Fiddler hadn't noticed me. I felt a strange impulse to leave before he saw me, but fought it down, feeling that perhaps this meeting was fated. The whole thing was peculiarly unsettling. There was comfort, at least, in knowing Fiddler was alive. Big Jim hadn't gotten him yet.

But what about Vera Ann? She was not here. I determined to find out about her, and so stood drinking my beer, staring straight at Fiddler and waiting for him to see me.

You've never heard as sour a fiddle drag as the one Fiddler Smith produced the moment his eyes met mine. Longhurst turned his head to hide his smile. It really was funny, as I think back on it, though at the time I didn't crack a smile. I kept my eyes focused straight on Fiddler's, taking a slow sip from my mug.

Somebody in the saloon gave a catcall. Fiddler ignored it and lowered his fiddle. He had stopped playing in midtune.

He glanced toward the door, licked his lips, then looked back at me. Resigning himself, he strode forward and joined me at the bar.

"Hello, McCan."

"Hello, Fiddler. I see you made it to Powderville."

"I made it."

"I'm glad. I was afraid something bad had happened to you. That happens sometimes, you know. A man can get hurt on the trail. Why, he might even get near-lynched by a mob that's mad because some fool burned down their watering hole."

Fiddler's face was as white as a sheet. "I owe you an apology, McCan. I shouldn't have hit you, and shouldn't have left you. I been worried about it ever since."

"Not worried enough to come back and check, I noticed."

He tried to swallow, but his throat must have been too dry. "I was drunk that night. I didn't know what I was doing. I was long gone from Walden City before it came to me that they might have found you lying out there."

"They found me. They came darn near to stringing me up. I'm lucky to be alive."

"I'm sorry. Really I am."

"Why didn't you come back, Fiddler? I thought you a better man than to run out on a friend. Or maybe I just thought I was your friend."

"Don't talk like that, McCan. You know I think the world of you. It was just the liquor, and being all crazy over Vera Ann. That's what did it."

"But you didn't come back. That's what galls me."

"I seen the smoke rising from the distance. I could see the light from the fire in the sky. I admit I was scared."

"They burned near the whole town, that mob. Burned it with Big Jim right at the head of it all. He was looking for you."

"Lord have mercy on me," Fiddler said. He leaned against the bar, laid down his fiddle and bow, and waved for a beer. As he drank it, his hands shook. Longhurst, seeing that this was not his affair, slipped off farther down the bar.

"Where's Vera Ann?" I asked

Fiddler looked pained. "Gone. She ran out on me."

"That right? How did it happen?"

"Out on the trail, it was. We were near the Black Hills. She told me the baby she's carrying wasn't mine, that she was already carrying it when she first met me."

"So I was right about her."

Fiddler grew angry at once. "Don't you talk bad about Vera Ann," he said. "I still care about that gal a mighty lot."

"Where is she now?"

"Still in the Black Hills. She said she had friends there, and made me take her over to Deadwood. I tried to talk her out of it. I told her I would marry her, raise that baby like my own." He shook his head and went red and moist in the eyes. "She wouldn't even listen to me. She shook me off like I was no more than a dog."

"So you came on to Powderville alone."

"Yeah."

"Did you find your brother?"

"I found him, all right. Found him in his grave." He wiped the back of his hand across his right eye. "He's been dead these three years, and I didn't even know it." He paused for a moment, looked away, then back at me again. "Why are you here, McCan? Did you come after me?"

"No. I'm heading up to Timber Creek and Upchurch. I've got some old friends to look up."

"Oh."

"Why'd you stay here, since your brother is dead?"

"A man has to stay somewhere. The fellow who runs the saloon gave me a fiddling job. Tips and free beer. Right now that's enough for me. There ain't nothing better worth doing out there, not with Vera Ann gone. I'm finding it hard to care much what happens to me now.''

I studied him silently. Though I was still mad as blazes at him, forgiveness was starting to slip in. Fiddler Smith seemed more worthy of pity than fury.

I gave a sigh of resignation. ''Well, I came out alive. You can rest your mind about that. Ike Walden wasn't as lucky.''

''What happened to Walden?''

''He's dead. Killed by that mob you stirred up. They blamed him for ordering the saloon burned. But it wasn't his fault, was it? It was you doing that on your own, trying to hurt Big Jim. Right?''

He lowered his head, ''Right.''

''You'd have been better off just to have shot that Indian instead of torching his building. He got out just fine, and now he's after you.''

''After me?''

''He found out where you were heading, and came after you. You owe some thanks to Vera Ann, Fiddler. She probably saved your life, diverting you off to the Black Hills when she did. I'm betting that Big Jim passed you by while you were there.''

Fiddler really looked scared now. He turned up his beer and didn't stop gulping until it was gone.

''Big Jim's after me?'' He said it as if trying to comprehend it. ''He was that set on finding me?''

''So I hear. That's what his partner told me when I saw him in a jail cell in Cheyenne.'' I took a softer tone. ''You got to consider he may still be looking for you, Fiddler. Watch out for him. If he finds you, he'll kill you.''

Fiddler nodded. He wore a blank, scared stare. "I thank you for the warning, McCan. God above, I'm sorry I done you like I did. Maybe I would have come back if I hadn't had Vera Ann to watch out for. Yeah, I would have come back—it's Vera Ann I was worried about."

Maybe it was true, or maybe it was just Fiddler looking for some way to justify to himself the wrong he had done me. It didn't matter now.

"Well, Fiddler, all's said that needs saying, as far as I'm concerned. Most likely our paths won't cross again. I forgive you for what you did." It took all my will to do it, but I stuck out my hand. "You watch out for yourself, hear? And keep a lookout for Big Jim."

"I will," he said. His handshake was trembly. "Bless your soul, Luke McCan. You're a better man than I'll ever be."

"There's none of us good men when it comes down to it, Fiddler. We're all just blind folks stumbling along as best we can."

When Longhurst and I left, Fiddler was drinking another beer. I gave him a long look from the door, figuring it to be the last time I would see him, then exited into the night.

Chapter 14

It's hard to describe my feelings when we rode into Miles City. My thoughts had lately been turned toward the future, but seeing this town again pulled me back into the past. Things had changed—the town was bigger, and somehow brighter—yet so much was the same. On main street stood the livery with its bow-shaped sign, the familiar blacksmith shop, the bakery, the Chinese laundry butted up against the meat market. My feelings ran counter to each other: I was home again, yet also a new-comer in a strange land.

Even in the bright sunlight I could feel ghosts of my past hovering all around me. Or maybe I was the ghost, visiting again the places I had haunted in life.

I looked for Maggie as I rode, though I had no reason to expect her to be in town. A question burned in my mind: Was Rodney Upchurch still alive?

Longhurst was in high spirits. He grinned at all we passed, and tipped his hat to the women. We were gritty and bearded from our long ride, so we found a hotel and checked ourselves in after stabling our horses at the livery. A barber's parlor next door offered baths, and we took advantage. The soapy water washed the dirt from our bodies and eased the aches of days in the saddle. So far, no one I had seen had given any indication of recognizing me.

I made conversation with the barber and found the answer I had been seeking.

"Rodney Upchurch? Oh, yeah—sad situation. The poor fellow passed away three weeks ago. I didn't know him, but they say he was a good man. I did know his father; he operated a big store right here in town for years."

Confirmation of Upchurch's death intensified my contradictory feelings. On the one hand it made me feel sad for Maggie, who surely was in grief. On the other hand, there's no denying that having my old rival out of the picture did open new opportunities for me.

"Who's running the big Upchurch store?" I asked.

"Maggie Upchurch, all alone. Quite a determined woman, that one. Pretty, too."

"Amen to that," I said beneath my breath. The barber heard me.

"You know Maggie Upchurch? I assumed you were a newcomer, sir."

"I am, in a way. But I lived here for a time, working for the Timber Creek Cattle Enterprise."

"You don't say? Well then, welcome back, Mr . . ."

"McCan. Luke McCan."

"I'll bet you've got lots of old friends to look up."

"I do—but don't spread word about me yet. I want to surprise people, you know."

Afterward, Longhurst said, "I thought you were in a big rush to find all your old buddies."

"I thought I was. Now that I'm here, it feels different. I want to settle in slow, not hurry anything."

"Maggie Upchurch in particular?"

"Yeah." I grinned self-consciously. "I guess I'm a little nervous about how she's going to react to seeing me. I might be the last person she wants to lay eyes on."

"Don't wait too long," Longhurst said. "She's a very marriageable woman right now. Somebody could steal her out from under your nose again. Heck, I might just do it myself!"

"You do, and I'll skin you. Stick to flirting with your saloon girls and leave Maggie to me."

Longhurst dug out his snuffbox. "Come on," he said. "We've got land and cattle to buy. Taylor Longhurst is ready to start ranching."

"Don't get yourself too worked up, Longhurst," I said. "It can take a long time to build up a cattle business."

My prediction, to Longhurst's delight, held about as much water as a bottomless bucket. Within three days he had scouted down a disgruntled small-time cattleman itchy to rid himself of both land and herd. He had suffered several strokes of bad fortune and felt pressed to return to Illinois to take care of ailing parents. Exactly one week after our arrival, Longhurst was passing money and signing papers in a lawyer's office—some of the money being mine, for I had decided to buy into the operation—

and we walked out onto Main Street as owners of what Longhurst dubbed the L&M Cattle Company.

It felt good to be part of the landed class. Of course, true to my nature, I had a thousand worries rolling around in my mind. I had gone at once from being a responsibility-free drifter to facing duties and risks. Longhurst and I would have to worry about weather, disease, rustlers, all the common threats facing cattlemen. And there were only the two of us to run the ranch, with little cash remaining to hire help. It would take time before we began making money. Within an hour of closing our transaction, I had already mentally mapped out a dozen potential roads to poverty, any one of which we might find ourselves on.

Longhurst, as usual, seemed to have no such worries. He knew less about the cattle business than I did, and felt sure that nothing but wealth lay ahead of us. As for our meager remaining cash, he was ready to spend a chunk of it on celebrating the founding of our enterprise.

I couldn't deny Longhurst that celebration, my thought being that we probably wouldn't be able to afford such frivolities for a long time afterward. That night we toured the Miles City saloons and dance halls. I was pleasantly surprised to find myself repelled rather than attracted by the gambling tables. Maybe this ranching investment was just what I had needed to steer me into a more stable course of life.

I met a couple of old acquaintances in one of the saloons. Neither was a close friend, but both found it big news that Luke McCan was back in the area and going into business. It would not take long now for word of my return to spread. Soon

Maggie would know I was back. I wondered how that would make her feel—if it would make her feel anything at all.

"It seems a prime time for you to go look Maggie up," Longhurst suggested. "Now you're a respectable man of business. She'll be impressed."

"I'll look her up soon," I said. "All in good time."

Two weeks went by and the good time never came. Partly it was because Longhurst and I were extremely busy, taking stock of the herd, repairing the dismal log ranch house that was now our home, and doing all the hundred other things required to revive a lagging ranch operation.

Our ranch house stood about midway between Rosebud and Miles City. The previous owner had let it, and the operation in general, run down considerably. The roof leaked, the walls were poorly chinked, and the dirt floor was uneven. By merit of my superior carpentry skills—and Longhurst's superior excuse-making—most of the repair work fell to me.

This kept me away from much human contact for many days. Though I griped enough about it to keep up a good front for Longhurst, I really didn't mind the isolation. For reasons I couldn't explain, I didn't feel the need for company. Some of it might have stemmed from my troubled times in Walden City. Some of it might have been because I still wasn't sure that I was ready to see Maggie. I was like the little storybook boy in London who longed to meet Father Christmas, then lagged back and hid his head in his mother's skirts when at last he met a man costumed as the character at a children's party.

As long as my reunion with Maggie was a dream, a thing as of yet not real, I could imagine it falling out the way I longed for it to. The real thing, in which Maggie's reaction would be controlled by herself, not my wishes, might be a far different affair.

My isolation was soon to end. Old friends, having heard I was in the area, began riding out to see me. Even bearish old Stewart Biggs, a veteran cowpoke who had tried to get my dander up when I was a greenhorn back at Timber Creek years ago, rode out to say hello and fill me in on news of the ranch. I could tell he wasn't happy there anymore; things had changed since the old days.

"Ever since we lost Dan Tackett and Abe Hunt, it's been a dee-cline, a steady dee-cline." That's the way he said it. "That little Iowa worm Henry Sandy is still there, running the place. He's losing money, so likely he'll be gone soon enough. Of course, I been telling myself that for the last two years, and he ain't gone yet." Biggs fidgeted. "I might just up and leave . . . if I had another good spread to go to work for."

None too subtle was Stewart Biggs. Unfortunately, I couldn't give him the answer he was fishing for. "Stewart, if I can ever roust enough work out of Longhurst to make a go of this place, I expect we'll have need of some good men. Right now, though, it's slim pickin's for hired work at the L&M."

He looked disappointed. "Well, then, I might come checking later—if you don't mind it."

"I'd be offended if you didn't. Thanks for coming to see me."

Biggs bowlegged it over to his waiting horse and

mounted with a loud wheeze of exertion. He was aging now; it made me sad.

"Oh!" he said. "I plumb forgot. Maggie Upchurch said to tell you hello. I was out by the Emporium before I come out here, and she sent the word."

I wondered if Biggs could see my shirt jumping from the pounding of my heart. "Tell her hello, too. How's she doing, now that her husband's gone?"

"Truth is, I think she's doing better than when he was living, even though it sounds a bad thing to say. She had to tend to him like he was a baby at the end. Now that he's gone, she can have some peace."

"I hope so." Biggs turned and began to ride away. I called to him and he wheeled again.

"Tell Maggie I'll be up her way in a day or two. I'll stop in the Emporium. I'd like to say hello."

Biggs touched his hat and nodded, then rode off. I watched his horse kicking up dust until it was far away. Entering the house, I looked myself over in the broken glass that served as our mirror. Unshaven, dirty, unshorn . . . I looked like I had just come off a long winter's line camp.

That night, over eggs and beef, I told Longhurst I'd not be working about the ranch the next day. I had things to do in Miles City.

"Like what?" He sounded grumpy; he knew that me away from the ranch would mean more work for him.

"Like getting a shave and a bath and some new clothes."

His brows went up. "Going up to Upchurch at last, I take it?"

"You got it right. I want to see that lady again. I've been too long a-waiting already."

Longhurst poked his fork at me. "Don't you up and get married on me and leave me to run this ranch alone."

"Run it? Run it broke, you mean."

"I think I'm doing a fair job so far!"

I grinned at him. "Reckon you are. Think you can handle it for a day without me?"

"Think you're pretty all-fired important, don't you! Of course I can handle it. But I mean it: Don't you go getting yourself married. Don't you do it. Hear?"

"I hear."

Chapter 15

In my time I've faced gunmen and rustlers, outlaws and lawmen. None of them ever put my nerves on edge nearly as much as the sight of the Upchurch Emporium when I rode over the slope and saw it gleaming in the sun on the flat below. The big white building hadn't changed a bit since last I saw it, except that what appeared to be a new storage room had been added on the west side, and the place was now surrounded by several more houses, stables, and such. There was no denying that the little Upchurch community had become a true town.

The house Rodney Upchurch had built for himself and the bride he had snatched from me was painted a clean light brown now, and looked smaller for it. There was Maggie's flower garden, still brown and winter-dried; there were her carefully nurtured young fruit trees. Across the backyard stretched a clothesline, some of Maggie's dresses flapping on it in the cool wind. Even from this distance I recognized two as dresses Maggie had worn during our courting days. I had to smile. Despite the success of the Upchurch Emporium,

Maggie remained a true daughter of the frontier: unwasteful, unprideful, frugal. She would wear a dress until it was threadbare, then rip it into rag strips and use them to make rugs. There was no room for waste in plains life.

Nudging spurs against horseflesh, I began my long, circling descent to the Emporium, feeling so nervous I had to laugh at myself. All I was doing, after all, was saying hello to an old friend. I wasn't riding down to propose marriage.

Who was I fooling? The possibility of eventual marriage was at the very heart of all I was doing. This first reunion with Maggie could prove a door to a bright future. That door had been closed in my face when Maggie married Rodney Upchurch and then again when Cynthia died. This time, heaven willing, it would open. The choice would be Maggie's.

An expensive carriage shiny with varnish and polish sat in front of the Emporium. I tied my mount to the hitchpost and looked the rig over in admiration. Maggie's store was drawing some big-money customers these days.

At the door I took a deep breath and forced myself to walk straight in. And there she was: Maggie, as pretty as ever.

She didn't notice me, for she was embroiled in seemingly intense conversation with two well-dressed men. These fellows had big-city money written all over them; they surely accounted for that fine rig outside. From their bearing and manner, it was clear that theirs was a business visit. Slipping over behind a display of fabric rolls, I remained hidden from Maggie's view, not wanting to unnerve her by a sudden appearance in the midst of what looked to be an important conversation.

I wasn't trying to listen to the talk, but the taller of the two men had one of those voices that crawls through the air and reaches every corner of a room even when softly spoken. I detected very quickly that these men were proposing to buy out the store.

"Mrs. Upchurch, I hope you'll reconsider," the tall one said. "A young widow such as yourself needs to be free of burdening duties such as this store imposes." The man's voice, though still low, had a quality that told me he and Maggie were in tense disagreement.

"Mr. Bell, I've been accustomed not only to operating this store, but doing so with an invalid husband who required nearly constant attention. Now that he's passed on, God rest him, the burden of my duties is lighter, not heavier. This store is my livelihood and I have no desire to sell it."

A short pause. "Mrs. Upchurch, I want this store. I've made you a good offer and I cannot understand why you won't take it!"

"I've explained myself clearly, I think."

Another pause—then I almost jumped out of my boots when the lanky Mr. Bell pounded the nearby countertop so hard that it rattled the candy jars on the far end. I came around from behind the on-end fabric rolls and saw Maggie stepping back, a look of alarm on her face. Bell swore in a most ungentlemanly manner.

Seeing him talk so to Maggie flew all over me. I strode forward.

"I think you'd best leave, friend," I said.

Three faces turned to me, all bearing expressions of surprise—Maggie's most of all. Bell lifted his hands and turned again to Maggie, keeping me in the corner of his eye. "Look, Mrs. Upchurch, I apologize. I'm a man of hot temper and it got the best of me."

"That's a good apology," I said. "Fine job. Now get on out of here."

Bell's partner stepped forward and said, "Now, listen here . . ." Bell put a hand on his shoulder and stopped him. Together they walked out. Bell was about to slam the door, but thought better of it and caught it before it hit. He eased it shut. A few moments later the fancy buggy clattered away.

"Hello, Maggie," I said, smiling at her.

She looked at me like I was foulness on legs, "Luke McCan, how dare you walk in here out of the blue and interfere with my business? Who do you think you are, anyway? My champion? I'm perfectly capable of dealing with my own affairs myself, Mr. McCan!"

She spun on her heel and stomped back to the little office at the back of the store, entered, and pounded the door shut. I was left speechless, alone in the midst of the big store.

A moment later anger came. I wheeled, and stomped back to the entrance. I wasn't as restrained as the last man to exit this door: I slammed it as hard as I could, hard enough to make sure Maggie Carrington Upchurch heard it back in her office.

She didn't seem surprised to see me when she emerged from the store that evening. I was leaning against a tree, smoking and waiting for her, for my anger had cooled—as I hoped hers had as well. She smiled and slowly shook her head as she approached. Time hadn't changed her at all; there wasn't another day of age in that perfect oval face, still girlishly freckled. Her dark hair did not frame her face as I remembered it. She wore it pulled up and tied with a plain ribbon—a merchantess's concession to practicality, yet it did not diminish her attractiveness one bit.

"Luke," she said, drawing near and extending her hand. "It's good to see you again."

I took her hand in both of mine—it was marvelous to touch her again after all this time—and gently squeezed it. "It's good to see you, too, Maggie. Reckon I picked just the wrong way to say my hello earlier today."

She smiled a healing smile. "I was on edge—it was me who was wrong, not you. I know you were just trying to help. That Bell man has been after me to sell out to him since just after Rodney's burial. Maybe now he'll leave me alone at last."

"Well, if he doesn't, you just let me know and . . ." I stopped. "Doing it again, aren't I? I can't seem to get it through my head that you're able to take care of yourself."

"I have no choice."

"I heard about that. You've got my condolences, Maggie. I know it's a hard thing to lose someone you love."

We walked together and talked for the next hour. She told me of the difficult long months of Upchurch's alternating improvements and declines; I told her about my time in Missouri and the loss of Cynthia. Strange, how easy it was to talk to her about Cynthia.

She was fascinated with the story of Walden City and Fiddler Smith, though the latter portions horrified her. "You might have been killed,

Luke!'' she said—and she said it like it was an important matter to her.

"I might have been, but I wasn't. I'm mighty glad, too. I would have missed the chance to see you again.''

"I'm glad you came, Luke. And I wish you and Mr. Longhurst the best of luck on your new ranch.''

"Thank you, Maggie.'' We stood silently, looking at each other until it felt uncomfortable. "Maggie . . . you mind if I come back sometime to see you again?''

"I hope you will.''

"Good. Good. I'll be back, then. Well . . . good-bye for now.''

"Good-bye, Luke.''

I sang all the way back to the ranch.

Two days later I was in Miles City buying nails and groceries, when I looked across the street and saw a sight that made me drop my bundles on the boardwalk. A woman was walking there, carrying a bag and looking as sad as she was pregnant. It was none other than Vera Ann Walden.

I found nothing pleasant in seeing her. Every bad memory from Walden City flooded back, along with new concerns. Why was she here? Fiddler had said she had intended to remain in the Black Hills with friends.

It would have been easy to let her walk on past, to ride back to the ranch, and forget about her. Yet I couldn't do that . . . especially not with her looking as forlorn as she did. If ever I had seen a woman in need of help, it was Vera Ann at that moment.

So I laid my bundles in the wagon, walked out onto the street, and called to her. She turned, surprised to hear her name called, and watched me cross to meet her. Surely she was as taken aback by the sight of me as I was in seeing her.

"Luke!" Her voice sounded weak and shaky.

"Vera Ann, I'm surprised to see you here. I thought you were in Black Hills."

"I was, then I had to—But how do you know about where I was? Nobody here . . . knows . . . oh, I'm so weak . . ."

"Vera Ann!"

I caught her as she started to fall. Her face was as white as milk. It made for quite a scene, me grasping at a fainting pregnant woman right on the sunny central street of Miles City. Several people came running up, alarmed. Is she all right? What's happened? Did you hurt her?

What had happened was that Vera Ann had fainted from hunger. I fanned her awake right there on the boardwalk and she admitted that she had not eaten a bite for two days.

"Well, you'll eat today," I said. "Come on— let's get you over to the cafe and put some victuals down you."

Despite her obvious hunger, Vera Ann ate slowly. Her hand shook every time she lifted her fork. Here was a woman who had been through hard times.

"Where did you see Fiddler?" she asked me, a desperate edge on the query.

"In Powderville. It wasn't a planned meeting, but I'm glad it happened. I was able to warn him that he was in danger."

"Danger? What kind of danger?"

"There's a big Sioux Indian after him . . . at least, there was. I don't know the situation now. It's an old enemy of Fiddler's, not to mention being one of the owners of the saloon Fiddler burned down outside Walden City."

"Burned? What are you talking about?"

I was amazed. Vera Ann didn't even know what had happened outside Walden City that night—either that, or she was putting on one convincing act.

I realized abruptly that there was one detail she could not know, and needed to: the death of her father. My strength drained away; I sank back in my chair, dreading what I had to reveal.

"Vera Ann," I said gently, "there are some things you must know about. One thing in particular I have to tell you, and it's not easy: Your father is gone. He was killed the night you left Walden City."

Vera Ann's eyes went red and moist. A tear trailed down her cheek and she lowered her head, saying not a word.

"I'll start at the beginning and tell it straight through," I said. "That's the easiest way to make sense of it all."

I laid out the story: the torching of the saloon, my abandonment by Fiddler, the destruction of Walden City by Big Jim's mob, and the defiant death of Ike Walden. She stared at her plate as I told it, asking no questions, making no comments.

"Now I want to hear what's happened to you since I saw you last," I said to her. "Why are you in Miles City?"

She spoke in a quiet, slightly trembling voice. Some of what she said I already knew. She had become pregnant sometime before Fiddler Smith and I had arrived in Walden City. Knowing her stern father would deal with her harshly over the pregnancy, she tried to lure either Fiddler or me to take her away before the truth was known. Fiddler had taken the bait, and she had sunk her hook deeper into him by telling him, falsely, that the child she carried was his.

Once far away from Walden City, however, the guilt of that lie had weighed on her, combined with a growing sense of doubt about whether she really wanted to spend her life with Fiddler Smith as her mate. She confessed to him the truth about her pregnancy, then made up the story about friends in the Black Hills as a way of getting him to set her free. He did so, however reluctantly, and took Vera Ann to Deadwood.

Life as a lone, unmarried, pregnant woman in a little western Gomorrah like Deadwood had proven far more hellish than anything Vera Ann could have imagined. She started out with a fair stash of the money she and Fiddler had taken from Ike Walden the night of their flight, but it didn't last long. What wasn't spent was stolen, and before long Vera Ann found herself with only three options: starvation, prostitution, or finding Fiddler Smith again.

The last option had been the most appealing. With charm and the last of her cash, she convinced a wagoner to take her from Deadwood to Powderville, where she hoped to find Fiddler still visiting his much-talked-about brother. But the brother was dead and Fiddler wasn't there. He had been there, folks told her, but he had left abruptly after talking to a couple of drifters who showed up to get some farrier work done.

With tearful pleading Vera Ann had convinced the wagoner to take her on one final ride, this time up to Miles City. There, she hoped, she would find Fiddler, or at least some other person who would help her out. She had never dreamed, she said, that that person would be me. She had never expected to meet Luke McCan again.

I reached across the table and patted her hand. "I'm glad I found you," I said. "No woman should have to go through what you have, especially while she's carrying a child."

"What can I do, Luke?" she asked. "I still have no place to stay." Her eyes became soft and sincerely pleading—no deception, no conniving this time. "Can I stay at your ranch? At least for a while?"

"That wouldn't do, Vera Ann. People talk, you know. But there's a place I can take you, a lady I know who I feel sure will be glad to take you in and give you all the help she can. She's a good woman, a friend of mine, and her name is Maggie Upchurch."

Chapter 16

She was just as kind and generous about it as
I could have ever hoped," I was telling Longhurst.
"Maggie took Vera Ann in without a moment's
hesitation, and before I left she was talking about
new clothes and fixing up one of the extra rooms
and getting a crib for when the baby comes." I
nodded my head admiringly. "Maggie's quite a
woman, Longhurst. Quite a woman. Everybody
talking about how fine she is, taking in a 'soiled
girl' like Vera Ann. That's how I heard somebody
putting it."

Longhurst took a snort of snuff, sneezed, and
said, "Vera Ann must think she's died and gone to
heaven."

"It'd take a lot less than heaven to make her
happy, with all she's been through," I said. "You
know, it's nigh as much her fault as Fiddler's, all
the trouble that happened at Walden City, but I
can't seem to hold my anger at her over it. I just
feel sorry for her, mostly."

Longhurst aimed a finger at me. "That's your
very problem, McCan! Always pitying folks too
much and getting messed up in their problems.

You'd get by better if you'd learn to mind your own business and stay out of everybody else's.''

Before the next week was out, Longhurst had proven himself unable to live up to his own standards—and in the process gave me one more occasion to marvel at how things that you think are over and done with can rise up again before your eyes. Running into Fiddler at Powderville and encountering Vera Ann in Miles City had already stripped away my assurance that the Walden City affair was behind me.

On the following Tuesday morning, Longhurst rode into Miles City to talk to another cattleman about a possible small-scale land lease. I spent my day on the range with the herd; that evening I came loping slowly in, thinking about Maggie and feeling good about the world. The sun was setting and my stomach was grumbling for a feeding of beef and biscuits, our most usual nightly menu.

I dismounted and led my horse around to the little barn to feed it grain. Stretching to relieve saddle cramp, I fished out my fixings and began rolling a smoke. It was one of those rare moments when life is moving at the most perfect, lazy speed, pressures and worries a long way off.

I lit the cigarette and looked up through the smoke to see Longhurst barreling in at top speed. His horse was lathered and panting. The evening light was casting a strange shadow across the left side of Longhurst's face—then I saw it wasn't a shadow, but a fresh bruise.

''What the devil . . .''

''McCan, I'm glad I found you. There's trouble.'' Longhurst swung down off his perch and ran the horse into the corral without unsaddling it.

"So I see—and from that shiner, I'd say you found your way into the middle of it."

"This is serious business, McCan. It's Fiddler Smith."

"What?"

"You heard me—Fiddler. He's in Miles City, or was until he ran out. It's a good thing for him he ran, too, for he came nigh to getting himself killed."

"You sure it was Fiddler?"

" 'Course I'm sure. I seen him with my own eyes, didn't I?"

Blast it all. I had hoped Fiddler Smith wouldn't come crawling back through my life again. Why would he be in Miles City? I had a suspicion that whatever his reason, it had to do with Vera Ann.

"So what happened?"

"Well, I'd gone into a saloon to wash the dust out of my throat about the shank of the afternoon, when out across the street I heard a ruckus. I downed my beer and went out to see about it— reckon I can't get the lawman out of my blood— and what did I see but Fiddler Smith with a knife out, swinging it at a couple of big gents who were yelling and cussing at him."

"I didn't know what it was about or who was in the right or wrong, but I couldn't just stand there. I took off and started out to help Fiddler, when he spins, slashes one of the others across the upper arm, then kicks up like a saloon dancer and boots me right in the eye. That's right—boot! Them lanky legs have a right wide stretch, I'm here to tell you. I suppose he thought I was coming to hurt him instead of help.

"I went down like a feed sack, and Fiddler

jumped right over me and headed for his horse. He rode out before anybody could stop him."

"Them two he had been fighting with came over and asked me if I was all right—I guess they figured, just like Fiddler, that I had been going to take their side in the fight. I asked them what it was about, and they said this one-eared gent had come into a saloon all drunk and rowdy, demanding to know where he could find his woman and Luke McCan. He said her name was Vera Ann Walden and he'd heard saloon gossip up around Glendive about Luke McCan taking in some pregnant female. I reckon he figured out it was Vera Ann."

"The story I get is that Fiddler's hot to take up with Vera Ann again. How he feels about your part of things I don't know. I'm thinking he may believe you've stole his woman, and may try to hurt you for it."

"Fiddler Smith's a fool," I said. "I wish he'd ride off as far away from here as he could go. Well, go on, Longhurst. Did the law go after him?"

Longhurst's face was lighted orange by the setting sun; his expression became even more intense. "Now, there's the most loco part of all, and let me tell you, it sends a chill right up my backbone! A deputy came sauntering over shortly after Fiddler rode off, and found out what had happened. I asked him if he was going to go after Fiddler and he said no, he didn't think he would. All he'd likely do if he caught Fiddler would be run him out of town, and he'd already gone off on his own, so there would be no point to that. But here's the thing that perked my attention: This deputy, as he's turning around, says; 'I've already had my fill of fooling with one-eared troublemakers today, anyhow.'

"First thing I thought of when he said that was this Big Jim character. I was putting two and two together, you see: if Fiddler Smith was about Miles City, then maybe Big Jim was, too. Maybe he'd still been looking for him and had followed him, you know. Sure enough, when I asked the deputy about it, he says this other one-eared man was a big ugly Indian, and he'd been going about town, scaring folks and asking real loud about a man named Smith, who he'd followed in from Glendive."

"Lord have mercy, Longhurst! You think Fiddler knows Big Jim is this close to him?"

"That I can't tell you. But I sure knew you'd want to know about this, in case Fiddler shows up gunning for you. Hell, he could lead Big Jim right here!"

"Or worse, he could find out where Vera Ann is and lead him up to Maggie's. Longhurst, do you know where Fiddler headed after he rode out of town?"

"No . . . but I can tell you that on the way here, I saw a durn big campfire burning along that little crick a couple of miles back."

My mind flashed back to that first night when Fiddler and I had shared camp, and how he had commented about never being able to abide a camp without a roaring fire. "It might be him—I'll go and see."

"You think that's smart, McCan? He might have designs to harm you, thinking you took Vera Ann and all."

"So he might—which means I'd rather find him than let him find me. Besides, whatever he may think about me, I want to warn him about Big Jim.

I won't do to him what he did to me when he left me for that mob to eat alive. Lord knows I hope I'm a better man than that.''

"You're too good a man—so good you'll get yourself killed one of these days. But if you're set on going, let me get a fresh mount and go with you.''

"Get the fresh mount, all right, but don't go with me. You've got to head up to Upchurch, fast as you can, and see to Maggie and Vera Ann until I can get there myself. I don't want Fiddler showing up there with them alone in that house and luring Big Jim to them.''

Even stubborn old Longhurst saw the sense in that and did not argue. We worked quickly, preparing for our divergent rides. What had happened to that lazy evening I had been enjoying? It had vanished. The night now was heavy with threat and cooled by an urgent wind that said hurry, hurry, get going before the trouble that always follows Fiddler Smith catches up with you . . . or with Maggie.

The night was cool against my face as I rode toward the wooded creek, praying it in fact was Fiddler's camp Longhurst had seen . . . and praying that if it was Fiddler's, I would reach him before Big Jim did.

The fire was somewhat burned down by the time I drew in sight of the camp; still, its flames danced hot in the night breeze. I looked for the silhouette of a human form about the blaze and saw nothing. Dismounting, I unbooted my Winchester and crept forward, wondering if I should hail the camp and risk Fiddler shooting me in anger, or come in secretly. Either way had its dangers.

I chose the latter option, partly because the closer I drew, the more unsettled and uncertain I felt. Something was wrong here. The atmosphere didn't feel quite right. Trouble was about—or maybe already had come and gone.

Don't let me find him dead, I silently prayed. Don't let Big Jim have already gotten to him.

Why did I care? I didn't know. Fiddler Smith was no true friend of mine . . . but I did care. I didn't want to see a man I had ridden and worked with murdered by the same big savage that had almost taken my own life.

There, by the fire . . . a dark heap. Maybe a bed-roll. Maybe a body.

Heart driving in my chest, I advanced. The wind moved the fire, sent sparks flying, made the circle of light dance and play over the mysterious heap that held my attention. It did look like a man now, a man in his blankets. Maybe he was sleeping— but if he was, why was there no motion of breath?

"Fiddler?" I said softly. "Fiddler, is that you?"

I kicked the blankets. Empty. Before I heard any sound, I knew I wasn't alone. Someone was behind me, and close. I spun on my heel and caught the flashing vision of a face not a yard from mine. Something swept down and struck the side of my head; I collapsed.

In that brief moment that I had seen the face, I knew what a terrible error I had made in coming into this camp. The face had been that of a big man, scarred and dark and missing an ear. The face of Big Jim.

Chapter 17

The next thing I was aware of was lying on my back, arms and legs outstretched. When I tried to move, I couldn't. My wrists and ankles felt like they were held in too-tight vises. Twisting my head, I saw that I was tied to four stout pegs driven into the earth. My head pounded in rhythm with the flickering of the big fire. So close was I to the blaze that sweat rolled off me; I was nearly being roasted alive.

Big Jim appeared above me, grinning down like a devil in a child's nightmare. He knelt, his swarthy face coming so near mine I could taste the foul breath blowing across his yellowed teeth.

"Looks like I caught me one of 'em, anyway," he said. "You're McCan."

"Let me go, Big Jim," I said in a gravelly voice. "You have no cause to hold me like this."

"Like hell!" he declared. "You got away from me once. Now you won't get away."

"What are you going to do to me?"

"Maybe nothing. Maybe you'll talk and tell Big Jim what he needs to know and I'll let you go."

That seemed unlikely; Big Jim didn't look the

sort to have an ounce of mercy in him. I felt like a fool, blundering into his camp as I had. In my zeal to find Fiddler, I had overlooked the possibility that my search would yield up the wrong man.

He leaned even closer. Firelight glittered on the ugly scar-nub where his ear had been, and on the ragged thing that once had been a nose. "You tell me where I can find Fiddler Smith and maybe I'll turn you loose."

"I don't know where he is."

"You know—you're his partner!"

"Not anymore. I haven't been his partner since Walden City."

He hit me so hard I fainted. When I came around again, he was kneeling on the other side of me, placing a flat stone beneath my bound left hand.

"What are you doing?"

"Nothing, if you talk."

"I told you—I don't know where Fiddler is!"

He lifted another stone, one almost as big as my head. "See if this helps you remember," he said. Then he brought down the stone.

I felt pain like I had never known, heard a mashing, snapping sound as he crushed my hand. I sent up a scream and almost passed out again.

"The next one will hurt even more," he said. "You talk to Big Jim now."

"I don't know . . . where he is . . ."

The stone came down again, and I did pass out. When I awakened, my hand had no feeling at all, and in a burst of panic I wondered if he had cut it off. Twisting my head, I was first relieved, then horrified. My hand was still there, but it was a pulpy, shattered thing, broken and bleeding. The numbness went away when I saw what he had done to me, and great throbs of pain rolled up my left arm.

"Where's Fiddler Smith?" Big Jim asked again.

"I swear to God above . . . I don't know."

"You like to hurt, McCan? I hope you do, because I haven't even started to make you hurt yet."

I closed my eyes and saw faces before me—people I had known and loved. Old friends from long past like Bill and Bob Webster, Caleb and Jerusha Black, Dan Tackett and Abe Hunt; my sister Martha . . . and my lost Cynthia. Then Maggie . . . and with her image came a burst of will. I had to get through this alive, to make sure that Big Jim never did to Maggie the sorts of things he was doing to me. I wished I had never taken Vera Ann to Maggie, for Vera Ann would draw Fiddler to where she was, and where Fiddler went, Big Jim would follow.

He was at my feet now, pulling off my right boot. I struggled and prayed toward the dark sky, asking for rescue, for whatever mercy God could grant a man who usually ignored him. I would have prayed for death, but death would wipe out any chance I might ever have to see to Maggie's safety. Maggie . . . I forced my mind to concentrate on her image. For Maggie I would have to endure Big Jim's tortures, and somehow come through alive.

I lifted my head and saw him at the fire, raising a burning brand. He was going to put fire to my bare foot. I tried to close my eyes and shut out the sight, but my eyes wouldn't obey me. I watched in terror as he began to kneel, a broad grin on his face.

I bit my lip, determined not to scream again, no matter what he did. And I didn't scream. I laughed instead, for from the brush beside the camp clearing, suddenly came a figure that I was certain was a guardian angel, sent in answer to my prayer . . . except it struck me as peculiar that this guardian angel carried a rifle, wore dirty clothing and a battered derby, and looked for all the world like Fiddler Smith. Apparently I fainted again, for all I can recall from the next moments is the sound of a shot, the noise of grappling, the shouting of most unangelic curses, then a second shot.

The face above me now was not ugly, like Big Jim's, but beautiful. Lean, whiskered, homely, single-eared—but beautiful beyond any face I had ever seen. Cold steel touched my right wrist and I felt my bonds being cut. He moved down to my feet and freed them, then to my shattered left hand. I heard him exclaim in horror at the sight of it; when he cut the bonds on that side, I felt a new wave of pain and almost fainted again.

"You're all right now, McCan," Fiddler Smith's voice said. "He's gone now and you're all right."

"Dead . . . is he dead?"

"Not dead, just run off. He will be dead soon. I'm going after him."

"Fiddler, is that you?"

"Sure as shooting. Sure as shooting. God, I'm glad I found you, McCan. He was going to . . ."

I faded out again and heard no more. When I awakened, the fire had burned down to embers and the camp was empty except for me. I lay still for a long time, my left hand pumping agony up my arm with every beat of my pulse. Slowly I sat up, then rose, and with my head swimming, I staggered to where I had left my horse. It was still there.

Somehow I managed to get into the saddle. Leaning over my saddle horn, my shattered hand pressed to my belly, I rode.

It was no longer dark, and beneath me was a soft feather tick, not the hard earth of Big Jim's camp. Sunlight poured in through a window to my right, and I didn't hurt anymore. After five minutes of staring at the ceiling, I slowly turned my head to the left and saw my hand, splinted and bound tightly in crisp white cloth.

A door opened and a slump-shouldered man with white hair and a pale face came to my bedside. "Hello, son," he said. "My name is Arnold York. I'm a doctor."

"You didn't cut it off."

"What's that?"

"You didn't cut off my hand."

He smiled with one side of his mouth, the other apparently stiffened by apoplexy. "No, I didn't. I thought it might prove useful to you to keep it."

"I feared I'd lose it."

"What happened to you, son?"

"An Indian. He tied me down and smashed my hand."

The doctor's eyes widened. "You're telling me there's some sort of Indian trouble about? I've heard of nothing like that."

"Just one Indian. He thought I knew something he wanted to know." I closed my eyes and smiled. "I feel good, Doc."

"You ought to. I've got you so opiated you ought to be floating on the brink of heaven."

"Where am I?"

"Miles City. This is my office."

"How'd I get here?"

"You rode in about sunrise. You were in a bad way. You've been sleeping all day."

"I want to sleep some more."

"Go ahead. It's the best thing for you—but drink some water first. You're dried out."

I managed a few sips. Drug-induced weariness began to crawl over me; as I drifted off again, I thought of Maggie, Vera Ann, and Longhurst, and wondered if all was well with them. Then I remembered Fiddler, heading off into the night to kill Big Jim. None of the thoughts brought me worry, for the doctor's medicines had robbed me of the ability to fret over anything. It was a blessed, needed relief.

By the next morning, pain was with me again—and so was Longhurst. He was at my bedside when I awakened.

"McCan, are you all right?" Longhurst's usual teasing tone was absent; he looked sincerely worried about me. I found it gratifying.

"I'll live, or so the doctor says. How much use of this hand I'll have I don't yet know. How's Maggie?"

"Fine. I rode like the devil after you sent me off and got to her in good time. Fiddler never showed up, and neither did Big Jim. Now tell me what happened with you."

I filled him in. Telling the story brought it all back clearly and made me realize how close to a slow and painful death I had come. Fiddler Smith truly had proven to be my guardian angel. Any hard feelings I had toward him were gone now; he had more than made up for abandoning me to that saloon mob outside Walden City.

"What I don't know is what happened between Fiddler and Big Jim after I rode off," I said. "Fiddler went off swearing to track him down and kill him."

"I'll see what I can find out," Longhurst said. "If there was a killing, there'll be a body, and those usually have a way of turning up, in my experience. The thing for you to do now is to not worry about anything but getting healed up."

"I want to see Maggie."

"She'll want to see you, too. When I told her you'd gone off looking for Fiddler Smith, she got fretful. But she doesn't know yet about you being hurt. I didn't know, either, until I rode back down to find out about you. When you weren't at the ranch, I came into town and asked around until I traced you down."

"Go back to her, Longhurst. Tell her I'm fine, and I'll be up to see her at first chance."

"I will. Reckon running the L&M Ranch is going to have to take a back seat for a few days, huh?"

"Reckon so."

"I'll be back to see you. You rest. The doctor tells me he's going to let you go soon, so you be patient, hear?"

Longhurst left. I lay there wishing I had thought to ask him to roll a cigarette for me, for I couldn't manage it myself with one hand bandaged up. In all my days on roundups, I had never learned the near-essential cowboy skill of rolling a smoke one-handed.

The doctor let me go the next afternoon, with stern instructions not to try to use my injured hand until

he gave the say-so. Maggie wanted me to come
back to Upchurch to continue my rest, and tempt-
ing though that sounded, I had to turn her down.
My place was at the ranch, far too neglected these
past days. So from Miles City we rode out to the
L&M. Maggie sat close to me on the wagon seat,
gently holding my injured hand in hers. The nightmare I had been through in Big Jim's camp seemed
minor compared with the happiness and hope for
the future that Maggie's unveiled concern gave me.

Vera Ann, for some reason, was silently tearful
and said nothing to me at all. As for Longhurst, he
looked weary and solemn all the way. I attributed
that to his extensive back-and-forth travel between
Miles City and Upchurch, but when we were at the
ranch, he pulled me aside and gave me news that
explained both his somber manner and Vera Ann's
emotional state.

"Yesterday I found where Big Jim's camp had
been," he told me. "I scouted around, looking for
sign of what might have happened after you got
away. Not a quarter-mile off, I found where they
must have met up again and fought. There was
blood on the ground." He stopped a moment and
swallowed. "And an ear."

I gaped, "An ear . . ."

"Yes. A white man's ear. No bodies—just the
ear."

I had to sit down. "So Big Jim got Fiddler instead of Fiddler getting him." The thought saddened me. "You figure Fiddler is dead?"

"I do. Most likely Big Jim hid the corpse somewhere. I guess cutting off the ear was his way of
marking the job done. The only thing I can't figure
is why he didn't take it with him. It seems the kind

of thing a man like that would do, you know.''

"Vera Ann's taking it hard?''

"Real hard. I think she's decided she liked Fiddler Smith a lot more than she had thought.''

"I know the feeling,'' I replied. "I really do.'' I stood and took a deep breath. "Fiddler wasn't a saint, but it's sad to me to think of him dead, especially after saving my life like he did.''

"What's done is done, McCan. We can take some comfort, at least, in all that trouble being over now. With Fiddler gone, that should be the last we see of Big Jim, and for that we can all say good riddance. Now come on—let's cook these women some supper.''

PART THREE

FIDDLER'S RETURN

Chapter 18

In every man's life there are many occasions when nothing goes as it should and every plan and dream shatters. Much more rare are those times when the dreams come true and the plans become reality, as if by magic. Rare times—but they do come, once, maybe twice, in the life of every man. The weeks following my encounter with Big Jim were such a time for me.

I suppose it was a new awareness of my mortality, prompted by my ordeal, that led me to evaluate my life and opportunities. Already my love for Maggie was fully reborn; now it blossomed. Beyond a doubt I knew that I wanted her for my wife, just as I had years ago. In those days she had seen me as only a friend. Now, I hoped, she would see me as more.

I remembered the frustration of watching her being taken from me the first time largely because I had assumed too much and acted too slowly. This time I wouldn't make that mistake. A mere month after my painful brush with Big Jim, I asked Maggie to become my wife . . . and she said yes.

Maggie's marriage ceremony to Rodney Upchurch had been a massive outdoor affair, appropriate to his station as a successful merchant. We opted for a quieter, smaller ceremony. In a tiny shingled chapel a few miles from the Emporium, I stood straight and proud with Maggie, Longhurst "best-manning it," to use his terminology, at my side. A few words from the preacher, and suddenly Luke McCan was transformed from a lonely, gambling drifter to the husband of the prettiest lady on the plains of Montana.

We returned to the Emporium after the ceremony, to enjoy a small, unpretentious reception. Longhurst meandered over and congratulated me, though in a downcast way. I pressed him to find what was wrong. "How the blazes am I supposed to run a cattle operation with my partner living a dang forty million miles away and all preoccupied with his sweetheart?" he asked me.

"You're exaggerating things just a little, Longhurst. You're going to find life easier, not harder."

"Huh! I'd like to believe that one!"

"Believe it. Maggie's a woman of some money, and she's offered to bolster up the ranch until things start ticking on their own—in other words, Longhurst, you can go hire yourself Stewart Biggs and maybe even a couple more to do your work for you."

Such a look of surprise and relief I've never seen. Longhurst kissed my bride, not bothering to ask my permission, and wandered off to spike the punch, take a few snorts of snuff, and talk boisterously to Vera Ann. She hardly said a word back to him and didn't even smile. Not that I had expected her to; she had been a sad young woman of late, and with good reason. She had first lost a father, then also the man who wanted to be her husband. All that lay before her now was a struggle to birth and raise a child without a husband to support her. I can't honestly say I liked Vera Ann, but I did feel sorry for her.

The demands of the L&M ranch and the Upchurch Emporium together made a honeymoon for Maggie and me impossible. Our first night was spent in Maggie's house behind the Emporium (now my house, too—the idea took some getting used to) in a new bedroom built on the east end. Maggie and I had agreed it would be best to begin our married life in a chamber unshadowed by personalities and sorrows now past. I wouldn't begrudge Maggie her fond memories of Rodney Upchurch, any more than she would begrudge my memories of Cynthia. Even so, we saw no reason to let those memories become a potential burden on our relationship.

These were happy days, if busy ones. Longhurst did hire Biggs and a couple of other hands, but it was still often necessary for me to travel back and forth between Upchurch and the L&M. Nevertheless, I had no complaints about it. I was married to my old love and nothing could dampen the joy of that.

Nothing, I should say, except Vera Ann Walden. The poor girl, growing bigger and slower by the week as her pregnancy advanced, reminded me of a comic picture I had once seen of a sad old woman who carried a rain cloud with her wherever she went. Vera Ann moped and cried and generally got in the way, and the times Maggie and I most wanted privacy were the times she demanded the most of Maggie's attention. Maggie, bless her, never complained about the burden, although it clearly was wearing her down.

For my part, I worried about what would happen once the baby was born. Would Vera Ann then remain in our home? She had no prospects of a livelihood on her own, and now that Fiddler was gone, no one was about who showed any inclination to take on her care. The situation seemed hopeless.

Weeks became months as the year slid past. Autumn came and brought the chill of a coming winter. Vera Ann fell sick as the end of her pregnancy neared; Maggie at last broke down and confessed she needed help in caring for her. I promptly advertised for a maid and hired the first person to respond: a skinny former schoolteacher with black hair pinned in a pie-shaped roll atop her head. She talked in a tightly clipped, high voice, wore spectacles, had neither lips nor hips, and, to top it off, was named Ambrosia Flatt. "Miss Flatt will be fine," she answered when I asked her what we should call her.

What Miss Flatt lacked in looks and personality she made up for in skill. She moved into Maggie and Rodney's old bedroom, took over much of the cooking and cleaning, and proved an excellent nurse for Vera Ann. Bit by bit the lines that had appeared beneath Maggie's eyes went away and life in our house became more pleasant, even if more crowded.

Longhurst met Miss Flatt on a Sunday afternoon when he came in for a visit and supper. I was both amazed and secretly amused to see he was immediately smitten with our new maid. "I'll be coming

up to see you more often,'' he told me before he
left. ''There's no reason for you to be riding out to
the L&M so much, with all you've got to do here.''

I smiled. Taylor Longhurst never volunteered for
any extra exertion unless he had something to gain.

Maggie received the telegram from Bozeman the
very afternoon that Vera Ann went into her travails.
A Bozeman cousin on her late mother's side was
very ill and required her help. Maggie, usually a
staunch woman, couldn't restrain her tears at the
prospect of leaving home for an indefinite period.
Just lately life had started being what we had hoped
it would be—and now this.

We had no time to talk the situation over that
day, because of Vera Ann's labor. Maggie and
Miss Flatt stayed at Vera Ann's side throughout the
all-night birthing. I didn't even go to bed; Vera
Ann's screams and moans wouldn't have let me
sleep anyway. I couched myself into a chair in the
sitting room and smoked the night away. At last
weariness overcame all else and I drifted off a little
before sunrise.

Maggie shook me awake an hour later. She
looked haggard but happy. ''It's a girl,'' she said.
''Healthy and fat and strong.''

I smiled. ''I'm thankful. How's Vera Ann?''

''Exhausted, but well enough. She's sleeping.
She named the baby Martha.''

''Martha . . . like my sister.''

''That's who she named her after.''

I was touched. Vera Ann had heard me talk often
of my late sister from Independence; naming her
child after her must have been Vera Ann's way of
thanking me for the roof I had put over her head

in a difficult time. Hard feelings I had aplenty for Vera Ann, but from that moment on they were substantially tempered.

Soon enough I would have reason to be glad for the softening of my attitude. Vera Ann was already a tragic figure to me; before long an even greater tragedy would descend upon her, one none of us could anticipate at that time.

I drove Maggie to Miles City the next day and she boarded a Northern Pacific train for Bozeman. "Don't be sad," she told me. "I'm not that far away by train."

"Any distance is too far," I replied. "I don't have a good feeling about you going off. The last time folks I care about climbed on a train, I never saw them again."

Her eyes flashed. "Don't say that," she said firmly. "Don't even think a thought like that. I'll be back, soon."

The train smoked and chugged as it pulled away from the station. I watched it until it was out of sight. My bad feeling lingered. I felt that trouble was on its way, and I hoped as hard as I could that it would not find Maggie.

Turning away, I returned to the buggy and drove up onto Main Street to the nearest cafe, for I had not eaten for hours. I was so low I didn't even taste the meal, good food though it was. From Miles City I rode out to the L&M to check on matters there. Longhurst didn't know I was coming—otherwise I'm sure he would have been out working with the hired men, rather than lounging back in a wicker-bottomed chair on the porch, writing on a pad of paper.

He stood quickly when I rode up, dropping the

pad behind him on the chair and looking embarrassed.

"Working hard, I see."

"Now, McCan, don't you talk smart-mouth to me. What I'm doing is important . . . at least to me. What are you doing here?"

I told him about Maggie's call to Bozeman, and about the birth of Vera Ann's baby. "Miss Flatt's taking good care of mother and child. I'm glad we hired her," I commented.

"Me too," he said.

I stayed the night at the ranch house. Longhurst went back to work on his pad right after supper, scribbling erasing, scribbling again until late in the night. The next morning he self-consciously handed me an envelope. "Give this to Miss Flatt, would you?"

"What is it—a love letter?"

"Mind your own business, Luke McCan."

The wind was up and kicking with the dawn, and blasted me all the long way back to Upchurch. I had tucked Longhurst's envelope into a coat pocket; a particularly powerful gust swept it out. Papers scattered and blew, and only with much exertion was I able to chase them down, all the while cussing at Longhurst for failing to seal his envelope.

I didn't deliberately try to read Longhurst's private correspondence, but stuffing the papers back into the envelope I couldn't help seeing what he had written. It was, of all things, a poem.

"Ambrosia, Ambrosia, name as sweet as honey, I'd rather look upon your face as find a pot of money . . ." Then farther down: "If I was a flower, I'd like to be a posey, and get plucked up by the roots and smelt by sweet Ambrosey . . .''

I was right: Longhurst was in love. Nothing but love could make a man write fool verse like that and think it good. I didn't know what effect the poem would have on Ambrosia Flatt, but it certainly lifted my spirits. I laughed out loud most of the way back to Upchurch.

Chapter 19

I dreamed about Fiddler Smith that night. Back in Walden City we were, in that little shack of a house Ike Walden had provided us. Fiddler was grinning around his secret whiskey bottle, reaching under that leather patch to scratch at the nub where an ear once had been, and rattling on about the wonder of women. He picked up his fiddle, drew the bow across the caked strings, and began to sing in that distinctive voice: "Love somebody and I do, I do, love somebody and I do . . ."

I awakened depressed. Sitting up in the dark room, I put my hand over to touch Maggie, only then remembering she was not there. At the moment, that was too much to abide. I rose, put on a pair of trousers and a shirt, and headed to the kitchen to roust up a midnight feast.

I was finishing off some cold ham slabs on bread when Vera Ann appeared at the door. She was wrapped up in one of Maggie's old robes, a thick woolen shroud Maggie had loaned her. Vera Ann smiled and nodded hello, then came and sat down across from me at the table. The lamplight spilling

onto her face showed the subtle lines and crevices
that had come onto her features over the past nine
months. Ordeals always leave tracks, and Vera Ann
had been trod upon by her share.

"Hungry?" I asked her.

"A little."

I shoved the plate toward her. "You take the
rest. I'm satisfied."

"I dreamed about Fiddler," she said abruptly.

"Really? That's a funny thing—I did the
same."

"Was yours a good dream?"

"Sad, mostly. It's always sad to me to dream
about somebody and wake up and remember
they're dead."

"Mine was a good dream." Her eyes were wist-
ful, staring into the lamp flame, then rising to meet
mine. "I don't believe he's dead."

"Vera Ann, you know as well as I do that—"

"Finding Fiddler's ear doesn't mean he's dead.
An ear isn't a corpse. Fiddler had one ear cut off
years ago, and he didn't get killed that time. Maybe
it happened again."

I had my doubts, but said nothing.

"I believe he's alive," she reaffirmed. "I believe he'll come back to me."

"If he's alive, I think he would have already
come back," I said gently. "The night he and the
Indian fought, Fiddler was out looking for me because he thought he could find you if he found me.
Likely he was jealous, too, thinking I had taken in
a woman he saw as his. Feelings that strong
wouldn't have just left him. If he had lived through
that fight, he would have kept hunting until he
found you."

She looked back to the flame again, her face more somber. "I don't care what anyone thinks," she said very softly. "Fiddler's alive, and he'll come back for me."

She rose and walked out of the kitchen and back toward her room. She had not touched the food on the plate.

Christmas came and went and Maggie still had not returned. Her cousin's ailment, from what I could tell from her letters, was centered in her lungs, was getting no worse, yet getting no better either. Thus Maggie was left in a limbo with no foreseeable end. The second day of the new year brought me a new letter from Maggie, with a despairing plea: Please come and see me, as soon as you can. I miss you terribly.

I smiled. Even before receiving the letter I had already decided to go see Maggie; being without her was becoming too much to bear. Her plea only made me more eager to go.

I almost missed the postscript at the end of the letter, for the paper had folded in such a way as to nearly hide it. When I read it, I rose from my chair, amazed. "P.S.—I think I saw Fiddler Smith in Bozeman today."

That's all it said.

Fiddler . . . alive? Could Vera Ann's intuition have been correct?

I stood debating about whether to tell Vera Ann about the postscript. She was down in the Emporium today, having begun working there, at her own request, a few hours each week. No, I decided. No point in getting up her hopes based on something this insubstantial. Maggie had never laid eyes on Fiddler Smith and knew him only by description. Probably she had seen someone else.

Longhurst arrived that afternoon. He came to Upchurch much more frequently than he used to, now that he and Ambrosia Flatt were courting. His poem had done the trick. After I delivered it to her—struggling to keep my composure—she had gone through some remarkable changes. Silence gave way to chatter, sternness to cheerfulness. And she started to eat—eat a lot. The results were initially positive—"rounding off the Flatt real nice and pretty," as Longhurst punned—but the woman was showing no signs of slowing down her consumption, and was starting to grow too plump. Romance gave her an appetite.

I told Longhurst of my coming journey to Bozeman and asked him to remain at Upchurch during my absence. "To see to the store, you know, and make sure Vera Ann and Miss Flatt are safe and sound." As I said it, I thought of the old saw about asking the wolf to guard the henhouse—but what choice did I have?

"I'll be glad to stay," he said. "I'll set up my cot down in the side room at the Emporium."

"Thanks. There's something else I want to mention to you, by the way. I got a letter from Maggie. She says she thinks she might have seen Fiddler Smith in Bozeman. That's all it said—no details."

"I'll be! Reckon it could be true?"

"Anything's possible, I suppose. I can't quite believe it, and I haven't said anything to Vera Ann, so don't mention it. While I'm in Bozeman I might check around and see what I can find out."

*   *   *

Bozeman was a fine and appealing Gallatin Valley town—the "Garden of Montana," some called it—that guarded the entrance to those vast mountains that rumple the western third of Montana and the upper portions of Idaho. It was named after John M. Bozeman, the famous trailmaker, and had quite a lively history. You might recall it as the town where back in 1873 vigilantes strung up "Old Man Tripp" Triplett and "Steamboat Bill" St. Clair to a beef dressing rack. Likely as not you've seen the photograph.

Maggie was waiting for me at the station when the Northern Pacific train finally screeched and steamed to a halt. What a sight she was! I hugged her until she expressed fear for the survival of her ribs. I hardly let her get the protest out before I cut it off with a kiss, and us right there on the platform where everyone could see us.

Maggie had brought her cousin's rockaway to pick me up in. We took the roundabout route back to the house, Maggie showing me the town, with its wide streets and nice brick buildings. A long team of freight wagons was rolling down Main Street as we went up it; the sight took me back to my old days of freighting between Pierre and Deadwood back in Dakota. It was good to see freighters at work; since the growth of the railroads, there was much less of that old-fashioned type of conveying going on.

"How's Freida?" I asked, Freida being Maggie's cousin.

"Better today—I'm hopeful of returning home soon, if she holds up."

"Lord have mercy, I hope she does. I've missed you terrible."

She asked about Vera Ann and the baby, and about Miss Flatt. I told her all were fine, and prompted a laugh from her when I described the growing romance between Longhurst and our housekeeper. "I just hope Longhurst will behave himself while I'm gone," I said.

"How does Vera Ann do with the baby?"

"She keeps it fed, and loves it dear . . . but beyond that it's Miss Flatt who gives most of the care. Vera Ann's not the most, well, competent mother I've seen. She's hardly more than a child herself, in some ways."

Freida Davenworth's house, just off Main Street, was a fine dwelling. Freida's husband had been a successful rancher who sold out at just the right time to reap a good profit and set his wife up in a fine home before drinking himself to death. Alcohol poisoning, the doctor had called it. Freida, childless, lived now on the substantial savings her husband had put by, and I admit I resented that she had called Maggie in to help her instead of hiring a nurse. Maggie had chided me for feeling that way, reminding me that we really couldn't know Freida's financial circumstances, and had to assume she spoke truly when she said she couldn't afford bought help.

Freida was sitting up in bed, looking pale but cheery in a sunny yellow gown and robe. She had me shake her wilted stem of a hand and told me how kind Maggie had been to her, and that soon Maggie would be able to return home to me. I hope so, I replied.

Maggie and I shared supper and stories that evening in the kitchen. In the midst of it all I recalled her mysterious reference to having seen Fiddler Smith.

To my surprise, she shuddered. "It was a horrible thing," she said. "I had decided not to even mention it to you, then on an impulse I scribbled that note at the end. Yes, I'm sure it was Fiddler Smith. It had to be."

"Where did you see him?"

"In a barroom . . . don't look at me like that—I didn't go in. I saw him through the door."

"What was the 'horrible thing'?"

"The night I saw Fiddler Smith, I was nearly robbed . . . maybe even worse. It was my fault, in a way. I shouldn't have gone where I did.

"It was evening, and I was out walking. Caring for Freida can be exhausting, and sometimes I just have to get away. I wandered too far and got onto a street at the far end of town. Nothing but saloons and a couple of dance halls. When I saw what I had stumbled into, I turned and started for home . . . then I heard music. The sweetest music I had heard for so long. It was a violin, playing something that sounded maybe Irish or Scottish, very pretty and sad.

"I know it sounds foolish, but I had to see where that music was coming from. I turned back around and went further up the street. Some men stepped out from beside one of the saloons and walked behind me, getting closer all the time. I walked faster, they walked faster . . . then I reached another one of the saloons and somebody opened the door. That was where the music was coming from. The door was only open for a couple of moments, but it was long enough for me to see who was playing that violin. A tall man, thin. And he had no ears at all.

He had grown his hair long and let it hang down the sides of his head to cover it, but you could still tell.

"I knew right away it had to be Fiddler Smith. I was surprised, but there wasn't time to think about it, not with those men behind me. I started to run, and they ran right after me. Almost caught me."

"My lord, Maggie!" I said, heart pounding. "How did you get away?"

"Some other men stopped them. There are gentlemen of sorts even in a place like that, it seems. I suppose they didn't like seeing a woman chased. I didn't stay around to say thank you. I ran all the way back to Freida's house, and never said a word about what happened."

I reached out to her and hugged her close. I remembered my bad feeling about her coming to Bozeman and wondered if it had resulted from some premonition of that evening of danger for Maggie. Thank God she had come through all right.

"I'm staying here with you until you can come home," I said, announcing a decision made on the spot. "I'll not have us separated any more. I'll wire Longhurst in the morning and let him know."

"But who will run the Emporium?"

"Longhurst and Vera Ann can handle it. Stewart Biggs can keep the L&M running without Longhurst about—it's winter, after all, and Biggs has really been running the operation anyway."

Maggie smiled and kissed me. "I'm glad you're staying," she said. "I've missed you so badly."

"You don't have to miss me anymore."

That night, for the first time in far too long, I

slept with my wife at my side, and I felt like one
of those biblical lame men made whole again. But
in the back of my mind I kept wondering if that
really had been Fiddler Smith Maggie had seen. I
had to know, and I determined that before I left
Bozeman, know I would. I would go to that street,
find that saloon, and if Fiddler Smith was there, I
would meet him and learn what happened that night
after he saved my hide from Big Jim.

I rolled over, put my arm around Maggie, and
went to sleep.

Chapter 20

I strode down the street and turned onto an avenue of run-down structures long ago claimed by equally run-down specimens of humanity. It was like a hundred other rows of dives and vice dungeons I had known in my day. Once I had been a part of this kind of world; now I felt a stranger. Luke McCan, I realized, had been changed much by marriage and responsibility, and I was glad of it.

Two drunks staggered past, jostling me without apology, probably hardly realizing I was there. They stank of liquor and sweat. Stepping over a big gap in the boardwalk, I studied the doors of the various saloons and wondered if I would find Fiddler Smith beyond one of them. Pulling my coat around me in the cold wind, I picked one tavern at random and made for the entrance.

Plenty of men inside, and a few human beings that once might have been ladies, but no Fiddler. I exited and made for the next saloon and had no better results there, nor in the next one. Walking onto the street, I considered giving up and heading home, when a most remarkable event occurred.

The next saloon down had a large window of red-and-white checkerboard glass. As I paused to roll a cigarette—still difficult because my injured hand remained stiff and nearly useless—that window exploded outward, and a big man tumbled onto the boardwalk. I leaped back. He lay there stunned, then rose groggily. He was hardly on his feet before another figure came through the window on a leap. It was none other than Fiddler Smith himself, fiddle and bow still in hand. He let out a roar and kicked the dazed man, knocking him onto his rump. Another kick sent him rolling into the street.

"Fiddler!" I exclaimed, stepping forward. A bad move—Fiddler turned and kicked again, his heel digging into my gut and doubling me over.

Three others emerged from the saloon, two by the door, one by the now-glassless window. I rolled to the side, trying to find my breath again, as Fiddler Smith became embroiled in a very major scuffle. The fiddle dropped and was crushed beneath a boot. Fiddler cursed, and gouged the crusher in the eye with the tip of the bow, snapping it. That put that man out of commission, but left Fiddler still facing the other two, one of whom had a knife.

By now I had managed to get to my feet again. Without a thought I waded in, swinging my fists and bringing down the knife-wielder. I stomped his wrist, stooped, and grabbed the knife, which I tossed onto the roof of the saloon. Fiddler, meanwhile, was pounding away at the remaining man, giving and receiving about an equal amount of damage. I joined him from behind. Balling my fists together, I brought them down on the brawler's head and knocked him to his knees. Fiddler let out a laugh and kneed the man on the chin.

"Come on!" I urged. "Let's get out of here!"

He only then saw who I was. "McCan! What the . . ."

"Run!" I shouted, for others were coming out the door toward us.

Quite a parade it was, Fiddler and I running down the boardwalk, pursued by three rowdies who looked twice as big as they probably really were. I don't mind confessing that it was mortal fear that drove me down that boardwalk, knocking over several unfortunate stragglers who got in the way at the wrong time. Fiddler and I rounded the corner onto Main and ran all the harder, until at last our pursuers fell away, waved us off with curses and bluster, and strode breathless back the way they had come.

Fiddler and I went a little farther and cut into an alley, where we leaned side by side against a wall, panting. Fiddler began to laugh.

"Fiddler and McCan, back at it again!" he declared. "Lord a'mercy, McCan, where in the devil did you come from?"

"I've been looking for you," I said. "My wife is here, and she said she saw you . . . aw, forget it for now. It's a long story, and I can tell it better sitting down."

"Come on, then," Fiddler said. "I'll buy you a whiskey."

"Make it a cup of coffee," I said. "I'm a more respectable soul than I used to be."

"All right, Saint Luke. Coffee it is. There's a cafe right across the street yonder."

"Sorry about what happened to your fiddle," I said.

"Forget about it. It went out like I want to, scrapping and gouging. My daddy would have been proud."

Fiddler had never been much to look at, but with both ears missing he was downright ugly. He wore no patches to cover either hole, and his longer hair didn't really hide the deformities all that well. "You'd be surprised how hard of hearing it makes a fellow when his ears are gone," he said. "When I put patches over 'em I can't hear a dang thing."

"I'm glad to find you alive," I said. "I had thought that Big Jim killed you. I owe you my life."

"You don't owe me," he said. "Ain't nobody in the world that owes this sorry old beggar a thing. Now tell me what you're doing here."

I told him about my marriage to Maggie, about her ailing cousin and her trip to Bozeman, and how she had spotted Fiddler inside the saloon. "I had to come and find you, and say thanks for what you did for me."

"Thanks accepted, if you got to give it. But like I said, you don't owe me a thing. You've helped me, and I helped you."

"What was all that ruckus over back yonder?"

"Nothing. One of them fellows took to calling me 'Earless Smith' and it riled me. You know how I am."

"I do. Now start talking. I want to know what happened with you and Big Jim that night."

"I killed him, that's what," he said. "I think I did, at least. I sure 'nough put a bullet in him."

He took a swallow of coffee, smacked his lips, and told his story, starting from the time he fled

Powderville after I warned him about Big Jim.

"Hearing Big Jim was that close put a scare into me, and I headed for Dakota. I got no farther than Glendive before I stumbled into some work, helping build a big horse barn. I kind of liked it there, and Big Jim never showed up, so I got it in mind that I might just settle in Montana. Then this drifter came through from Miles City. He was a big talker, this one. He said there was a new cattle operation over near Miles City, run by a man named McCan and a partner. I told him I knew you, and that's when he told me that you had took in some pregnant woman who passed out on the street. I figured it right off to be Vera Ann.

"I'll admit it square: it made me mad to think of Vera Ann being with you. Jealousy, I reckon. The way this fellow told it, it sounded like she was living with you, you know, like a wife. I fumed over it until it got the best of me, and got on my horse and went to Miles City to find you, not knowing that Big Jim had sniffed me out again and was right on my tail. I got drunk in town, made a little too much ruckus, and had to run. I had heard that your ranch was west of town, and headed out that way to find you. And find you I did, all staked out in Big Jim's camp. You know what happened from there."

"It's what happened after that I really want to know."

"Not a lot to tell. I tracked down Big Jim and we fought. He got me down, sliced off this other ear of mine, and was set to cut my throat when I got my hand on my pistol—I'd dropped it during the scuffle. I put a bullet into his side and he scampered off. I must have passed out, for when I came to, he was long gone. I looked for him and never found him.''

''So you don't really know he's dead.''

''No . . . but he's got to be. That was a bad wound I give him. And he never came back. I think he crawled off into a hole and died.''

''There was no body found—my partner looked. All he found was blood on the ground, and your ear.''

''Well, I can't explain it. But I still think he's dead.''

''I hope he is, for your sake.''

Fiddler grinned. ''That kind of talk makes a man nervous.''

''Sorry. You know me—I worry a lot. But tell me, why didn't you come to find me when it was all over?''

Fiddler shook his head thoughtfully. ''Don't know that I can answer that. All I can tell you is that as I sat out there nursing this chopped-off ear stump, I had time to sober up and think. I started seeing things different. I figured Vera Ann was better off without me, that she was probably happier being with you. So I patched up my ear, said my good riddances to Big Jim, and started riding west. I wound up here in Bozeman, and have been here ever since.''

''Vera Ann never was with me, not like you were thinking,'' I said. ''I took her up to Upchurch and asked Maggie to take her in. She's had her baby now, Fiddler. A fat little girl she named Martha, after my sister.''

Fiddler's eyes went moist. ''Martha. That's a fine name. I'm glad to hear about it . . . I feel like she's half mine, even though I really wasn't her father.''

"So come and see her. I think Vera Ann would be glad to see you, too.''

"What's she doing now?''

"Clerking at Maggie's store a little. That's about it. She still lives with us.''

"Vera Ann," he said, just to hear the name. "Vera Ann.''

"Come back to Upchurch with me, Fiddler. Come meet that baby.''

"I can't.''

"Why not?''

"Because if I see Vera Ann, I'll want to marry her, and that can't ever be. I ain't fit to be a husband, much less a father. She's better off alone than with me. Hell, McCan, you know how it is with me. Everybody I get close to I bring trouble to. It's always been that way.''

I didn't know how to respond to that, so I said, "She'll at least be glad to hear you're alive. All this time we've been thinking Big Jim killed you. She's resisting believing it. She dreamed about you the other night, she told me. Dreamed you were alive and so now she really believes you are . . . and me all the while trying to make her believe you're dead. I guess the joke's on me.''

"The only joke here is sitting in front of you. Keep on telling Vera Ann I'm dead until she believes it. It's for the best.''

I crushed out my cigarette, dismayed to see how low an opinion Fiddler had developed about himself. It was downright saddening. "All right," I said. "I won't tell her, if that's the way you really want it.''

"It is."

We parted shortly after. I watched Fiddler Smith's lean figure stride off in the darkness. I felt sorry for him, sorry for Vera Ann, and sorry for little Martha, whose future seemed so unsure. What would become of her, growing up fatherless?

That thought stayed on my mind all the way back to the house, where Maggie awaited me.

"Did you find him?"

"I found him."

"I knew it had to be him, I knew it!"

"I asked him to come back with us. He said no. And he doesn't want us to tell Vera Ann he's alive."

"Why?"

"He thinks it's better that way. But you know, Maggie, I believe he still loves Vera Ann. He just thinks himself too worthless to have her." I sat down beside her. "I've been thinking. I want us to ask Vera Ann if we can adopt Martha. Raise her as our own. What would you think about that?"

Maggie smiled. "I think it's a wonderful idea, Luke McCan. And I think you're a wonderful man for thinking it."

She kissed me. The touch of her, the scent of her, filled me with warmth. I stood, swept her up like she was a child, carried her to our room, and closed the door behind us.

Chapter 21

Maggie and I returned home by the Northern Pacific two weeks later, after Freida rallied and declared herself fit for normal living. I had not seen Fiddler Smith since that one encounter, and as Bozeman disappeared behind us, I expected never to lay eyes on him anymore. All the way home I thought about him, and about Vera Ann's determined belief that he was alive and would return to her. She had been right about the first part, not the second. Fiddler had convinced me he would never come back for Vera Ann.

He was right, I decided. It is best that she keep on thinking he's dead. Better that she feel the pain of loss instead of the pain of rejection—though from Fiddler's viewpoint, he wasn't rejecting Vera Ann by declining to come for her. He was rejecting himself.

We found the Emporium and the L&M all operating in fine form, though the store was dirty and sloppy from Longhurst's overly easygoing management. As for the L&M, its temporary loss of Longhurst during my absence was actually its gain; Stewart Biggs had been running things and doing a better job of it than Longhurst ever had.

Vera Ann looked fitter, slimmer, and healthier than when last I had seen her, and the baby had grown like a summer weed, apparently racing the now-rotund Ambrosia Flatt to see who could put on weight the fastest. Miss Flatt had a strong lead. She also had her ring firmly through Longhurst's nose; his heart-on-his-sleeve devotion to her was as strong as ever. He had been living in the side room of the Emporium, no doubt spending more time courting Miss Flatt than doing any honest work.

He wasn't all that happy to see me return, for that meant his time at Upchurch was over and it was back to the L&M for Taylor Longhurst. "I don't cotton much to going," he admitted privately. "I doubt you've noticed it much, but me and Ambrosia have sort of an interest in each other now."

"You don't say. When's the wedding?"

"I ain't asked her . . . yet."

Miss Flatt was depressed after Longhurst left. She moped through her tasks and cared for little Martha without enthusiasm. A woman in love if ever I saw one.

We wasted no time in approaching Vera Ann about the adoption of Martha. I had no idea whether she would react with shock, sorrow, or relief. What we got was a combination of them all—and then, agreement.

"Thank you, Vera Ann," Maggie said. "You can know that Martha is going to be raised in a strong and loving home. We'll treat her as our own child."

Vera Ann smiled the saddest smile I'd ever seen. "And what about me? What will happen to me?"

"Now's not the time to worry over that," I said. "Things will work out right. They most always do."

Things will work out right. They seemed innocent and empty enough words at the time, but they weren't empty. They were filled with irony that would reveal itself only later—irony so bitter it hurts me even as I write it into this narrative.

If only we could see tragedies before they come.

Winter, like a kitten too high in a tree, released its clawing grip with the greatest reluctance. At last the warm winds of spring blew across the plains and the brown land began to turn green. These were the days of rebirth, and the days the trouble came.

A scream awakened me one night, a scream from Vera Ann's room. The voice, however, was not Vera Ann's, but Ambrosia Flatt's. I leaped from my bed, dragged on my trousers and grabbed my pistol, and darted out the door to find out what had happened.

Miss Flatt, holding a lamp in one hand as she pressed the other to the side of her head, stood in the door of Vera Ann's room. A trickle of blood ran down between her fingers. She slumped against the doorframe as I reached her.

"Ambrosia!" I said, in my distraught state forgetting her preferred mode of reference. "What happened?"

She sank to the floor. "He hit me, knocked me cold . . . and now he's taken Martha!"

"Who, Ambrosia? And where's Vera Ann?"

"Gone . . . with him. They were together. He was horrible, ugly . . ." She began to cry. "He had no ears, just ugly holes where ears should be!"

Fiddler. I stepped back, disbelieving. Fiddler Smith had returned after all—returned for his woman and the baby that now legally was mine and Maggie's.

"When did this happen?"

"I don't know . . . I was unconscious for I don't know how long. He hit me! I can't believe he really hit me!"

Maggie showed up; I told her what had happened. "Luke, you've got to go after them! They can't take Martha!"

"Thank God Longhurst is here," I said.

Longhurst was down in the Emporium tonight, having been up to visit Miss Flatt. He had quit bothering with business pretexts for these now-frequent courting journeys. I dressed and hurried down to the Emporium to roust him.

Distant thunder rumbled as I told him what had happened, then a light rain drizzled down, peppering the roof gently as the big Emporium echoed and amplified the sound. "We can't track him in the dark," Longhurst said. "There's nothing to do but wait until first light—then we'll go after him even if it's raining fire and brimstone."

"Why did he come back, Longhurst? Why, after all this time, did he change his mind?"

"Love, that's why. He loves that girl, McCan, and he couldn't stay away from her."

"But why did they have to take Martha? She's not Vera Ann's now—she's ours."

"You got a piece of paper with lawyer writing on it that says she's yours. Vera Ann's got more— she's got her blood in that child's veins. I expect she couldn't find it in her to leave Martha behind."

First light found us mounted and armed. Fiddler

and Vera Ann had taken one of two flatbed wagons that were property of the Emporium, and the tracks were clear on the rain-matted spring grass. Longhurst and I galloped along the path, my optimism growing as we went. Surely we could overtake them.

They were heading north, toward the Missouri. I knew this country well, having traveled it aplenty back in my earlier roaming days. "There's an old line camp up a couple of miles," I said to Longhurst about midday. "Maybe they waited out the storm there. I hope so, for that would help give us a jump on them."

"I been trying to figure, McCan. I don't see how Fiddler can figure he could get away with something like this. He was bound to know he'd be chased—else he wouldn't have gone about things like he did. But why'd he take a wagon? Surely he knows we'd catch up to it."

"He had a woman and baby to haul," I replied. "What else could he do?"

"Something about this don't sit right with me," Longhurst said. "It smells like fish bait sure as this world. I think old Fiddler might be trying to trick us, McCan."

I should have listened to him, for he had lawman instincts, honed by years of tracking and trailing a lot more difficult than what we were doing now. As it was, I didn't even answer him. All I knew was that my adopted baby girl was taken, and the tracks pointed me north. On we rode, toward the river.

The old line camp cabin was so squat and plain that you could pass within a quarter mile of it and never know it was there. Even Longhurst's keen eye might have missed it had it not been for the figure that ran toward us from the cabin's direction. It was Vera Ann, alone and distraught, hands waving above her head as she stumbled toward us.

"Thank God, thank God you've come!" she said, flinging her arms out to hug me hardly before I had time to fully dismount. "If you'll hurry you can stop him—you've got to!"

"What are you talking about, Vera Ann?"

"Fiddler! Oh, Lord help me, he's taken my baby and run off! He's left me here alone!"

I looked at Longhurst and read on his face the same bewilderment I felt. "I don't understand, Vera Ann," I said.

"Fiddler's cast me off," she said, "He came to me in the night—oh, I was so happy to see him alive that at first I thought I was dreaming again— and he told me he had come for me. He said we would be a family, he and Martha and I. But Martha's not mine anymore, I told him. She's adopted by the McCans. Fiddler said it didn't matter, to take her and go away with him. I did it—I know it was wrong, Luke, but I did it.

"We took the wagon and rode in the dark, and at first it was so wonderful—Fiddler talking about the life we would have. But he was drinking while we rode, and he started to change the drunker he got. He talked bad about me, called me terrible names, said I wasn't fit to marry him or care for Martha. When he saw that old cabin yonder he threw me off and rode away with Martha, saying he was bound for Glendive. Oh, Luke, I'm so scared—you've got to go after him and get back Martha!"

"We'll go, all right," I said. "We'll chase him all the way to hell if it takes it. Can you make do in that cabin until we get back?"

"Yes, yes! Please, just go!"

"Hop up behind me on my saddle here and I'll ride you over to the cabin," Longhurst said.

"No!" she declared. "There's no time—just go after Fiddler!"

"She's right," I said. "Come on, Longhurst—we got no time to waste."

Longhurst was looking at Vera Ann in the strangest way, and appeared hesitant to leave. As for me, I was nearly panicked over the thought of a drunken Fiddler Smith having my adopted baby daughter out there on the plains. I wanted to race as hard as we could toward Glendive to intercept him. Longhurst's silent dawdling made me mad.

"In the name of God, Longhurst, let's ride!"

He never took his eyes off Vera Ann. "All right. You're the boss."

We came across Fiddler's wagon tracks again, double furrows through the new grass, and leading from the old line camp on a straight course toward the still-distant community of Glendive. All appeared to be just as Vera Ann had described: her abandoned, Fiddler and the baby gone.

Still Longhurst lagged back, looking around the horizon and back over his shoulder. "What the devil are you looking for, Longhurst?" I bellowed. "We're wasting time!"

"My suspicion exactly," he said. "I think we're making a bad mistake, McCan. I believe Vera Ann was lying to us."

"You're loco," I declared. "Loco and lazy and slow, and if you cause me to lose Fiddler Smith's trail, I'll put a bullet in you, I swear it!''

It was one of the harshest things I had ever said to a man who had done nothing to earn my displeasure. If I had only let him have his say and let his trained instincts guide us instead of my panic, a great tragedy might have been averted.

I know that now. I didn't know it then. We rode on, following Fiddler's wagon tracks.

Chapter 22

Look yonder," **Longhurst** said, pointing ahead of us. "I see it," I said, squinting my eyes. "Now why do you think Fiddler would abandon the wagon here in the middle of nowhere?"

"Not only abandon it, but take the horse," Longhurst noted.

He was right. The wagon was sitting empty and the horse was gone. I checked the ground and found its tracks, heading northward. I was amazed. What was Fiddler doing—and where was Martha?

Longhurst had dismounted and was also examining the tracks. "It's just like I figured," he said. "He's dumped the wagon, unhitched the horse, and now he's started circling north. He'll cut back to that line camp and get Vera Ann, then the three of them will be off with a fine jump on us. Not a bad plan, huh? He probably had a saddle in the wagon bed. It all makes sense now. I wondered why Fiddler would have told Vera Ann he was going to Glendive if he was really wanting to get rid of her."

"You mean to say he's riding with a baby in his arms?"

"No, no. Fiddler never had Martha out here."

"Where, then?"

"Didn't you notice how keen Vera Ann was to keep me from getting up close to that line camp cabin? Didn't you notice how she ran out to meet us well away from it, and shooed us off before we had a chance to get close enough to hear anything like, say, a kid crying or talking? Heck, he might have even had fresh horses hid around that line camp somewhere, if he planned this out as close as I bet he did."

I could only stand and stare at the north-bound horse tracks and think how gullible I had been. My old Walden City partner had played me like his fiddle, and I had been too panicked to see it.

"We've got to get back to that line camp, then," I said. "They'll have left a trail."

"And we'll be riding worn-out mounts by the time we get back. He's made two idiots out of us, McCan, no denying."

It was so ironic, so hopeless, that I might have laughed . . . except there was nothing funny in the thought of Martha being taken away from me and Maggie. We had grown to love that little girl; she might as well have been flesh and blood of our own.

We mounted and rode back the way we had come, pushing our mounts as hard as we dared, knowing all the while the entire effort might now be futile.

I had expected to find the line camp empty and the tracks of their horses already fading. But as so often happened when Fiddler Smith was about, what I expected wasn't what I got.

They were there, the three of them. Martha was tossing playfully on her back atop a blanket spread on the earth, happily waving chubby little fingers at the clouds. Fiddler sat about ten feet away from her, cradling Vera Ann's bloody head in his lap while he cried. I could see even before I got close that she was dead. There was blood on her chest—the stab wound that had killed her was there—and also on the left side of her neck and down her left shoulder. That blood had streamed down from the place her left ear had been.

Longhurst and I dismounted and walked slowly toward them. Fiddler was weeping like a child, saying over and over again to Vera Ann, just as if she could hear him, that he was sorry, so sorry he had left her. I went over and scooped up Martha, hugging her close and closing my eyes. Thank you, Lord, I prayed. Thank you for keeping my little one safe.

Longhurst went to Fiddler and knelt beside him, examining Vera Ann's corpse. "Big Jim?" he said.

"Yes," Fiddler replied. "Oh, God, oh God, what have I done to my sweet lady? What have I done?"

"You didn't do it," Longhurst said. "It was Big Jim. You couldn't have known he would show up."

"I should have known—I knew he was after me again. But I didn't know he was this close, I truly didn't. I wouldn't have left her if I had. God help me, he got to her before I could double back."

"He must have been close when we were here, McCan," Longhurst said. "He might even have been watching us."

If you've ever seen the top of a Rocky Mountain

pine literally explode into flame in the midst of a big forest fire, you have an idea of the way anger suddenly flared in my mind. It was sparked by a realization that overwhelmed me. I strode forward, grabbed Fiddler by the collar, and pulled him to his feet. Vera Ann's corpse flopped sickeningly to the earth, half-open eyes staring right up at me.

"You mean to tell me you took my baby girl even though you knew Big Jim was after you? What kind of man are you? What kind of trash?" And then I hit him, hard.

Fiddler fell back on his rump with a loud "Oooof!" Sitting there, he closed his eyes and cried even harder. "I deserve it, I do—I want you to shoot me, McCan. I don't deserve to live."

"Reckon you don't. But I'm no murderer."

"Calm down, both of you," Longhurst said. "There's nothing to be gained by nobody shooting nobody. Just be glad the baby's safe—that's the thing to do."

I turned away, rolled a smoke with shaking hands, and let the tobacco fumes settle my nerves. When I turned again, flipping the stub away, Fiddler was sitting by Vera Ann, stroking her hair. It was a pitiful sight. Longhurst was holding Martha, poking her belly with his finger and making her laugh.

I went over and crouched beside Fiddler. "So how long have you known Big Jim was alive after all?"

He sniffed and wiped his sleeve under his nose. "I found out maybe three, four days after you and me talked in Bozeman. I swear I don't know how he lived after the hole I put in him. But he did, and came looking for me."

"How'd he know to look in Bozeman?"

"He didn't. I was on the boardwalk and he was on the back of a prison wagon rolling through Bozeman when we saw each other. We had drifted over into the same parts, and he got himself arrested for one thing or another. The day after I saw him, I heard talk about a big redskin knocking a jailer cold and walking out free. It put a mortal fright into me, for I knew he was coming after me. He found me, too, saw me right across that same street you found me on. I ran like Old Scratch. Stole me the first horse I saw and rode east. I thought I'd shook off Big Jim, really I did.

"That's when I got the notion of coming back to get Vera Ann. She'd been on my mind ever since you talked about her, just weighing on me. So I changed my tune about not coming back to her. I knew she'd never go off with me without her baby, and I had a feeling that if we took the baby you'd chase us. So I came up with this scheme to throw you off track until we could get far away. It would've worked, too . . . except I didn't know Big Jim was so close." He started to weep again. "Why didn't I just let things be? If I'd stayed away, Vera Ann would still be alive."

"I wonder why Big Jim spared the baby?" Longhurst asked. Just hearing the question made me sick to my stomach.

"I think I know," Fiddler said. "I think he didn't know the baby was there. When I found Vera Ann, she was a long way off from the cabin. I believe she ran so he'd chase her and miss the little one."

"Like a mamma quail leading the dogs away from her young," Longhurst said. "What do you think of her doing that!'' He said the last in an admiring tone, looking at Vera Ann's still form.

"I found this on her body,'' Fiddler said. "He left it for me. He must have known I'd come back.''

He pulled a crumpled paper from his pocket and handed it to me. I unfolded it, swallowed, and read: "Your woman's life for my family's life. Now the score is even.''

"You understand what this means, Fiddler? He considers it through. He's not going to chase you anymore.''

"I know.'' Fiddler's face hardened like stone. "Now I'm going to chase him.''

"I figured as much. I'm going with you.''

"No need for that—it's my duty, not yours.''

"Vera Ann Walden lived under my roof. She gave birth to the baby that's now mine—that's right, Fiddler, Maggie and I adopted Martha since last we talked. Vera Ann was murdered, and I won't let the man who murdered her walk away from it.''

Fiddler stood. "He can't be far away. Let's get started.''

"What weapons you got?''

"A shotgun, yonder with the horse, and this pistol.''

Longhurst stepped up. "Wait a minute, gents,'' he said. "We can't go after Big Jim with this youngun to be cared for.''

"No, we can't,'' I replied, "That's why you're going to take her back to Maggie while Fiddler and I go after Big Jim.''

He protested loudly; he wouldn't be left to tend children while we went after a killer. He was the former lawman, after all; it made more sense for him to go than for me. Martha was my child; it should be me, not him, who took her home.

He made sense, but sense made no difference. I lifted my crippled hand. "It was me who felt Big Jim crush my bones, and who almost had a foot burned off by him. I'm going, Longhurst, and there's no more arguing about it."

He lifted his brows, took in a loud breath through his nostrils, and nodded resignedly. "So it is, then. You take care, Luke McCan."

"I will, don't worry. Get Martha home, quick as you can. And tell Maggie that I'll be back. Tell her not to worry."

"She won't need to worry," Longhurst said. "I'll be doing enough of that to count for everybody."

Longhurst gave Fiddler his horse, a better riding mount than the draft horse Fiddler had been upon. We checked weapons, tightened saddles, and I kissed Martha good-bye. She was fussy now, probably from hunger.

We carried Vera Ann's body back to the line camp and laid it out. Burial would have to wait; now there was neither time nor means for it. Fiddler stroked the hair back off her brow one last time, then turned his back and looked at her no more. We mounted and began our journey, following the sign Big Jim had left.

Side by side Fiddler and I rode, moving east, for the tracks of Big Jim's horse led that way. "He's going toward Glendive, just like you did," I said.

"McCan, I want you to know something," Fiddler said. "I've done plenty of wrong in my day, and I rode with the Independent Army, which was

as bad a bunch as I've ever been with. But I swear
on my mother's grave, I never killed Big Jim's kin,
and I never took his ear. The man that did it blamed
it on me when the Sioux caught up with us, trying
to keep them from taking their blades to him. Big
Jim believed him, for he had been out cold when
his ear was cut and never saw the face. He's hated
me all these years for a thing I never did.

"I want you to believe that, McCan. It's important to me that you believe it."

I looked in his face in the waning afternoon
light. Studying his eyes, I looked for signs of deception and found none. "I believe you," I said.
And I really did, then and forever thereafter.

Chapter 23

We rode until the fading light forced us to stop, then spent a nearly sleepless night beneath an intensely black sky. When we awoke the next morning, Fiddler was in a despairing mood. In the previous twilight we had wandered off Big Jim's trail; now there seemed no hope of finding it again.

"We can only go on to Glendive and hope that's really where he's bound," I said. "Though he could have turned off at any point. Do you think he believed you'd come after him?"

Fiddler replied, "He believes it. He knew I couldn't let him kill Vera Ann and just leave him be."

"In that case, he's probably either trying to get as far away as he can . . . or he's planning an ambush."

We made a quick breakfast on some of the bread and dried meat I had brought for Longhurst and myself. I wondered if he had made it safely back with Martha, and hoped that Maggie wouldn't be too worried about what I was doing. It seemed half-loco, when I thought about it. This was between Big Jim and Fiddler . . . no. That was true no longer. The killing of Vera Ann had changed that. It was almost funny—here I was, again championing Vera Ann, just like I had against that harasser back in Walden City. Except now it was too late to do her any good.

In midmorning we saw something far ahead of us on the grasslands. As we drew closer we discovered it was a parked wagon, surrounded by a family in very plain black clothing that marked them as Mennonites. A wheel was off the wagon, but that only partly accounted for them being stuck out here, far from help or shelter. Leaned up against one of the intact wheels was a young man, maybe nineteen or twenty. An older woman, apparently his mother, was squatted beside him, tending to a nasty-looking gash in the side of his head.

The bearded father stepped forward as we rode up. "Do you come for good or for evil?" he asked, and it struck me as a peculiar question.

"For good, I would hope," I replied. "My name's McCan. You appear to be in a fix here."

"We've found misfortune with the breaking of our wheel," he replied in his Iowa Amish accent. "And more misfortune has since found us."

I dismounted and walked over to the injured young man, who was quite dazed. "Did this misfortune come in the form of a big one-eared Indian?"

The man nodded, an expression of surprise on his face. "How do you know this?"

"The story's not worth telling. Suffice it to say we need to find that man. Why did he hit your boy?"

"He was stealing from our wagon, stealing without apology before our very eyes. We had thought

he had stopped to help us repair our wheel. Young
Zeke grew angry and I'm afraid made himself look
threatening. The Indian struck him down. I believe
he was unaware of our peaceful ways.''

"Peaceful ways and Big Jim the Scarnose are
unacquainted with each other,'' I said. ''Which
way did he go?''

"From here, north. He had asked us where we
were bound, and I told him we were on our way
to New Hazelton. He seemed very interested to
hear of it, and I think he went looking for it.''

"New Hazelton? That's been sitting empty for
years.''

"We are going to reoccupy it and rebuild it.
Others are following us. Forgive me for not iden-
tifying myself: I'm William Bund, newly come
from Iowa. This is my family.''

"Pleased to meet you, Mr. Bund, folks. This
man with me is Fiddler Smith. Can we help you
set your wagon right?''

"Thank you, sir. You were surely sent of God.''

Now that we knew which way Big Jim was going, Fiddler was impatient to head after him.
"Keep your shirt on,'' I side-whispered to him. ''It
won't take us long to help out these folks.''

When the wheel was fixed, I dusted off my
hands and asked Bund, ''Why would the Indian go
toward New Hazelton? Doesn't he know there's
nothing there?''

"I don't know, sir,'' Bund replied. ''But I think
he might see it as a place to hide. It was my suspicion that he felt pursued—he looked back the
way he had come quite a lot.'' Bund gave us a
knowing look. ''It was you he was afraid of,
maybe?''

"Likely so."

"You are men of the law?"

I nodded. "That's right, or close enough."

"Big Jim's scared," Fiddler said with a tone of satisfaction. "Dogged if he ain't scared of me!"

Bund looked confused. To him I said, "If you think the Indian went to New Hazelton, I advise you to delay going there yourselves until we've had a chance to deal with him."

"I'll heed that. Young Zeke could use the rest, and I have no desire to meet that Indian again."

"Good luck to you, Mr. Bund."

"God bless you, sir."

We mounted and rode north, heading for New Hazelton. Seven or eight years ago the little settlement had been formed by a band of Iowa Mennonites, then abandoned when a plague of illness, followed by a harsh and biting winter, decimated their numbers. Now all that remained was a cluster of empty buildings. The cattlemen had been glad to see the simple agrarian folk leave, cattlemen almost always despising tillers of the earth. Now it appeared New Hazelton was on its way to rebirth.

I had all but forgotten the empty little Mennonite haven. If it was Big Jim's idea to hide there until any potential pursuers went by, I had to give him credit for good thinking. Few would think to look for him there.

"McCan, when the time comes, I want it to be me who kills him," Fiddler said as we drew within two miles of the empty former settlement.

"We'll hope it doesn't come to that," I said. "I'd like to see him stand trial and hang."

"There'll be no judges for Big Jim except me

and almighty God,'' Fiddler said, ''I'll kill him, or he'll kill me, one or the other.''

Fiddler crouched, studied the tracks in the earth, then looked up to scan the brown, dreary cluster of buildings that had once been places of shelter and livelihood for a good and faithful people. Now, the fresh tracks told us, they were giving refuge to a man much different than those who had built this place.

''He's here,'' Fiddler said. ''Somewhere in there we'll find him.''

My skin seemed to tighten and chill on my frame as I examined the empty community. ''Reckon he sees us?''

''Don't know. We'll know he's seen us when we hear the first shot.''

''If we live long enough to hear it.''

Fiddler turned to me. ''Go on back, McCan. You don't belong here. Let me go in and find him.''

''We've already been through all that, Fiddler. We're both going.''

''You got a family, McCan. I got nothing to lose but a wasted life and too many guilty memories.''

''Shut up, Fiddler. I'm going with you.''

I unbooted a Winchester from my saddle and Fiddler pulled out a fearsome-looking shotgun. We circled to the west end of the vacant town, where the central street ended right on the grasslands, and entered the town, walking side by side, between our mounts, heads crouched low so he wouldn't be able to get an easy shot at us from any angle. Even so, I felt like a target on legs.

From one end of the street to the other we walked, and nothing happened. At the far end we turned left and went between two buildings. "Where the hell is he?" Fiddler said.

"If he's here, we'll find him . . . or he'll find us."

We changed our tack, leaving the horses in the alley and exploring the town together, guns at ready. Around corners we peered, through doorways, into glassless windows filled with cobwebs. Nowhere was there evidence of human life other than our own.

"I think he's gone, Fiddler," I said.

Fiddler lifted his hand. "Listen!"

I had heard it too. The faint whicker of a horse—on the side of the settlement opposite that where our horses were.

"Let's go," I whispered.

The horse was in a stable; a saddle was tossed over the rail. "So he is here, and hiding," I said.

Fiddler stepped out of the stable into the street. "I feel him," he said in a near-whisper. "He's close . . ."

"Yes," I said, for I felt the same prickle in the skin that Fiddler must have. "It's like I can almost smell him."

Have you ever had something happen to you so abruptly that for a good while you can hardly realize it has happened at all, or even know what has occurred? That was how it was for me when my feet suddenly were under me no more, the dirt was in my face, and something that felt like a slab of granite was on my back. I heard a shout, the roar of a shot, then felt a great throbbing explosion in my skull. The weight left my back; I rolled to the side, head spinning.

"Fiddler! Fiddler, where are you?"

My eyes were open, yet saw nothing but vague
shapes and light. Whatever had struck me had
dazed me worse even than that befuddled Mennonite propped up against the wagon wheel. Gripping
the back of my head, I felt blood.

He must have dropped on me from above; Big
Jim had probably hidden on the stable roof, waiting
for us to get into just the right position. I was grateful he hadn't snapped my spine. Who had fired the
shot I heard? I had been in no position to tell; all
I had heard was an indistinct roar that might have
been Fiddler's shotgun, or Big Jim's pistol firing
close to my ears. The echo of it still rattled around
inside my skull.

More gunfire, from around the corner. I groped
for my pistol . . . gone. Big Jim must have swept it
from my holster. My rifle was gone, too.

I was unarmed in a town occupied only by shadows and two other men, each determined to kill the
other.

Part of me wanted to run as hard as I could, to
get on my horse and ride out—for if Fiddler Smith
died here, Big Jim would come for me. The thought
of being hunted among this gathering of empty
buildings, hunted like a mouse by a cat, was more
terrifying than any nightmare. I would circle
around to the horses, mount, and get out.

No . . . no. I couldn't do that, not and leave Fiddler here alone. That would be a coward's way.
Somehow I had to help Fiddler—but with no
weapon, how could I do it?

Again there was a burst of gunfire, farther away.
The last blast was unmistakably that of Fiddler's
shotgun, followed by silence. I grinned. Fiddler had

gotten him! But immediately two pistol shots resounded, and I heard a scream.

Fiddler's scream.

I darted onto the street. Where were they? "Fiddler!" I yelled, "Fiddler, are you alive?"

Onto the street he stepped, coming from the far side of one of the empty houses. He grinned, smoking pistol still in hand. His scarred face was all the more fearsome for his smile.

"Now it's your turn, McCan," Big Jim said. "Now you'll die like Fiddler died."

"I have no weapon," I said, backing away. "You can't shoot me unarmed."

"I can't? Then tell me how it is I can do this!" He fired the pistol; my left leg buckled beneath me and blood streamed down my thigh.

"You're a coward, Big Jim!" I yelled. "Only a coward would gun down a man who's got no chance to fight back!"

"For that I'll cut out your tongue, before I give you the chance to die," he said, lifting the pistol again.

The shot echoed among the buildings. I had closed my eyes instinctively, and when I opened them again, what remained of Big Jim's head was not anything I wanted to look at long. Fiddler's shotgun blast had taken him right in the side of the head, striking him, ironically, on his single good ear. The results you can probably imagine without me spelling them out.

"Well, now it really is done," Fiddler said as the shotgun fell from his fingers. He slumped down to his knees, then leaned to the side. Blood poured from a hole in his chest.

I pushed myself up on my bleeding, numb leg.

To my surprise I was able to stand; the wound was grazing and superficial, nicking a vein and numbing a nerve, but doing little beyond that. I went to Fiddler's side.

"I'm thinking I might need some help, McCan," he said weakly.

"Can you ride?"

"I got my doubts."

Panic was beginning to well; inspiration, fortunately, overtook it. "Bund! I'll go back to Bund and bring that wagon up, then we can ride you to help. Fiddler, I'm going to get you into this building here and cover you up . . . you rest until I get back with Bund's wagon—you understand?"

"Don't think . . . I'll be dancing any jigs . . . while I wait . . ." I could hear the hurting in his voice.

"It's going to be all right, Fiddler. I promise you, everything's going to be all right."

"He's dead, isn't he . . ."

"He's dead. Big Jim can't bother you anymore."

"Not until . . . I meet him on the other side . . . likely we'll be in the same place, me and him . . ."

"Shut up and lie down. I'll be back, fast as I can."

I made him as comfortable as I could, then limped across to the horses, and rode out.

Epilogue

Longhurst inhaled what looked like a palmful of snuff, sneezed, and wiped his nose with a handkerchief. We were in the front room of our house, me with my bandaged leg propped up on a stool. I touched the sore place gingerly with my stiffened hand, thinking how my adventures with Fiddler Smith had left their marks on my physical person. My inner person, too—I wouldn't be quite the same again, having known him.

"Now, wait a minute," Longhurst said. "Let me understand this. You rode out of New Hazelton and found this Mennonite fellow again, and when you got back on the wagon, Fiddler was gone?"

"Vanished like a ghost. There was Big Jim's corpse, just as before, but Fiddler was gone. His horse, too. Yet he couldn't have ridden out—he was in no shape for it. The only thing I can figure is that someone came along and found him during the time I was gone, and took him away, and his horse with him."

"Took him away—dead or alive?"

"I like to think the latter. I'm inclined more to believe the former."

"It's a sad thing," Maggie said, holding Martha on her lap and looking at her as if she feared she would vanish before her eyes. Since Longhurst had safely brought the child home, Maggie had been like that with her, doting and loving and clinging to her every moment. "His life seemed so . . . wasted, I guess."

"He held the same view himself," I replied. "As for me, I'm not going to judge him. He had good in him and bad. We're all that way, just with different mixes."

"I still can't figure it, him vanishing like he did," Longhurst said. "It's surely a mystery. And why, McCan, if somebody came along and hauled off his corpse like you think, didn't they haul off Big Jim's corpse too?"

For that I had no answer; it was a point well made. Even so, I remained sure my partner from Walden City was dead; I felt it more than knew it.

Fiddler was gone, and with him the trouble that always came along with him. Life could now become what I wanted it to be—Maggie and Martha and I, at home, at work, and at peace.

But before the peace would come the tears, and that night I shed them. Tears of grief for two shortened and tragic lives: those of Fiddler Smith and Vera Ann Walden.

Longhurst and Miss Flatt were married in the summer in a flamboyant ceremony and reception the likes of which the Emporium hadn't seen since Maggie's marriage to Rodney Upchurch. By now Miss Flatt—who after the wedding proudly informed us we could feel free to call her . . . no, not Ambrosia, but Mrs. Longhurst—was twice the weight she had been when we hired her. Longhurst had his own name for her—Fats. The funny thing was, she didn't seem to mind it.

The L&M thrived and grew, and over the years Longhurst actually became a good cattleman. The Emporium also thrived—but the best thriving was done by little Martha, who turned from a chubby baby to one of the prettiest little girls I had ever seen. In time she gained playmates, children born to Maggie and me, all of them dark-haired like their parents. Martha stood out; her hair was shining gold.

The mystery of Fiddler's disappearance was never solved. In fact, the mystery only deepened. Two years after that final shoot-out in the empty Mennonite settlement, an envelope addressed to Martha McCan showed up in the mail. Inside was two dollars. No note, no marks to indicate who had sent it, or why. Three months later another envelope came, only a dollar inside this time. From then on such mystery gifts arrived at irregular intervals, containing varying small amounts of cash. All were addressed to Martha, the name and address crudely scrawled.

"It's Fiddler," Maggie would say. "It's his way of trying to do something good for the daughter of the girl he loved."

"Fiddler's dead, Maggie," I would reply. "I know he's dead."

"You don't know it," she countered. "You just think you do."

And perhaps she was right, for one autumn evening in Sheridan, Wyoming, a long time after, the year of 1897, there happened an incident that left me wondering.

I was there on business, having traveled alone. The business finished, I was on my way back to the hotel, when I passed the open door of a saloon. Nothing about the place caught my attention and I gave it not a glance as I swept by . . . and then I heard it. Music. Sweet, high-toned fiddle music played in a flourishing style that was as familiar as this morning yet as distant as memory.

I froze at the saloon doorway, staring straight ahead. The music bubbled out, pulling from my mind a voice singing the words of this very tune: "Love somebody and I do I do, love somebody and I do . . ."

For several seconds I remained where I was, still looking ahead. One glance inside would have answered the question. I started to turn my head . . .

Then I bolted forward, having never looked. The music faded behind me. When I reached my hotel room my heart was racing.

I was glad I hadn't looked. There are some mysteries best left unsolved, some questions best left unanswered, and some memories best left as memories, and nothing more.

Author's Note

Renegade Lawmen is a work of fiction, but makes reference to some historical places and events, a few of which are worthy of note. There really was a mining town named Craig City in Colorado, and the Independent Army described in this novel did operate there, did collect Indian ears for bounty, and was substantially wiped out in a responding Sioux massacre. There never was a Fiddler Smith in the Independent Army, however; he, like McCan, is a fictitious character.

Walden City is also fictional; I have located it approximately in the area actually occupied at the time by the gold-mining town of Manhattan, about forty miles west of Fort Collins.

The settlement of Upchurch, Montana, is a fictional community I introduced in the novel *Timber Creek*, which tells Luke McCan's story prior to the period of *Renegade Lawmen*. New Hazelton is also a fictional community. Miles City, Powderville, Glendive, and Bozeman are among the actual Montana locales mentioned in the book.

Lastly, the train accident in Chatsworth, Illinois, to which the death of McCan's fiancée is attributed in the novel, actually occurred as described. It took the lives of a hundred people and injured many more, and was considered one of the worst such accidents of its time.

CAMERON JUDD
April 2, 1991